A Winter Rose

by

Amy Craig

A Winter Rose

Cover Art by *Diana Carlile*

The Wild Rose Press, Inc.
PO Box 708
Adams Basin, NY 14410-0708
Visit us at www.thewildrosepress.com

Publishing History
First Edition, 2021
Trade Paperback ISBN 978-1-5092-3629-9
Digital ISBN 978-1-5092-3630-5

Published in the United States of America

She smiled. "We have work to do."

Shrugging, Michelle turned to her sister. "I'm not sure inspiration boards are relevant anymore. When the last digital scrapbooking company went public, they made headlines for the wrong reason. Their IPO flopped."

"But their CEO is intense. Can you imagine having him as a coworker?"

"That's the wrong platform," Michelle said.

"Are you sure?"

The older sister nodded. "I know which founder you're thinking about. His last venture made billions."

Serah scratched her head. "Maybe. Either way, he's hot."

Eliza searched a wall of shelves holding salvaged containers and antique finds. Letting the sisters talk, she located a creamy milk glass vase, set it on the table, and kicked the ground. *Maybe they didn't catch my drift.* She cleared her throat. "I don't care if their CEO is the pope. I've known you two since you were toddlers, and I have a stack of embarrassing photos in a shoebox back at the farmhouse. Do you want to revisit your middle school makeup choices for #ThrowbackThursday? That pale blue shimmer shadow would definitely stand out in my news feed."

Michelle's skin paled.

She smiled. *Now I have your attention.* "Let's focus on the present. You only have to remember three things to do your job: a woman is getting married next Saturday, she told us what she likes, and the residents of Skagit Valley expect us to meet and exceed her expectations."

Dedication

To Grace Oulton,
who nurtured the students in her English classes.

Chapter One

"I don't think this is the right floral design." Eliza surveyed her assistant's sketches. The strict formality of the experimental arrangements looked more appropriate for a hotel lobby than a white clapboard church. She took the Valentine's Day wedding to keep Michelle and Serah busy during their school break, but she never anticipated them rejecting the bride's farm-to-table dreams. "The pomanders are clever, but they're too modern for this bride. She wants soft pink flowers, rustic details, and local touches."

Michelle rolled her eyes. "That was so 2000."

Taking a deep breath, Eliza focused on colorful spools of ribbon decorating the barn's far wall. The structure had weathered decades of cold, wet, cloudy Washington winters, but to keep up with Hartley Farms, she and the building would both have to evolve. The spools of color softened her frustration, and she wondered if her daughter created the rainbow design. The girl inherited a world of make-believe from her Norwegian father, and his influences continued to lighten their days.

Glancing at the plant clippings scattered along the workbench, she sighed. Bits of foam, wire, tape, and glue proved her two teenage assistants spent the day overhauling her classic arrangements. *The florist business is supposed to be a side gig.* She rubbed the weariness from her eyes. *I never dreamed a pair of interns would require this much supervision.*

She scratched the back of her neck and flicked a piece of straw from her fingers before focusing on Michelle. "I don't care if *Vogue* dropped a headstone on 'rustic'. The bride showed me a whole binder of shabby chic pictures. She cut them out of her favorite wedding magazines, doodled little hearts on the edges of the pages, and spent two hours walking me through her vision."

Serah stopped working. "Like, a literal binder? Why didn't she use an online inspiration board?"

Michelle glanced at her younger sister and toyed with her long brown ponytail. "I dunno, Serah. Maybe she's a Mormon."

"Mormons use social media. Is she Amish?"

The teenagers went back and forth while a pile of roses waited on the big wooden worktable. Seeing Serah put down her florist wire, Eliza realized they forgot her presence. She took a moment to study them. Of the two sisters, Michelle had the advantage of age, but she figured Serah's work ethic and gold-streaked hair would take her farther in life. *If Michelle reins in her attitude, she could go places.*

Rubbing her temples, she let the barn's humming floral coolers calm her mind. When that technique failed, she removed her wide-brimmed hat, set it on the worktable, and swept her bangs out of her face. Clearing her throat, she slammed a drawer.

The teenagers startled.

"Ladies, the bride's religion doesn't matter, but she's plain ole Catholic."

Serah and Michelle stared, their mouths reforming

the name of the religion.

She smiled. "We have work to do."

Shrugging, Michelle turned to her sister. "I'm not sure inspiration boards are relevant anymore. When the last digital scrapbooking company went public, they made headlines for the wrong reason. Their IPO flopped."

"But their CEO is intense. Can you imagine having him as a coworker?"

"That's the wrong platform," Michelle said.

"Are you sure?"

The older sister nodded. "I know which founder you're thinking about. His last venture made billions."

Serah scratched her head. "Maybe. Either way, he's hot."

Eliza searched a wall of shelves holding salvaged containers and antique finds. Letting the sisters talk, she located a creamy milk glass vase, set it on the table, and kicked the ground. *Maybe they didn't catch my drift.* She cleared her throat. "I don't care if their CEO is the pope. I've known you two since you were toddlers, and I have a stack of embarrassing photos in a shoebox back at the farmhouse. Do you want to revisit your middle school makeup choices for #ThrowbackThursday? That pale blue shimmer shadow would definitely stand out in my news feed."

Michelle's skin paled.

She smiled. *Now I have your attention.* "Let's focus on the present. You only have to remember three things to do your job: a woman is getting married next Saturday, she told us what she likes, and the residents of Skagit Valley expect us to meet and exceed her expectations."

"Why did she pick Valentine's Day?"

"Three things, Serah." She picked up a second vase and put it on the table, smiling as she set the groundwork for a trap. "Actually, I have one more thing to say."

Both assistants looked at the vase.

Amid the scratches of roosting chickens and the subtle grunts of pigs, she dropped her voice to a whisper. "I'm not your bestie. I'm your boss."

Both assistants frowned and leaned forward.

"I'm your boss," she repeated with more emphasis. "If I tell you to put cornstalks in the vase, you put cornstalks in the vase." She unsettled the vase, and it teetered on a rim before falling to the worn work surface.

Serah righted the vase. "I've always liked that vase."

Michelle rolled her eyes. "Whatever." She turned back to the spiral notebook holding her designs, flipped through the pages, and stroked her thumb along a pen and ink drawing. "Cornstalks? Seriously?"

"I pay the bills, cash the checks, and make sure you receive your wages," Eliza said. "I like your ideas, but you have to respect my livelihood." She reached for Michelle's notebook and rotated it until she saw the large rose pomander from the teenager's perspective. Crystal studs and wisps of foliage altered the classic design of tightly bunched roses. She returned the notebook to Michelle. "The concept is pretty, but this bride has other dreams."

"This design received a lot of likes on my personal account."

She exhaled, wondering how she missed such a

monumental shift in popular culture while she worked on her knees planting bulbs. "Your friends like pomanders?"

"They're not only her friends." Serah came to her sister's side, her chin high. "Michelle's Marvels has six thousand followers."

Eliza looked at the teenagers and cataloged their strengths. She knew their parents, they clocked in on time, accepted the rural facilities, and Michelle would leave for college in the fall. "That's fantastic, Michelle. The Hartley Farms account only has a few hundred followers. Maybe you could give me some tips."

"You've only made like, ten posts." Michelle twirled her hair and picked up her phone, turning the device so Eliza saw a screen full of tiny, multicolored thumbnails. "You need to generate more content, or you're not relevant."

Eliza rolled her eyes and added "content generation" to her mental task list. It sat somewhere below paying the property taxes and making sure Skye read a thousand books. "I've been a little busy."

Spying a chicken walking down the concrete center aisle, she scooped up her daughter's pet. The hen flapped at the indignity. Ignoring the animal's protest, she returned it to the far end of the barn where pigs and chickens sheltered in old horse stalls. She deposited the hen in the coop and surveyed the cobwebs in the eaves. *I'll get Gabe to sweep them out.* She brushed her hands on her jeans. *I don't need chicken droppings on my worktable, and I don't need deferred maintenance when I have paid help.*

When she returned to the table, she considered her assistants and their interest in all things related to technology. The teenagers might not qualify as stoic and dependable help, but they brought a certain joy to her days and made her think of the potential beauty lying dormant in the fields. Growing flowers required endless days of toil and perseverance, but the blooms made every day worth the effort. She hoped the same rule applied to teenagers. "Did either of you follow-up on the negative reviews for Hartley Farms? I hoped the wedding website had a mechanism for conflict resolution."

Michelle returned to flipping through her notebook. "I haven't seen anything."

Eliza drummed her fingers on the old table. "Can you believe what the last website review said? 'The stale designs reeked of a funeral parlor. The blooms were so old they dropped their petals the second I opened the box.'"

"Weird."

Eliza looked at the hothouse blooms perfuming the winter air. *You couldn't get fresher blooms unless you cut them from the fields and carried them inside in your arms.* She shook her head and rolled her shoulders. "I'll have to call them again. I can't imagine who left such hostile feedback."

"Have you considered succulents?" Michelle asked as she turned a page.

"Succulents? In the middle of winter?"

"They're very popular on the blogs. Brides love the soft white textures."

Eliza rubbed her temples. "I don't think our bride wants to evoke Palm Springs. She said 'local' and 'rustic'."

"Well, I mean, pink roses aren't really local right

now either. Your fields look like a thorny mess." Michelle shrugged. "Our winter stock all comes from hot houses anyway."

Eliza closed her eyes and focused on taking deep breaths. "How many Washington state hot houses are growing succulents?"

"Somebody is doing it," Serah said.

Eliza looked at the younger sibling and bit her lip. She imagined their Valentine's Day bride surrounded by snow-bound cacti. *Succulents*? "Well, I don't know those growers."

"How about rhododendron and a collar of big shiny leaves?" Michelle asked. "They would go well with the shape of the tulip and narcissus petals."

Cocking her head, Eliza considered the suggestion. "The paddle-shaped leaves are pretty."

"But?"

"But I didn't get that vibe. The bride specifically mentioned roses and dusty miller."

Michelle rolled her eyes and closed her book. "Dusty miller is not local."

The women stared at each other like one cookie sat on the table, and they all wanted it.

A list of tasks crept into Eliza's consciousness, and she blinked first.

Michelle winked at her sister and took a step toward her boss. "You know what I think about when I see the silvery-white foliage?"

Eliza feared she knew the answer. "What?"

The high school senior picked up a discarded stem and pulled off a leaf. She dropped the naked stem to the floor, held the leaf in her hand, and met Eliza's gaze. "Succulents."

She shook her head and exhaled. *So much for collaboration.* "Michelle, I really appreciate your creativity, but the bride found us through the Farmer-Florist Collective. Do you know what that means?"

"She knows how to use the Internet?"

Clever. At least she didn't say "cornstalks." Eliza took a deep breath and summoned the patience she used for her daughter's tantrums. "It means she could have chosen any florist in Seattle, but she picked us because we're committed to locally sourced flowers. We have to honor that intent."

The teenager crossed her arms. "It's February. We've already established nothing's blooming."

Eliza gestured to the roses, stacks of foliage, and dried accents waiting in the coolers. "And yet, we have a cooler full of local stock from local hot houses. All I'm asking is that you follow my designs. Do you have a problem with that directive?"

"Fine." Michelle kicked the packed dirt of the old barn floor. "But what do you want to do about the cedar and boxwood garlands? They're stuffy."

Eliza shelved a tool lying on the worktable and fingered the waxy leaves she bound with floral wire before the sun came up. "I think they're romantic."

"Can we add some eucalyptus? It'll make the church smell fantastic."

Eliza shook her head. "No eucalyptus. No crystals. No avant-garde touches. I want you to stay true to our mission. Local blooms and local color."

Michelle pursed her lips. "Your mission has a twenty-percent approval rating."

So does your work ethic. Eliza bit back the bitter words and rolled her shoulders to loosen the rigidity in her muscles. "I'm working on that." She grabbed her pea coat, opened the heavy double doors, and faced the blowing wind. The warm barn felt like a sanctuary, but she had too much work to spend the day battling her assistants' micro-aggressions. She pulled her hat low against the sharp winter light and glanced over her shoulder. *Sometimes making it through the day is enough to earn a pat on the back.*

****

A stand of cedar trees sheltered the gravel drive, but Eliza slipped past the barrier and headed toward the fallow fields. The rows waited with latent promise, willing to produce blooms if her team's hard work and ingenuity could sow the seeds. Since Erik's death, the bulk of the planting designs came from her ingenuity, and she intended to walk the designs she stayed up late last night to finish. She tromped through the waterlogged rows and relied on her sturdy boots to protect her feet. She catalogued the conditions of the field and let the land tell her where her designs went wrong. *Too tight, too wet, too shady.* She dragged her rubber boot along the rich soil. *I need to work harder to get things right.*

Woody brown stems swayed in the icy February wind like forgotten wheat. She stopped in the middle of the field, picked a dried pod, and rubbed small, black seeds between her fingers. *Will you bloom again?* The wind lifted her hat, and she pulled it low against the sight of standing pools of water. The accumulations rippled with the wind, the shifting gray hues of the sky, and the promise of snow. She shook her head and surveyed the canvas, primed and ready to plant. *What about the elements I can't control?*

A snow goose eyed her from the new row and cocked its head. Eliza smiled, imagining her presence from the goose's point of view. *Am I intruding on your breakfast? Sorry, buddy, it's my field.* The animal's red feet and black-tipped wings shone against the mottled landscape. She admired its bravery and looked at the remainder of the flock foraging near the weathered posts and wire fencing of a field trial. She ignored the wild birds gobbling up her seeds and scanned the twenty acres of farmland her father left her in his will. Come summer, the rich river land would sway with rows of pink-tipped ranunculus, glistening tulips, and pastel anemones. "Where on Earth did Michelle get succulents?"

The audible comment startled the intrepid goose, and it honked and returned to the safety of the flock.

Eliza smiled. *You've got to be tough to make it out here.* She kept walking until the stand of cedar and alder trees bordering the farmland stopped her progress.

Neighboring farms rippled across the Skagit Valley and climbed into foothills of the Cascade Mountains. The eroded silhouette of Mt. Rainier dominated the purple-tinged horizon, but she turned north toward Mt. Baker. *I kept asking Erik to let me lead. Now that he's gone, I can't find my rhythm.* She stared at the imposing mountain, stark against the gray-tinged sky. *Maybe the accident should have taken me instead.*

When the mountain remained silent, she sat on a granite boulder and pulled a knee to her chest, knowing the people in the barn and the old, white farmhouse would have a hard time seeing her at this distance. Safe from their judgment and expectations, she wrapped her arms around her leg, rested her chin, and stared at the river and trees sheltering the family farm. *Maybe I took on too much too soon. Mom wants me to move back to town, but this farm feels like home.*

After a while, the soft sway of the brush and the windswept silence of fallow farmland soothed her. Knowing the geese and the mountain harbored few answers, she sighed and felt the weight of her obligations. *Living in town would be easier, but I want to make this lifestyle work for Skye and for myself.* The thought of imitating her daughter's wails and frustrated cries promised a quick release, but experience taught her when the endorphins faded, she would still have the right and burden of managing the land she owned and loved. She squared her shoulders. *I've shed enough tears in the preceding years.*

Fat raindrops tapped the rim of her hat, and she pulled a two-way handset from her tool belt, resolving to get back to work. "Gabe, the forecast says it's going to snow. Do we have enough frost cloth for the hoop houses?" She waited for the foreman's reply and watched the flock of geese scrounge for their feast. The handset remained quiet, and she checked the radio frequency. "Gabe? Are you there?"

Three white SUVs slowed at the river gate.

She straightened, assuming they would turn at the property line. Instead of retreating, the vehicles advanced on a seldom-used gravel drive leading to Hartley Farms. She strode toward the buildings to intercept the visitors, then squinted and swore as she picked out the light bars and the emblems for Immigration and Customs Enforcement. Changing the frequency on the radio, she spoke into the handset. "Mom, keep Skye in the house."

"What's wrong?"

Claire's terse response reflected the note of alarm in her command. "I don't know yet"—she broke into a run—"but nothing good will come of it." She sprinted across the fields and cursed the soft ground as the geese took flight. Her boots kicked up debris and splattered mud on her worn jeans as she ignored the burn of the winter air and struggled to breathe. She stopped in the barn doorway, panting and nearly out of breath as she confirmed ICE officers occupied the building.

"Where's Gabe Arellano?" the tallest officer asked Serah.

The sisters grabbed each other's hands and cowered near the floral coolers. Instead of answering the man, Serah looked past him and focused on Eliza.

Eliza nodded to reassure the teenager whose eyes widened as a shaft of sunlight caught her gold-streaked hair. *They're kids.* She drew in a ragged breath and maneuvered her body to defend the space between the terrified assistants and the uniformed agent. The room's occupants focused on her, and she removed her hat and slapped it on the table to buy enough time for another breath. "Why are you looking for Gabe?"

The tall man's gaze narrowed. "Are you Eliza Edwards?"

She nodded and stood straight before accepting an intimidating stack of paperwork from the officer.

"We have a search warrant for Hartley Farms. Mr. Arellano is unlawfully working in the United States."

Eliza looked over her shoulder and jerked her head toward the rear of the barn.

Understanding the wordless command, Michelle pulled Serah toward the comfort of the chickens and pigs.

Their sudden movement triggered the officers, who shifted en masse toward the threat of two teenagers with flower petals stuck to their shirts. The lead officer put a hand on his gun. "Don't move."

The teenagers froze.

Eliza locked gazes with the officer and switched the frequency on her radio. "Gabe, please report to the barn."

When the radio remained silent, Serah started to cry. Her sobs echoed in the weathered building.

A hen cried out, and the threat of violence hung in the air like suspended dust motes.

"Gabe. I don't want these men in the farmhouse," Eliza said into the radio, adjusting her stance to keep the officers at bay while she waited for Gabe to make his final decision on her farm.

"I'm in the greenhouse," the foreman's voice echoed over the handset.

The lead officer nodded and dispatched his team. The men and women fanned out to scour the greenhouses and the soft-sided hoop houses. Within minutes, they returned with the foreman in handcuffs, Gabe's defiant brown eyes snapping as he struggled against their hold.

Eliza met the foreman's gaze and shook her head, telling him she could do nothing to help him.

Gabe exhaled, and resignation settled his shoulders. He looked at the floor and then raised his gaze. "I'm sorry, Eliza."

"You should have told me," she said, restless as she paced the work area.

"You don't understand. My family doesn't have

any resources."

She stopped and looked at the man. "I could have helped you."

"How?"

She took a deep breath, unable to answer the foreman's poignant question without knowing the specifics. "I would have wanted to help you."

"How far would you go for your family?" he asked her.

She thought of her six-year-old daughter, knowing she would shelter Skye as long as she could. *Empathy might be the first step to forgiveness, but I still have a business to run.* Knowing the officials saw one problem and expected two more, she faced the ICE officer and cleared her throat to grab his attention. "Everyone else is above board."

The lead officer raised his eyebrows. "Are you sure? Your foreman gave you forged paperwork, and you didn't know it."

She crossed her arms. "True, but your agency took two years to figure that out."

The man sneered. "Do you make a habit of harboring illegal immigrants?"

No, but this spitting contest is ruining my afternoon and terrifying my staff. "Do you make a habit of intimidating American citizens?"

The man smiled.

I'll take that as a "yes." She took a step toward him, recognizing her ignorance of Gabe's circumstances meant she did nothing wrong. "These women are students at Mount Vernon High School. Instead of sitting on the couch during ski week, they're working to save money for college. I've known their family for fifteen years."

"Then why do they look so scared?"

"Why did you bring ten men to a flower farm?"

An agent at the rear of the group laughed.

The lead man scowled. "I'm doing my job."

"So am I," she said. "Go bully the illegal growers tearing up the Cascades."

The officer narrowed his gaze but signaled the men holding Gabe. "Let's go."

Two ICE officers funneled Gabe to their waiting SUV.

He shook his head and looked at Eliza one last time.

I'm sorry too. But she kept her thoughts to herself.

A light rain fell as the remaining men followed the leader's signal and exited the barn. Truck doors opened and closed before powerful engines growled to life, and the vehicles kicked up a cloud of dust on the gravel drive.

Serah collapsed in her sister's arms and continued to cry.

Unsure whether to hug the teenagers or give them room to comfort each other, Eliza picked up her hat and held it in her hands. She radioed her mother. "All the agents left the property."

"Thank goodness," her mother said.

Serah looked up, wiping her eyes. "I always liked Gabe."

"Are you okay?" She took a cautious step toward them. "Do you want me to call your mom?"

Both girls shook their heads.

"We did nothing wrong," Michelle said.

"No, of course not." She kicked the ground and

looked up. "Did either of you know about Gabe?" The harder questions lodged in her throat, their implications broader than the continued presence of the foreman. *Do my people trust me? Do they respect my authority and the commitment I made to keep them safe and provide for them?*

The sisters looked at each other.

Michelle nodded. "We knew. Or, at least, we guessed."

She exhaled. *They all know I'm a stickler for the rules. What else am I missing?* Softening her stance, she recalled her confusion standing on the cusp of adulthood. "Is there anything else you want to tell me?"

Both assistants shook their heads.

"Okay. Pack up the arrangements and take off the rest of the day. Go tell your mom what happened before she hears it on the news. I'll take care of the mess."

"Are you sure?" Serah asked.

She nodded and stooped to pick up a trampled bloom. Dark lines marred the rose's soft pink petals, but the center held firm. She lifted the flower to her nose and inhaled a soft perfume of lemons and honey. Notes of musk followed the sweet crispness, and she thought of summer's warmth and the promise of growth waiting in her fields. "We've got good stock. This is a setback."

"Not for Gabe," Michelle said.

"True, but he made his choices like the rest of us." She scanned old growth beams supporting the barn roof. Hay peeked from the overhead loft, and a series of heaters warmed the cavernous space. Pigs and chickens nestling in the old horse stalls, but little about the barn had changed since her childhood. *Now I'm the one taking the chances and bearing the consequences.* She inhaled and smiled for the benefit of the teenagers. "Don't worry about it. I'll find another foreman."

"My uncle has a friend…" Michelle said.

She held up her hand and shook her head. "I appreciate the offer, but I want someone with experience."

The sisters nodded and packed up the arrangements. They grabbed their purses and coats, left the barn, and piled into Michelle's car without saying another word.

Alone in the barn, she rummaged through a pile of supplies occupying a horse stall and withdrew a roll of frost cloth. A quick calculation told her the fabric remaining on the roll fell short of the amount she needed to save the young plants in the hoop houses from the coming storm. She dialed the local hardware store and waited for Luke's wizened practicality.

The owner answered on the second ring. "What do you need, Eliza?"

"Frost cloth."

"You and everyone else in the valley," he said. "Don't people know how to read a weather forecast?"

She laughed. "Well, there's a difference between reading it and believing it."

"Smart woman, like your mother."

She waited while he checked his inventory and came back to the phone offering to deliver the cloth. She appreciated the gesture but wanted to avoid calling in favors unless absolutely necessary. "I don't need to make more work for you, Luke. I'm sure Claire has a list of errands and groceries, so I'm coming to town." She paused. *Wait, what if he wants an excuse to make the delivery?* "Unless…"

"That's fine. I'll see you soon." He hung up the phone.

She closed the big barn doors and walked toward the farmhouse. Last year's profits went to fresh white paint and gleaming solar panels. *Daddy always taught me to take pride in the things I own.* Removing her boots to keep mud from the freshly swept floors, she found Claire and Skye in the cozy kitchen.

Claire maintained a clear view of the barn and guided Skye through a recipe for spiced butter cookies. Bottles of cinnamon, cardamom, cloves, and ginger littered the laminate countertop.

"What are you making?" Eliza asked.

"Daddy's favorite cookies!" Skye said.

Claire met her gaze.

Eliza felt the weight of a thousand unasked questions. "That's exciting."

Skye's vigorous strokes sent flour skittering across the countertop.

Claire took control of the wooden spoon. "Try to keep it in the bowl." Demonstrating, she used her steady left hand to scrape the bottom of the bowl with long, sure strokes. The indulgent weariness of her smile lightened her reprimand.

Skye watched her grandmother's demonstration and reclaimed the spoon as soon as the older woman loosened her grip.

Eliza considered the pair. *I don't know what I'd do without my mom. I keep thinking about Skye as a toddler, crying and confused when Erik failed to come home from his trip and wrap her in a warm hug. Mom's been a constant in Skye's life through the good times and the bad.*

She looked at her mother and smiled. Claire's bright blue eyes and silver-streaked blonde hair shone beneath the warm kitchen lights. She wore pastel wool sweaters and gauzy scarves like a uniform. The clothes covered her softening waistline and permitted more than one savored indulgence, but a crisp white apron protected the soft materials and allowed Claire to sift sugar with her exuberant granddaughter and end up none the worse for wear.

Eliza unbuckled her tool belt and set it on the kitchen table. The tools settled with a heavy thud, but the conditioned leather kept them from leaving a mark.

Claire glanced toward the barn.

Eliza shook her head. "He's gone."

"That's too bad," Claire shook her head.

Skye stopped stirring. "What's too bad?" A diminutive apron kept her white-blonde braids from falling into the mixing bowl.

Eliza brushed a streak of flour from her daughter's forehead. "Nothing, Sweet Pea."

The girl eyed her caregivers. "Granny said I could lick the spoon."

Eliza sampled the buttery sweetness of the dough. "It's delicious, but keep it in the bowl, or you won't have much to eat."

The girl looked at the old barn. "Do you think the *nisse* wants one?"

"I don't know, Sweet Pea." She toyed with the soft hairs escaping her daughter's braids. You're our expert on the little people."

"I bet he'd eat a cookie."

Eliza met her mother's indulgent gaze and smiled.

"Who could resist Granny's recipe?"

"The *nisse* and I love Granny's cookies!" Skye looked back and forth between her caregivers. "Maybe he'd like two of the sugar cookies we baked yesterday."

"Only one." She watched the girl palm two cookies with the skill of a cat burglar testing her limits. Raising her eyebrows, she waited for her daughter to accept her first offer.

Skye reached for the mixing spoon and stuck it in her mouth. "Fine."

Trusting her mother to keep Skye from overloading on sugar, Eliza focused on the needs of the farm. "I'm headed to the hardware store to pick up supplies. I'll get groceries while I'm there."

The older woman nodded. "Take Luke a box of dahlia bulbs."

"What will Luke do with a box of dahlia bulbs?"

"Plant them?" Claire shrugged. "It's not my call."

"It could be your call."

Wind rattled the windowpanes as the two women stared at each other. Eliza decided to borrow a page from Skye's playbook and test the limits of her mother's patience. "Do I need to bring him soil and a pot?"

Claire put her good hand on her hip. "Don't talk back to me, Eliza Jane. The man owns a hardware store."

She grinned. "Maybe you would like to come along and bring him the bulbs."

The older woman crossed her arms. "Does that mean you're cooking dinner?"

Skye wrinkled her nose.

As she recognized the familiarity of her mother's

gesture, Eliza conceded their point. She grabbed a handwritten list from the refrigerator. "I'll do a grocery run while I'm in town."

"Be careful on the roads, Eliza. I wish I could be more of a help."

"You're a huge help, Mom. Keep everyone warm and cozy until I return."

The older woman nodded and scanned the acreage beyond the kitchen window. "That's one thing I can do."

Eliza kissed her daughter's head, grabbed her tool belt, and left the kitchen. She sat on a bench near the front door to pull on her boots, but a glass vase collecting dust on the coffee table caught her eye. Last week, she replaced the Christmas nutcracker with a vase of rosy-pink glass pebbles and sprouting bulbs. The vase looked empty near a haphazard pile of picture books, but within weeks, tender leaves would grow and a bloom would fill the room with a sweet smell. At the thought of bulbs heralding spring, she smiled. *I should bring some flowers to the house, but I don't want to trump Luke.*

The thought of her mother exchanging valentines with the store owner made her shake her head. She slipped her foot into the still-warm boot and wondered what the old man would send in return for the dahlia bulbs. *Daddy's been dead for a decade, and Skye's getting easier to manage. It's time for Mom to look after herself.*

Then Eliza caught her reflection in the hall mirror and shook her head. The aftermath of her late nights ringed her jade green eyes with plum-colored shadows. Dry air chapped her cheeks and lips until they were pink. The look fell short of the gloss of makeup, but she brushed aside her light brown bangs and opened the door to focus on her priorities. A light rain fell as she picked up the grocery list, buttoned her coat, and went back out to face the cold. *Mom can't be selfish until I'm in control.*

Chapter Two

The rain intensified at the same moment Julien spotted a hardware store in the small town of Mount Vernon. He slowed his motorcycle, found a parking spot, and put down his left foot on the slick asphalt. Raindrops ran down the shield of his helmet. Cutting the engine of the performance motorcycle that carried him from Louisiana, he smoothed back his unruly dark hair.

As the luxury engine quieted, he rolled his shoulders, wincing at the stiffness in his muscles. Below his knee, the tender nerves in his residual limb ached from three hundred miles of jarring road vibrations. *A cross-country expedition seemed like a good idea, but the physical therapist was right. Stretch breaks can only get me so far. Maybe I should have extended my stay in Las Vegas.*

A flock of geese flew overhead.

He disconnected his headset and stowed his helmet out of the rain. Without the noise and distractions of the highway, he examined the deserted streets of Mount Vernon and squinted through the rain. Not trusting his vision, he shook his head and looked again. *You've got to be kidding.*

Every storefront in the town glinted with a rain-streaked tribute to Valentine's Day. Eight blocks of small businesses shimmered with doilies, garlands of hearts, and posters for a tulip festival. He looked toward the river and spotted a festooned mailbox glittering outside the post office. *Isn't that illegal?* The old movie house on his left advertised fancy cocktails and a run of black-and-white musicals. The Italian restaurant sported bright polyester flags with red and pink stripes, heavy from the storm. He eyed the houses up the hill and gave them a nod of approval. *At least they're safe from this flood of commercial sentiment.*

He turned to the curved glass façade of the hardware store. The dependable, small-town bastion of self-sufficiency sported advertisements for tools and automotive supplies. As he strode toward the front door, he smiled at the promise of grease and shoptalk. *That's more like it.*

When he spotted the store's seasonal window painting, he stopped short. A chubby cupid winked and pointed his arrow beneath a shower of cartoon tools and falling hearts. After considering his options, he decided to ignore the plump infant and to reach for the door.

A bell chimed, and a long-haired man sat on a stool holding a cup of steaming coffee between two hands. The clerk's cargo vest teemed with mechanical pencils and an assortment of tools. His beard balanced a salt-and-pepper ponytail and partially obscured the glint of metal dog tags hanging against his chest. He caught Julien's gaze and nodded. "Hello."

Julien approached the counter and returned the man's greeting. "I'm looking for engine oil."

"Aisle three."

Turning, he walked toward the aisle.

"You feeling okay?" the man asked.

He paused. "Yes, sir."

"Been on the road a long time?"

Without turning his head, he raised his pant leg and revealed the green metal prosthesis below his knee. He gave the clerk time to react, looked over his shoulder, and made eye contact, watching for signs of pity.

The man nodded and took a sip of his coffee. "Going to be slippery tonight."

"I haven't taken a spill in a while."

The man jerked his heard toward the store's curving windows and the drops of rain sliding down the plate glass. "I meant on the bike."

Julien turned and stared at the high-end machine. "The bike has winter tires."

"Only a fool rides a motorcycle in the middle of February."

He clamped his lips together. "I prefer stubborn."

The clerk shook his head. "That's not a good excuse."

"Do you ride?" Julien considered the man's long gray beard and bedraggled ponytail.

The man shifted on his stool. "When the weather's good."

"Then you know how to adjust your machine. In conditions like this, I ride in a higher gear for better control," he said.

The clerk looked out the window. "How do you operate the rear wheel brake?"

"The anti-lock brake system interconnects the front and rear brakes. I thought about installing a hand brake, but I found I didn't need it."

The man nodded. "My old bike has a toe lever." He turned to Julien. "You got a leak?"

"Appears that way."

The man tapped his chin. "You handy?"

"I can fix anything with the right set of tools." He crossed his arms and raised his right eyebrow, daring the man to test his claim.

"Good. I have a feeling you'll need it." The clerk smiled and sipped his coffee.

Sensing his dismissal, Julien nodded and scanned the bright white aisles. Stately, brass pendant lights hung from the painted ceiling and made it easy for him to check the tidy shelves for the right additive. He found the oil he wanted and glanced at the small brass frame advertising a fair price. Even the divider strips in the green-flecked terrazzo floors carried a brass tinge. When he saw his trail of wet boot prints, he winced. *Somebody put a lot of love into this store. If my mama were here, she'd hand me a bucket and a mop to polish it up.*

"You from the South?" the clerk asked.

The man's voice echoed through the store. Julien fell back on decades of social training. "Louisiana," he called back.

"I thought I recognized the accent. Is your family still there?"

He picked up the item he needed, made his way back to the counter, and put down his item. "A hurricane couldn't force them to move."

The man nodded. "I grew up in Virginia."

Julien shook his head. "That's borderline."

The men stared at each other before the older man laughed and extended his hand. "Luke Wilkins."

"Julien Kroger."

"What brings you to Mount Vernon?"

"Doing my best to stay off the interstate."

The clerk nodded.

Julien glanced at the bits of grass stuck to his leather boots. He raised his gaze and felt like a twelve-year-old kid again. The novel sensation made him shake his head and laugh. "This is the cleanest hardware store I've ever seen."

"Used to be a pharmacy, but it turns out you only need one of those in a small town."

"Seems like the locals have a thing for hearts and flowers."

"Beats logging and mining. It didn't take long before the valley's white settlers figured out the fertile bottomlands were their best assets. These days, Skagit County has about a million tulip bulbs in the ground, but the farmers grow all matter of crops."

Yep. Julien settled in for a lecture. *Just like landing in the principal's office.*

"Skagit County's a special place. My late wife grew up running through the tulip fields, and she wanted to come back here after I left the service." He glanced at a photograph of a smiling woman with old vintage charm. "We ran the store together before she passed away."

"I'm sorry for your loss."

Luke nodded. "She was a sweetheart. Could have been a starlet if she set her mind to it." He took another sip of coffee and winked. "Don't know why she picked me."

Julien looked at the late afternoon light beyond the store's curved façade and maintained his smile while memories chipped away at his heart. *Sometimes it's better not to know why people choose one another...or don't.*

"How long are you staying in town?" Luke asked.

"Not sure."

"Where are you headed next?"

Julien peered beyond the rain, but humidity fogged the glass. *Back home, we know better than to blame the humidity on a temperature difference. Life is what it is.* He smiled and remembered the drawings he and his brother made on the single-paned glass shielding their family home from the elements. The sashes had shifted with time, and insects found their way into the house. Sometimes he wondered about the point of having the glass at all. "North? The plan was to go coast to coast."

"Maybe you should stick around and wait out the storm."

The hint of criticism raised Julien's hackles and sent his memories racing back to the tedium and rebellion of detention. He crossed his arms over his chest and looked at Luke, but the man refused to blink. "I'm fit to ride."

"I never said you weren't."

"Any other questions?"

Luke nodded and sipped his coffee. "How'd you lose your leg?"

"Oilfield accident."

He raised his eyebrows. "Seems like you'd want to keep the other one."

"Most people are polite enough to avoid mentioning it."

The clerk grinned. "I've seen worse."

Julien glanced at the man's dog tags and took a deep breath. He leaned his hip against the counter and took the weight from the prosthesis. "I'm sure you've seen plenty. I guess I should have said thanks for being so upfront."

The man let him linger.

"Most of the country's inhabitants go silent when I enter the room."

Luke nodded, rolled up a sleeve, and exposed a jagged white scar. The mark ran from the crook of his elbow to his sturdy wrist. He ran a thumb over the smooth white skin before raising his head to meet Julien's gaze. "Living with new scars."

Julien nodded and shifted his weight. "Even harder when you can't forget them."

"I needed years before I could pass a knife without thinking of this wound." He gestured to a display of wooden figures. "I finally took up carving to get over my nightmares."

The cold seeped past Julien's jacket, and he shivered. A tool pusher had yelled to warn him of the swinging load the moment before it crashed to the rig floor and shattered Julien's leg. "I'm not taking up industrial power supply to get over mine."

Luke laughed. "Folks don't like to think about their own mortality."

"But you?"

"I'm too old to observe the niceties."

Julien grinned. "Does that help you win friends and influence people?"

"You're the first customer I've had all day." He took a sip of his coffee.

Julien laughed. "I'm sure it's the weather."

The man smiled and checked his watch. "I expect one or two more before the storm rolls in. I'm not one to meddle…"

Julien raised an eyebrow.

"But you really might want to call it a day. Nothing to do with your leg. The roads north of here get dark and curvy past twilight. There're too many trees and shadows for good visibility. Plus, the rain will freeze when the temperature drops. Snow's your best bet." He paused. "What happens if you get ice?"

Julien squinted to read the wall-mounted thermometer hovering near the freezing point. He thought of a light frost glazing the cane fields back home. Snow seemed as soft and benign as the powdered sugar coating a beignet. "I didn't consider the possibility of ice."

Luke nodded. "You're a long way from home."

"Seven years in the oilfields taught me two things: there's always time to do it right, and there's always the risk of an accident." He looked at the rain-drenched windows and wondered which outcome would prevail if he stayed on the road. The local deserved a point for experience and possessed more knowledge than he could transfer over the course of an afternoon. "What's the best hotel in town?"

"How much do you want to spend?"

"The cost doesn't matter."

Luke turned to a display case and selected a crisp white business card. "Try the Darling Bed and Breakfast. Skagit County's maintenance team will plow the roads in the morning, usually by nine o'clock. I'll throw in some water repellant in addition to the oil."

Julien nodded his thanks.

The older man turned toward the register. "It works well on the slush."

"I'll bet it does."

The over-the-door bell chimed.

A trim woman entered the store carrying a cardboard box. She shook a shower of lingering raindrops from her hands and transferred the box to her hip.

Julien smiled as she removed her dripping hat and brushed aside a mess of light brown hair. *Maybe Cupid did his job after all.* The woman's bright green eyes flashed with curiosity as they looked at each other. Julien opened his mouth to greet the woman.

But she walked right past him.

Won't be the last time it happens. He checked her ring finger and consoled his ego. *The lady probably has a million preferences that have nothing to do with my amputation. Single doesn't mean interested.*

Undeterred, he focused on making his selections, but the labels blurred together. Shaking his head, he admired the fit of the woman's worn jeans and purple plaid shirt. Her work-worn garments skimmed her hips and subtle chest, making him think she might also appreciate the pleasure of a job well done. If that turned out not to be true, the faded seams stretching across her high, toned butt did plenty to hold his attention.

"Luke! I'm here for the frost cloth!"

"I'm right here, Eliza. The beard doesn't make me deaf."

The woman put her box on the counter and pushed it toward the clerk. "I'm sorry. I've had a trying day. My mom sent these bulbs as a gift for Valentine's Day."

Luke's impassive features quivered until a bushy eyebrow rebelled and rose to attention. "Is that what she said?"

"More or less. Do you want planting instructions?"

The man grimaced. "I'm a Vietnam vet, Eliza Edwards. I can figure out how to plant a few dainty flower bulbs."

They stared at each other until Luke pulled out a hand-carved wooden spoon and pushed it across the counter.

"Did you make this for Claire?"

"I made it."

The woman raised her eyebrows.

Julien wondered if the two stubborn fools had more in common than they cared to admit.

"Your mother's an obstinate woman."

Eliza smiled. "It runs in the family."

"I can see that. Now tell me what happened to your foreman?"

"ICE raided the farm and took Gabe into custody. They gave us zero notice, and now I have an absolute mess on my hands."

"Are the girls all right?"

She tapped blunt fingernails on the countertop. "I sent Serah and Michelle home for the day. They're supposed to be padding their resumes, not pondering the injustices of life. I'm thankful Skye was in the house with Claire."

Luke stilled the woman's rhythmic movement with a hand over hers. "I'm sorry about Gabe. The last year's been rough, and he worked hard to help you out."

Eliza sighed. "I wish I could have done more to help him. I hate feeling helpless."

Julien shied away from the sincerity of the moment. He returned to the automotive aisle and made a point of looking for the rain repellant, if either of them cared to notice. Despite his effort, their voices carried across the store's polished surfaces like a PA system, and he figured he might as well enjoy the conversation and his view of the woman's backside.

"What are you going to do now?"

"Drink more coffee." Eliza picked up a glittered heart keychain and checked the price tag. She sighed and set it down. "Trudge along until I find someone else to help with the workload."

"You have an army of elves I don't know about?"

The woman smiled. "Just one."

Julien and Luke both stared.

She met Luke's gaze. "I have my mom."

The clerk nodded. "Your mom's got a heart of gold, but she doesn't know a thing about farm labor."

"She's a mean cook, and she loves Skye." Her expression softened, and she fingered the keychain again. "What more could I ask for?"

"A lick of common sense."

"I need more than common sense." She straightened her shoulders. "I swear I've had a string of bad luck."

Luke sipped his coffee. "You don't believe in luck."

"You're right. I believe in hard work, but this disruption couldn't have come at a worse time. I planned to use the cold months to prepare for springtime. Without Gabe, I'll be fighting maintenance fires. I want to be ready to plant the moment the spring sun warms the earth." She stared out the window. The wind shifted, and the rain pelted the window. "Who will I find on such short notice?"

"What about Brian McDuff?"

She shook her head. "He's leading daytrips on the

river."

Luke grimaced. "This time of year? What about Lucy Hudson?"

"She's pregnant with twins, and her OB put her on best rest."

Luke cleared his throat.

Julien smiled to see the edge of the man's tolerance for practical matters. He returned to the counter and set down the bottle of water repellant he selected. The pair glanced at him, but they continued to trade names and excuses like he had ceased to exist. When neither of them showed signs of slowing down, he cleared his throat and opened his mouth to ask for a purchase total.

Luke jerked a thumb toward Julien. "What about him?"

"What?" The woman pursed her heart-shaped lips and faced him.

Her head came up to his shoulder, but she appraised him with the frankness of a cattle baron. He bore her scrutiny.

She shook her head and turned back to Luke. "I need a steady, reliable hand."

Julien crossed his arms. "What's wrong with mine?"

"You look like you spend your days pumping iron and taking selfies."

I've never taken a selfie in my entire life, but I'm glad you're not immune to my workouts. He debated whether to lay on the charm or play it straight with the stubborn woman. "Ma'am, you look like you're playing dress up with the big kids."

She grinned. "I am the big kid. Do you know anything about running a farm?"

"My family has grown and milled sugar cane for one-hundred-and-fifty years. We produce over 350 million pounds of sugar and a few million gallons of molasses. Our mill processes over 40,000 acres of cane from the surrounding Louisiana parishes."

The woman raised her eyebrows.

Julien kept talking, as much to drive home his point as to brag on his family's heritage. Brandon might run the show these days, but Julien still felt proud of the family business when he walked into the cane fields and listened to the song of blades and stalks swaying in the breeze. "Our sugar mill is one of eleven mills still operating in the state. The refineries in Gramercy and Chalmette get national attention, but I promise you, Kroger Industries is thriving."

"So, what are you doing in the Pacific Northwest?"

"Too many sticks in the sugar kettle."

She stared and cocked her head before looking to Luke. "What is he talking about?"

The clerk raised his hands and picked up a pencil to leave himself a note. "Damned if I know."

"My older brother runs the family operation," Julien said. "Competition pushed much of the sugar industry into the Caribbean, and I don't need to stick around Louisiana and dilute his momentum. I've always been the second son."

Eliza nodded. "Fair enough, but my scale would bore you. I've only got twenty acres."

He thought of a farm smaller than four city blocks and nodded. "Probably so." Then he pulled out his credit card and pushed the automotive gear toward Luke. "Can you ring me up?"

The clerk shook his head and abandoned his pencil

35

to mutter something about southern idiots. He named a total, ran the credit card, and dropped Julien's items in a brown paper bag. He glared at Julien and pushed the bag across the counter. "What happened to 'there's always time to do it right?' "

Don't pin me down, old man. It's a catchphrase. He rolled his head and squared his shoulders. "What happened to choosing your own battles?"

Luke's gaze narrowed, but he nodded.

Julien headed for the door. He put a hand on the old brass bar and glanced over his shoulder at the slim brunette.

The woman toyed with the wooden spoon Luke gave her.

"Take the keychain for Skye," Luke said.

"I don't need handouts."

The man grinned. "It's a gift."

Julien sniffled, surprised by the sincerity of the gesture. *The South can't claim a monopoly on small-town charm.* He shook his head and dismissed his reaction. *Get it together, Julien. It's a keychain for a kid.*

The woman looked up and met his gaze.

He recognized the hints of fear and uncertainty behind her determination. *You'll get through this, lady. You might feel like your life is falling apart, but take it one day at a time.*

She looked away and sighed.

"Ma'am, sounds like you're having a rough day, but I admire your commitment. It really doesn't matter what you're growing. Farming's hard work and a bit like gambling. You can do everything by the book and still end up on your ass." He watched as the last ounce of fight left her shoulders.

"That's what I'm worried about the most."

Julien considered a variety of ways to dislodge his foot from his mouth. "Ma'am, everyone has a rough…"

She pointed the spoon at him. "Stop calling me ma'am."

Her show of defiance gave him a reason to smile. "What do you grow?"

"Flowers."

He looked to Luke for confirmation.

The clerk nodded.

"I'm not much good at delicate," Julien said.

"Flowers are more than pretty petals. Hartley Farms is part of the sustainable flower industry. We specialize in growing local and seasonal flowers to support a regional farmer-florist collective. We also make wedding arrangements during the off-season."

He looked at the thermometer and watched the temperature drop a degree. Nothing but chilled glass separated him from a quick escape, but he stepped away from the door. "Why would you choose such a pain-in-the-ass crop?"

She crossed her arms. "A crop is still a crop. I'm taking my cue from the organic farmers and selling a premium product."

Julien shook his head. "Flowers already cost a premium."

"We're pitching farm-to-vase instead of farm-to-table."

"I doubt you're in this industry for the money."

Eliza grinned. "Why not? We all have to eat. Americans will spend nearly two billion dollars on cut flowers for Valentine's Day." She raised her eyebrows.

"Why shouldn't I sell what people want?"

Julien crossed his arms and widened his stance. "Grow soybeans."

"Soybeans don't glitter with dewdrops. They don't sway in the soft spring breeze and bring a smile to my face. I love planting flower seeds and watching them bloom."

She rubbed her fingers together like she could feel the soft petals between them. His fingers itched to feel them too.

She smiled. "Every day those plants grow taller, I know they're getting closer to leaving my farm and helping someone express their love without saying a word."

He glanced at the backside of the smiling cherub and snorted. For a moment, her words carried him away from the cold reality of the winter day, but he felt the dull ache of the prosthesis. "Love is fickle. Maybe you should take another look at soybeans."

"Maybe, but I'm not interested in growing beans."

He nodded, determined to leave the hardware store better off than he arrived. "Yes, ma'am."

Luke coughed. "You know what's better than a hotel?"

"What?" He feared the man's intervention.

"Gainful employment and a furnished cottage."

He shook his head and glanced toward the door. "I'm not looking for work."

Eliza nodded. "Don't worry about me, Luke. Let the pretty man go back to the gym and the cane fields where he belongs."

Luke rolled his eyes.

Suppressing a smile, he wondered if Luke knew

Eliza well enough to dismiss her like a defensive teenager. The man's gaze focused on him.

He jabbed his finger on the counter. "I was wrong. You're not a fool. Only an idiot rides a motorcycle in the snow, dismisses Claire's cooking, and ignores a woman in distress."

So much for the niceties.

"Eliza doesn't need you to play Rhett Butler. She needs you to mend the leaks in the irrigation lines and weather-strip the greenhouse so she can get her work done."

Thirty-two years of Southern manners urged him to assist the woman, whether she thought she needed it or not. Julien took a deep breath, then felt the two ounces of wet synthetic fabric chaffing his residual limb. He transferred the bag to his left arm and revealed the transtibial prosthesis. "I'm not the right man to help you."

She considered his sophisticated green hardware before she met his gaze. "Nice rig. What happened?"

"A chunk of west Texas heavy equipment fell on my leg."

Her green eyes narrowed. "You said you're from Louisiana."

"Yes, ma'am. I also told you my brother runs the family farm."

She nodded. "My name is Eliza."

He dropped his pant leg and stood straight. "I heard your name. Doesn't mean I'm required to use it."

She raised her eyebrows.

"My name's Julien." He told himself a small concession would help him gain ground.

"Julien, I have a tip for you. This is Washington."

She crossed her arms. "Nobody has time for your gothic charm."

Laughing, he joined them at the counter. "Noted, but I gather you've never set foot in a cypress swamp?"

"No."

He lowered his voice. "The moss and the shadows might seem a bit spooky to outsiders, but we've come a long way from the dark ages. My mama does the accounting and runs the local auxiliary association, but she still taught me the four Rs: reading, writing, arithmetic, and respect."

Eliza scanned his rain-soaked jeans and steaming jacket.

A litany of southern defenses sprang to Julien's mind.

"Your mama might have omitted a few topics," she said.

He swallowed his laughter. "Of that, I have no doubt." Rubbing the stubble on his chin, he thought about her circumstances and what he would do in her situation. *Work myself to the bone most days.* He glanced at the shadows beneath her eyes and wondered if insomnia or early mornings put them there. "Right now, it sounds you've got a long list of tasks and zero resources. You might have to take what you can get."

She tucked her bangs behind her ears and cocked her head. "Do you have any other antebellum values I should know about?"

He smiled. "I open doors and pull out chairs."

"Why?"

Julien struggled to give her a meaningful answer, but the question hung between them like a sweet Vidalia onion. Layers of complexity hid behind a cavalier skin. The life he fled represented a portfolio of memories and regrets. "I'm holding onto the best remnants of Southern hospitality."

"Why would you idealize the past?"

He took a deep breath and exhaled. "Because I can't make any promises about the future." He stared as the distance between them shrank like two vines reaching for the same steady support.

Then Eliza nodded. "Julien, I could really use some help."

"Yes, ma'am. How long?"

"Until? Until I find someone else?"

"How long do you expect that to take?" He calculated the impact of the delay and wondered if the weather patterns would hold long enough for him to reach Canada.

"Less than a month? We see a lot of seasonal laborers when the weather warms up."

"Yes, ma'am."

Eliza opened her mouth but stopped short of speaking.

Julien watched her purse her lips. *What thoughts are going through that woman's head?* Beyond her chapped, pink lips and wind-kissed cheeks, he noticed the fine lines teasing the edge of her features. They made him think of days spent working in the sun. *A lot of women don't leave the house without makeup, but she's as pretty and determined as a wildflower.*

She sized him up for a third time and nodded before she turned back to the clerk. "Luke, how much frost cloth do you have?"

"As much as you need."

"All right, Julien, last chance. Are you in or out?"

He grinned. *Smart woman. You're making this my choice instead of leaning on Luke's guilt trip.* Determined not to let five-and-a-half feet of determined woman get the best of him, he smiled and crossed his arms. "Pull your truck around back, and I'll get the cloth loaded."

She nodded and walked out of the store.

Did I catch the hint of a smile? He followed her outside and flipped his collar to ward off the rain. A cold wind blew off the river. He did not need the store's thermometer to know the temperature dropped while he lingered inside. He put his purchases on top of his motorcycle seat and reached for his stowed helmet. Glancing over his shoulder, he realized she had stopped short. *Did you lose your nerve, pretty lady?*

Eliza gestured toward the motorcycle and bit her lip in the rain. "Is that yours?"

He nodded and unbuckled the chinstrap on his helmet.

She shook her head. "You can't bring your motorcycle to my farm."

"Why not?" he asked.

"My husband died in a motorcycle accident. My daughter is terrified of the machines."

He swallowed. *Losing my leg on the rig floor wasn't the worst thing that could have happened.* He looked back at the hardware store and locked gazes with Luke standing in the doorway. The older man crossed his arms and nodded like he knew how to put life's pieces together long before either of them drew their first breath.

Julien stowed his purchases beneath the motorcycle's leather seat, flipped his key to the clerk, and unhooked the duffle that served as his overnight bag. "Not a problem, Miss Eliza. We'll take your truck."

"It's Eliza."

"Yes"—he cleared his throat in deference to her loss—"you're the boss."

She nodded and put her hat back on her head.

The wide brim shielded her face, but Julien glimpsed a full-blown smile.

She climbed in an old truck with a covered bed and left him standing in the rain.

Hell. He shook his head and headed toward the back of the hardware store. *If I get to see that smile again, she can be my chairman and my CEO.*

Chapter Three

Eliza parked the truck at the back of the hardware store, took a deep breath, and examined her reservations about the brawny stranger who might be her salvation or her latest mistake. As she moved the groceries and made room for supplies and Julien's duffle, she exhaled and wondered if she was doing the right thing by letting Luke push them together. *The man's a great judge of character, but who knows if I'll regret this decision?*

She looked for Julien and spotted him turning the corner, walking through the cold rain as confidently as if he possessed two solid legs and a few more tucked up in storage. *I came into town for supplies, not a charming Southern amputee.* He defied her expectations of an oilfield hand, but she looked at his scuffed leather boots, thick and sturdy with reinforced toes. The elaborate stitch work might be a vanity, but his quality footwear told her more about his work ethic than the presence of his rippling muscles. All things considered, the man could use a shave, but sturdy, worn boots counted for a lot on a day like today.

She considered his chiseled profile and caught herself replaying his reluctant smile when she claimed the upper hand. She shook her head. *I came to town for supplies, and I have a business to run.*

Julien reached the overhang of the loading dock, pulled a frayed baseball cap out of his duffle, and tucked the hat in his chest pocket.

The boyish gesture amused Eliza and settled her nerves. The man might have pushed back against her authority in the hardware store, but his warm brown eyes simmered with amusement when she refused to back down. Seeing him walk to her side and stow his baggage in the back of the truck, she eyed his muscled form. "So, you're not afraid to get wet?"

He laughed. "Nope. Let's get started."

Eliza nodded and walked to the loading dock where Luke stood. She grabbed a box weighing close to fifty pounds.

The older man nodded but did not offer to help.

Julien grabbed the next box.

She tried not to notice how he lifted the package like it might house florist's foam.

He picked up two additional boxes, and his thick arms flexed as he adjusted the weight.

"Don't overdo it," she said.

He met her gaze, eyebrows raised.

Instead of taking the bait, she rolled her eyes and dropped her box in the back of the truck. The box landed with a resounding thud.

Julien set down his load before he returned for more.

Show-off.

Despite the rain, she lingered near the safety of the truck and evaluated him with the intensity of an employer, the interest of a woman, and the protectiveness of a mother. *Have his arms always been out of proportion with his frame? Is he compensating for losing his leg? Is his injury the only thing that sent him fleeing to the Pacific Northwest?*

Julien shook the raindrops from his shaggy black hair, consulted with Luke, and reached for three more boxes.

She exhaled and grabbed the last box, then lingered beneath the protection.

"Why don't you have a hoop house?" he asked.

"I have three of them." She trusted the predictability of farm conversation. "Last month, I lost a crop of anemones. I'm doubling down on frost protection with the cloth."

The man muttered something about flowers.

Luke laughed.

Eliza hid her smile and ignored the derision in Julien's response, but the man's soft rolling accent and quiet deference gave her hope the man would put in a hard day's work when push came to shove. Whatever his thoughts about her crop of choice, he still carried her supplies through the rain, and his work ethic mattered more than the words he said. She met Luke's overseeing gaze and smiled. *He could talk down a cougar from the treetops, but I never expected him to find me a new foreman.*

The clerk surveyed the loading dock. "That's the last box out here. Do you need more from the storeroom?"

Eliza shook her head. "Thanks, Luke, I owe you."

The man jerked his head toward Julien. "I hope he works out."

She nodded.

Julien returned to the dock. "You good to go?"

Shifting the box in her arms, she cocked her head as he reached to take the load from her arms. Their fingers brushed, and she inhaled as the casual touch seared her skin beneath the freezing rain. She gave him the box and turned to hide her reaction. "I'll go warm up the truck."

"Yes, ma'am."

She looked over her shoulder.

Julien shifted the box in his arms, wiped the raindrops from his eyes, and shook Luke's hand.

He felt nothing. She blinked and left the men to exchange words while she cranked the ignition and turned on the heater to repair her senses. *Luke's probably warning him that whittling knives can cut more than wood.* The older man's protectiveness made her smile until she thought of her late father. *He should be the one staring down my new foreman, but he took the easy way out.* After a few minutes, she honked the horn.

The men on the loading dock looked up and scanned the yard.

Eliza crossed her arms. *You two can chitchat all day, but I have a farm to run.*

Julien walked toward the truck, opened the door, and used the grab handle to climb into the cab. He secured his seatbelt and pulled the frayed baseball cap over his head. "Time's a'wasting."

"Says the man standing in the rain on a loading dock."

"The old man had a few things left to say."

She stared, waiting for him to replay his conversation with Luke.

He remained silent.

"That hat would have kept the rain from your eyes," she said.

He settled into the seat and adjusted the vent. "Do

you like it when your hat gets wet?"

She glanced at her leather hat on the back seat and shook her head.

Julien rubbed his hands in front of the heater. "Can we stop for food?"

"Sure, but the farm isn't far. Can you make it twenty minutes?"

He grimaced. "You ask a lot of a man."

"My mom will feed you."

Nodding, he settled into the seat. "Luke said she's a good cook."

She shook her head. "He'd get more dinner invitations if he manned up and asked her out."

"Maybe he's got his reasons," Julien said. "I reckon you don't live that long without learning a thing or two."

"Maybe." She checked her rearview mirror and put the truck in gear. The combination of heat, warm bodies, and wet clothes fogged the glass as they left downtown.

"Slow up a minute." At the stoplight, he pulled a bandanna from his jacket and handed her the worn fabric.

She dismissed the offering and adjusted settings on the center console. "The truck has defrost."

"The cloth will work better."

She considered blowing him off but took the bandanna, leaned forward, and cleared the windshield. The fabric smelled of laundry soap and a subtle musk that intrigued her senses. "Do you want your hankie back?"

"No, you keep it."

Tucking the damp cotton between the seats, she

wondered if hiring him was the right decision. She glanced at him. "Any other suggestions?"

He shook his head.

Smiling, she focused on the road. "Are you a backseat driver, too?"

The worn springs creaked as he settled into the seat. "Do you need one?"

"Absolutely not." She took her foot off the brake and turned onto the county road, navigating in silence as the cloud-soaked sky loomed above brown winter fields. Despite the rainclouds, light slipped from the setting sun in the west and lit the underside of the clouds with a soft red light. *I can bring him back to town in the morning if the dynamics don't work out.* She liked how he scanned the traffic patterns at every intersection but cautioned herself not to read too much into his behaviors. Maybe he thought she was a terrible driver and feared for his life. She smiled and let the speedometer climb. The truck's sturdy heater kept the cab warmer than the cold promise of the snow-capped mountains. *What if he's a great fit?*

"You're speeding."

"Thanks." The sun slipped below the horizon. She dismissed the easy freedom of the open road, slowed the truck, and turned on the headlights. *I'll give the man twenty-four hours.* The last streetlights disappeared from the truck's rearview mirror, and the golden hour gave way to early darkness. Raindrops pelted the windshield, and wind blew dry leaves against the glass. The truck's wipers caught the traveling foliage and dragged the leaves across the glass. She turned up the wiper speed, and the leaves flew free. Smiling, she stole a glance at her passenger. "We should talk about compensation before we get much farther."

"Pay me the same as your last foreman. I'll find out if you're cheating me."

She tightened her grip on the steering wheel. "I'm not a cheat."

The man settled his hands over his stomach. "Then we won't have a problem." He reached for the bandanna and cleared the foggy side window that obstructed his view. "Luke mentioned greenhouses and irrigation lines. What other kinds of work do you have?"

Content to return to the practicality of common ground and the predictable hierarchy of the farm, Eliza nodded. "Gabe oversaw all the field production, greenhouse construction, soil work, irrigation, and delivery. The acreage is small, but he spent a lot of time on his feet." She decided not to ignore his injury. "Let me know how often you need to take breaks and whatnot. I expect you to work hard, but I don't want you to overdo it."

"Don't worry about my leg, Eliza. It's my job to handle it."

His curt response dispelled the intimacy of the drive, and she adjusted the heater. *It's only a short-term arrangement. Nothing says "at-will employment" like the day-to-day toil of farm labor.* The silence between them felt cold and impersonal. She inventoried the work required before she could end her workday.

"Tell me why you're going…farm to vase."

The open-ended question startled her, but she recognized an opportunity to reestablish a working relationship. Taking a deep breath, she resolved to treat the man like any other new employee. "Hartley Farms offers a superior product. Eighty percent of all flowers sold in the U.S. are imported. Most of them come from South America, and those flower farms carry a legacy of fertilizers, pesticides, and nonexistent labor laws. Did you know Customs Enforcement has to fumigate commercial blooms before they allow them into the country?"

Julien nodded. "The Food and Drug Administration runs a tight ship."

"I mentioned I'm part of a farmer florist collective. During the winter, I can manage both hats while the fields lie dormant, but I booked a wedding this weekend, and I'm stretched too thin to do it all on my own. The ICE raid was a terrible way to start off the week."

"I doubt they considered your needs when they decided to pick up your foreman."

"No, probably not." She left downtown Mount Vernon and eschewed I-5 for the back roads. The local country radio station filled the air space as Dike Road skirted a patchwork of farms.

Julien looked out the window. "It gets rural fast."

"You'd never know we're an hour north of Seattle. My farm fronts the river. We're pretty close to the Skagit Wildlife Area and the rich delta of the estuary."

"I like the small towns. I took State Route 9 from Arlington and meandered through the lakes. I was making my way toward the border in Sumas."

"What stopped you?"

"Engine oil. Then Luke was generous enough to warn me about the possibility of ice. I might be stubborn, but I draw the line at blatant idiocy."

The truck's headlights glinted on the river. She

smiled and made a right turn on Fir Island Road. "The weather can be unpredictable this time of year. You made a good call getting off the road."

"That's what I heard." He cleared his throat. "Are there fish in the river?"

The unexpected question startled her. "You like to fish?"

"Yes, ma'am."

She glanced at him and raised an eyebrow.

He smiled. "What kinds of fish are in the river, Eliza?"

"Anything you're patient enough to catch. Tourists come here for Steelhead, Coho, and Chinook, but local anglers go after a whole list of species. The water plummets from the mountains, rolls through whitewater rapids, and spills into a complex network of tributaries. I understand it's some of the best sport fishing in the state."

"That's quite an obstacle course."

She nodded. "You'll see more than fish out here. Huge seasonal flocks of snow geese and trumpeter swans over-winter in the fields. We also get raptors, bald eagles, and an occasional blue heron. A family of river otters lives upstream from the farm."

"You obviously enjoy the land."

"But I don't fish," she said.

"What do you like to do for fun?"

Fun? She shook her head and wondered how much time had passed since she made time for fun. Her father's suicide and Erik's death upended her world and erased the word from her vocabulary. She kept her gaze on the road. "I spend every minute growing flowers or finding a moment to connect with my daughter. I don't have time for hobbies."

He nodded and returned to staring out the window.

The dried brown fields dappled with evergreens looked as common as snow geese, but she wondered how he viewed the landscape. The awkwardness of their new acquaintanceship gave her time to second-guess her decisions, but she spied Snow Goose Farm Stand.

"That farm stand sells organic produce and some arts and crafts." She softened the coldness of her overworked remark.

"It's the middle of winter."

"My daughter loves their ice cream."

"What's her name?" he asked.

"Skye."

"Good name for a farmer's kid."

"My late husband picked it out." She adjusted her grip on the steering wheel like Erik sat in the backseat, poised to correct her driving habits.

"I'm sorry for your loss."

She heard the politeness behind his condolences and sighed. *Where's the sweet spot between protective defenses and open communication?* "Do you like kids?"

"I like my cousins. That's about the extent of my experience with them." He remained silent for a moment. "My brother's wife is expecting."

She smiled. "That will be fun for your family."

He coughed. "Something like that."

"Skye's a handful." She filled the gap before their conversation lapsed to uneasy silence. "My mother does a great job of helping me." Unable to set aside her responsibilities, she considered the worst possible outcomes of hiring a man on the spot. "Would I find anything to worry about if I ran a background check?"

"No, ma'am."

She exhaled and wondered whether to believe him. "That's what Gabe said, too."

"The foreman?"

She nodded and bit her lip, wondering how she could trust a man who worked at her side for years and reserved so much of himself. Inhaling, she shook her head. *Dwelling on the past won't help me now.*

"Well, run the check if it makes you feel better."

"I might." The truck's headlights illuminated the darkening road. She told herself to respect the man's autonomy, but she rationalized her next question by assuming it would be too obvious if she avoided asking it. "So, what happened to your leg?"

He crossed his arms and leaned back against the old fabric seat.

For a moment, she wondered if the question went too far. Then she turned, and the headlights of an oncoming car revealed the quick flash of his smile.

"I wondered how long before you asked. I had my money on you making it to the farm."

Laughing, she gestured toward a turnoff she could find blindfolded in the dark. "We're almost there."

He cleared his throat. "I was in the wrong place at the wrong time."

A familiar pothole bounced the truck. "What does that mean?"

"It means a weld broke on the rig, and a piece of heavy equipment fell from a significant height. The safety lead should have cordoned off the area beneath the lift, but I shouldn't have been there either."

"Was the wound clean?"

"No, it was a mangled mess."

She winced and empathized with his physical pain. "I'm sorry."

The song on the radio changed, and he took a deep breath. "It wasn't your fault."

She glanced at him, knowing how many sleepless nights she spent considering the culpability of her personal losses.

"The emergency personnel took a while to reach the west Texas field. The medics arrived on site and stabilized me before the helicopter took me to a hospital in San Angelo. The trauma surgeon did his best to stabilize the carnage, but not much of my leg was left to save. He amputated my right leg at the knee and"—Julien cleared his throat—"a second flight took me to Houston to save my life."

She swallowed, following the story without imagining too many of the graphic details. Memories of Erik's broken and bloodied body waiting in the sterile white hospital room still haunted her dreams. "Did you have anyone with you?"

"A corporate lawyer."

She snapped her head and looked at him. "What? No family? What about your brother?"

He looked away. "They met me at Hermann Hospital when they got word."

"Would you rather not talk about the accident?" She stopped at an intersection and stared at the traffic signal to mitigate the intimacy of their conversation. *How can I ask him about his tragedies and not confess my own?*

"I don't mind the questions, but the days after the accident are a medicated blur. I lost count of the number of medical procedures and eight-hour surgeries. Three weeks passed before the wound closed. Rehab. Prosthesis. Gait Training. That year felt like a decade."

She imagined the prolonged pain brought on by a year of surgeries and rehabilitation. The man deserved credit for maintaining that stamina and perseverance without cracking. *He might be quick with a joke, but what was he like before the accident?*

"Two years have passed since the accident."

She swallowed. "I honestly couldn't tell in the hardware store until you mentioned it." The light changed, and she looked at his features, illuminated by the dashboard and the spare glow of the intersection.

The side of his mouth ticked up. "You had other things on your mind."

Like ogling your ass? She cleared her throat. "What did you do after rehab?"

"I tried to put my life back together, but that turned out to be more complicated than I expected. So, I've been meandering across the country for six months to sort it out. I started in Louisiana, skirted Texas, and spent a few weeks in the southwest desert. When Vegas failed to hold my attention, I poked around the Tetons and the Rockies until the weather turned cold, and I headed for the coast."

"And what's next?"

"Canada? I had some thought of riding to Alaska, but a few weeks of manual labor for the benefit of a pretty lady suits me fine."

The compliment brought a flush to her cheeks, but she wondered if she should feel offended. *It's one thing to admire his assets and another thing to admit the admiration, even if the feeling is mutual. I wouldn't turn him down based on his looks.* She cleared her throat and raised her chin. "Do we need to talk about boundaries?"

"Nope."

"Good." The truck's headlights illuminated deer grazing on the side of the road, and she cut her speed.

"Unless you want to talk—"

She held up her hand. "Julien, I'm up to my neck in problems."

"I'm teasin' you, Eliza. I know you've got a mess on your hands. Don't worry about me. I could use the break of these coming weeks."

"Most people don't consider manual labor a break."

"Well, most people aren't me."

The teasing banter felt refreshing, but the thought of losing his help before it began roiled her stomach. "What happens if you go home? You mentioned too many cooks in the kitchen."

"I said too many cooks stirring the kettle."

She shook her head. "I have no idea what that saying means."

"They used to crush the cane and evaporate the juice in large, cast iron kettles open to the air."

"Hopefully, their processes have improved."

"The sugar industry exists in a strange miasma of hatred and desire. It's a bit like having an extended family. I miss it, but I don't think I would ever choose it."

"We don't have that problem with flowers." She smiled. "Everybody likes them."

He made a noncommittal noise. "If you really want to appreciate history, stop by the Bayou Teche Museum in New Iberia. It's all there, the good and the ugly. When push comes to shove, people don't have a problem overlooking our industry's sordid past and putting a five-pound sack in their grocery cart to bake a cake."

His voice warmed as he spoke of Louisiana. She pushed her bangs out of her eyes and wondered if Julien's heritage prevented him from seeing the possibilities of further reform. Her interim foreman spoke with the conviction of a man who accepted the past, but she wondered if he saw the possibilities of the future. "We used to harvest whale oil to run our lights. Times change, and society evolves."

"Exactly. Most Americans still want to buy the product. Obesity and added sugars are contentious, but what's the alternative? A load of chemicals?"

"Honey." His silence gave her courage. *Now's probably not the time to debate whether his family should move away from synthetic chemicals, pesticides, and fertilizers.* She cleared her throat. "Skye has a raging sweet tooth. I'm hoping she'll grow out of it."

"It's more than a biological preference." The seat creaked beneath his shifting weight. "I grew up pouring cane syrup over my pancakes and expecting the rich tang of molasses in my mother's cookies. I associate it with happiness."

Stubborn man. "I would be happy if Skye ate a few more apples."

"Are you one of those over-principled vegan princesses?"

"No." She laughed and dodged a pothole. "I spend a lot of time worrying about my kid."

"Fair enough. You're too pretty for that Earth

mother shit."

She raised her eyebrows. "Careful. You're not in Louisiana anymore."

He resettled his muscled frame in the worn passenger seat. "Here's what I know. You said, flowers glitter with dewdrops and sway in the soft spring breeze? Well, cane stalks soak up the summer sun and drive local economic development. The other parts of the state rely on petrochemicals and tourism. My family? We grow sugar. That's my crop."

"Then why were you working in the oilfield?"

"I enjoy getting my hands dirty."

She nodded. "Well, we've got plenty of dirt." She put on her signal and slowed for a thirty-foot wide dirt and gravel access road leading to her farm. The road bisected a field of tall brown corn stalks, and she turned on the high beams so he could see more than the road in front of the truck. "This is the Smith Specialty Potatoes Farm. They grow red, white, yellow, and purple potatoes."

He leaned forward.

"It's an impressive operation." The truck bumped along the access road. "The corn is mostly a rotation crop. The Smith family sponsors the Winter Festival and maintains a good team onsite to manage the farm logistics while they're away."

He scratched the stubble on his face. "Why are we driving through their farm?"

She kept her hands on the wheel and decided to suspend the history lesson. *Some memories are less painful than others.* "It's a private access servitude."

"Is this the only way to your farm?"

She shook her head. "I have an access point from

the river road, but from town, this road is the fastest way to come and go."

"How big is this potato farm?"

"Close to a thousand acres."

Julien whistled. "They've got you blocked in."

"Like I said, the river road is the other point of access."

"How'd you end up living at the end of Potato Alley?"

Eliza took a deep breath. *Word travels fast in the county. I'd do better to get ahead of the gossip.* "The land used to belong to my family."

"Ancient history?"

She took a deep breath. His honesty and self-awareness gave her courage. "My father sold off the land piece by piece to pay his gambling debts. He softened the blow by giving me first right of refusal on future sales, but I doubt I'll ever invoke those rights."

Julien shifted in his seat. "I'm sorry."

Eliza shook her head and ignored the note of empathy in his voice. "Don't be. He also put me on a pony as soon as I could hold the reins. When I was a kid, I didn't know what they discussed behind closed doors, but I knew I loved him."

Chapter Four

Julien thought about the people he loved in Louisiana. Their kindness smothered him and kept him from sharing his thoughts. *We don't upset Mama. We don't rock the boat.* He smiled. *Eliza wouldn't last a week down there, bless her heart.*

She slowed the truck to a stop and hopped out of the vehicle to unlock a farm gate. The wide, metal barrier stayed open as she navigated across old metal pipes that might have once kept livestock on the land.

The rain slowed.

Julien put a hand on the door, prepared to jump out and do something useful. "Do you want me to close it?"

"I can do it." She navigated the gravel drive to the farmhouse. The truck's high beams merged with the security lighting and flooded the yard with yellow light. "That building is the foreman's cottage and summer bunkhouse. The wooden barn with the security lights houses the florist business, and the greenhouses support the farm."

"You need all this infrastructure to grow flowers?"

She frowned. "The big white structures are the three hoop houses where I grow early blooms. I have a seed propagation greenhouse, too. You can't see the river through the trees, but if you climb the bank in the morning, you'll catch an amazing view across Saratoga Passage, Skagit Bay, and the Whidbey and Camano

Islands."

I bet you'd love the marshes back home. He shook his head, remembering her quick correction when he tested the waters between them. *Look, but don't touch. It's like Vegas.* Then he thought of the professional women who overlooked club rules at the first sign of crisp bills. *Except it's not.*

Eliza parked in front of the farmhouse and turned off the truck.

Her comments kept him on track, and he focused on evaluating the farm buildings.

"The fields start on the other side of the drive and follow the rising elevation until they run into a stand of trees separating us from the potato farm. You said you spent some time in the Tetons? Well, when the sun comes up, you'll find we've got great views of the Cascades and Olympic Mountains."

Julien opened the door and listened to the cold night air. "We're close to I-5?"

She nodded. "I have a new septic system and a solar array connected to the power grid. I aim for self-sufficiency, but a couple of generators provide automatic backup power. Like I said, it's rural."

"I'm sure it's a pretty piece of property," he said.

She exhaled and reached for the door handle. "Like I said, wait until the sun comes up."

Climbing out of the truck, he yawned and stretching his arms above his head. "Do you want some help with the groceries?"

"Yeah, but the groceries will keep." She walked to the back of the truck. "I'll introduce you to Claire and Skye before I let you loose on the farm. I don't want them to feel uncomfortable seeing someone new around the yard, but let's walk though the other buildings first. We can start with the cottage."

He let down the tailgate and considered his duffle before deciding he could always come back and get the bag. His leg ached from hours on the motorcycle, but the ride from the hardware store gave him more to think about than muscle pains. He considered calling Brandon but figured his big brother had more important things than to keep track of his movements.

Eliza approached the barn and stopped short. "I thought I forgot to turn off the work lights." She shook her head. "I didn't see their car beside the greenhouse. They shouldn't be here this late."

Julien tensed. "More trouble?"

A smile broke through her worried expression. "No, a couple of headstrong teenage girls."

He laughed and followed her into the illuminated barn. Instead of livestock and fresh hay, the room smelled of roses and cut greens. He blinked to get his bearings and thought of cane fields after harvest, shorn clean before the burn. Then the two teenagers came into focus, and he recognized their guilty looks.

"We, uh, decided to stay and put in a few more hours." The one with a long brown ponytail scratched her head.

The younger girl nodded. "You need our help."

Her eager-to-please gaze remained focused on her boss. He let Eliza handle her assistants and looked at a series of vases on the far counter, half-filled with vibrant blooms. A sinuous rope of greenery snaked around the old wooden worktable in the middle of the room, and he lifted his nose, catching the ripe scent of livestock hidden in the recesses of the barn. *Pigs. She said nothing about pigs.*

"I told you to go home after ICE left."

"Well, Claire said we could stay."

"We've been over this." Eliza put her hands on her hips. "I'm your boss."

"You don't have to pay us." The younger girl mimicked her boss' pose. "We're trying to help you."

"Of course, I'm paying you!"

Julien smiled, imagining himself as a teenager more interested in getting into trouble than helping his father run the farm. *Brandon was always the good son.* Two curious gazes focused on him. He shifted his stance and lifted a hand. "I'm the new foreman."

The teenagers looked to Eliza.

She nodded.

Interesting. They might enjoy butting heads, but they still defer to her.

She stepped closer to the teenagers. "This is Julien Kroger. Luke talked him into helping us out now that Gabe's gone." She gestured toward the older girl. "Michelle's a senior in high school, and Serah's two years younger. Their mom would have called them home by now, but school's on break, and they overruled me in favor of finishing their work."

"Not a bad choice." He offered his hand to the oldest girl. She appraised him with the brazen confidence of a teenager verging on womanhood, but he nodded politely and broke the connection. *You can't handle me, girl.* The other sister took his hand as well, but she barely looked at him and kept her attention focused on Eliza.

"Does he know what he's doing?"

Eliza crossed her arms and nodded. "I think so, but

why don't you ask him?"

The teenager with gold-streaked hair and dirt on her cheek looked at him like Eliza picked him out of the supermarket's bargain bin. *Well, you should have seen the other specimens left in the bin.* He braced himself for the teenager's interrogation.

"Eliza's got twenty acres."

He scanned the weathered surroundings. "She mentioned something about a farm."

The worry lines between Serah's eyebrows deepened. "Gabe worked hard. Back in November, we helped him tuck tens of thousands of spring flowering bulbs into the ground. He dug those trenches by hand, and we loaded them with enough bulbs to fuel Eliza's cut flower production and field trials."

Julien shifted his weight. "Good thing I know how to use a shovel."

"The last thing she needs is someone who doesn't know how to drive a tractor."

He raised his eyebrows and looked at Eliza. "You said nothing about a tractor."

She shrugged. "All the modern conveniences. I assume you can drive a stick."

"Yes, ma'am." He hoped the teenagers missed his wink. "About as well as you can."

Eliza blushed.

The older sister groaned. "Come, on, Serah. Either he'll figure out how to be useful, or Eliza will fire him. We have enough to do before the weekend wedding without managing the help."

Julien suppressed laughter at Michelle calling him "the help" but noted how the girl composed her crestfallen features and recovered from his simple rejection. He focused on the younger sister to establish where they stood. The younger girl's fierce loyalty toward Eliza deserved his respect, but he had no intention of making a pint-sized enemy on day one. "I'll make you a deal, Miss Serah. You see me doing something wrong, you let me know about it. Otherwise, I'll assume we're all good friends and here to make Ms. Eliza's life a little easier."

Serah nodded, her slow smile building into a welcoming grin.

He returned the smile and gestured toward the floral tools scattered across the worktable. "Don't ask me to arrange the pretty flowers. That's your department."

Eliza kicked the ground.

Turning to her, he looked for signs of approval.

She looked up. Her lips twitched with the hint of a smile.

Unable to sheath his own, he grinned and tallied a point for himself. He respected her desire to draw a thick black line between her family and her professional interests. *I would do the same, but life on a sugar farm often crosses boundaries. The families are so entwined with the land we can't see the dangers lurking on worn paths.* He raised his eyebrows, wanting her to understand he knew and respected her limits.

She nodded and strode past him.

He logged her approval and fell into step behind her. His background check might come back clean, but his mama taught him to let his behaviors lead by example. Then the soft sway of Eliza's hips and the tension of the worn denim stretched across her ass erased every thought of home. *I can maintain boundaries as long as you want me to, Ms. Eliza, but as soon as you give me a sign, I'm more than willing to test the limits between us.*

"If Claire said you could stay, then I assume she made enough food for dinner. Let's get these arrangements put away and tidy up the garlands so we can work on them tomorrow," she said.

Michelle shelved tools in labeled drawers. "You'll be busy showing your new foreman around the farm."

He winced. Each clunk of metal a confirmation Michelle believed her role in the business outweighed his presence.

"Don't worry about this mess. We'll take care of it."

"We all pitch in," Eliza said.

Her tone sounded as firm as her ass. The clunking metal slowed. He nodded, looking for something helpful to do in the women's domain. *I thought I had a soft spot for soft feminine curves, but I've always admired a fit woman.* He thought of his brother's curvy wife and shook his head. *I have no reason to compare the two women. They're both off limits.* Spotting a broom and a trashcan, he swept floor cuttings into a small, dusty pile. The three women moved around him, their movements like a complicated dance.

The younger sister opened a large cooler and placed the half-constructed arrangements back on the wire shelves. "Aren't they pretty?"

He looked at the pale pink roses and fuzzy white leaves of the arrangements. *They're flowers.* "Prettiest I've seen in a long time."

The women shrugged, their expressions unimpressed by his general praise.

Julien leaned on the broom. "I like the color palate."

Serah giggled.

Michelle frowned, her thumb caressing the handle of a knife.

The blade looked wickedly sharp.

"Do you know anything about flowers?" she asked.

He ignored the question and kept his gaze trained on the blade. The practiced motions of the female crew left him feeling out of place, but he had no intention of making the local news as an unidentified body. "That's quite the knife."

She looked up from the blade and slipped the tool into a leather scabbard. "A design knife. Serah still uses clippers, but a design knife lets me arrange the stems much faster." Fanning her fingers, she displayed the pale pink skin of recent scars. "I cut myself every so often, but the pain is worth the inconvenience."

"Michelle's passionate about her work." Eliza closed the distance between them and placed a hand on Michelle's shoulder.

I bet. His stomach rumbled.

Serah giggled again.

"Pardon me." He ignored the hunger pangs and returned to his task, watching the specs of hay float in the work light above his growing pile of leaves and bits of wire. A hot drink and a leather recliner sounded more appealing than busywork, but he refused to give Eliza a reason to doubt his word. Their encounter at the hardware store suggested the woman needed reassurance as much as she needed a capable hand. He shook his head and reached for the dustpan. *Set me loose on the farm. I can work all day in this weather without breaking a sweat.*

Michelle jerked back from the arrangement and stuck her finger in her mouth. "Ouch! I didn't see that thorn."

Eliza stopped tidying the workspace. She offered the teenager a bandage from a small pile waiting on the desk. "How many times have you done that?"

Serah rolled her eyes. "A thousand. Between the knife and the thorns, most normal people would learn to slow down."

He struggled not to laugh. *The younger sister isn't milk toast.*

Michelle refused Eliza's bandage, glared at her sister, and stuck her finger in her mouth.

He pushed his pile of clippings toward Eliza and jerked his head toward the sisters. "You have your hands full."

She looked at the sisters and shrugged. "They learn at different paces."

"Don't we all?"

She raised her eyebrows. "I can't afford to pay you to come up to speed."

"Set me loose on the farm, Eliza. I can handle it."

"Too good to sweep the barn?"

He tipped his head. "You're the one paying the bills."

"I know it." She picked up a box of vases and climbed a stepladder.

Leaning on the broom, he watched her maintain her balance with her arms full of glass. *It's one thing to run a crew of rough and tumble men who are too gruff to show their feelings. It's a whole 'nother ballgame to play mother hen to a couple of moody teenagers, a six-*

year-old, and her widowed mother, but she's doing it. I have to give her credit for that feat. "I promise, you're getting a good deal."

She nodded from the stepladder. "I'm counting on it."

A chicken sauntered down the hard-packed aisle and examined him.

He wrinkled his nose. "You didn't mention poultry."

"I had other things on my mind." She climbed another rung, then paused and looked over her shoulder. "Don't worry about the chickens. They're basically pets."

He nodded and wondered what other surprises waited on the farm. Holding her gaze felt awkward, so he looked away and watched the determined hen go after a brown marmorated stinkbug. The insects feasted on a variety of crops, including vegetables, fruits, and berries. *I wouldn't put it past them to go after her flower crop, too.*

The hen claimed her prize.

He smiled and started sweeping again. "Looks like the hen's earning her keep."

"Ugh," Michelle said. "I hate those bugs. We never had them when I was a kid. They smell so damn bad."

Eliza lifted the box of vases over her head. "Watch your language."

The two teenagers looked at each other and smiled.

He moved toward the stepladder. "Do you want some help?"

She climbed down the stepladder, muttering about bosses and mentors. "Nope." She dusted her hands on her pants and surveyed the room. "All right, that's good enough. I know Julien's hungry, and you two were born starving. Let's go see what Claire made for dinner."

The teenagers nodded and moved toward the door.

Eliza reached for Michelle's arm and stalled her progress. "I know I sent you home, but I appreciate that you stayed late."

The older girl nodded.

"Please don't do it again," she added.

"You don't always know what's best."

Eliza raised her eyebrows.

Julien imagined the thoughts going through the teenager's head. *She doesn't appreciate us. She's heavy-handed. I know better.* He knew the dangers of those teenage thoughts and recognized Michelle's proud scars as a desire to prove her worth. *I know you want to prove yourself, but hurting yourself in the process won't get you there any faster.* He recalled his seesawing emotions in the months following his accident. Brandon's overbearing presence had not helped, and Julien had lashed out more than once. He looked at Michelle and Eliza and shook his head. *Hell, I'm in no place to give advice. Sometimes I wonder if I'll ever grow up.*

"And you know what's best?"

The teenager opened her mouth.

Serah took her sister's hand and pulled her toward the door. "Come on. I'm starving."

Eliza raised her eyebrows.

Michelle closed her mouth and followed her younger sister toward the door.

Eliza rubbed her hands over her eyes. "Good call, Serah. The next thing I know, I'll have labor relations knocking on my door."

Serah grinned. "Maybe we should unionize."

Michelle rolled her eyes. "What do you know about unions?"

"More than you. I'm not the one who failed American history. Twice."

"Let's focus on food." Eliza ushered them toward the door and turned to meet his gaze.

"I have no objections to food."

She waited until he passed the threshold and reached for the light switch.

The audible click removed the sweet warmth of the barn's interior. He pulled his damp jacket close to his neck to block the wind and the coming cold and then followed the trio into the waning light. *What have I gotten myself into?*

Chapter Five

Eliza led Julien and her assistants to the front porch of the farmhouse.

Claire cracked open the door. "Late night."

"Sorry," Eliza said.

Her daughter came out of the warm interior wearing a wool nightgown and fuzzy slippers. Backlit by the house's warm yellow lights, her pale hair glowed, and her shadow flooded the worn wooden steps as she slipped past Claire.

Eliza opened her arms wide. "Hello, Sweet Pea,"

Skye raced down the steps and wordlessly hugged her hips. She snuck a look at Julien, scrambled back to the safety of her grandmother's hand, and ignored the assistants' greetings.

"Skye, this is Julien," Eliza said.

The girl stared with wide eyes.

Her unabashed curiosity was empowered by the safety of her family's presence. Eliza smiled at Skye's interest and courage. She second-guessed change but knew her chubby toddler had willowed into a curious girl. *Two years passed since the accident.* "Julien will replace Gabe. He'll help look after your chickens and pigs."

Julien wrinkled his nose and glanced over his shoulder at the silhouetted barn. "I thought I smelled pigs."

She glanced at the barn and wondered if she needed to spend more time taking care of the livestock. "We have a few American Guinea Hogs. They're very calm and docile."

The man's jaw twitched.

"Skye loves them, and they help clean up the summer rows." She wondered what Julien looked like without the mess of floppy hair and cropped beard. In the bright lights of the hardware store, something in his bearing exuded strength, yet the man knew how to wield a broom.

He shook his head and grinned at Skye. "Then I guess they're earning their keep as well."

Skye let go of her grandmother's hand and came down to the bottom step. She inspected him at close range, her gaze traveling from his hair to the top of his boots. "I named my pets after the US presidents. We're not eating them."

He dropped to one knee and winked. "I don't like to name my dinner either."

Eliza grinned and thought about doubling his pay. She wondered how much the physical accommodation cost him, but lowering his frame to Skye's level ensured her undivided attention.

The girl took a step closer. "Do you believe in little people?" The cold night air amplified her stage whisper.

He looked to Eliza and raised his eyebrows.

Replaying the way he managed Serah and Michelle, she shrugged and decided to let him find his own ground in the world of make-believe. "Your call."

Turning back to the girl, he shifted his weight. "What was the question?"

"Do you believe in little people?" Skye asked.

He shook his head. "I've never seen a little person myself."

"They don't like to be seen. It ruins the magic."

He nodded. "Makes sense."

He knows how to walk the line.

Claire stamped her feet on the top step. "It's cold out here."

Eliza looked up and watched her mother's frown deepen. She understood Claire's boundary conditions. *We have more than enough room for Julien at the table, but she's harder to win over than Skye.*

Claire jerked her head toward the truck. "You're bringing up the groceries?"

Julien rose to standing. "Yes, ma'am."

Claire nodded. She focused on Serah and Michelle and inclined her head toward the door. "Come on in, girls. No reason for you to be standing outside in the cold."

We'll review double standards another night. She watched the teenagers scamper up the steps to obey.

Skye reached for their hands, and the threesome disappeared in Claire's wake.

Julien went to the truck and hefted the first bag of groceries.

Some change is good, but Skye needs to know the important things in her life will always remain the same. Her daddy and I love her, even if he's not here. She picked up a bag brimming with vegetables.

"Well, that went better than I expected," he said.

Mostly. She wondered what Claire told Skye about Gabe's departure and added the issue to the list of topics she would discuss with her daughter's therapist.

"She liked you well enough, but sometimes Skye's too trustworthy. I hope she toughens up before school in the fall. Claire's been homeschooling her. I mean, kindergarten is optional, but"—she shifted the grocery bags in her hands—"I don't want her to fall behind her peers."

"It's a lot to manage."

"It is."

He followed her up the steps, giving her space on the frosted steps, but she felt his presence and caught the warm musk of his skin when the wind shifted. She stopped under the glow of the porch light and watched him position his body near the handrails, even if he failed to use them. "You need to tell me if it's too much." The swishing movement of the river, the distant rumble of the interstate, and the chattering night bugs buffered her words from inquisitive ears.

He stepped onto the porch. "Too much what?"

"Too much family dynamics. Too many pairs of eyes watching you work. Too much distraction." She took a deep breath. "I don't want to worry about any more accidents. I saw how Michelle tested you"—he opened his mouth and she shifted the bag to one hip to hold up her hand—"but you did a good managing them. You did a good job with Skye. Hell, you even deferred to Claire."

He laughed and set down his load, then lifted her bag from her hip and set it down beside the others. Stepping closer, he rubbed a strand of hair between his fingers. "I have absolutely no interest in your teenage assistants."

"Good." She swallowed any further words on the subject, but he stood so close she felt the warmth emanating from his body. Hints of cedar stirred between them, and she inhaled the alluring combination of male sweat and subtle aftershave. *I started this banter. I'll feel better knowing where it might end.* "What does interest you?"

He raised his eyebrows. *"Do you know the first thing I thought when you stepped into the hardware store?"*

"Look at that crazy woman who is about to lose her mind?"

Laughing, he dropped the tendril of hair. "Close."

She exhaled at the lost connection but struggled to decide if losing contact relieved her or grieved her. She wondered if Julien's palms matched the texture of his boots, well worn and sturdy. The thought startled her, and she blinked. *A man's touch hasn't seemed like a priority in a long time.*

He reached for her hip, his hand branding her skin where the cold bite of the wind buffeted her side. Fighting the urge to recoil and shelter her feelings beneath layers of responsibility, she inhaled and met his gaze.

"I never doubted your sanity or your capability. I thought you looked as good in your jeans as any woman I've seen in a long time. I also thought you might appreciate the pleasure of a job well done."

"I do." She swallowed. "I hired you to help me with the fields."

"You did." He dropped his hands and shoved them in his pockets. "You're like a tightrope walker, Eliza. One of those nimble exhibitionists in a pretty uniform. I forget you carry a long, thin pole to maintain your balance and keep it all together."

She frowned, thinking she liked it better when he admired her butt.

"The pole keeps people away," he said, "but you know the secret to staying upright?"

"A short walk?"

He laughed. "Carrying the pole helps the walker concentrate more weight below their center of gravity. It also helps them maintain balance when all gazes are on their performance."

"Seems like a good plan." She crossed her arms.

Again, he reached for her hair. "Sure, arm yourself with a big stick, but sometimes you should take a deep breath and ask yourself why you're alone on the wire, walking a tightrope, and worried about the fall."

She thought of Claire's scheme to move the family to town and sell the farm. "I'm the only one left who's capable of doing what needs to be done." She closed her eyes, remembering that last time she found herself on a winter porch, skittish and intrigued, wondering what the future held. *Now Erik's dead.* She shuddered.

Inside the house, Skye squealed.

Two teenagers who felt like family members laughed in response.

"You're awfully philosophical for a farmhand, Julien Kroger," she said.

He laughed.

The door opened, and Claire's narrowed gaze took in the minimal distance between them. "Did one of the bags break?"

"No, ma'am." He reached down and picked up his load. "I stopped for a minute to catch my breath beneath a beautiful night sky."

Claire glanced at the cloudy sky. "It's going to

snow. You'd better get settled in the cottage before you lose your way in the dark." She lifted a bag from Julien's hands, favoring her good arm over the one damaged by a stroke. "I can take it from here."

Yep, just like high school. Eliza picked up her grocery bag and one Julien still held. *One step forward and two steps back.* "Sorry."

The man shrugged.

Skye poked her head out of the door. "Mommy, aren't you coming inside for dinner?" She cocked her head and stared at the three of them.

"In a minute, Sweet Pea. Go back into the house with Serah and Michelle to have your supper. Granny will save me a plate. I'll get Julien settled in the cottage before I come read you a story." She ferried the bags into the warmth of the kitchen, ignored Claire's gaze, and left her daughter to chatter while Serah and Michelle filled water glasses.

Julien stood near the truck with his bag on his shoulder. "Care for a nightcap?"

She laughed and pretended not to understand his real question. Mutual awareness pulsed between them, but Claire was right to interrupt them on the porch steps. *I have more important things to worry about.* Walking past him, she shook her head and hoped the shadows of the security lighting hid her wistful expression.

She led him to the wood frame cottage, opened the door, and turned on the lights. "The cottage is one of the newer buildings on the property." She heard him close the door and headed straight for the thermostat. "Last summer, Gabe added a pad with a barbeque pit next to the covered porch. The building has a large bedroom, a kitchen, a bath, and an extra bedroom with bunks for seasonal workers or grooms."

"Grooms?"

She paused. "My father used to train racehorses when we had more land."

"Is that what led to the potato farm next door?"

She looked over her shoulder, wondering how much time remained before he put two and two together. "He was successful for a while."

"Most good gamblers have a lucky streak." He held her gaze without flinching.

The implications of her ancestry settled between them, and she swallowed, wondering how much time would elapse until he added up the rest of the variables and realized her father not only lost bets, but he buckled under the weight and consequences of his actions. She looked away and ground her emotions as she took in the comfortable and worn furniture of the cottage. *It's a small town with very few secrets. Julien will figure out I'm barely holding onto what we have left, and then he'll leave before the thaw. My success doesn't depend on what he thinks of this place.* Without the flow of fresh air, the interior of the cottage smelled of dust and wet carpet. She wrinkled her nose and ignored the intimacy of Julien's observations. "Gabe's things are still in the house, but I'll help you box them up tomorrow."

He set his bag on the worn oak table and surveyed his new accommodations. "The man didn't have a lot."

She put her hands on her hips and exhaled. *I thought he enjoyed living a simple life. He never asked for more.* "Gabe lived here, but his heart must have been somewhere else. I wish I could have done more to help him."

"How long did he work here?"

"Ever since my husband died. We worked hand in hand for nearly two years."

"Sounds like plenty of time to warn you about his undocumented status."

She nodded and picked up Gabe's faded sweatshirt, draping it over a kitchen chair like he might walk in the door at any moment. "I don't really care about the man's origins, but his deception frustrated me, and I'm not about to let that type of secrecy become a hallmark of my life." She gestured to the books and magazines stacked on the coffee table. "The pots, pans, and household things belong to the farm. I'm not sure what will happen to all his stuff, but use your discretion and stay out of his personal things."

Julien smiled and took a step closer. "I am the soul of discretion."

She scanned his biceps and wondered how he could still make passes after glimpsing the complications in her life. "I doubt that."

Taking the hint, he opened the refrigerator and scanned the contents. "Not much to eat."

"Claire will bring you some food. She's an amazing cook."

"Luke certainly agrees."

She wrinkled her nose, wondering how to extract herself from the intimacy of the room. "The cabinets probably have some chips or snacks you'd want." Silence filled the space between them, but she failed to move.

He stepped closer.

Choose, Eliza! How many chances will you get?

She considered the pleasure of rolling around the cottage with a hot-blooded male who thought she looked good in a pair of jeans. *I don't care if he has an itch to scratch, but what happens in the morning when I still need help?* Putting the needs of the farm above her own prickling desires, she retreated until her back touched the cold door and brushed the hair from her eyes. "I'll check on Skye and meet you in the hoop house after you've had your dinner. I want to get the frost cloth over the rows before the temperature drops."

"Yes, ma'am." He grinned.

She found Claire putting away the groceries. Skye colored at the kitchen table while Serah and Michelle finished the last of their meals. All four faces looked up and acknowledged her before returning to their tasks. She made her way around the kitchen, used to skirting the perimeter of Claire's kitchen until the day's work ended. *I'm starving.*

"Where'd you pick up the stray cat?" Claire asked.

Shit. I knew bringing Julien onboard wouldn't be so easy. She made a plate, dropped to a chair, and looked at her mother.

Claire blinked.

"Luke made the introduction," she said.

Her mother raised her eyebrows, opened a sack of cornmeal, and poured the grain into a large storage container. "Fair enough. Where does Julien call home?"

"Louisiana."

Skye stopped coloring. "Where's that?"

Eliza looked at her daughter. *I should have known they were all listening.* "All the way at the bottom of the country, where it's warm." She wondered if her daughter picked up the context of Claire's comment.

He's not a stray. He's far from home, and he's going back there.

Serah and Michelle exchanged looks.

She realized she had more than one impressionable mind to manage. "Mr. Kroger is staying on the farm to help us manage logistics like Gabe did before he left. His family grows sugar cane, and I think he'll be an asset during the winter months. Come spring, he'll probably go somewhere else. He wasn't planning to stop here, but he was nice enough to help us out. In the meantime, I want you all to be helpful, and I'll keep looking for a long-term foreman." She hoped the older girls heard the subtext of her statement. *Don't get too attached, and don't get any ideas.*

"Okay," Skye said.

Eliza exhaled. "Did you pick out your stories?" She rose and popped a mug of water in the microwave before she turned to face her daughter.

The girl shook her head, and her white-blonde braids bounced along her shoulders.

One day she won't want me to braid her hair like that. "Brush your teeth?"

"Not yet."

Michelle and Serah carried their dishes to the sink and thanked Claire for the meal.

The older woman nodded, handed them both an extra cookie, and walked them to the front door. "We'll see you tomorrow."

"Thanks for the help." Eliza turned and focused on Skye in the quiet kitchen. "Run upstairs and brush your teeth, Sweet Pea. I'll be right up."

Skye's face pinched. "Do I have to?"

No, you don't have to do anything, but what

happens next? We stay up half the night being silly, and I still have a farm to run in the morning. She kissed the top of her daughter's head and thought of the soft milky smells she remembered from Skye's infant days. "Don't make me say it again."

Claire returned to the kitchen. "Listen to your mother."

Skye scowled at both of them and tromped up the stairs.

Unperturbed, Claire turned to her daughter. "What else do you know about the man?"

"He knows his way around a farm. He has a prosthesis on his right leg. Michelle got sassy, and he put her in her place easily enough." She swallowed. "He hasn't shown an interest in anything but helping me out of a tight spot."

Claire raised her eyebrows.

She held her mother's stare, hoping the older woman would skip her obvious interest in the man. *Okay, I might have omitted my attraction.*

"What happened to his leg?" Claire asked.

"Some type of industrial accident." She decided to let Julien tell his story on his own terms.

"Are you sure he can he do the work?"

She swallowed. "I think so."

Claire glanced out the kitchen window at the shadowy buildings. "He's not bad looking."

"Mom."

The woman shrugged, her good shoulder lifting higher than her bad one. "What?"

Eliza smiled and pulled the hot water from the beeping microwave. She dropped a tea bag in the cup and waited for the leaves to steep. "He's easy to look at, but that doesn't mean I'm interested. I have plenty of complications in my life."

Claire nodded and folded a dishtowel. "You said he's here until spring?"

"Not sure. Like I said, Luke roped him into the job." *And I owe Luke more than a wad of cash if the arrangement works out.*

The older woman shook her head. "None of you have any sense."

Look who's talking. She kept her mouth shut and decided to play offense. Pulling the wooden spoon from her coat pocket, she presented the gift to her mother. "Funny. Luke said the same thing about you."

Claire reached for the spoon and inspected the wood's smooth grain. Pleasure widened her gaze, and a soft smile lifted her lips.

She deserves to be happy. "He made it for you."

Claire looked up. "Did he?"

Pleased to regain the upper hand, if only for a minute, Eliza smiled. "More or less."

Chapter Six

Julien emptied a bag of the last foreman's potato chips, changed out of his damp clothes, and headed outside where a low fog hovered above the fields. The wind caught his neck, and he pulled his jacket tighter, glancing at the old farmhouse glowing against the cold blue sky. Turning, he walked toward the sound of the river. *I have a basic grasp of the layout, but I have no intention of stumbling into a drainage ditch or finding myself on the sharp side of a forgotten farm implement.*

Trees thinned as he climbed a small dike and spied the water rippling across a bed of stones. Mist floated above the surface, and vapors spilled over the banks, hiding stranded puddles and unseen footfalls. He inhaled. *I feel good to be back amid nature. That west Texas rig site was too dry and barren for my tastes. I'm used to the shadows at the edge of the cane fields and moss hanging from the cypress trees.*

A fish jumped, and an eagle swooped from the trees to snatch it.

He frowned. *The species of fish waiting in the river doesn't matter. I need more time before I feel confident navigating this type of terrain, much less casting graceful arcs or landing anything that counts.* He turned back toward the farm.

Two figures ran toward a sedan and closed the doors. The car sped down the gravel drive.

Michelle must be driving. He retraced his steps and

faced the first of three hoop houses. The taut fabric reflected the moonlight, and the sturdy structure held fast against the wind. He peered inside and inhaled warm, moist air. He flipped on a series of lights hanging from the structure's steel ribs, closed the door, and started transferring boxes from the truck. Not knowing which flowers Eliza valued the most, he staged the bundles between all three structures and hoped she bought enough cloth to protect everything in sight. Then he got to work.

Twenty minutes later, Eliza pulled back the exterior fabric and scanned the space.

He stopped examining the heat mats and rubbed the thick, white fabric between his fingers. The plants looked healthy, but he had a hard time comparing them to his experiences with cane. "The fabric won't smother the seedlings?"

"No, they're sturdy enough."

He thought of the acres Brandon managed back home. *Nothing but starlight and prayers to protect that cash crop.* Temperatures near freezing would kill the terminal buds and brown the leaves, but the plants would recover. Low twenties could cause terminal damage, but the family had never been that unlucky. He imagined the setback of losing acres of commercial crops. *Would the roots even survive?* He considered the tender green leaves in the hoop house. *What type of woman insists on nurturing seedlings through this weather?* Shaking his head, he focused on completing his task, but he could not bide the awkwardness of silence between strangers. "This is quite the setup. I've never seen the like."

She dropped to her knees and pulled a utility knife

from her belt. "My late husband and I built them. We'd only been on the farm for a week before we realized we needed cold protection. Horses live in barns, but flowers don't." She opened the first box and nodded, her fingers rubbing the fabric. "Frost protection sounds obvious, but we were learning on the fly and building a new dream from the ground up."

"His dream or yours?"

Turning, she met his gaze. "Mine, but Erik deserves the credit for making it happen."

"Having a partner lessens the load." The childhood phrase slipped from his lips without forethought. He expected amicable agreement, but he watched Eliza pause before she returned to the packaging. His quip felt awkward, and he scratched his head, not knowing where he blundered.

"My family used to raise apples on this land. Then horses when I was young," she said.

"Before the acreage went to potatoes."

She nodded. "The equestrian side ended before Erik showed up, but he understood my connection to the acreage. When I told him about my dream to grow flowers, he did his part to make this our home."

"That was gallant."

Her hands paused, and she looked up. "Sometimes gallant can backfire. I spent months pitching my dreams before Erik would consider jeopardizing our urban accomplishments." She tucked her long bangs behind her ear. "But you're right, when push came to shove, he made it happen." She brushed her hands on her pants and looked past the taut fabric of the hoop house. "At the first hint of cold weather, we found schematics for the hoop houses, dug the troughs for the plastic baseboards, and stretched fabric over prefabricated bows we ordered from the hardware store."

"You did good."

She looked at him. "Constructing the hoop houses gave us a jump-start on the growing season. It felt like magic."

He stretched his lower back and adjusted his perspective to understand a crop that went from seed to harvest in under a month. *What does a jump-start get you in Louisiana? Growing cane with a marketable sugar content means we need twelve to fifteen months without a touch of that stalk-ripping frost. I'm not ready for magic.* "Who decided to rig up the overhead lights?"

"That was my idea. They're for warmth and visibility."

"Interesting move."

Her hands stilled for a moment, but she resumed unboxing bolts of fabric. "I admit it's unique."

He rushed to clarify his interest and purge any hints of criticism from his voice. "Do you worry about the structures getting too hot?"

Her shoulders relaxed. "I open the plastic ceiling vents in the morning and close them in the afternoon. It's easy enough to moderate the temperature and let the plants breathe."

Reading this woman isn't easy, but damn, she's worth it in those jeans. He exhaled. "I'm impressed." He faced the rows of young plants with bolts of cloth in his arms. Dirt spacers ran between the rows and left enough room for a person to stand. "I'm also realizing I have a lot to learn."

"Flower crops have to be cut-and-come-again or succession-planted with faithful precision." She stared at the seedlings. "That rigor means timing is critical, and the sooner I start, the better chance I have of coming out ahead. I need interesting blooms with substantial vase life to keep customers coming back to my partner retail locations."

"Like the farm stand."

She nodded, leaned down, and examined the bright green leaves of a young plant. "This structure houses ranunculus and anemones. They're the backbone of many florist arrangements."

He nodded, waiting for her to guide their conversation. "And the others?"

"A mix of flowers and foliage. Some greenhouses house two-year-old saplings. Erik thought he could turn a profit on a tree farm, but I'm not sure who has that type of long-term stamina."

He swallowed a laugh and kept his mouth shut until he understood her sense of humor. *Easy, stallion. You've known her less than four hours, and she's your boss.*

"Kale and lettuce take up a small portion of the back house." She looked upward and smiled. "Claire likes to have her salads."

He cleared his throat. "So what goes in the fields come springtime?"

"You'd recognize the blooms from the grocery store. Roses, sunflowers, lilies, zinnias..." She ticked off the names on her fingers, then went full-on into flower mode, her animated gestures lending a rhythm to the cadence of additional names.

As the list of unfamiliar names lengthened, he focused on her voice and the work at hand. *Southern women take pride in being eccentric. This dedication doesn't make her less appealing, but a good portion of the South would wonder if she's speaking in tongues.* He struggled to hide his grin before she caught onto his amusement.

She adjusted the bolt of cloth in her arms. "Fluttery scabiosa, stiff celosia, and papery statice to give the bouquets interesting texture. I'm always on the lookout for new ideas." She finally looked at him. "I scavenge greenery and filler whenever I find something that catches my eye."

He shrugged. "You lost me at zinnias."

She blinked. "Really?"

"Really." He smiled to soften the blow.

Shaking her head, she began draping the fabric. "Let's cover these plants first. If the forecast turns out to be accurate, the frost cloth will buy me a few degrees. Start at the end of the row and place it in line with the rows. Use a stake every five feet to give the fabric height, and be careful of the foliage."

He nodded and got to work.

"They each have their charms. Take the roses, for instance."

Her voice softened with the cadence of free-flowing thoughts and short pauses. He craned his head to catch her words.

"I picked a site with good drainage, but most of the plants in the fields are old garden roses, developed prior to 1867. It's really important to guard their roots."

He liked listening to her as much as he liked looking at her ass. "What happened in 1867?" he asked to keep her talking.

She brushed her bangs from her eyes and squinted.

Feeling like a local who never left the swamp, he

shifted and increased his pace.

"The world met the first Hybrid Tea Rose."

He grinned. "Of course." *A one-word answer doesn't exist in Louisiana, but thorns or not, it's hard to get a grip on this woman.* "I've heard of tea roses."

"Most old garden roses are own-root roses. They don't have a root graft to provide the strength and stability commercial growers covet. If winter temperatures kill a grafted plant, the rootstock can take over and send up its own blooms." She took a deep breath. "I don't worry about the weather affecting my field roses. If the plants survive, I know they will send up consistent suckers in the spring. Babying them all year long pays off because they're both beautiful and dependable."

Like you? He looked up. "This doesn't seem like the right time to ask about your favorite color."

Laughing, she straightened the cloth in front of her. "Lavender, but don't cut anything without asking me first. Your time at Hartley Farms might be good for a laugh, but when you leave here, you'll know the difference between showy crap and a good bouquet."

Looking at the naked dirt and tender seedlings, he tried to remember the last time he ventured into a florist's shop or glanced at the flowers in a grocery store. He came up short. *Don't count on it.* The steady *pat-pat* of returning raindrops kept him company while he worked in silence. The rhythm of the drops reminded him of the urgency of their task while the sheet plastic rippled beneath the wind's impact. He changed his posture to avoid muscle cramps, but by the time he reached the last row, his stomach and his muscles both ached. *I should have insisted on real food.*

Eliza reached the end of her row and glanced over.

The purple shadows beneath her eyes made him feel guilty for admiring her figure. *She needs help, not a roll in the hay.* He shook his head. "What would you have done if I hadn't shown up at the hardware store?"

She climbed to her feet. "Worked twice as long."

Nodding, he followed her to the second hoop house.

Dropping to her knees, she unrolled another bolt of cloth. "Tell me more about Louisiana."

He smiled. "It's muggy. Animals thrive where people can't put down roots."

"Animals?"

"Snakes. Gators. The terrain requires a special person to eke out a living down there. Or a desperate one. What do you want to know?" He answered her questions about food and music to help pass the time.

"And Mardi Gras?"

His nose itched, and he swiped his thumb along the side. "I prefer our country celebrations. They're more authentic."

She laughed. "I can't imagine being decked out in plastic beads."

The offhand comment sobered his thoughts. "Why not? I used to be the life of the party."

"I bet."

He shook his head, wondering what she saw as he knelt by her side. A broken-down Cajun desperate to make a buck? The settlement money in his accounts did little to fill the void where his self worth and direction once pulsed. *What does life feel like when you wake up each morning and feel excited about*—he shook his head—*fluffy scabiosa?*

93

Eliza rocked back to her heels.

The movement startled him. "You quitting early on me, Eliza?"

"Nope. I'm admiring the view."

Her slight smile might give a man reason to mistake her intent, but her narrowed gaze suggested she had something more than work on her mind. He scanned the tight enclosure and shifted his weight.

"I think I got an upgrade," she said.

He scratched his jaw. "How do you figure?"

"Gabe? He wouldn't be out here this late, but you're here with me."

He laughed. *So much for thinking she admired my assets.* "So, you're just happy you're not doing this alone?"

"Well, that helps, but you're kind of intimidating." She smiled. "I'm glad I took a chance. Luke caught me at a weak moment."

He shelved his thoughts and focused on work, letting conversation fill the uneasiness left vacant by his thoughts. "The old vet seems very protective, but when the novelty of my presence wears off, you won't have any trouble running me off."

"What if I don't want to run you off?"

He started. *And here, I thought I was the only person doing the looking.* A slow, speculative smile warmed his skin. "What happened to boundaries?"

She laughed and returned to her work. "Take it up with HR."

Just like that? We're done? Determined not to let the moment pass, he cleared his throat. "I made my interest clear when we stood on the porch."

"Claire interrupted us."

"And while you walked me to the cottage?"

She looked over the rows of tender plants. "Too much, too soon."

He followed her gaze and surveyed the sheltered plants. *She has too much to lose. Two steps forward and one step back. Let the lady lead.* He sighed, watching her shake her head and get back to work. *Not the first time a person's used me for their own benefit, and it won't be the last.* "You give me the word when you've sorted it all out."

She wiped the sweat from her forehead. "I've developed a reputation for being irritable."

"No way." He stretched the phrase into comedic disbelief, testing her limits. "Irritable women can't be as beautiful as you are."

Looking his way, she rolled her eyes. "I might make an exception for your accent and easy charm."

"You let me know." He exhaled, wondering if he came on too strong. *Easy charm?* He shook his head and thought of the reasons women sought his attention. Wealth and local prestige used to rank high on the list, but features matured, and curiosity climbed the rankings after he left the small town where he grew up. Then the rig's heavy load came crashing to the ground.

He wanted to ignore the interested stares of women who caught sight of the prosthesis, but he understood the difference between admiration and idle curiosity. *What does Eliza know about me, a roughneck from a southern parish?* The silence stretched between them. He cleared his throat. *I can't remember the last time someone looked at me with honest appreciation.* The thought of mixing labor and lust appealed, but this situation felt too uncertain for anything more aggressive than a compliment. If he pushed her too far, he might end up flat on his ass on the side of the highway. Then again, her ability to deliver on that threat turned him on. The moving river water and shifting tree branches caught his ear. "The rain's stopped again."

She stuck a stake in the ground. "We're almost done." Five minutes later, she left without saying a word.

He followed her outside, where a cloudless sky greeted him, and a full moon glowed above the treetops. The cold, clean air filled his lungs. "The temperature's dropping." He waited for the easy banter to return but watched her fold her arms in front of her chest. Her face no longer reflected playful admiration or the quiet intimacy of the hoop houses. Its wide-eyed gaze scanned the fields, accepting the elements and the consequences to her livelihood.

"We'll see what survives," she said.

Hating the vulnerability in her voice, he reached for her to offer warmth.

She stepped away at the last second.

He drew back his hand and ran it through his hair. "I can't get a read on you."

She nodded. "You're not the first person to say that."

"Were any of them successful?"

"Once or twice, I thought someone might have a chance, but I still have to get the job done." She looked at the old farmhouse and tucked her hands in her pockets. "Good evening, Julien. Good luck getting settled."

"Evening, Eliza. Tomorrow's another day."

She nodded and left him.

Without the need to disguise his discomfort, he favored his leg and made his way back to the cottage. His residual limb throbbed, his back ached, and he wanted nothing more than a hot shower and rich meal. Well, he wanted Eliza, but their tug-of-war offered more than a shallow reward and a heavy sleep. As soon as the cottage door closed, he stripped out of his damp clothes and pulled a pair of dry boxers from his bag. *Stupid northwestern rain, leaving a man uncertain of where he stands. Give me a good ol' fashioned thunderstorm, and let's be done with it.*

He opened the refrigerator and thanked Gabe for leaving him a sugar-laced Coke. The old couch looked clean enough. He opened the bottle and propped a chair under his scarred knee, polishing off the fizzy drink while the metal prosthesis hung cantilevered in the air. He stared at the contraption like an unwanted friend but unstrapped the green metal contraption and laid the high-tech device on the worn carpet. His muscles relaxed without the added weight, and he peeled off the liner sock, considering the angry red scar at the end of his knee. A day of physical punishment left its mark, but he closed his eyes and ignored the punishing feedback. *Damn, work feels good.*

The front door opened, and Eliza's mother walked into the cottage without bothering to knock. She cradled a casserole dish under her left arm. "Thought you might be hungry."

The food carried the rich scent of melted cheese. He started to stand and eyed the prosthesis. Practicalities overrode his principals and his impulse to defend his domain. Remembering his boxers, he grabbed a pillow to cover his lap. "Howdy, Claire."

She put the Pyrex dish on the beaten-up kitchen table and looked at his injured leg.

He returned the favor and glanced at the droop in her right arm.

"Stroke," she said, "we'll make quite the pair."

When do Eliza's burdens end? Her mother's impairment seemed minor, but he encountered people who treated an amputee like an oddity worth collecting or a missing slot on their intimate bucket list. He took a deep breath. "Does your daughter have a soft spot for damaged goods?"

The woman opened a kitchen drawer and withdrew silverware. "She has a soft spot for her Skye. The rest of us have to fend for ourselves."

He laughed, using the noise to disguise his relief. "She works herself to the bone."

She nodded and produced a plate.

The plum-colored shadows beneath Eliza's eyes lingered in his memory. *Her skin's as smooth and still as the waters of the bayou. She might be in the business of cultivating delicate blooms, but I suspect she's as stubborn as a snapping turtle.* He thought about times she showed interest and shook his head. He might be out of practice, but he knew better than to compare a woman to a reptile. *Maybe a heron?*

Claire filled a plate with cheesy casserole and set the dish on the coffee table.

Nodding his thanks, he shifted the pillow to guard his assets, reached for the plate, and took a healthy bite of the casserole. The rich saltiness of the dish filled his stomach, but he struggled not to make a face as he explored the chewy texture of an unfamiliar grain. *Not as good as my mama's rice casserole, but I'll take it.*

Claire took a seat in the scarred leather recliner across the room. She caressed the worn leather. "This was my husband's chair."

"When did he pass?"

She shook her head. "That's old news. We're doing the best we can without him."

Julien raised his eyebrows. "What happened to Eliza's husband?"

Claire flexed her palms on the scarred armrests. "Died in a motorcycle accident."

Nodding, he took another bite. "She told me to leave my bike at the hardware shop."

Claire looked up. "I'm surprised she even spoke to you."

"She didn't know about the bike."

The woman nodded. "Erik was traveling on Mount Baker Road with a couple of friends. He was an experienced rider. I understand the crash was a chain reaction."

He shook his head. "That's a shame. The man left behind a single mother and a struggling farm."

"He didn't do it on purpose."

Julien conceded the point but wanted to plumb the murky depths of Eliza's operation and see where he landed. "The buildings are in good shape, but the greenhouses could use work."

"Every year on a farm is a challenge. You win some, you lose some."

That's a trite excuse. He cocked his head. "Eliza said her father was a gambler."

Claire sat in silence.

He wondered if his comments went too far.

She squared her shoulders. "Arn thought he could

beat the odds, but they ended up destroying him. I watched him sell off pieces of pastureland when bets fell through or horses failed to place. His sleepless nights and negative account balances tested our marriage, but I made the choice to marry him." She rubbed her arm. "Eliza didn't have that luxury. She cried for days when he sold her horse. Erik might have done better than her father, but he's gone, and I'm grateful for the struggling farm we have left. I don't want Eliza and Skye to live through the stress I experienced."

He scratched his beard. "Seems like she's doing a lot with twenty acres."

"I don't know how she settled on flowers, but the crop doesn't matter. It's still work."

"Farming's an honest trade."

She raised her eyebrows. "They'd have an easier time in town."

"Do you think she will fail?" He took a bite.

"No, but I want her to have something left if it happens." She stood.

Julien took another bite, put down his plate, and looked up at the woman. *Eliza doesn't seem a woman who would go down without a fight. Even if she folds, the decision should be hers.* "What's the alternative?"

"Sell the acreage and reinvest the proceeds in a business. Let other people take risks."

He shook his head. "I don't think she wants to do that."

Claire tapped her fingers on the worn table as she passed it.

He smiled, recognizing the gesture from the hardware store. *Eliza might favor her daddy's ambitions, but Claire left her mark as well.* He glanced at his pants, wondering if the older woman would turn away or stare at his backside while he got dressed. Then he looked at Claire.

She raised her eyebrows.

Damn woman's got me pinned.

"I trusted Gabe. I don't trust you," she said.

He frowned. "Why not?"

"That man was very transactional. He clocked in, and he clocked out. Eliza said your family grows sugar cane."

Julien nodded.

"Are they any good at it?"

He reached for a paper napkin. "Kroger Industries is thriving."

Her gaze narrowed. "You don't need a day laborer's wage."

The woman's forthrightness amused him. He imagined her going head to head with his mama and stifled a grin. "No, ma'am."

"Then why aren't you where you belong?"

"I don't want to wrestle my brother for daily control of the farm." He shrugged.

"Surely there's room enough for two?"

"Cane is a multi-year crop, but we burn it to the ground after we harvest it."

Her mouth hung open. "That's ruthless."

"That's life." He ran a hand through his hair. "To be honest, I made too many memories running through the fields and scaling live oaks to let Brandon dictate my days. The scale of operations is vast, but farming gives a man a sense of ownership. It's difficult to know where to draw the line." *Why am I telling her my life story?* He shrugged. "The accident ended my oilfield career, but I'm not ready to sit in an office chair. What's the alternative? Flipping hamburgers for minimum wage?"

"It's a paycheck."

He made a noncommittal sound. "A road trip seemed like a good way to clear my head."

She raised her eyebrows. "You're running out of open road. Maybe you decided to change your tactics and saw a pretty woman with a chunk of land?"

"I don't want your daughter's farm." He laughed. "She's a beautiful woman, but I only stopped my road trip to help her out of a tough situation."

She leaned forward. "Why?"

"Your daughter looked like she was about to break." The truth of his statement hung between them.

Claire shook her head. "My daughter can find someone else to do this thankless work. Someone who won't get bored and needs the money from an honest job."

He glanced at the darkness waiting beyond the cottage window. "Fair enough. By then the weather will be warm enough for me to hit the road."

She stabbed the table. "In and out. I knew it! You're not here to put down roots."

Damned if you do, damned if you don't. A few decades of strong southern women taught him to choose his battles. He smiled. "Isn't that what you wanted to hear?"

She peered at him. "Keep your gaze focused on the land."

He reached for the prosthesis and snapped it into place. The sound echoed in the small cottage. "Ma'am,

I have nothing to gain from sticking my foot in my mouth. Hell, I only have one foot left. I won't deny I've wondered whether Eliza and I could do more than business, but that's her call too, and I didn't make her any promises."

"Good." She nodded.

"So in the meantime, teach me everything I need to know about growing zinnias and"—he searched his memory for the name of another bloom—"anemones?"

She snorted.

He grasped the edge of the pillow and started to stand.

Claire held up her hand. "I'll feed you, but the rest is up to you." Retreating to the door, she paused and looked at him. "I'm counting on you to make sure no one else gets hurt."

He watched her leave and wondered why the cottage felt emptier without her protective presence. *Feisty, old she-dog. She's guarding what's hers.* He removed the prosthesis, stashed the device in the bunkroom, and palmed the wall to make his way to the shower. Steam filled the room as he stepped under the spray, using the wall to keep his balance. Streams of soap and scalding water washed away the evidence of his labors as he replayed his conversations with Eliza. When the hot water ran out, he made his way to the bunkroom, pulled back the covers on an unused bed, and collapsed on the crisp white sheets. The lingering smell of laundry detergent gave him permission to smile. *Not that it matters. I've tried $30 motels and $3,000 suites. Neither option has helped me sleep.*

Picking up his phone, he dialed, and smiled when Brandon answered his call. Despite the time difference, he listened to his brother clear the sleep from his voice and excuse himself from his south Louisiana bedroom. He tried not to think about the woman sharing his brother's bed.

"I was about to call the police and report you missing," Brandon said.

"Less than a week passed since I checked in."

"Where are you?"

He glanced out the window at the moonlit fields and the shadowed buildings of Hartley Farms. Brandon's voice conveyed the entitlement of an older brother, but Julien wondered why he continued to provide answers. "I stopped in Washington."

"Good call. You turning back or shipping the bike home?"

"I'm staying here for a while." He smiled, hearing his speech pattern slip into the familiar rhythm of their family drawl. He picked up the long vowels and soft inflections of his brother's voice without thinking about the habit. Eliza called the accent charming, but she might not be ready for the full effect. Yet, on a lonely moonlit night, hearing his brother's voice reminded him life in Louisiana encompassed so much more than "ma'am". *I answer his questions because he would come for me in a minute. I would do the same for him.* "I found some work to keep me busy."

Brandon stayed quiet for a moment. "You get plenty of royalties from the cane."

Big brother always knows best.

"If that's not enough, you can live off your settlement check. Come back here where you belong. Start your life over and build something you're proud to call your own."

He took a deep breath. "I was in your way."

"You weren't."

He smiled. "Y'all were coddling me like an orphaned calf."

Brandon snorted. "We were worried."

"Yeah. I caught on to that fact." He struggled to view his family in a positive light, hating how his mother cosseted and prayed over him during his time at home. *Doesn't she know cake, booze, and prayer can't mend all wounds? Doesn't she know how depression lingers at the periphery of my thoughts?* He excused her actions, knowing she loved him. *Why can't we be honest with each other?* "A few manual tasks help a man feel useful."

"I have a generation of work for you."

Life requires more than a bottom line. Where's the fun in padding Brandon's pockets? Eliza needs the help. He closed his eyes. "How's the distillery coming along?"

"Good. Fine. Hell"—Brandon exhaled—"Tharpson got a jump-start on us with Cane Cut. I'm not sure we can catch up to his operations. The Kroger brand needs a proper name and more attention than I can give it. I scheduled interviews for a head distiller. Come home and help me weed out the trash."

"Find someone else to plug that hole. You know I gave up drinking."

Brandon laughed. "You could write a book on rum without tasting a drop."

"Doesn't mean I should. How's your wife?"

"Still pregnant," Brandon said. "She has a wall of names picked out."

"Brandon James Kroger IV. All hail the king."

"Not if I can help it."

He considered mentioning Eliza but decided to hold off until he understood the tension he felt. *Is it merely lust?* He took a deep breath. "Tell Mom I'll be back for the baptism."

"That's a long way off. Will you make it for Easter?"

"Probably not."

"Mama will be disappointed."

"She'll get over it." He cleared his throat, hating the note of resentment in his voice.

"Tell me where to send your mail," his brother said, breaking the silence.

"All my bills are on auto-pay."

"A Valentine's Day card from Mama."

He sighed. "Hartley Farms, Mount Vernon, Washington." He waited while his brother scratched the information on a piece of paper.

"What crop?"

He took a deep breath and mentally braced himself for his brother's reaction. "Flowers."

Brandon remained silent for a second, but then he cleared his throat. "You've got to be kidding."

"Never been more serious."

"Well, I'll be. You can take the boy off the farm…"

Julien smiled. "Goodnight, old man. Get some sleep. I sure as hell need it." He rubbed his face, waiting for his brother's retort.

"Come home," Brandon said.

The wavering, quiet request caught him off guard. His feelings for Eliza compelled him to stay in the Pacific Northwest, but his love for his family made him consider the benefits of returning to Louisiana. *How can I choose between my future and my past?* The thought of seeing Caroline waddle around the old plantation house tipped the scales toward Washington. He and Brandon competed for the woman's attention throughout high school, but the wedding of Brandon Kroger and Caroline Nelson mandated a concession speech that still left a sour taste in his mouth. Acknowledging his complicated feelings for the 2006 Sugar Queen, he shifted in bed and considered a range of affectionate, expletive-laced send-offs. "I'll think about it." He lied to ease his brother's mind. "Goodnight, Brandon."

"Goodnight, Julien."

Peering out the window, he watched a bald eagle circle the farmhouse and land on the roof of the barn. *I hope the fishing's good for both of us.* Letting his head hit the pillow, he watched falling snow accumulate on the cold ground. The white powder dampened the call of the river and the sounds of the night faded into white noise, as soft and comfortable as a lullaby. Surrounded by another man's things, he finally closed his eyes and buried his thoughts. *The weather might be cold as hell up here, but life as a foreman has to be better than coveting my brother's life.*

Chapter Seven

Eliza awoke on the window seat and peered through the condensation fogging the old glass window. Snow fell overnight, heavy and wet. In the soft blue light before dawn, it blanketed the landscape and gave her a quiet moment to think about the practicalities of her life. *Had the seedlings survived? Would the hens lay a full clutch?* She let her mind drift as lowlights filled the sky, and the sun rose with a promise of warmth over Mt. Rainier. Checking the forecast, she stood, knowing she needed to clear the drive and stomp down the paths. *Coffee comes first.*

Claire padded into the kitchen and pulled down a stained mug.

Eliza filled both cups and shared a moment of silence with her mother as she took her first fortifying sip.

"How late were you up?" Claire asked.

"Too late."

"Did the cloth work?"

She looked at the snow-topped greenhouses. "I hope so."

Claire took another sip. "You wouldn't have this problem if you moved to town."

She glanced at the fields. "I also wouldn't have this view." The women stared at each other like dueling cowboys.

Skye arrived and asked for pancakes.

Eliza hugged her sleepy-eyed daughter. "Are you feeding the animals today?"

"Feed me first." The girl rubbed her eyes and yawned. She left one eye closed and eyed her mother. "Please?"

Eliza and Claire swapped smiles, knowing Skye would fuel up and become a tumbling, snow-suited mess once the mixture of buckwheat and syrup hit her system.

"Why doesn't Julien have a haircut? Is he a hobo?" Skye asked.

Eliza struggled not to choke on her coffee. *Had Claire used that antiquated word?* "What?"

"His hair is too long for a boy."

She glanced at her mother, hoping Claire would offer a quick correction.

The older woman smiled and cracked an egg in a bowl. She reached for Luke's wooden spoon and mixed the yolk with her good hand.

Looks like I'm on my own. Meeting Skye's sleepy gaze, she wondered what other questions would come tumbling out of her daughter's mouth. *What will she say when she catches sight of his prosthesis or hears the easy rhythm of his words?* "Sweet Pea, I don't think right and wrong ways exist for boys to wear their hair."

"But you make me braid my hair."

She brushed Skye's hair. "To keep it out of your eyes."

Skye's gaze narrowed. She looked at her mother's messy bun. "Does that mean he has to wear a ponytail?"

"I'm not sure his hair is long enough." *It's*

probably healthy she's finding similarities with a stranger, but I'm not sure how I would have spun "hobo" into a compliment. I guess Julien is a migratory worker, but where did she even learn that word? She cleared her throat, praying her daughter abandoned her interest in the derogatory term. "Did you notice Mr. Kroger walks a little funny?"

"Nope." Skye pulled a fork from the silverware drawer and placed it on the table.

Half the utensils pointed the correct way. She took a deep breath. The girl asked enough "why" questions for an encyclopedia. If she forgot to stick to the facts, she would end up explaining world oil conglomerates. She weighed her child's innocence against Julien's sensibilities. "Julien had an accident that injured his leg. The doctors gave him a fake leg to replace it."

Skye shrugged and reached for the napkins. "Okay."

Okay? She watched her daughter's features shift like she struggled with unspoken thoughts.

"Are the pancakes ready yet?"

I guess hunger won. "Be patient with your granny."

Skye pulled out a kitchen chair and rested her chin in her hands. "I still think Julien needs a haircut."

"Mr. Kroger's an adult and can wear his hair whichever way he chooses."

Skye grinned and raised an eyebrow. "But aren't you the boss?"

"Yes! Don't let Serah or Michelle tell you otherwise."

Claire laughed and poured batter on the griddle.

It sizzled in the hot grease. Eliza shot her mother a warning look. She took a deep breath and smiled at her daughter. "I trust Mr. Kroger to help me take care of the farm. I'm not at all worried about how he looks while he does it. He's a smart man; let him worry about keeping his hair out of his eyes while he does it."

Skye looked at the crock of kitchen utensils sitting on the kitchen counter. A pair of stainless shears shone in the yellow light. "Maybe he'll let me cut his hair."

She smothered a laugh, swallowed, and thought of the bangs Skye gifted her first big-girl doll. *At least she hasn't applied the scissors to her hair.* "I doubt it. Let's leave haircuts to the professionals."

Skye frowned.

"Maybe he'll tell you about the alligators where he grew up. Maybe you can teach him about our town and the things you like the most."

Skye straightened and swiveled her chair toward the bunkhouse. "Does he like ice cream?"

Sensing the return of familiar ground, she smiled. "I'm sure he does, but don't get in his way while he's working. You have your own work to do."

The girl pouted. "I don't want to feed the chickens."

"Hmm." Claire opened cupboards and moved casserole dishes. "Where did I put that recipe for chicken stew?"

Skye's mouth fell open. She stared at her grandmother.

The older woman turned and winked. "I won't cook your chickens, but your mother's right. You need to take care of what's yours." She set a plate of pancakes in front of the child and slid the syrup across the table.

Eliza smiled, sensing an end to the conversation.

"You take care of me, Granny. Does that mean I'm yours?"

Skye's question ripped the bandage off her worst fear. Eliza blinked back tears.

Claire's face softened, and she walked toward Skye and dropped a kiss on her head. "People don't belong to each other. We're a family, and we work as a team. Your mommy loves you and takes care of the farm so I can spend my days playing letter games and baking your cookies. I think I got the better end of the deal."

Eliza nodded, wishing she could sweep her child into her arms without unbalancing the girl's emotions. *How can a simple morning turn into such an ordeal?* She resolved to spend more time with Skye. "I don't think anyone in town would doubt we're a team." She lifted the girl's chin and pressed a kiss to her little nose. "Except maybe on the days when you skip your bath and smell like you belong in the barn."

Skye stuck out her tongue.

Eliza smiled. *There's my brilliant, resilient girl.* She pulled out a chair and asked Skye about her homeschool curriculum, watching as the girl polished off her pancakes. Immune to the lure of syrup, Eliza filled her stomach with yogurt and granola.

Claire glanced at the clock.

"I'm headed out." She wished she could stay in the kitchen all day, but she ruffled Skye's hair, grabbed her hat, and left the warmth of the farmhouse to the generations who needed it. Her boots sank six inches in the snow, but she tromped toward the barn, intent on accomplishing work.

A wolf whistle pierced the morning air.

Looking up, she found Julien standing on the

cottage porch and took in his muscled frame and the worn baseball cap covering his unruly hair. *Well, that's a sight to get your blood flowing in the morning. He might not be Sampson, but damn, he looks good.* Instead of mentioning the man's bedhead, she chose to focus on more practical matters. "You're up early."

He nodded and examined her winter gear. "So are you."

"Twilight crept in near six forty-five. It's almost seven thirty now."

He glanced toward the farmhouse. "I saw your light on well past midnight."

She crossed her arms. "So?"

"So, I had a long night, too. Yet, here we are."

"Here we are." She almost asked him what kept him awake, but the shadows beneath his tanned skin suggested the answer might not be an easy one. *Does his leg pain him?* She kicked the ground. "I hope the quality of the bed didn't keep you awake."

"The bed's fine."

She looked at the snow-covered hoop houses. Wintry accumulation strained the ribs and flattened the top of the arches. She needed more than a little help on the farm, but she hoped Julien respected their arrangement. *What kind of man would renege after one sleepless night in the cottage?* "Let's get to work knocking the snow off the hoop houses and the greenhouses."

"Can you bring me a shovel?" He toed the snow in front of him with a leather work boot. "I'd rather not step off this porch and fall flat on my face."

The specter of workers compensation stopped her in her tracks. "What happens if you fall?"

He laughed. "You tell everyone it was graceful."

She exhaled and made her way to the wooden barn to retrieve a shovel. The moment she opened the old doors and walked inside, the smells of fresh hay and warm animals gave her a reason to smile. *This building has always been my favorite place. Did I tell Skye I used to sleep with the horses?* She glanced at the humming coolers and sighed, wondering how long before Serah and Michelle arrived for work. She collected the shovel, a wide push broom, and a lighter-weight kitchen broom and stepped outside. Blinking against the sunlight, she carried the shovel to Julien and left him to clear his path.

The hoop houses glistened beneath the bright morning sun. Carrying the brooms, she took a deep breath and pulled back the fabric. The thermometer mercury read thirty-five degrees. On the ground, it read thirty-three degrees. She exhaled, glanced over her shoulder, and beckoned to Julien.

He peeked into the tunnel, his features muted by the shadows and the thick layer of snow. "How'd we do?"

She handed him the thermometer. "So far so good. Let's knock the snow off the structure."

"I hear snow can insulate."

"The forecast says the temperature will be forty by mid-afternoon."

"Yes, ma'am." He stepped past the entryway, grinned, and reached for the light switch. "Good call on the lights."

"Thanks." She picked up the kitchen broom and ran her broom along the underside of the tunnel fabric to dislodge the wintry precipitation. Her movements sent clumps of snow cascading down the exterior of the structure. They mounded on the ground like silhouettes of the distant Cascades.

Julien followed her lead.

The slow, manual process strained her back, but a patchwork of light brightened the tunnel. She stretched, flipped off the lights, and nudged the remaining pockets of snow to dislodge them. "The plants don't need the lights. They need the sun."

"Don't we all." He gazed at the sagging roof above his head and grinned.

Stop staring at the man and get back to work. By the time she and Julien finished the third house, she felt her heart racing and perspiration dripping down her back. The heat and humidity made her think of lazier days and gym memberships. *This sweat is worth a thousand hours on the elliptical. We did it!* She led him out of the structure and leaned on her broom to admire their work. Remnants of snow rested on the ribs, but she grinned, flush with accomplishment. "That work qualifies as the day's cardio."

He turned his head and appraised her figure. "You don't need any more exercise."

The warmth beneath her jacket rose several degrees. She forgot her reservations and grinned. "Was that a compliment?"

"Maybe. I'm out of practice." He brushed a stray clump of snow from her shoulder.

She shivered. *Did his hand linger? Is his proximity fueling my body's response?* "Most men start with my lips."

Laughing, he pulled out a bandana, wiped his forehead and winked. "Your skin is smooth, like the still waters of the bayou."

If only. She smiled. "Too far. The elements aren't kind to me. Every time I look in the mirror, I see lines."

"I only see your vivid green eyes."

She laughed, too pleased with their progress to come down hard on the man. "Get your eyesight checked. Right now, we need to return to work."

He smiled and rested on his broom. "You started it."

I did, didn't I? I can't afford to start things I'm not willing to finish. She met his gold-flecked gaze. "Julien, I admit I'm attracted to you, but I don't have time for this banter."

"Eliza, there's always time for this banter." A soft smile lingered on his face.

"I knew you would be trouble."

Gesturing to the three hoop houses, he raised his eyebrows.

"Fair enough." She braced her hands on her hips. "I couldn't have done the work on my own."

"Sure you could." He scanned the snowy farmyard. "It would have taken much longer."

She thought of Skye's question at the kitchen table. *Do I belong to you? Julien's not a luxury, he's a necessity. If things go sour between us, I'll have to run him off.* She retrieved a knotted old rope and threw one end over the top of the structure. "Don't get ahead of yourself. We're not done yet."

Grasping the concept, he walked to the far side of the hoop house and grabbed his end of the coarse tool.

She worked with him to pull the rope back and forth across the fabric skin. Released from the last of the flattening weight, the ribs sprang back and resumed their shape.

He walked to her side. "The hoop houses are well-made if they can take this abuse." A clump of snow landed in the top of his boot. He shook his head at the nuisance. "Well, that's one benefit of a prosthesis. I can't feel the cold."

She laughed and let the comment stand, unsure of how else to respond.

"This crop is a lot of work for something I can't eat."

"Some flowers are edible, but the blooms don't taste good." She coiled the rope, heavy and wet with melted snow. "They're mostly for show."

"Right now, I'd settle for a cup of coffee from a familiar brand."

"I have plenty of coffee in the barn."

He took the rope and settled it on his shoulder.

She led him inside and showed him where to hang the rope before encouraging him to look around the barn while she started a pot of coffee and fired up the computer. Free of looming tasks, she watched him examine the floral coolers and spools of ribbon, kick the edge of the concrete aisle, and test the beams of an old horse stall. When animal sounds lured him to the back of the structure, she found him eye-to-eye with a hen perched on top of the coop.

"You've got containment issues." He jerked his thumb toward the fowl.

"My husband built the coop out of wood and secondhand materials. He used old posts, boards, pallets, and a crib rail he found at a garage sale. The nest boxes are repurposed cabinet drawers, and the horse mesh is mainly there to keep the pigs out of the coop. We weren't going for industrial confinement."

"I'm sure the hens like the nice high perches."

She shrugged and tossed a scoop of feed to the animals. "The design was a bit of a guessing game. I worried about keeping them away from the heat lamps, but they seem to have an ounce of self-preservation. Skye collects the eggs and keeps the feeder and drinker full. I don't ask her to replace the straw. Maybe in a few years."

"What about predators?"

She shook her head. "The barn is buttoned up tight each night."

He rolled his shoulders and nodded. "So, changing straw goes on my list of duties." Adjusting his stance, he peered at the accumulated tools in an old stall. "Where does the rest of the day fall on the spectrum between farmer and florist?"

"We've got a bit of everything today. As soon as the county plows the roads, I need to drive up and down the access road to tamp down the snow and keep them out of the ditches." She shook her head and walked toward the coffee pot. "On days like this one, I can't imagine managing more land."

He followed her and accepted a cup. "You have ambitions?"

She poured half-and-half in her cup and handed him the carton. "And memories. The farm used to be much larger. My dad always said things would improve. I have a thirty-year option to buy back parts of land he sold. I can't take on a thousand acres, but I waste plenty of nights imagining how I would plow up those potato fields."

He leaned against a post and sipped his coffee.

"What would you plant?"

She shrugged. "Perennials? Fields of cash crop peonies? Tulips for the tourists?"

"You don't sound thrilled about those options."

She wrinkled her nose. In a good year, small-scale, high-intensity production techniques let her gross $50,000 to $60,000 per acre, but she also loved the varieties she grew. *Peonies?* She shook her head. *Where's the character?* "I don't want people tromping through my fields for a pretty picture."

"What about running a plant nursery? The tree farm you mentioned?"

"Too demanding. I can't stomach pansies, and garden nurseries make their profits by selling the same annuals year after year. I have the greenhouse space, but I don't like direct retail."

He lifted his cup and frowned. "Why not?"

She grinned. "Frankly, it's boring."

Taking a sip, he smiled and straightened. "You don't strike me as a woman who likes to be bored." He rolled his shoulders.

She watched the tendons in his neck flex, then she blinked and met his gaze. "You don't strike me as a man who likes to sit still."

He raised his eyebrows.

She kicked the ground. "Why don't you bring your coffee outside and look at the greenhouses? I'll do my best to clear the drive and help you find the tools you need to repair them."

An hour later, she found him with a disassembled greenhouse crank and a can of spray lubricant. "You don't waste time."

"It wouldn't budge, and you said ventilation is

important for the plants."

She stared at the ancient hardware and wondered when the rust set in. "Propping open the door works fine."

"Well, I don't mind fixing it." He tugged at two pieces, but they resisted.

She nodded, pleased with his willingness to tackle the job, and walked away.

"I walked down to the river last night."

His soft rolling accent stopped her. "In the snow?"

"It hadn't set in yet." He brushed rust from the joint until the pieces popped apart.

"What did you think of the scenery?" She scanned the winter fields.

"Pretty enough. I saw a bald eagle."

"They're not nocturnal animals."

"Well, it was nighttime, Ms. Eliza, and I saw one grab a fish."

"Maybe it was a trash panda peering through the trees."

He straightened and turned. "How dumb do I look?"

She kept a straight face. "That's an open-ended question."

Scowling, he put down the lubricated pieces.

I liked it better when we were flirting. She smiled. "So maybe it was an eagle. Most of the wintering adults arrive in November and February. They breed farther north, in Alaska and Canada. I've seen eagles as early as October, but I don't know why you and the bird bonded over a midnight matinee."

"Maybe it was restless?"

"Maybe it was hungry," she said. "Your eagle

might be up late because it's bad at catching fish."

He shook his head. "It looked healthy enough."

She glanced toward the river, wondering why the transplanted southerner spotted an eagle before she did. "I hope you're right. I have a thing for eagles."

"Is that so?"

"As a kid, they really confused me. Like, if the birds were so rare, how did they become an American symbol? I asked my mom about it, and she said she'd never actually seen one either. Convinced my first grade teacher was smarter than my mom, I asked her what happened, and she explained how DDT almost extinguished the species. My mom and I both cried. It's no wonder she never saw an eagle; the birds were gone from Washington by the 1950s."

He nodded and reassembled the crank parts. They slid together with zero resistance. "The pesticide basically weakened their eggs, and the breeding pairs smothered their own offspring."

"It's a terrible story." She swallowed to contain her emotions. "I keep thinking of those confused birds, trying their best to raise the next generation with no ability to control their situation."

He opened his mouth but shut it and shook his head. "Well, you have a bird on site. But I think it's a male."

She frowned. "How do you tell the difference?"

He picked up the crank and smiled. "Just a hunch."

Undaunted by his explanation, she shook her head. "I still don't understand why you saw it at nighttime. Maybe it was injured."

He glanced up. "You think we had a little man-to-man, handicapped moment?"

"You're hardly handicapped."

"My physician calls it 'medically impacted.' "

She smiled. "Well, that's better than 'disabled.' "

He winked. "Yes, ma'am, it is."

The moment lingered, and she smiled, content to reclaim any easy camaraderie. "If you see the bird again, look at its feet. A raptor rehabilitation facility is up the road, and the facility tags birds with silver leg bands before reintroducing them to the wild. I've heard the rehabilitated birds can struggle to establish themselves once released." She debated pushing his buttons. "Your eagle might be tagged and failing to thrive."

"The bird wasn't failing to thrive." He picked up the lubricant and gathered the tools from an old toolbox. "The animal looked perfectly healthy."

"We'll need to find a spotting scope to read the numbers on the band. The federal bird banding lab maintains records on birds that are found deceased or injured."

"Eliza, the bird was fine."

"Hunting at night is not normal behavior, Julien. It's atypical."

"Maybe it needed some air."

She bit her lip to keep from smiling. "It's a bird. It's got nothing but air."

His laughter filled the warming air, and he considered the far-off mountains. "Where I come from, those birds nest on top of transmission towers or old, blown-out cypress trees. My brother and I often saw them when we were fishing. They always choose the highest ground."

"Not a lot of options in a swamp," she said.

"When we spotted an eagle nest nearby, we knew we were in a good fishing spot."

The conversation no longer felt like easy banter. She scanned the fallow, snow-covered fields and recognized the compliment behind his words. "This farm is a good place. We'll see if your bird has the good sense to stick around." Turning, she left before he could respond.

Serah and Michelle's sedan passed the farm gate and parked near the barn.

Michelle stayed in the car, checking her makeup in the visor mirror.

Serah popped out and bounded over to greet her. "Can you imagine all this snow?"

Eliza looked at the fields. *If we get this volume of moisture any later in the season, spring rains will inundate the soggy fields, and drainage will become an issue. It's a pretty sight for a postcard, but we dodged a bullet. The fields will turn into stream-fed mud pits if it happens again.* She kept her thoughts to herself, unwilling to spoil the moment. "It's beautiful."

Serah smiled and walked toward Julien. "What are you working on?"

He handed her a metal component.

"Eww."

He retracted his grease-covered palms. "I guess I should have worn gloves."

She looked at the crank and wrinkled her nose. "I'm glad it's you and not me." She sauntered back to the barn.

"I can tell," Julien said when she was out of earshot.

"She meant nothing by it," Eliza said. "She's still a

teenager. Empathy hasn't kicked in yet."

"I know." He grinned. "I mouthed off with the best of them."

Thank goodness he's resilient. She smiled and recalled the thick calluses on Julien's palms. She thought about him crouched in the hoop house, helping her drape frost cloth over young plants. *I keep pushing him away and making excuses, but I'm not fooling anyone. He said he's no good at delicate, but he keeps surprising me. I like everything else he has, so why wouldn't I like his hands and the parts I've seen?* She imagined peeling the layers of clothes from his skin and revealing his muscles. Raising her hand, she felt a flush heat her cheeks and cleared her throat. "See what you can make of the tool and supplies inventory."

"Yes, ma'am."

She considered softening her approach, but the two teenagers in the barn waited for her attention. Leaving Julien to his tasks, she entered the barn and found the sisters loitering over their phones. She squared her shoulders. "Come on, you two. We have a lot of work left on the wedding arrangements." *I need time to figure out what to do with the new foreman.*

Chapter Eight

Late in the afternoon, Julien finished the tool and supply inventory. He appreciated the opportunity to limit his movements but questioned Eliza's motives. *Did she really want an inventory, or did she feel like she needed to give me a break?* He shook his head and closed the doors protecting an old stall. *I don't need her pity.* Memories of his recuperation confused his responses to offers of help.

One night, his mother cracked open his bedroom door and caught him burning prescription slips in the flames of a glass lantern. He kept his gaze on the flame. "Give me space, Mom. I'm a grown man." His request ignored her concern and the advice of his rehabilitation psychiatrist to confide in the people he loved. Instead of fighting his willfulness, she fled. Brandon saw through his bravado. Their relationship straddled a fine line between rivalry and brotherly competition. He kept Julien within sight, and the oversight rankled. *Why do I have so much trouble accepting help?*

Instead of reporting on his inventory findings, he let himself into the vegetable greenhouse and used a grease pencil to mark the weakest parts of the steel and glass structure. Knowing he could make necessary repairs if he got his hands on arc welding tools, he pulled out his phone and dialed the number of the hardware store.

"This is Luke. What can I do to help you?"

He cradled the phone against his shoulder and tested the resistance of a support beam. "This is your friendly, neighborhood drifter."

The older man laughed. "You survived the snowstorm?"

"More or less."

"Travelers reported black ice north of here."

"Should I tell you that you were right?"

"It'd be nice to hear that once in a while," Luke said.

The beam wobbled in Julien's hands. He looked at the tracks along the drive and the puddles of snowmelt forming in the fields. "Luke, the farm's more than a bit frayed at the seams."

"Women in charge."

"No, Eliza's running a tight ship. She hasn't stopped working since the minute she stepped outside of the house. I'd cast my doubts on Gabe and whoever came before him."

Static kept the line open. Luke cleared his throat. "What do you need?"

"Welding tools. These greenhouses are about three seconds from falling to the ground." The rest of the equipment needs came in second place, and he considered how to repair the structure.

Four chickens strode into the greenhouse, clucking and pecking as they walked through the rows of vegetables.

"What about your bike?" Luke asked.

He kept his gaze on the birds. The soft sounds of the animals reminded him of home, but he knew the fowl could be destructive. *They'll forage for bugs, eat the plants, and scratch up the layer of mulch Eliza put down for weed control. I don't care if they eat every stinkbug on the property, they still have their place in the world.* When his bold gestures failed to deter the birds, he strode toward them, preparing to end the call. "Luke, I gotta go."

"Wait a second. Did Claire like the spoon?"

He scooped up the nearest animal, ignored its flapping protestations, and headed for the greenhouse door. "Probably. I wasn't there when Eliza gave her the spoon."

"Not letting you in the house, eh?" Luke laughed. "I hope she liked the gift."

He snorted. "Come out here and see for yourself. I'm not playing Cupid, old man."

The man laughed, promised to arrange for the tools, and ended the call.

Julien headed toward the barn with his feathered hostage. He found Skye standing in the winter sunshine and stopped short. Two braids hung over a dark purple pea coat, and she wore colorful, insulated rubber boots against the snow. Her easy smile made him think of sassy laughter cultivated by a free-range childhood. When she looked up at him, hints of jade green shone in her hazel eyes. *Skye has her mother's eyes, but Eliza's green eyes hold greater depths, like she understands the consequences of tough love and tender resolve. What happened to Eliza to reveal such faceted depths? My interest started as lust, but when did it evolve?* He took a deep breath and focused on the girl. "Hi, Skye."

"Hi, Julien." She reached for the bird in his hands.

He relinquished the bird, startled to find it still in his possession.

She settled the bird on her hip and stroked its feathers. "Where did you find Miss Guinea Heny?"

He frowned. He knew Guinea fowl hens. The dominant creatures chattered incessantly. He scanned the animal for defects, but its shining feathers testified to a life of ease. "That is not a guinea fowl."

"No, she's a bantam! But she likes to roost near the guinea hogs, so I call her Miss Guinea Heny."

He decided not to argue with the child. "How many chickens do you have?"

"Four."

He nodded. *I can manage four pampered fowl.* "What are their names?"

"Miss Guinea Heny, Foxy Soxy, Turtle Dove, and Sparkles."

Narrowing his gaze, he kept his questions to himself. "Sparkles?"

"The *nisse* likes her. I always find Sparkles next to his porridge bowl."

Is she all there? He scanned the buildings, hoping a *nisse* referred to some colloquial aspect of farm life that never reached the south. "And what's a *nisse*?"

"The little man that helps to take care of that farm. My daddy said he was probably the first man to live here, and he's never gone away."

He opened his mouth but settled for adjusting his cap.

"The *nisse* likes to work alone at night when no one can see him. I stayed up late one night and saw his eyes glowing like a cat or a raccoon."

He shook his head. "Probably lightning bugs."

"What?"

He shrugged.

She jutted out her chin and put her free hand on her hip. "I know the difference! Animals don't move like little people. I turned on the lights and saw his red hat for a whole second. It was very jaunty."

Jaunty? She's a smart kid, but I bet she gives Eliza fits.

Skye smiled. "He wore a tattered, gray pullover with short pants and a belt. The red hat gave him away, because cats don't wear red hats. And we don't have a cat."

Julien nodded like he understood her whimsical madness. *Where is Eliza?*

"Sometimes, I see his footprints in the dust." She transferred the hen to her other hip.

He sighed. *What's the harm in make believe?* Shifting his weight, he considered the possibility of the *nisse.* "Does he work for free?"

Skye nodded. "I leave him little gifts to say thank you, but my dad told me I have to be careful not to think of the gifts as payment. The *nisse* can be very"— she shifted her gaze around the room—"proud."

He leaned closer to hear the whispered last word.

"Mr. Kroger, if you see our little man, never mention his shabby clothes or insult him." She looked around the farm and frowned. "He might leave us or make our lives harder."

He straightened and scanned the mottled, snow-covered acreage. Motes of dust floated through the sunlit air, and he imagined a small garden gnome mocking him from the shadows of the barn. *I hope the nisse brought some helpers. We have plenty of work.* A flock of geese flew overhead. Instead of finding the charm in the girl's fable, he sensed her vulnerability and wondered what fears lurked in her dreams. *I don't want to get involved in nonsense and family dynamics, but Eliza doesn't seem to cosset the kid. Skye seems pretty resilient. I guess that's a testament to Eliza and her mother. I don't know how I would have coped with that trauma.*

Her lip quivered. "My daddy said he'd always look after me."

"That's what daddies do."

The child's serious expression dissolved into laughter.

Wondering what he did wrong, he widened his eyes.

"No, you silly. The *nisse*. He will look after me because we look after the farm. I pay special attention to the chickens and the pigs because the *nisse* likes them the most. Don't tell Granny, but I always remember to feed the animals. Eventually."

"Don't you think you're a little more important than the chickens and the pigs?"

Skye shifted the chicken in her arms. "No. Everyone works together on a farm."

"That's true." He scanned his limited experiences with children and wondered how to extract himself from the conversation without putting a foot in his mouth. Recalling their conversation on the farmhouse steps and the way Eliza let Skye's comment about "little people" pass without making a fuss, he resolved to do the same and follow her lead. "Well, I don't see any mythical creatures, but the rest of your feathered crew is in the vegetable greenhouse. Can you catch them and take them home?"

"Oh no!" Skye dropped the hen and slapped her

cheeks. "The vegetables!"

Julien changed course, fearing he would find himself in charge of the pampered fowl. "I'll catch the chickens if you carry them home."

"Good plan." She pointed toward the sky. "To the chicken coop!"

Julien recalled the jumble of spare parts he saw last night. *Of course. The coop's right next to the pigs.* He scooped up the abandoned chicken. "Okay, you hold"—he searched his memory and passed her the bird—"Miss Guiney Heny while I round up the next one. Can you hold two birds?"

She took the bird and pivoted. "To the greenhouse!"

"Perfect." He injected calmness into his tone. "We'll carry them two by two."

She preceded him into the greenhouse, scooped up a second animal, and kissed its feathered head.

"Wait a minute. I thought you couldn't catch them."

Skye cocked her head and smiled. "I never said that." She ambled toward the exit, two feathered tails peeking through the space between her arms.

The hens' plumage mocked his valiant attempts to play hero. Left with two animals, he snuck up on Sparkles and hoped the beady eyes of the fourth animal belonged to Turtle Dove. The hen eluded him for twenty minutes. By the time he made it to the barn, Skye had a case of the giggles, but he grasped the remaining two animals like football trophies.

"Hello, Sparkles! Hello, Foxy Soxy!" Skye's voice rang through the winter air.

Eliza and her assistants stopped working and

watched the parade.

He shrugged as best he could with two chickens in his arms. "Y'all come down for Mardi Gras if you want a real show."

Eliza whistled.

Winking, he trailed Skye to the end of the stalls and tossed the birds over the horse mesh.

She grabbed a corncob and pointed at the swine. "I told you, they're guinea hogs."

Afraid to ask, he took a deep breath regardless. "What are their names?"

"Lincoln, Jefferson, Hamilton, and Petunia."

"Hamilton wasn't a president," he said.

The girl stared. "Neither was Petunia."

"You should rename the little guy. I might be from the bayou, but I understand life didn't work out like Mr. Hamilton planned."

She nodded and stared at the misnamed animal. A slow smile spread across her face, and she looked up. "I'll let you re-name him if you help me take care of him."

He shook his head. *Clever girl. I've considered the joy of progeny, but I've already done several rounds of 4H, and I have no intention of starting my adult endeavors with a pig.* "Maybe you're right. Names are important, and you shouldn't change them. He might get confused."

Eliza walked up. "How about Grant?"

"Boring." Skye stuck out her tongue.

He thought about his suggestions. "Roosevelt?"

The girl frowned. "I don't want him to eat the field roses."

"Ford?"

She peered at his legs and tilted her head.

He smiled. *Apparently, word of the prosthesis has gotten around.*

"How about Peg-leg?" she asked.

"Skye!" Eliza reached for her daughter.

The girl ducked away and grinned.

He crossed his arms and raised an eyebrow. "I'm not a pirate."

She laughed and wagged a finger. "That's what a pirate would say."

Eliza caught her arm. "Apologize. You're being rude."

He waved off the exchange and watched Skye flounce through the sunlit barn with the confidence and amusement of a child. "Don't worry about it. No offense taken."

"She has a kind heart," Eliza said.

"She meant no harm. You're doing a good job with her."

"Am I?" Eliza exhaled and looked at the ground.

He wanted to raise her chin and tease a smile back to her lips, but he swallowed and crossed his arms. "She's kind to the animals."

Eliza nodded and looked up. "We need to get back to work."

He watched her stride through the barn, the efficient sway of her hips erasing his ability to make decisions. *Should I leave now? They could do a lot worse than Peg-leg. Voyeur? What did Mama teach me about coveting what I can't have?* The light-filled space where Eliza and her assistants assembled flowers for a wedding had nothing to do with him. *This dream doesn't involve me. I'm here to work and help her out of a tight spot. Slipping out amid the chaos of the wedding might be easier.* He moved to pass the group with a tip of his cap.

Eliza met his gaze.

Her furrowed brow caught his attention. *I can't get a handle on you either, lady.* He smiled and forced himself to keep moving. *How long since she sported the same untroubled expressions as her kid? Will I leave her with more grief?* Returning to the vegetable greenhouse, he tagged the remaining work and figured he could make the necessary repairs and leave town before anyone formed an attachment. Deep in logistics, he registered a honk from the assistants' departing sedan but kept working.

Claire brought bag lunches to the greenhouse. "You want one sandwich or two?"

"Two." He reached for a screwdriver.

"Men."

She muttered the word like an insult and placed his lunch on the worktable scattered with pliers, chisels, and rags. *Ornery old woman.* By five, his stomach rumbled for dinner, and he wondered if he should expect a casserole. Wiping the sweat from his brow, he looked up and spied security lights illuminating the buildings and the yard. *I hope Luke gives Eliza a discount on supplies. At least I'll leave the place better than I found it.* He entered the barn for a notepad and a pen, but instead of raiding the desk, he found Eliza perched on an old wooden ladder built to slide along a set of rails like an antiquated rollercoaster. Years of oilfield training taught him to inventory the dangers of the situation, and his pulse skyrocketed. *Those metal rails and rusted screws are poor insurance against an accidental fall from height. The woman should wear fall protection or have a spotter to keep the ladder from sliding out beneath her.* "What the hell are you doing up there alone?"

She removed two items from the storage area and climbed down two rungs.

The ladder shifted.

He lunged to steady it.

Glancing down, she smiled. "I'm glad you're here. Can you take these boxes?"

After receiving the dust-covered boxes, he put them on the worktable. "Why don't you come on down?" He took several deep breaths.

She remained on the ladder.

Tucking his cap in his back pocket, he grabbed the lowest rung of the ladder and braced his weight. *Fine, if you want to work at heights, I'll spot you.* He looked up and swallowed. Her denim-clad ass filled his field of vision, and he found looking away more difficult than he cared to admit.

She shifted, rearranging the items in storage.

Shaking his head, he focused on the flower-strewn chaos of the barn. Containers and foam bases on the worktable overflowed with blooms. He sighed, realizing the progress meant she stayed up later than he had. "You don't quit."

"I don't have time to quit." She climbed another rung and leaned into a dark storage space. Her torso disappeared into the shadows, putting her backside on full display.

This arrangement was a mistake. "I'm not saying you should quit," he said. "Just slow down and get some help."

"That's why you're here."

"By chance. What if you fell?"

She straightened and spied the distance to the concrete floor. "I'd survive."

He thought about the weeks he spent going in and out of surgeries, wondering if life justified the pain and effort. The prospect of learning to function without a lower leg would daunt most men. Unfortunately, Caroline switched allegiances and doubled his self-doubt. Even as he said good riddance, the emotional injury overloaded his brain. He spent sleepless nights struggling to process her decisions before the nurse arrived and medicine numbed his pain. Unwilling to let Eliza experience that type of upheaval and self-doubt, he decided to drive home his point. "There's more to life than survival."

"It's a ladder, Julien."

"Claire can't take care of this place on her own."

"Now you sound like Luke." She blew her bangs out of her eyes.

"Maybe he's on to something."

She straightened and looked down. "Excuse me?"

"What would happen to Skye if you got hurt?"

He faced the fury of a slighted woman, and twenty-four hours of playful banter disappeared from his memory. *I'm playing dirty, but it's worth the risk. She needs to put in the extra effort to minimize her risks.*

Eliza shook her head, climbed down the ladder, and stood amid the straw littering the floor.

Outrage brought a flush to the woman's cheeks the wind could never achieve. Dust marked her forehead, and a string of cobwebs rested on top of her light brown hair. He resisted the urge to clear the silvery strands, swallowed, and had second thoughts about making his point. "All I'm saying is…"

"You can leave now." Her eyebrow twitched.

He put his hands on his hips. "What?"

"I don't need you to ride into town on a surge of testosterone and save me from my foolish ways. I'm doing fine on my own, Julien." She pointed to the ladder. "I've been up and down that ladder a million times without your help. The ladder has been there since before I was born, and it has never failed me. If I thought the ladder was a risk to myself or to my family, I'd be the first person to remove it."

Damn ladder.

She dropped her hand and crossed her arms.

If she's kicking me out, I might as well go down swinging. He took a deep breath. "Exactly. You don't see the risk because you've been up and down that ladder a million times. What happens if the wood's icy and you slip? You have a seizure? A snake bites you on the ass?"

Her jaw dropped. "A snake?"

He crossed his arms and mimicked her stance. "It could happen."

"Most of the snakes in Washington are nonvenomous. And it's winter."

"A spider?" He raised his eyebrows.

"How will a snake get to my butt?" She rolled her eyes. "I'm standing on a ladder."

He shrugged at her obstinacy. *I could have come up with a better scenario if I hadn't been ogling her figure.* "You never know what's going to happen."

"You're right." She dropped her arms and her shoulders sagged. "Your best friend could crash his bike and take you out with him. That's what killed my husband, but I'm still here."

He swallowed.

"You're the one riding a deathtrap after losing part of your leg. You want to talk about minimizing risks? Look in the mirror and start with yourself."

"I have nothing to lose," he said.

"What does that mean?"

"Nothing." He uncrossed his arms.

She shook her head. "My point is that I've already had my bad luck. I don't have time to slow down and worry about hidden risks. The list would never end. So, stop worrying about me or hit the road."

Stubborn woman. He turned to leave.

"Idiot," she said.

The flimsy insult hit home. He spent the last twenty-four hours pulling weeds, clearing snow, and doing Eliza's bidding for a shade above minimum wage because he thought the work might matter. He thought the repairs might make a difference in her life. *Idiot.* He turned and met her gaze. "You need more than a foreman." He prided himself on a level tone, but frustration gave him an excuse to raise his voice. "You need a lick of common sense and a hard look in the mirror. You're fighting so hard to prove yourself you'll be lucky if falling off the ladder is the only thing that happens. Slow down and spend some time with your daughter. Help your mama in the kitchen. Sell the farm if you can't figure out everything. At this rate, you'll burn out and find yourself old and gray with nothing but pride to keep you company."

She widened her gaze but, instead of fighting back, she bit her lip.

Hating the show of vulnerability, he grabbed her hand to reassure her. The contact sent a shock through his body. Instead of letting go, he tightened his grip. "I'm sorry."

Taking a deep breath, she nodded. "You're not wrong, but I liked you better when you were greasing joints and staring at my ass."

He squeezed her hand. "I almost lost everything, Eliza. I'm still digging myself out of that hell. I don't want the same thing to happen to you."

"There's more than one way to burn," she whispered.

Pulling her close, he lowered his head and brushed her lips with his own, waiting for confirmation. She tasted like sun-drenched honeysuckle and heady sweet wine, but he gave her space to pull back and set him straight.

She closed the distance between them.

Then the soft warmth of her skin anchored his senses. Permitting himself to savor the moment, he forgot about the cold dampness of the barn and the pain in his leg. He forgot about months of depression and the self-reflection chasing him across the country. The beautiful woman in his arms had looked mad enough to spit, but she was certainly kissing him back. Then she wasn't.

She tore her lips from the warmth of his mouth. "You can't just kiss me. I'm your boss."

He laughed. "Not a problem, pretty lady. I quit."

"Of all the ass-backward, Neanderthal things to do…"

He shook his head, cutting her off before she had time to complete the insult. *I'll take "idiot" but I'm only going so far down that path.* He rolled his lips and caught the lingering sweetness of honeysuckle. *Hell, she can call me anything she wants.*

"Is this how you do things in the South?"

"No, ma'am. Southern women have more common sense than the northern populations."

Her eyes widened. "What does that mean?"

Crossing his arms, he wondered if he could claim another kiss without getting slapped. *In for a penny, in for a pound.* "They know when someone's trying to help them."

Her mouth fell open. "I'm going back to the house."

"Not so fast. From the moment we laid eyes on each other, you've been batting your eyes at me and pushing me away. That's your prerogative. I have the strength to let you make up your mind. If you're too scared to choose a course of action, I'll be the one who walks away."

She put her hands on her hips. "Is that a threat?"

"Foolish woman. I thought you were brave." Shaking his head, he exited the barn. *I should have tested my luck against the black ice. At least the ice wouldn't haunt my dreams.* Blinking at the blinding whiteness of the landscape, he pulled on his cap and waited for his heart rate to slow. He had half a mind to return to the barn and apologize for his behavior. The other half wanted to grab Eliza and confirm her desires. *Stopping in Washington was a mistake. I might need a few weeks to forget her, but I'm a patient man.* He pulled out his phone and searched for a ride service. The app promised a ride in thirty minutes. He swore.

A plaintive wail filled the stillness of the fading

light.

He scanned the snow-covered ground and searched for Skye amid the farm buildings. The day's activities left footpaths between the buildings, but a smaller trail veered from the greenhouses. He followed the footprints and found Skye crouched in the snow amid the remnants of a summer garden. Tears stained her cheeks, but she appeared unharmed. Piles of weeds littered the plot, and her flock of chickens milled around her feet, searching the damp straw mulch for seeds. *So much for keeping their feet dry.* He closed his eyes and took several deep breaths, crouched beside the girl, and waited until she looked up. "What's wrong, darlin'?"

She held up a dark brown feather and thrust it toward him. He wondered how any child could commit to a vegetable garden and get excited about kale, but he realized some people probably felt the same way about catching fish. "Woo-ee. That's a fine eagle feather. Where did you find it?"

"In my garden!"

"So, why the tears?"

"This"—her eyes narrowed—"eagle will eat my chickens!"

He smiled, containing his laughter. *I wouldn't worry about the eagle, kid. Your grandma makes a mean chicken casserole.* Instinct urged him to ease Skye's pitiful expression, but he held back and reached for the feather, running his hands along the glossy, dark-brown barbs. "You're in luck, small fry. I'd be worried if this feather belonged to a peregrine falcon. They have a taste for quail and small flightless birds." He eyed the chickens barely worth the effort to pluck.

"Even a golden eagle would have me worried. But this feather? This fine specimen is a bald eagle feather. And do you know what bald eagles eat?"

Skye shook her head and wiped her nose. Her small eyes looked hopeful.

"Fish!"

She tested the word, opening and closing her mouth. Squinting at the river, she wrinkled her forehead and pursed her lips. Turning back, she tilted her head and looked. "Fish? Only fish?"

"Nothing a bald eagle likes better than fish. I saw one last night, pretty as a picture over the water. It scooped up a quick flash of silver to keep its belly full then claimed a perch on top of the barn."

Skye reached out and petted the nearest chicken, her motions hesitant and rhythmic.

This child understands loss.

"You'll be okay, Sparkles," she said. "Bald eagles only like fish."

He waited until she stopped stroking the feathered animal. "You have bigger problems on your hands."

Her face fell, solemnity weighing down her shoulders. "I knew it."

He considered the wisdom of his joke. *Hell, children need room to grow.* Lowering his voice, he held up the glossy talisman. "This feather is contraband."

"Contraband?"

She stumbled over the word she might not recognize, and her confusion warmed his heart. He whisked the feather behind his back. "You shouldn't have this feather. I happen to know it's illegal to collect eagle feathers. They're protected under the Migratory

Birds Treaty Act and the Bald and Golden Eagle Act."

"But I found it!"

"Tsk-tsk." He shook his head. "I once heard of an Indian tribe that wanted eagle feathers for a headdress. Two years passed before they could collect enough feathers from the National Eagle Repository."

Her eyes narrowed. "But that one's mine!"

"Keep it safe." He handed the feather back and winked. "It's a treasure."

She eyed the prosthesis. "Like pirate treasure?"

He pushed himself to stand and brushed the snow from his pants. "I am not a pirate." He gave her a moment to process the statement. Then he comically lunged for the feather, over-shooting her trembling hand. "And pirates take treasure." His cap fell in the snow, and the chickens scattered.

Skye squealed and ran off with her prize.

Her flock regrouped and followed in noisy pursuit.

"She favors her father," Eliza said.

Turning, he found her leaning against the back of the greenhouse. Picking up his cap, he brushed the snow from the bill. "How long have you been there?"

"Long enough to say thank you."

"You're welcome." He wondered how to address the ensuing silence.

"The last two years were hard for her," Eliza said. "She remembers Erik, but then she forgets a trivial fact about him. Her physiatrist said she could take years to process the loss. That's why Claire and I decided on home schooling."

"Parenting her has to be rough."

She stared at the barn and frowned. "She's worth the effort, but the smallest things set her off. I wish I knew she would be okay."

He thought about the little girl's belief in helpful elves. "She's finding harmless ways to cope, like the bits about the little people or the *nisse* and whatnot."

"Erik used to read her Norwegian bedtime stories." She smiled. "It was his way of teaching her hard work. The *nisse* only stays if you treat the animals well and do your best to take care of the farm. Maybe the tales help her feel closer to her father."

"No harm in that." He stood beside her and watched Skye herd her chickens into the barn.

"I think the folktale is a healthy way for her to feel connected to her dad. She thinks the *nisse* will protect her like he protects the animals."

He scanned the glistening farm. "Not much to fear out here."

"It's hard to be six." She sighed and turned. "Hell, it's hard to be thirty-four."

He scanned her tight jeans and wondered if her curves continued beneath her boxy plaid shirt. "I wouldn't put you a day past thirty."

She raised her eyebrows. "And yourself?"

He grinned. "I'll be thirty-two for the rest of my life."

"That's too bad. I don't go for younger men."

Brushing his overgrown hair to the side, he pulled his cap over his unruly hair. "Good thing you fired me."

"You quit."

Well, she got me on that. "I should apologize."

"Because you crossed a line?"

He took off his cap and ran a hand through his hair. "It was just a kiss."

"I'm talking about what happened before the kiss.

This land was my family farm. I pushed Erik to come back to Skagit County, raise flowers, and support the cooperative. He turned out to be too good at grasping my dream and running with it. I thought I lucked out in life by finding such a capable partner, but he took over managing the farm until everyone deferred to him."

"He pushed you out?"

"More accurately, he pushed me into the kitchen." She glanced at the farmhouse and shifted.

At that moment, Claire turned on the porch light.

"I tell myself I'd do anything to have him back, but that's not the truth." She shook her head. "I'd do anything to have another chance to reason with him and exert myself."

He liked it better when they were discussing kisses. "I'm sure you two would have worked it out."

"Erik was a proud man. The fairytales were sweet, but they were more than stories of elves and gnomes. He was obsessed with *Jante* Law."

"Come again?"

She smiled. "A notion runs through Scandinavian cultures that encourages people to live thoughtful and modest lives. Nobody is supposed to think they're special. Erik kept repeating that idea. 'You're full of good ideas, Eliza, but you think you're the only one who is special.' "

"That's bullshit." He stood straighter. "Everyone deserves to feel special."

She laughed and tucked a strand of hair behind her ear. "You're thinking like an American."

"Fine. I agree with the basic idea, but as long as you're responsible, your ideas count. We're not talking about running for office. We're talking about sharing ideas with your spouse and working out how to run the land."

"I'm bothered by how much I love running this place, but sometimes I let it go too far. I've apologized to my assistants more than once for getting heavy-handed. Now, I feel like I should apologize when I don't spend enough time with Skye."

Hearing the uncertainty in her voice, he closed the distance between them. "Should I apologize for kissing you?"

"No, but you might need to shave."

He rubbed the stubble on his face and felt the rough hair. "Picky woman."

She smiled. "It's my face you're scratching up."

"Fair enough." He considered embracing her but held back. *Too much, too soon and I'll scare her off.*

"You're right about a few things, Julien. I'm barely hanging on. I don't need to take unnecessary risks, but don't get me wrong."

Her gaze blazed with pride.

"I love what I'm doing," she said.

Screw the distance. He reached for her hand and warmed it between his own. "Superwoman couldn't manage twenty acres, a kid, and a side business."

She stared at their hands. "I had a foreman."

"You need a new one, and I'll stick around until you regain your momentum."

She looked up. "It's the wedding this weekend."

He raised her hand and brushed her knuckles with his lips. "You took on too much."

Her gaze narrowed.

Wondering whether she felt the heat of his lips or the brush of his overgrown beard, he smiled and dropped her hand before she could bolt. "I'm not leaving you stranded, but if you stopped raising your hackles and pulling back to keep me at a distance, we'd both be a lot happier."

She tilted her head. "Are we bargaining?"

He laughed. "No, because I'm not your husband, and I have no interest in taking over your business. I'm proposing a little"—he winked—"stress relief."

"We'll butt heads while you're here."

"Is that a euphemism for sex?"

"Nope," she said.

He sighed. "That's disappointing."

"Well, those are my terms. Take them or leave them." She pursed her lips. "No more kisses."

He smiled at the memory of her flushed response. "You like my kisses."

"I do not."

"You kissed me back." He raised his eyebrows.

"A momentary lapse of judgment."

"The story of my life." Laughing, he watched her grin and wondered if any of her flowers could put on such a dazzling display. He thought about stealing a kiss to prove his point.

Skye rounding the barn with the eagle feather tucked in the top of her braids. Hay clung to the girl's jacket, and she cradled a content chicken in her arms. "Mommy, my tummy hurts."

Eliza bent and felt her forehead.

The universal motion touched his heart, and he thought of his mama making the same gesture.

"You don't feel hot, Sweet Pea. Are you hungry?"

"I'm not hungry!"

Skye yelled with the ferocity of a feral cat.

He rubbed his ear.

The chicken squawked.

Eliza swallowed and met his gaze.

Oh, no, lady. That's your kid.

"Okay then. Let's go inside and see what Granny is doing in the kitchen." Eliza took the chicken, handed the animal to him, and winked.

"She's probably still cooking."

Skye's voice came out defiant, yet weak. He stifled the impulse to pat her shoulder and offer comfort. *Her mother knows best.*

"Uh-huh." Eliza nudged Skye toward the white farmhouse, leaving her hand on her daughter's back.

Skye planted her feet. "Julien is hungry, too."

"Granny will bring him a plate when he's finished working."

The girl looked at him. "But I want to hear more about eagles."

He braced his hands on his knees so he and Skye could talk on the same level. "How about we walk down to the river and look for the bird tomorrow?"

Skye pulled the dark brown feather from her hair and examined it. She turned to her mother "Eagles eat fish." Her lip quivered.

He waited with the stillness of a hostage negotiator.

A tear slipped from Skye's eye. She glanced at the fowl in his hands. "Are you sure they eat fish?"

"Positive." He nodded.

"What if this bird's an omnivore?"

"Darlin', that doesn't…"

Eliza held up a hand. "Just bring the bird inside, Julien. We'll be out here all night if the two of you go head to head."

He stared at the feathered animal in his hands. Its beady eyes stared right back. "Chickens do not belong in the house."

"It won't be the first time," Eliza said. "Plus, it's my house."

He held the animal aloft. He had a one-in-four chance of guessing the animal's name and securing his ticket to a hot dinner. "You're a lucky bird, Sparkles."

Skye giggled and reached for the animal. She tucked it under her arm and handed him the eagle feather. "You can hold my treasure. Sparkles likes you, and she's my favorite."

He tucked the treasure in his jacket and nodded his thanks.

Skye led him to the farmhouse steps. "Will you read me a book after dinner?"

Turning, he searched Eliza's face for guidance. The security lights surrounded her with golden light, but he caught the indecisiveness playing across her features. *I should have claimed another kiss when I had the chance.* The thought of tasting her sweet lips distracted him. He stumbled and grabbed the porch handrail to arrest his fall.

Eliza placed a hand on his back. "You okay?"

The pressure of her palm burned through his jacket. He thought about more than the pleasure of a kiss. *Slow down, Tiger. The terms may shift, but she hasn't yet thought through the implications.* Conscious of their audience, he winked. "Remember, if I fall, you tell everyone it was graceful."

She nodded and bit her lip.

He jerked his chin toward Skye. "Are you okay with this arrangement?"

"It's one meal," she said.

Skye preceded them through the front door.

"You're the boss." He paused on the threshold and looked over his shoulder at the fallow fields. *But what does that make me?*

Chapter Nine

Skye dropped her chicken near the door, pulled off her shoes, and flung her body on the couch with the athleticism of a budding gymnast. A heartbeat later, she yawned, and her moment of accomplishment collapsed into an unpretentious sprawl. Eliza shook her head, turning to watch Julien navigate the threshold. She tried to ignore the prosthesis, but his stumble focused her attention on the vulnerability. Claire's stroke taught Eliza to pay attention to subtle clues, but she forgot about the hardware.

His pace slowed, and he tested the flooring's unfamiliar traction. Within the span of Skye's yawn, he shifted his weight to the prosthesis and moved forward.

How could any woman resist that combination of strength and discipline? She imagined his recovery and the pain of putting one foot in front of the other. *I don't know if Erik could have managed a year of recovery and rehabilitation. He would have dismissed the whole idea of gait training.* She grimaced. *His injuries from the wreck could have been so much worse.*

Julien looked past her. "Dinner smells good."

She inhaled the rich smells of roasting pork, garlic, and fresh rosemary. "It does."

Skye climbed across the couch and toyed with their converted Christmas tree. A shiny, pink, plastic ornament swung from side to side. "My tree smells good, too."

He approached the large fir and examined the pink, shatterproof ornaments. "Y'all are really into the holidays."

"Skye removed the Christmas ornaments and added the pom-pom'd skirt and blinking white lights to keep the tree relevant for Valentine's Day," she said. "The tree has stood there for three months without dropping its needles."

He raised his eyebrows. "That's a fire danger."

She shrugged. "That's why engineers invented smoke detectors." She waited for his counterargument.

"Why do the decorations stop before the top?"

Exhaling, she smiled at the pockets of pink-hued festivity. "That's as far as Skye can reach."

Skye stood on the edge of the couch and demonstrated her reach.

"No standing on the couch. You know better." She grabbed the child around the waist and deposited her back on the floor, tugging her braid to soften the admonishment.

The girl pouted and glanced at Julien.

Crossing his arms, he stood in silence by the twinkling tree.

Skye changed tactics, settling on the old cushions.

She thinks she rules the house, and she might be right. Scanning the rest of the living room, she wondered if Skye's antics were enough to distract Julien's attention from the curtains' frayed edges or the couch's faded upholstery. Most of the furniture pieces predated her childhood, but the solid wood furnishings felt sturdy. Skye and the land needed her attention more than the farmhouse needed a makeover. She straightened a pile of picture books and moved a throw pillow. "Here, take a seat."

"That's all right. I'll stand," he said.

She frowned. *Claire might have called the man a stray, but he's as stubborn and persistent as a goat. Does he keep standing because it hurts to rise or because he's worried about what happens if he remains still?* She took another look at the furnishings and shook her head. *Whatever. Our living room is more comfortable than the cottage.*

He set down his frayed baseball cap and leaned against the wall.

She reached for it and brushed his hand.

Claire carried a vase of flowers into the room. The vase fell from her hands, and a thousand shards of glass scattered across the hardwood floor.

The chicken screamed and flapped its wings.

"Skye! Don't move!" Eliza yelled.

Skye froze and burst into tears.

She released her breath, made her way to her daughter, and felt glass grinding the wooden floors beneath her work boots. "I'm sorry, Sweet Pea." She swooped her daughter into her arms. "The noise scared me."

Skye dropped her head to her shoulder and choked back tears. "It scared me, too."

Claire kneeled and corralled the glass with her hands. "I'm such a fool."

"Mom, don't touch those shards." She weighed the importance of her daughter's affection and her mother's efforts to repair the damage.

Julien remained against the wall.

Adjusting Skye's weight, she looked at him.

"Julien?"

He straightened, picked up the abandoned chicken, and booted it from the house. "Here, let me help you, Ms. Claire."

His drawn-out words comforted Eliza's frayed nerves.

He crouched at Claire's side. "Where's your broom?"

Claire sniffled and turned her back on him.

"Ma'am, I know how to operate a broom."

Eliza suppressed a smile and jostled Skye in her arms. "Go look in the closet off the kitchen." She watched him make his way through the unfamiliar house. Her stomach rumbled. "Where do we stand on dinner?" she asked her mother.

Claire rose from the floor, her knees wobbling as she regained her balance. "Twenty more minutes in the oven."

"I'll pull it out when the timer goes off."

Claire bit her lip.

"Why don't you take Skye up for a bath?"

Smoothing her apron, Claire took mincing steps between the pieces of glass and made her way to the stairway.

Eliza put Skye on the bottom step and smoothed her hair. She wondered if Claire's kneejerk reaction had been more than a reflex. *Her physician told me it's important to recognize the early warning signs of a stroke.* Scanning Claire's face, she looked for lingering symptoms. "Is everything okay?"

"I'm fine. I'm just a clumsy fool," Claire muttered. She brushed a hand along Skye's pale blonde braids. "You have hay in your hair, Sweet Pea."

"I found a feather!"

"Where is it?" Claire asked.

"I gave it to Julien."

The older woman glanced at the kitchen and narrowed her gaze, but she took a deep breath and focused on her granddaughter. "Let's go draw your bath."

Sighing, Eliza watched her family climb the steps. *Am I doing the right thing by upsetting the balance and letting Julien into the house?* As soon as the pair moved out of earshot, she felt Julien return to her side.

"What happened?" he asked.

"Claire's grip isn't what it used to be."

"She told me she had a stroke."

She considered him, standing amid a scatter of glass with a broom and a dustpan in his hand. The overhead pipes knocked and rattled. Skye's light footsteps echoed along the floorboards. She smiled at the signs of normalcy and relaxed her shoulders. "When did she tell you that?"

"She brought food to the cottage last night, caught me in my boxers, and gave me her thoughts on life. I was either too polite or too hungry to move."

She's not gone yet. "Crafty."

He rolled his eyes. "Something like that."

She took the dustpan and gestured toward the couch. Sweeping up the remnants of the shattered vase soothed her nerves, and the task set a rhythm that made it easier to talk. "I remember Claire tripping on the steps outside of Skye's preschool. Then she complained her foot felt heavy at dinner and said her vision wavered from time to time. Erik and I listened, but we failed to connect the irregularities as a series of

155

emerging symptoms. I was too busy fussing over the baby, and he was too busy planning the future. I didn't realize my mom's ailments added up to something scarier than old age."

"We don't expect our parents to get old until it happens," he said.

She nodded and swept the dust and glass into the pan. "I didn't expect her to have a series of mini-stokes. The doctor called them TIA's, or transient ischemic attacks. Looking back, I feel like I should have helped or caught the symptoms earlier."

"Eliza, you're not a doctor, and nobody would fault your work ethic."

His soft, counseling tone threatened to unleash her emotions.

He stood and walked toward the collected pile of glass and dust.

She shook her head, keeping her eyes on the floor.

"Let me help you," he said.

"You might cut yourself." The admonishment lingered between them. "I can do it."

He dropped to one knee. "At least let me hold the dustpan."

Frustration clogged her throat. "I can do it." She coughed to clear the sudden tightness in her chest.

"Eliza, look at me."

Biting her lip, she complied and looked up, knowing he would see the tears sliding down her cheeks. His warm and compassionate gaze scanned her face. Sniffling, she held back the frustration and fear flooding her system.

"Your mama is still here. She's upstairs bathing your baby girl."

"What if she crashes the car with Skye?" She wiped away the tears. "What if she has another stroke and nobody's in the house to call an ambulance? The next one could be worse." A ragged breath escaped her lips. "A broken vase shouldn't set me off, but anxiety and uncertainty keep me awake some nights. Both generations are squeezing me. They deserve my support, but I feel like my life's one misstep from falling apart."

He abandoned the dustpan, stroked her cheek, and tucked a loose strand of hair behind her ear. "You're letting your fear get to you. It's the dead of winter and you can't do much but prepare and try to keep up. You don't quit, and I reckon these fields will be a riot of colors come springtime. Claire doesn't look like she's ready to slow down yet, so let her set the pace."

"But Skye?"

"She's a clever girl and old enough to stay out of most mischief." He smiled. "Hell, she's got a guardian elf. Keep her out of the passenger seat if that's what worries you the most."

"My mom would be livid." She sniffled.

He laughed. "A small price to pay, but I'm pretty sure you can handle Claire."

Smiling, she nodded and inhaled the crisp musk of his presence. "I'll tell her it was your idea."

He leaned toward the side of her face. "I have many ideas, Eliza Edwards. Riling up a stubborn, old she-cat is not at the top of my list." His hand cupped her waist.

Grinning at the innuendo, she took a deep breath to get her bearings. "She's not that bad."

He pulled back, eyed the faded couch, and

scratched his chin. "How long is Skye's bath?"

"Absolutely not." She laughed. "I knew this attraction would be a problem."

"Nah." He used the calloused pad of his thumb to wipe away her tears. "You've a whole list of problems, but what's going on between us isn't one of them."

He kissed her lips with an unexpected softness. The soft give and scratch of his beard teased her senses before she felt the warmth of his skin. Clutching his shirt, she let the smell of clean sweat and lush earth surround her. Desire coursed through her system. Realizing she wanted more than a kiss, she captured his bottom lip and pressed her body into his warmth. His appreciative growl urged her to continue, but she pulled back and assessed his stance. *Can I lean on him?*

He pulled back. "I won't fall," he whispered.

She nodded.

Wrapping her securely in his arms, he increased the pressure of his kiss.

His tongue slipped and teased as the sweet heat of the kiss climbed higher and drove away her fear. For a moment, she relaxed against him and savored the unchecked satisfaction of exploring an unknown landscape. Despite her reservations, she thrilled at his body pressed against her body, ripe with mutual attraction. The heat and rhythm of his touch lured her into a lazy exploration. She took the lead and let go of her worries. *This desire could be enough.*

The oven timer went off.

Her six-year-old streaked down the stairs in underwear and socks. Flying past them, she demanded milk. "Is it time for dinner yet?"

Eliza closed her eyes, stepped away from Julien,

and smoothed the front of her shirt. "Skye, go get your pajamas. Dinner is almost ready." She looked at Julien without shielding her pleasure, grinning like no one could see them.

Claire cleared her throat from the top of the stairs.

She glanced up and locked gazes with her mother. *Well, it's my house, too.*

The standoff lasted until Claire grabbed the handrail and descended the stairs.

Her measured footfalls sounded as loud as a gavel.

She appraised Julien, pursing her lips. "You might as well be useful. Go set the table."

"Yes, ma'am." He winked at Eliza and turned to do the older woman's bidding.

Eliza watched his long strides eat up the floorboard. *I'm beginning to appreciate that phrase.*

A sheet pan of roasted root vegetables stretched the meal. Julien declared the pork loin tasted as savory and delicious as the smells portended. "Not much a man won't do for roasted garlic and meat juice."

Claire cracked a smile, then narrowed her gaze. "Humph."

He ignored the censure and told stories from bayou country to entertain Skye.

Eliza wondered if the man could be any more charming. "It sounds like a different world."

"The South is unique," he said, "but Louisiana is a true melting pot. They call New Orleans the northern-most Caribbean city. Historic decisions steeped the river parishes in petrochemicals and agriculture."

"Like sugarcane," Skye said.

He winked. "Up north, Shreveport is dry and religious. They ought to re-draw the state lines, let New

Orleans merge with the coastal ports, and give Shreveport to East Texas. I'm sure they'd love to be known as 'Little Dallas'."

Claire put down her fork. "I admit my knowledge of the South is limited to movie theaters and textbook caricatures. Is it still racially divided?"

Eliza winced.

He glanced at Skye and nodded.

Accepting his answer, Claire turned to her granddaughter. "It's time for bed, Sweet Pea."

She rubbed one eye. "I'm not tired."

Claire exhaled. "I am."

On any other night, Granny's tone should have been enough to close the discussion, but Julien's presence added excitement to the girl's evening. *I'm not immune to his presence either.*

Skye squared her shoulders. "Julien said he would read me a story."

She decided to mediate the generations. "One story."

"Yes!"

Julien and her daughter retreated to the couch.

I'm still in charge, aren't I? She rose and helped Claire clear the table.

In the living room, Julien began a favorite old book.

She caught herself listening to the cadence of his words and shook her head to avoid the distraction.

Claire clucked her tongue. "Do you know what you're doing?"

"No." She set a load of plates by the white farmhouse sink and turned to her mother. "Living by the seat of my pants?"

"That's not like you."

She nodded. "Let's talk about something else."

"Like what?" Claire asked.

"How about your relationship with Luke?"

Claire handed her a plate. "How about not."

She smiled and turned on the hot water. "It's almost Valentine's Day."

The older woman shook her head. "I have enough problems closer to home. Cupid doesn't track dirt into the house and disappear when he gets bored."

"It's not like I could ask him to take off his boots." She glanced over her shoulder.

"Why not?" Claire handed her another plate.

"His leg? I don't know. How does that even work?"

"You don't need another project."

Shifting the flatware in the soapy water, she stood straight and rolled her shoulders. "He's not a project. He's working as hard as Gabe ever did."

Claire glanced at the fields.

Eliza followed her mother's gaze and admired the soft contours of the land beneath the moonlight. The illuminated hoop houses shone like beacons against the shadowed barn. *I bought myself time. That's the only thing that counts. He'll be gone before the solstice.*

Claire shook her head. "Gabe never came inside the house."

Julien entered the kitchen and cleared his throat. "Skye's waiting to go upstairs. Can I help with the dishes?"

She judged her mother's tight smile. *Let him fend for himself.* She handed Julien a drying towel. "Thanks, I'll get Skye into bed." She led Skye up the stairs,

161

turned on the nightlight, and tucked her daughter beneath a warm duvet. Lying still and listening to Skye's stream of consciousness felt like a luxury. The intimacy of the moment warmed her heart.

"And then the chickens and the *nisse* raced. The chickens won, but the *nisse* could have won if he hadn't taken a break."

"Why did he take a break?" she asked.

"Haven't you seen his long, white beard? He's older than Granny Claire."

Eliza smiled. *The therapist told me it's healthy to appreciate her unique perspectives. Before long she'll go off to school and join the cult of pink princesses and soccer cleats. Maybe I should get her another doll.* She smoothed the pale hair from her forehead. "What do you think of Julien?"

"I don't think he likes to race."

"Because of his leg?"

"No, because he talks slower than I do." She looked up, her eyes wide in the soft glow of the nightlight. "He said he's not a pirate."

She raised an eyebrow.

Skye exhaled. "That's too bad, but I like him." She demanded two more stories and a patchwork of folk songs and lullabies.

Eliza complied and let her words fade into a soft hum.

Within seconds, Skye closed her eyes and drifted to sleep.

She descended the stairs and spotted Julien and her mother leaning over the dining room table.

Claire unrolled a long ream of paper and pointed out pink-hued sticky notes.

They marked the peony varieties Eliza debated planting in expansion fields. Another sheet held notes on sprawling blueberry plants, prickly raspberry bushes, and neat apple trees. She had considered a hundred opportunities to keep the farm profitable. *What would Julien think of my whimsy?* She watched the pair debate her plans with the sensitivity of investment bankers.

Claire stuck a finger on a design. "This idea has merit, but peonies are a risky expansion for Hartley Farms. The down payment would wipe out her resources, and establishing perennial plants takes time. Maybe three to four years before she could have a commercial harvest."

Julien trailed a finger along the plans. "But she could do it."

"She can't keep thinking of these plants as romantic flowers. They're crops. To have the best chance of success, she needs to ditch obscure blooms and cultivate pretty varieties with fragrances worthy of a bouquet. Brides like Sarah Bernhardt peonies. They're big, light pink, and have a peppermint smell. I've seen them in all the magazines."

They're also boring. Eliza shook her head. *Did you even read the notes? I want to plant uncommon varieties. I want people to gasp and smile when they see my flowers for the first time. How do I make you understand this crop is more than a business?*

"Growing the plants is only half the battle. Commercial growers have to time the market, dry store their cuttings to stretch longevity, and compete with established peony farms for market share." She turned to the Southerner and braced her good hand on her hip. "Did you know they've started growing peonies in

Alaska?"

He shook his head and ran a finger along her notes, repeating the varietal names aloud. "Looks like she's done her homework."

"She needs less to worry about, Julien, not more."

"Yes, ma'am. I hear what you're saying. She'd have to manage another mortgage and a more complex operation, but she seems capable of doing it. What's holding her back?"

"An abundance of caution," Eliza said. Julien and her mother looked up, but only Julien had the decency to blush. She descended the rest of the staircase. "I hate to interrupt this little strategy session, but I'll have you both known I'm a grown woman. I can tolerate risks. I can decide for myself on the right time to make a move."

Claire rolled her eyes.

She dismissed her mother's familiar retreat and focused on Julien, who seemed confused about the privileges that came from two brief kisses. "I didn't ask for your opinions on my business plans."

He toyed with his nascent beard. "Consider it a little bonus, Eliza. A little *lagniappe*."

Struggling to make sense of his feedback, she repeated the unfamiliar word.

Claire leaned on the edge of the table. "Leave the man alone, Eliza. He asked questions, and I answered them. I keep telling you peonies are a ridiculous idea. Every farmer in Washington can grow them. We already have a field of roses we struggle to unload."

"So, when did you switch sides?" she asked.

Claire raised her eyebrows. "When someone listened."

Eliza blew her bangs out of her eyes. "Roses don't compete with peonies. You want to talk about crops? Let's talk about revenue per acre." She walked around the table and traced the familiar patterns. The fanciful names called to mind scents and viewing notes. Determined to ignore the romanticism of the blooms, she cleared her throat. "Once these plants are established, they're almost maintenance free. Very limited fertilizer costs. Minimal pruning labor. Wholesale pays between two and five dollars a flower. You can't touch that profit with roses."

"How many blooms per acre?" Julien asked.

"About twenty-five thousand."

He whistled. "You're projecting between $50,000 and $125,000 per acre?"

She smiled like she claimed the last cookie.

"If everything goes right," Claire muttered.

"I've done my research, and I know how to calculate the bottom line. I've spent years working on these plans." She gestured toward the drawings and tried to contain her frustration. "I don't appreciate your little show and tell."

Claire blushed.

"Mom, I know you're trying to help me, but it hurts me when you're so cavalier with my thoughts and opinions."

Julien cleared his throat. "You're not making calculated business decisions."

She whipped around to face him. "Excuse me."

He ran a hand against the grain of the sticky notes.

The notes ruffled like the feathers of an exotic bird.

"You told me the farm grosses about sixty thousand an acre right now, but the numbers you're throwing around for peonies dwarf your current profit. Why would you do all of this research and then let it sit?" He shook his head. "Hell, I've barely seen you sit in the last twenty-four hours. If you were solely focused on cash flow, you would have laid down a dozen acres of…Sarah Bernhardt and called it good. The plants would already be in the ground."

"It's more than money." The admission left her feeling naked. *The peony plans don't feel right, but I can't base my decisions on emotions.*

"Don't turn up your nose at good money," Claire said. "You don't know what it's like to exist on the brink of poverty."

Her parents sheltered her from the worst of their financial discussions, but she wondered if that decision did more harm than good. *At least I might have guessed what was coming.* "I can manage the farm's finances."

"Don't forget about your kid." Claire shook her head and tucked her errant scarf over her shoulder. She disappeared into her first-floor bedroom, and the closing door echoed in the silence.

Eliza stared at plans lying on the dining room table. She checked the positioning of her notes and started to re-roll the softened, white paper. "She has zero faith in my ability to manage this farm on my own."

"I think she means well," he said.

"No. She had faith in Erik." The admission still hurt. "I started this design the year we got married. My mom thought the research and doodles would keep me busy until a baby came along. She used to stay up with me and research varietals. Now, she thinks moving to town is my only alternative."

"She's protecting you."

She stiffened. "I don't need protection."

Julien arched an eyebrow.

Remembering Claire showed him the plans, she exhaled. "I have Erik's life insurance money, but I'm not sure if the peony plans make sense. They can make a profit, but something about the field designs nags and worries me. They don't feel right. It sounds silly, but sometimes I dream about wading through a sea of sweet-smelling blooms. It should be a happy dream, but I'm never sure if the sea belongs to me, or I'm drowning in it."

He nodded. "My mama tried to grow peonies once. Turns out we don't get the hard freezes they require. She tended the plants for years, dug up the tubers, and stored them in the freezer. They made a pretty bush, but they never bloomed or gave off the scent she craved."

"It's hard to resist their allure." She smiled at the frustration of nurturing the crop in an unsuitable climate. *Don't we all force the things we want the most?*

He took a step closer. "Some people don't go for delicate."

She held up a hand. "I want people to gasp and smile when they see my flowers for the first time, but I want to do the same thing every time I walk out the door. How can I look at a sea of blooms and know I planted the flowers for my bottom line?"

He laughed. "Eliza, my family doesn't love sugarcane. We're just good at it."

"Anyone can be good at peonies in the right climate." She shook her head and looked out the window. "My mother's right. I should stick to investment berries. They're less pretentious."

He pulled his baseball cap over his dark hair. "Seems like you made your decision. It's not a good fit. Throw away the plans."

She examined the reams of rejected possibilities and felt the weight of Skye's future and the untapped potential waiting beyond the front door. "I have to expand to turn a profit. To keep things going for myself and Skye."

"What're you good at doing?"

"Bossing people around? Wasting an inordinate amount of time nurturing rare varietals?"

Again, he laughed and leaned down, kissing her cheek. "That's the problem with being the boss, Eliza. Make decisions. If you can't get excited about the bottom line, find a way to profit from what you love."

She touched the warm imprint of his kiss, struggling to keep her mind focused on proving her point. "It's not that easy. Sugar is a global commodity."

"You don't need a formal market to sell a superior product." He walked toward the door. "Go settle up with your mama, or you'll never sleep. Come find me tomorrow and point me in the right direction."

"Tomorrow?" She bit her lip, holding back a tear that threatened to fall from her eye. *He didn't quit.*

Raising a hand over his shoulder, he walked out the door without looking back.

His footprints marred the polished wood floors. She sighed. *Mom will have a fit.* Returning to the kitchen for a mop, she stood in front of the sink and filled a bucket, wondering how many times Claire did the same thing. The faucet ran, but her mind drifted. Beyond their acres, hilled potatoes filled the former pastures, their vines brown and flaccid along the frost-covered ground. *How did Claire navigate the stress of living with Dad? What did she tell herself when the Smiths grew in prominence and she watched her world shrink year after year? Would Skye fare better if we moved into town?* She ran the wet cotton mop head across the dusty footprints and thought about Julien's challenge. *The potato plants are a solid crop, too, but who could love such boring little blooms?*

Chapter Ten

Cold air, good food, and a steady day of work gave Julien's body a reason to relax in the cottage bunkroom, but his mind lingered on the memory of Eliza's lips. *Her expansion plans have more to do with pinning down her tastes than balancing her bottom line, but she met every one of my suggestions with stubborn pride.* He closed his eyes. *It's easier to be the outsider looking in. We're just not there yet.* Another hour passed without sleep. Pulling back the curtains, he confronted the farm's moonlit terrain.

Opening the front door, he took a deep breath and felt the cold bite of the air burn his lungs. He left the cottage and walked past the big, wooden barn. At the river's edge, a murmur of high-pitched whistles and piping notes filled the air. Abandoning his view of the water, he scanned the treetops and found the bald eagle perched in a craggy ash tree. The large bird's golden eyes and distinctive white cap glowed in the moonlight. The standoff persisted, and he tested the allure of a long, beckoning whistle.

The animal cocked its head.

"Pretty bird," he said.

Screeching, the eagle flapped its immense wings.

"Handsome bird?" He scanned the treetops for a nest. Standing still, he felt the damp cold seeping past his jacket. "A storm is coming. Go home." He watched the haughty animal stare back and step sideways on a naked branch. "Suit yourself, bird." Turning away from the mist-draped river, he retraced his steps to the cottage, stopped on the porch, and looked at a single light shining from the second floor of the farmhouse. *Is she still wide-awake, worrying about her crops? That's the thing...I can tell she cares.* He thought of her controlled fury when she descended the stairs, her voice as chilled and measured as a block of ice. *I have a few ideas to help her thaw out.*

The eagle flew to the top of the barn and screeched.

He grinned and took the hint, returning to his place on the farm. Instead of lying in bed and replaying the last few years of his life, he settled on the cottage floor and stretched to warm his muscles and vanquish insomnia. Wind battered the windowpane. He began a routine designed to maintain his abdominal muscles, obliques, and the stabilizing muscles of his lower back. His physical therapist taught him the subtleties of the crunches and bird dogs. He completed the moves on autopilot until he no longer felt the weariness of the day's pain radiating up his leg. Sitting on the rumpled bed with sweat dripping down his chest, he took a deep breath. *Exhaustion has always been the solution.*

He slept better than he had in ages, got out of bed with the sun, clicked on the prosthesis, and made a cup of coffee from a package with a foreign label. Light spilled over the snow-dappled fields as he drank the strong brew. The caffeine kicked in, and he stretched. *Sitting still feels too dangerous.* Dropping to the ground, he counted push-ups until his muscles burned. The pain helped him recall the exhaustion of his first weeks in rehabilitation. The surgeries had stopped, but five weeks passed before the prosthetic leg arrived and gait training began. The first time he tried on the device, he compared his discomfort to the stiff leather of new boots.

Sterling, his physical therapist, laughed.

His view of the device went downhill from there. After a full day of rehabilitation, his mangled body hurt like hell, the device gave him blisters, and he considered chucking the device out the window. "I'm so over this crap."

"If you stop moving forward, you won't like the outcome."

"Whatever, man."

Sterling crossed his arms.

Alone in his room, Julien used the pain as an excuse to drink. Doubt crept into his consciousness. He wondered what people would say about him if he quit. *That kid was always second best.* The empty bottle rolled from his hand, and he passed out.

"Inactivity breeds discontent," Sterling said the next morning. "It's dangerous to sit still."

"I'd settle for a dark room and a bottle of pain relievers."

Sterling smacked his shoulder. "Leave your doubts in the past and greet the dawn." He stretched wide his arms and grinned.

Julien winced at the volume of the man's voice. "Asshole." He refused to drown his pain. Giving Sterling a hard time became the high point of his day. They bashed Southeastern Conference rivals and ragged each other about cheap beer and Tex-Mex oddities. At the end of his rehabilitation, Julien responded to the therapist's encouragement, tolerated the setbacks, and had pushed his body through the necessary exercises without complaining.

Thank God, he was willing to be my friend. Is that what Eliza needs? I can't treat her like one of the guys. He spread his legs and reached for a towel, thinking of the time his car broke down and confined him to a wheelchair. He had spent the better part of the summer months pushing himself up and down the driveway of his parents' house to avoid Caroline's social calls. He sent Sterling a picture of the mottled skin and a punctured wheelchair tire.

"Wait, just one?" the therapist asked.

For the first time in a month, Julien had smiled.

Now far from home and far from his lowest point, he stood and put his coffee cup in the sink. Beyond the cottage door, pink and gold morning light spilled over the mountains. Eliza's fields waited in the shadows, fit for blooms but heavy with the daily maintenance of farm work. As he descended the steps, the sun rose higher, and light illuminated dormant plants and patches of glistening snow. *I don't want to be her friend, but I also don't want her to know how far I've come.* He advanced on the spiky nubs of dormant roses, walking between frost-covered bushes sparkling like the centerpieces of a Mardi Gras ball. Eliza called them "old garden roses", but he doubted spring would bring a field of uniform pink buds. *She likes a challenge.* He pressed a thumb against a thorn and smiled at the sharp bite. *A flash of pain for a beautiful reward.*

Geese landed in the field and searched for their morning meal. His progress disturbed their grazing. They honked and hissed.

"I haven't had breakfast yet either," he said.

The nearest animal thrust its beak toward his leg.

"Point taken. I'll fry up the eggs in the refrigerator."

The bird lunged again.

Smiling, he returned to the greenhouses and reassessed the length of his repair estimates. *I told her I would only stick around until she found help, but that was before I tasted her lips and before I saw her sprint across broken glass to gather her daughter in her arms. Reprimanding her on the ladder made me feel foolish, but a decade of safety training and a view of her pert behind were more than enough provocation to overrule my good judgment. I crossed a line. I can either stick around or hit the road when she finds someone else to fill my shoes.* He closed his eyes. *Sticking around means making a commitment.*

The weight of the decision felt too heavy. He climbed the dike and eyed the cold river water for signs of fish. *The only breakfast better than fried eggs would be a cast iron skillet full of buttery speckled trout.* He frowned. *Eliza's not paying me to fish.*

A string of long, piping sounds called his attention to the top of the ash tree. The bald eagle's golden eyes stared right at him.

"So, you're staying?"

The eagle turned its head.

"What's so special about this place?"

The animal's immense, dark brown wings stretched. It dove toward the icy Skagit, its yellow talons stretched for a catch before they plunged into the water. The bird skimmed the surface of the river and rose with a triumphant silvery fish.

"Touché. Are you sharing?"

The animal settled at the top of the tree and pecked at its meal.

He shook the hair out of his eyes. "Selfish bird." At the cottage, he fried the last of the eggs Gabe left behind and set about finding his boss. The lights in the barn indicated she had come and gone. He opened the door of the first hoop house and found her on her hands and knees weeding the rows. "Do you ever rest?"

"Nope." She wiped the sweat from her brow and smiled.

He debated a morning kiss and decided to wait and see how she reacted. *Her interest might have waned after she slept on the day's events. Then again, this pit stop has been full of surprises.* He sighed. *If I wanted to weed flowerbeds, I could have stayed home.* He thought about the things he would rather be doing. "Do you plan to spend the entire day on your hands and knees?"

She shifted into a crouch. "Only if you'll join me."

He raised his eyebrows. "I always reciprocate."

Laughing, she grabbed a trowel. "Get to work."

He eased his body to the earth, found his balance, and trailed a hand along her back. Stopping above her waistband, he leaned over and kissed her cheek. "Good morning to you, too."

"Your beard's damp from the mist." She smiled but stayed put by his side.

Pushing aside a toothy leaf, he examined the nearest plant. "What are we looking at?"

"Anemones." She parted the leaves of a larger specimen and revealed a flower bud. "They're sometimes called wind flowers. The petals are bright and distinct, with pretty black or yellow centers. They're a good substitute for brides who have their hearts set on off-season peonies but can't afford the expense."

"Are you sure you don't want to plant peonies?"

She smiled. "Mostly."

"Did you and Claire make peace?" he asked.

She bit her lip.

He decided to move on. "Is your Saturday bride counting on these anemones?"

"No, but she specifically requested the roses in the barn. I sourced the blooms from a Seattle greenhouse. These flowers won't be ready for a few weeks."

He pulled a weed. "Valentine's Day seems like a lousy time to get married."

She stopped working. "Have you ever been married?"

"No." He struggled to keep the disappointment of old relationships from coloring his response. *My family expected it the minute I graduated from college. I could feel the pressure, but I couldn't pull the trigger.* "Never found the right woman who could put up with me and my family."

Her gaze softened, and she rooted through the seedlings, her hands moving with quick precision. "Working as a florist taught me weddings are really about creating new families. The day shines a spotlight on the bride, but nine times out of ten, the party turns into a family reunion. I've heard more than one guest recount their first brush with romance in a drawn-out speech. From my point of view, Valentine's Day is the perfect day to get married. It's a day full of hope for new beginnings."

He yanked out another weed. "Tell me about your wedding."

"It was small. Neither one of us had much family, but I thought the day went well."

At the thought of her in a white dress, surrounded by sunshine and happy faces, he smiled. *She must have been as sweet and tender as an emerging bud, but these days, she carries more than the weight of a pretty bouquet.* He shook his head and added to his pile of weeds. *She still deserves light and happiness. Life has so many seasons. Can I give her a taste of happiness?*

After finishing her row, Eliza stood and bridged her hands behind her back. "I saw your eagle earlier this morning,"

He looked up. "Me, too. It caught a fish."

She nodded. "Skye is still worried about her chickens."

"The bird won't go after them."

"They're opportunistic carnivores. They'll eat just about anything," she said.

He smiled. "Yeah, but I think this bird has good taste."

She raised an eyebrow. "It's a predator."

"I bet the eagle took one look at those gamey fowl and opted for fresh fish."

Looking toward the river, she yawned and rubbed her chin "Maybe I should keep the chickens in the coop for the rest of the winter."

"I'll watch them," he said.

She faced him. "You can't be everywhere."

"They like me." He shrugged. "I'll put a little corn in my pocket."

"Does that work with the ladies?"

Laughing, he rose and claimed her opening before she could change her mind. He dropped a hand to the swell of her ass, wondering what could better, and felt her settle into his arms. "I'm willing to try. You tell me if it works."

She moistened her lips. "You might not need the corn."

Lowering his hand, he brought her flush against his arousal, desperate to see if she would run. Instead of pulling away, she shifted her weight and rubbed against him. His thoughts skipped over playful kisses and went straight to the homely cottage where he hung his hat. "Eliza…"

She shook her head and nipped his bottom lip. "I'm taking Skye into the city to meet with her therapist. I'll be gone until late afternoon."

He closed his eyes and eased his hold. "And when you get back?"

"I'll count the chickens."

Laughing, he released her and watched her walk away. *If I do my job right, you won't remember how to count.*

****

Prepping the greenhouse joints with a wire brush felt tedious, but he passed the time singing old gospel songs. Scraping away the accumulated rust, scale, paint, and dirt worked up a sweat and he stopped to wipe his brow and remove his jacket. *Who gets the blame for the state of these facilities—Erik or the deported foreman?*

A shiny, black SUV came down the long driveway leading from the potato farm. A man in jeans and an ironed shirt opened the gate and reclaimed the steering wheel, leaving the gate wide open after he drove past. He stopped the conspicuous SUV in the middle of the gravel drive.

Julien put down the wire brush and faced the vehicle.

A couple in matching getups climbed out of the vehicle. Their orange tans and blinding white smiles set them apart from the local wool and all-weather boot crowd. *These people either skip coffee or pay their dentist too much. Either way, I'm guessing they don't belong here.* He looked toward the farmhouse, knowing Eliza and Skye were in the city.

Claire showed no sign of emerging from the farmhouse.

Brushing the dirt off his hands, he walked forward and offered the man a brief nod. "Welcome to Hartley Farms."

The man stuck out his hand.

He made a show of testing his grip, but he had no problem matching the silent show of force.

The man released his hand and slapped him on the shoulder. "Beautiful piece of property!"

"I agree, but it's not mine."

The man's smiling veneer faltered. "It's not yours? Who owns it?"

"Who's asking?"

"Steven Warly. This is my wife, Nicole."

Julien offered the woman his hand. "Please to meet you." He hardly felt her squeeze as she made contact and dropped his greeting with a frosted-pink smile.

"We've been scouring the area for a home site and noticed the pretty farmhouse from the road."

Julien arched an eyebrow and glanced at the acres of potatoes separating them from the main highway. "You saw this land from the road?"

"Steven's being modest." Ms. Warly stepped

forward. "We did a bit of modern scouting using satellite maps and property records. You have twenty acres?"

Modern scouting, my ass. He probably knows the property taxes and the acres of river frontage to the foot. "I told you it's not my farm."

"You're not Erik Edwards?"

He crossed his arms and braced his weight, summoning patience to deal with the glossy pair. "No, ma'am, it's not mine." *If it was, I'd have thrown you off the land by now.*

The man consulted his phone. "Is Eliza Edwards here?"

He narrowed his gaze. "Sir, can I help you?"

"We'd like to make her an offer. Seven hundred and seventy-five thousand for the house and surrounding acreage."

The offer sounded low, but buyers valued land for different attributes. *Eliza can duplicate the soil, but memories and hope anchor her dreams for this place.* "I don't believe the land's for sale."

"This site has incredible potential. People will love the rocky outcroppings and natural vistas."

"People?"

The couple looked at each other and smiled.

He thought about calling the sheriff, but he exhaled. Knowing he had no reason to engage Mr. and Ms. Warly, he recalled Claire's admonishments and Eliza's lingering indecision. *The farm is a significant undertaking. She's capable of running it with help, but where's the harm in collecting information and giving her options?* "Why don't you leave your contact information? I'm sure Ms. Edwards will consider your offer and be in touch. If she doesn't want to sell the house, she might part with some acreage."

The woman thrust a card into his hand. "Oh, we want all of it."

Nodding, he tucked the heavyweight paper into his back pocket. "Yes, ma'am. I'm sure you do." *But I'm not in a position to make the sale.* He scanned the dormant fields. *Will Eliza waver with an offer in hand?*

****

He heard Eliza and Skye return after sunset. Emerging from the barn, he wiped his hands clean of sawdust. "Good trip?"

Eliza picked snacks from the truck's floorboards and tossed them to the ground. Straightening, she arched her back and smiled.

Skye ran up and down the driveway, spouting a symphony of high-pitched gibberish.

As she darted from place to place, the flashes of motion lingered in his vision, like a streak of light photographed with a slow shutter speed.

"An ice cream cone will do that," Eliza said.

He scratched his chin. "In the middle of winter?"

She nodded. "Skye is a connoisseur."

"Skye doesn't seem too worried about her pets." He watched a quick smile flash across Eliza's face. *Count your chickens, Lady. I'm ready to make you beg.* He considered detailing his plans for the night but realized the day had deepened the shadows beneath her eyes. *I'll start by rubbing the tension from her shoulders. The rest is her prerogative.* Stepping to the side, he stopped imagining the outcome if she chose more than a backrub. "How was your trip?"

"Exhausting. What happened on the farm?"

He cleared his throat. "I made progress on the welding prep. Serah and Michelle stuck to the barn. You had some visitors."

She frowned. "I wasn't expecting anyone."

He removed the business card from his back pocket and handed it over. "A couple showed up around noon and said they were interested in buying the house and the acreage."

She slipped the card into her shirt pocket and kicked the dust with her boot. The brim of her hat hid her gaze. "What did you tell them?"

"I told them you would consider their offer."

She snapped up her head. "You had no business encouraging them."

Her sharp reprimand startled him. "Eliza, I hardly acted encouraging. My mama would have kicked my ankle for being that rude. The visitors dressed like city folk. They're probably canvassing the entire road for prospects and handing out cards left and right. I thought you might want the information, but you don't have to act on it."

She exhaled. "Answer is still the same."

"Fair enough." He nodded. "Do you even want to know their offer?"

"Nope." She marched toward the farmhouse and paused to look back over her shoulder. "Stick to the foreman's tasks, Julien. I don't need a business manager, and I'm more than capable of speaking for myself."

To temper his response, he bit his cheek. "Yes, ma'am."

She paused but then kept walking.

Wiping his hands on his pants, he exhaled. "What

should I have done, Eliza? Pulled out a shotgun to run them off?"

"That's an option," she called back.

"A bad one." His shout filled the widening distance between them.

She gave him the bird but did not stop.

He shook his head and tabled his plans for a backrub and a satisfying roll in the hay. *She looked like she needed a hand in the hardware store, but I should have known better than to think I could make a difference.* Fixing his hat, he shook his head. "Stubborn woman."

****

At the end of the day, he opened the cottage door and found Claire holding a container of beef stew and a loaf of sourdough bread. The woman's businesslike expression warned him he would have to work for his meal, but his mouth watered in anticipation of the tangy reward.

She walked past him and set the items on the worn kitchen table. "How much was the offer?"

So much for a preamble. He pulled a bowl from the cabinet and met her determined gaze. "Eliza said she wasn't interested."

Frowning, she pulled out a chair and sat at the table. "I am."

He set the bowl on the table and crossed his arms. "Who owns the farm?"

She pinched her lips. "Eliza inherited it from her father."

"Then why does the price matter to you?"

"Knowing the price will tell me how hard to push her."

His burgeoning loyalty to Eliza felt too nebulous to make him choose sides. Deciding to stick to the facts, he relayed the price and watched Claire for a reaction.

She shook her head. "That's not enough."

He served himself a heaping portion of stew, put the plate in the microwave, and leaned against the counter. "Not enough for what?"

"To get them settled in town."

Running his hand through his hair, he replayed Eliza's quick rejection in the yard. "Your daughter doesn't seem real interested in that option."

"It's what she needs. A house in a good school district." Her eyes narrowed. "A steady income."

The microwave dinged, and he removed his plate. Sitting at the table, he lifted a forkful of stew to his mouth and savored the first meaty bite. "This is good. Thanks."

"It was better fresh from the pot. Add a little salt."

Reaching for the plastic saltshaker, he complied and took a bite. "I didn't get a dinner invitation today."

Claire smiled. "No, she's in a temper."

"I noticed." He eyed the leftovers in the container. "I appreciate the meal, but you don't have to cook my dinner every night. If you'll pick up groceries for me, I can manage."

"You can't carry much on a motorcycle."

"No, I can't."

She stood, pushed back from the table, and surveyed the cottage. "I see no reason for you to cook. I've made farm meals for forty years. Why should I stop now that we're down to a hard-headed Southerner?" She walked toward the door. "I'll do my best to make sure Eliza considers the offer."

"Claire, where would you go if Eliza sold the farm?"

She stopped retreating and turned. "I'm not sure."

The uncertainty in her gaze tempered his approach. *I learned to handle my mama with kid gloves instead of brute force.* "Your daughter would miss you. Skye would miss you."

Her gaze softened. "They need to start a new life. I won't be too far away."

"Florida?"

She grunted. "Hardly."

"Mount Vernon?"

"Perhaps. Depends on where they settled."

He considered his words and decided he and Claire understood each other. "Whether Eliza stays on the farm, Luke seems like he would welcome your company in town."

She put her good hand on her hip. "Am I that old, Julien? I'm down to good company?"

He swallowed. "I'm not much good at playing Cupid."

Shaking her head, she reached for the door. "Stick to your tasks."

These women have no qualms about putting me in my place. Alone in the cottage, he shook his head at his circumstances, raised a critical eye to his surroundings, and decided to finish his stew. *At least they keep me well fed.* He thought of the deep shadows beneath Eliza's eyes. *She's beautiful, but I fear beauty won't be enough to keep me here.*

****

Moonlight glowed behind the curtains as he checked the clock and realized less than two hours passed since he fell asleep on the couch. He stretched the cramps from his good leg and worked through some exercises. "I need more than a nap." After twenty minutes of stiff-muscled pain, he felt his cramping muscles release. The lack of tension gave his mind room to wander, and he pulled back the curtains. Lights shone from the barn. He pulled on his jacket and trudged to the wooden structure, intent on apologizing to Eliza and pulling his foot from his mouth. Classic rock slipped past the weather stripping. He opened the door.

A vibrant arrangement of pink flowers sat on the large, wooden table. Eliza stared at the blooms.

"Is that for the weekend wedding?" he asked.

She shook her head.

Closing the door, he walked into the barn. "Your dining room table?"

"Try again."

"A funeral?"

She adjusted a fuchsia flower. "It's too colorful for a funeral."

He stood on the opposite side of the table, giving her space and testing her interest in his presence. "Some people want to be remembered for the good things they've done."

A slight smile appeared on her face. "Well, maybe if they're a cosmetics saleslady."

"That pyramid scheme made it up here?"

"Barely," she said.

The music changed, and The Rolling Stones' "Dead Flowers" filled the barn with heroin-laced references. He watched her fuss with the arrangement. The track changed to The Doors. Zero reaction. He caught the sound of animals rustling in their coops. The coolers hummed and maintained a bass line against Morrison's lonesome lyrics. Tugging on a spool of ribbon, he considered the wisdom of his next words. "Do you ever worry you're wearing out yourself?"

"I picked up the flowers while I was in Seattle. They'll only be fresh for a few days."

Lifting his nose, he appreciated the rich floral scent above the motes of dust and hay. "I'm talking about more than this arrangement. I meant what I said, Eliza. Being the boss has its risks and its rewards. I was never cut out for it. That's one reason Brandon's running the sugarcane farm and I'm traipsing across the country on a bike."

She tugged on a piece of greenery. "I'm working on a book proposal for a children's book about cut flower gardens. Instead of organizing the chapters around growing, harvesting, and arrangements, I plan to focus on color." Her shoulders relaxed, and she looked at the spools of ribbon arranged on a wall. "Skye loves the rainbow. If I give her a bundle of flowers, she ignores the shapes and sorts them into colors. Kids have a different way of looking at the world."

"Make-believe gives kids a chance to impose rules and order."

She turned a flower and displayed its face. "Skye's therapist said something similar. Using her imagination is good for her."

He considered the flowers. "Is this the first arrangement you've done for the book?"

She grinned. "No, I saved the pink flowers for the end. I'm using tulips, sweet peas, zinnias, echinacea, ranunculus, roses, and dahlias. Children respond to the big, bold blooms. I want to get the bouquet right before I show Skye."

"What about the boys?" he asked.

She gestured toward a binder full of plastic sleeves, color images, and handwritten annotations. "Flip through the pages. I tried to create something for everyone."

Following her instructions, he flipped through the mock-up. Most of the arrangements looked at home in a florist's shop, but he inspected an arresting display. Unable to identify the species, he read the text describing the rugged, organic blooms. Grasses, ivies, chocolate cosmos, cattails, and dark red sunflowers spilled from the wooden egg crate. The dark blooms made him think of drawing lessons and high school art classes. "What about black?"

"Flip the page. Double Hellebore. Commonly called a Winter Rose."

"That's catchy."

She laughed. "A good number of hellebore species are poisonous. Life comes with tradeoffs."

He read a poem scratched along the margins of the page.

The winter rose is a steady bloom
Her petals shine at dawn.
But I daren't kiss her lovely lips.
The heart before mine is gone.

"The hellebore plants teach us beauty is worth the risk," she said. "You have to know what you're doing and work hard enough to earn it. The flowers I use are all easy enough to grow at garden scale. I've even considered packaging the book with seeds to make a little kit."

"I like the idea of a kit. It seems like the type of gift that would land on a top ten list for West Coast liberal parents."

She smiled. "Don't mock the vegans, Julien. They'll hear you."

He re-read the poem. "How poisonous is this flower?"

She moved the arrangement to the cooler and faced him. "Touching them might bother gardeners with sensitive skin. Consumption causes the most severe poisoning cases. Symptoms include burning sensations, vomiting, abdominal cramping, diarrhea, damage to the nervous system, and possible depression."

He swallowed. "Maybe those blooms are a poor choice for a children's book."

"Why? Kids have to learn discretion."

"My mama favored discipline."

She tucked a piece of hair behind her eat. "Did that work?"

"No, ma'am."

She laughed. "The species can also be medicinal. Most folktales and rhymes convey knowledge. Kids will think twice before they pick a hellebore."

He watched her lean into the bouquet and inhale the aroma of the blooms. Her breasts pressed against the lush greenery, and her wide smile lit up the room. *They might be a handful, but damn, they're worth the risk.* He cleared his throat. "Where'd you learn about flowers?"

"My father taught me about plants, about which grasses the horses should eat and which would twist their stomach into knots. I noticed the details and never looked back." She swallowed. "Erik coached me to consider profitability."

He let that comment die. *I don't want her thinking about him.* "I like the sci-fi fantasy theme. How many books do you need to sell to break even?"

"I have no idea," she said.

"So why do it?"

"It's a gamble, Julien, just like everything else. I've done guest magazine articles and blog posts about our flowers. I've made contacts. I hope the arrangements and notes turn into a book proposal, but the idea might go nowhere. I'm willing to take the risk."

He shook his head. "You're gambling with your time and resources."

Her gaze narrowed. "You told me to make a decision."

"Fields are tangible resources."

"I'd rather fail than sit on the sidelines," she said. "A successful book would inspire Skye and pad her college savings account."

He weighed the intimacy of their kisses against his desire to get involved with more than a foreman's duties. "Are you running short every year?"

She spread the petals of a rose. "I'm doing everything I can to keep the farm afloat. Skye's growing up. Claire's growing old. Life will only get more expensive."

"If Claire's worried about your finances, your husband's life insurance settlement can't be huge. You have absolutely no interest in selling the farm?"

She placed the arrangement in the cooler and slammed the door. The frame rattled. Placing her palm on the glass, she exhaled. "Did Claire send you in here?"

"Claire didn't send me." Understanding he owed her a full apology, he sighed. "I came over here to say I'm sorry. When those yahoos made their offer, Eliza, taking a card seemed like a sensible step, but if you'd been here, I would have deferred to you. I know the farm is yours."

She faced him and put her hands on her hips. "Why in the hell did you tell my mom how much they offered?"

Seeing the flush on her cheeks, he widened his stance, prepared to go a few rounds with an angry, beautiful woman to clear the air. "She asked?"

"Claire means well, Julien, but you have to pick a side."

I've been on Eliza's side since the beginning. He stepped closer, curious if to see if she would bolt. "Seems like y'all would be on the same one?"

She shook her head and rounded the table, fussing with her tools. "Claire wants me to buy a house outside of Seattle and run a cutesy shop. I'd be stuck on a street corner like a bug with a pin, desperately waiting for fickle customers to cover my margins. Let someone else do the selling. I want to be on the land. I want the connection of watching seeds turn into blooms and weighing a full harvest." She stared at the bouquet of pink blooms in the cooler, took a deep breath, and sighed. "I know my life could be easier. But I want what I want."

He gravitated toward the flash of pleasure on her face and inched closer. *I wish I saw more of that look.* "You deserve to get what you want out of life."

She laughed. "Everyone else disagrees."

"I'm not everyone else."

She stopped messing with tools and looked at him. "No, you're not."

The music kept playing. "If you run, I won't chase you."

She frowned. "What's your family like?"

He cleared his throat, wondering if he missed his chance. "My family?"

She leaned against the table and crossed her arms. "Do they push you? Claire never lets up."

"She wants what's best for you." He swallowed, hoping Eliza understood his allegiance.

"She wants to retire."

"I get the impression she wants to know you and Skye are in a good place." He trailed his hand along the work surface, surprised at the work-worn smoothness of the grain. *Eliza's life hasn't always been smooth. She works so damn hard.* He looked up and smiled. "If you push Claire and Luke a little harder, you might have another wedding on your hands."

She drummed her fingers on the table. "Claire needs to do something for herself instead of managing my life."

He laughed. "Good luck explaining that to your mother. Mine is a force of nature. The order varies, but she's devoted to God, her family, and her camellias."

Tilting her head, she leaned her forearms on the table and stared. "Was she worried about you after the accident?"

"Her concern was almost too much. I love her and thank her for everything she's done, but I had to get out of Louisiana." He rounded the corner of the table until he stood next to her. Aching to reach for her and smooth the worry lines from her skin, he settled against the table and smiled. "Nothing ruins a steak like a review of your shortcomings at the dinner table. I couldn't stomach any more family prayers for my health and speedy recovery."

She frowned. "You don't believe in God?"

"I believe in something." Willing to be honest with her, he reached for her hand and traced the lines on her palm. "I went to church with my family, but I couldn't stand the looks of pity and refused to go again. My mother got creative when I pushed back, but I got little out of live-streaming the service." He looked up from her palm and waited for her reaction.

She bit her lip. "They should have known not to pity you. You strike me as a determined man."

"My neighbors still see an altar boy making faces. Growing up in a small town is hard."

She pulled free her hand. "When are you going home?"

He closed the distance between them and set the tools to the side. "I might stick around a little longer than I thought."

"Or keep traveling?"

He smiled. "I'm here now."

She raised her arm and toyed with a button on his shirt. "Life is full of surprises."

Covering her hand, he stilled her nervous gesture. "Some of them are better than others."

"I hope your mother never called the oilfield accident a blessing in disguise?"

He laughed, grateful she had the courage to call a spade a spade "No, but it sure as hell pointed me in new directions."

She smiled.

"Let's stop talking about my mother." He lowered his hands to her hips and waited.

She unhooked the button on his shirt.

Shaking his head, he lifted her ass to the surface of the worktable.

Grabbing his shoulders, she frowned. "What are you doing?"

"Gold-plating my apology." He stroked the side of her breast, gauging her response.

She sighed and leaned into his touch. "Apology accepted."

He grinned and cleared his throat. "What else makes you happy, Eliza?"

"How happy are we talking, Julien?"

He lowered his hand and spread her legs, his intent as clear as the warm yellow light shining above them.

Her eyes widened. "Too much time has passed since anyone else has made me…that happy."

"That's a shame."

"I've been busy." She ran a hand along his shoulder and traced the tendons in his neck.

Her touch felt as light as the mist. "Time to take a break."

Smiling, she spread her calloused fingers, traced his collarbone, and grazed his pecs. "I have a bed."

He inhaled, imagining her spread naked amid tangled sheets.

Her hand skimmed his abdomen.

Feeling his cock straining against his jeans, he considered abandoning his plan for the pleasure she offered. *I need to distract her before I give into those bedroom eyes.* Giving thanks for the barn's heater, crossed his arms, and pulled off his shirt.

Her eyes widened. "Oh."

Smiling, he watched her take in the muscles of his chest.

Her green eyes narrowed as she traced his muscles with her fingertips. She licked her lips.

Relearning to balance had some added benefits. I'd do a thousand pushups a day to keep her looking at my body like that.

Her hand reached for his belt.

He shook his head. "I came over here to apologize, and I mean to do it."

She wrestled with the belt buckle. "Apology accepted."

He let her pull off his belt before he pried the thick leather from her hands. "I asked what makes you happy?"

She frowned.

Desire and confusion warred across her features. Taking pity on her, he offered her the momentary relief and promise of a kiss. Feeling her lips part, he cupped her cheek and indulged the ache in his chest, thinking of how good she would feel in bed.

She matched his rhythm.

The taste of honeysuckle flooded his senses. Feeling the warmth of her body on his exposed skin, he pulled her closer and wondered if he possessed the will and experience to hold back.

"Your kisses make me happy," she said.

Lifting the weight of her hair, he let the strands fall, as soft as silk. He cradled her head and placed his hand on her chest, lowering her body until she relaxed against his strength and let him settle her across the wooden table. "Not good enough."

Her gaze widened.

He popped the first button on her shirt. "You blew by me in the hardware store."

"Tastes change." She propped herself on one elbow. "Wait a minute. I told you I would have been too intimidated to…"

Guiding her back to the table, he smiled, unwilling to revisit his past mistakes. "People say a lot of things they don't mean. You called me an ass-backward Neanderthal."

Sighing, she leaned on both elbows. "Did that oilfield accident damage your memory? I said kissing me was an ass-backward thing to do."

He popped the next button. "Close enough."

She stared at his fingers.

Descending to the last button, he slipped the small pearl from the slot, locked gazes with her, and watched the heat shimmer in her eyes. "I got the message when you flipped me the bird."

"About that…"

Shaking his head, he freed the last button and parted the fabric to reveal her pale skin. The swell of her breasts straining against her bra brought a smile to his lips. Running a hand from her sternum to her soft stomach, he spread his fingers wide and grinned at the pleasure awaiting both of them.

Her stomach hollowed.

She relaxed against his touch. "You're the boss, Eliza." He met her gaze. "Tell me what makes you happy." Her cheeks blushed as pink as a rose. He watched her open her mouth and close it.

"Go down on me," she said.

Smiling, he ran his thumb beneath the metal button

securing the waistband of her jeans.

"Please." She sighed.

"With pleasure." He pulled down the zipper and tugged the denim from her hips to reveal soft, white cotton underwear. Watching her raise her body from the table, he cradled her ass and slid the denim fabric over her hips. Clothes piled on the wooden floor. He smiled at the sight of her skin, running his fingers beneath the side elastic and feeling the soft give of her curls.

"Julien, I didn't…"

He ignored her protestations and removed the practical cotton until he could stare at her sex—wet, glistening, and waiting. *Thank God for self-control.* Instead of uttering his desires, he rubbed the pad of his thumb over her clit.

Her hips bucked off the table.

"I'd put up with a year of your teasin' to get a taste of this sweetness." At the prospect of going down on her, he grinned like an idiot.

She took a deep breath and held his gaze, propped on her elbows.

He dropped his mouth and tasted her sex. The aroma filled his senses, headier than sweet wine. Each swipe of his tongue elicited a moan, and he watched her eyes close as she relaxed and responded to his touch. He licked her folds and found the rhythm that brought her to the brink, writhing for satisfaction and release. Hearing her moans change pitch, he increased the pressure of his touch until she came apart beneath his lips, chanting his name as a guitar solo floated through the space between the rafters. Julien raised his head and smiled.

Her chest rose and fell, eyes closed, as she

struggled to catch her breath.

His cock surged, but he braced his arms on the table and held back.

She opened her eyes.

Pulling her up to sitting, he shared the taste of her sex with a heady kiss.

She licked her lips and reached out her arms.

Shaking his head, he stepped back and picked up her clothes, dropping them on the table. "Now who's the boss?" The whispered challenge should taunt her into a lazy smile.

She lunged and pulled him close, biting his earlobe. "I am."

Laughing, he picked up his shirt and shook his head. "Yes, ma'am." Her smile stayed with him long after he returned to the cottage.

Chapter Eleven

"Wake up, Julien! We're going to Seattle!" Skye banged on the door of the cottage, tried the handle, and kicked the door.

Wincing, Eliza crossed her arms across her daughter's chest. "Sweet Pea, wait for him to answer!"

The girl glanced up, frowned, and wiggled free. She tried the handle again.

Julien beat her to the door. He met Eliza's gaze with a lopsided smile. "Good morning to you, too."

She smiled and glanced past him to see a cup of coffee and a plate of scrambled eggs waiting on the kitchen table. "Good. Claire stocked your refrigerator." She returned to the angles of his profile. "You shaved."

"I did." He rubbed the smooth skin along his cheek and grinned.

Warmth flooded her cheeks. "Sorry for the intrusion. Skye's excited to get off the farm."

The girl streaked past him and bounced around the room, touching his personal effects.

"I can tell." He stepped back and held open the door.

Picking up his coffee cup, he took a long sip. "Why are we going to Seattle, darlin'?"

"Mama needs more flowers for the weekend wedding. She said she might as well show you off." Skye put down his wallet and mobile phone. She cocked her head. "Are you a flower?"

"Do I look like a flower?"

She giggled. "You're not pretty enough."

Eliza gasped. "Skye!"

He shrugged and laughed. "Well, at least she's honest."

She hoped homeschooling would meet Skye's academic needs, but the six-year-old said everything that popped into her head. *How much time should I spend enforcing manners versus being thankful that she's happy?* The silence in the room felt awkward. *Perhaps I should work on my etiquette before I criticize hers.* She cleared her throat and smiled at Julien. "I told you Hartley Farms is part of a Washington farmer florist collective. Our integrated network supports local farmers and showcases local blooms."

He sat and finished his eggs. "That's a clever idea."

"I'd rather buy local blooms than order a box from South America, but in the middle of winter, that commitment means a trip to Seattle." She fidgeted, uncomfortable in a house she owned. She replayed his very satisfying apology and felt heat flush her cheeks. *It's one thing to wake up happy, but I can't spend the whole day thinking about his shirtless chest.* She kicked the floor. "A prominent national florist started the business model like a hundred years ago. You've probably heard of the company."

He shook his head. "I've never paid much attention to flowers."

"What?" She stared, dumbfounded. *This man saw me naked.*

He shrugged. "They're growing on me."

She cleared her throat. "The company started as a

non-profit corporation so florists could fulfill each other's out-of-town orders. Our collective doesn't have national ambitions, but we didn't invent the idea of banding together. We're merely keeping each other in business."

Skye looked up from arranging Julien's credit cards by color. "You have to drop things off in Seattle too, Mommy."

That girl hears everything. I need to be careful what I say around her. She scanned the homely living room and made a mental note to inventory the furniture and see what she could do to replace the crappiest pieces. "Yep. Church garlands for the wedding. I should have done it yesterday, but I didn't want to manage the timing with Skye's appointment. Plus, it's a good chance for Julien to meet members of the collective." She turned, checking his expression. "I mean, if you plan to stick around, meeting them would be good."

He stood and ferried his dishes to the sink. "I can't drive to Seattle on my own."

She considered the logistics of two pedals and frowned. "Why not? I can drive with one foot."

Laughing, he leaned on the counter and crossed his arms. "I don't think that's safe or legal."

"Well, we can modify the truck if we get that far." Impatience crept into her voice, and she blew out her breath. "Do you want to spend the whole day with Claire and the assistants or come with us?"

Skye picked up the salt and pepper shakers sitting on the table. "You should come with us. You're fun."

He winked. "What a sweet thing to say. How can I resist that charm?"

Skye nodded.

Eliza rolled her eyes. *I'll make you forget all about Southern charm.* She ushered Skye out the door.

The girl raced down the front steps and took off toward the house.

Her boots crunched on the cold gravel. She turned to Julien, who looked smug standing inside the warm cottage. "I would like you to come along, please."

He took a slow sip of coffee. "You're the boss."

Is he screwing with me? She bit her lip. *Not yet.*

The man winked.

Her stomach dropped. She turned toward the door and shook her head. "I'll see you in fifteen minutes."

Serah and Michelle arrived in short order and helped her load the garlands in the truck. Fir and cedar boughs filled the small space with the smell of crisp evergreens and subtle camphoraceous undertones.

She put her hands on her hips to stretch her back and focused on giving her assistants instructions. "We have two days until the wedding. The arrangements are nearly done, and we've had a couple of website inquires. That work should keep you busy for the day."

Michelle handed her a garland. "I guess the bad reviews didn't make a difference."

She loaded the fragrant foliage. "Reputation means more in this state than anonymous statements." Michelle's comment sank in, and she turned to the teenager. "You should know that fact."

"I mean, it's so close to Valentine's Day." Michelle turned to her sister. "Isn't it late for placing orders?"

Serah shrugged.

"They're thinking about fall weddings," Eliza said.

"Send them our information packet by email and call to set up consultation appointments."

"Yeah, I guess."

Serah followed her sister to the barn.

Alone for a moment, Eliza toyed with the pieces of lunaria, sedum, and echeveria woven into the garlands to add texture and color differentiation. The pieces would glow by candlelight, complement the bride's dress, and pick up hints of white in the bouquets. *Love shouldn't be complicated.* She sighed and considered her personal life. *There's a big difference between love and lust. You loved Erik, and you ended up second-guessing every choice you made. Take it one step at a time with Julien.*

"I think it will be a lovely wedding." Serah carried the next garland to the table.

Her voice sounded as cheerful as birdsong. Eliza smiled, remembering Serah as a sweet-natured little kid. She toyed with a pink rose lying on the table. I wonder what type of flowers Skye will choose when she grows up.

"The roses look pretty nestled in the dusty miller. When you get up close, they smell soft and sweet. The scene will probably calm the bride's nerves, too. It's no wonder rustic charm has defied Internet trends." She held out the garland. "I mean, who wants cold and sterile on their wedding day?"

She thought of the dormant fields, ready to bloom under the right conditions. *Cold and sterile are a matter of opinion.* "I'm glad you like the garlands." She walked around the worktable and inspected the finished bouquets. "Can you put one of the finished centerpieces in a galvanized pail and take a picture? Michelle's right about needing to generate more content for social media, but we won't post the image until after the wedding."

"That will be pretty. Maybe next to a chicken?"

She laughed and turned her back on the coolers, content with the arrangements waiting to complement the bride. "Good luck with that approach." She walked outside and inhaled the fresh morning air. *I love this place.*

Skye appeared with Claire and a large container of cheese crackers.

Eliza opened the door to the backseat. "Hop up!"

Scrambling into her booster seat, Skye waved her snack cup in the air. "Granny packed me snacks for the road!"

Feeling her mother behind her, Eliza stepped back.

Claire leaned in the vehicle. "Let me check your buckle."

Skye shoved a cracker in her mouth. "I can do it myself!"

Her garbled words made Eliza smile.

"Uh-huh. And can you drive, too?" Claire asked.

"That's Mommy's job."

"Hmm." Claire adjusted the straps. "Maybe she needs help from time to time."

Eliza winced. *Okay, so she's still mad about last night.*

Reaching into the footwell, Claire pulled up a wicker basket filled with hidden picture books, water pens, stickers, and small stuffed animals. "Do you want some toys?"

Skye wrinkled her nose. "I looked at those books yesterday."

"What about the water pens?"

She consented to the entertainment.

Eliza relaxed. *Thank goodness for the wonder of toys.*

Claire backed away from the vehicle and nodded.

Julien appeared with a travel mug. "Do I get snacks, too?"

Claire shook her head. "Losing the beard was a good start, but you need a haircut before I'll consider letting you back in the house."

He laughed and walked toward the passenger seat.

That man's in a remarkably good mood for someone who sauntered out of the barn with a raging hard-on. She analyzed his movements, watching him grab the overhead handle and hoist his large frame into the passenger seat. His arm flexed, and his upper body strength relieved the pressure from his right leg. *Did the muscles come before or after the accident? I don't mind taking advantage of the secondary benefits.*

Shutting his door, he met her gaze through the window.

She raised her eyebrows. Amusement lightened his features and gave her a glimpse of the man before the accident. *Which man would have stopped his road trip to help me?*

Claire cleared her throat. "Are you planning to leave before lunchtime?"

She shut Skye's door, stamped her feet in the cold morning air, and turned to face her mother. "I might be in over my head."

Claire nodded. "You've always been stubborn."

"I wasn't aware I'd made up my mind." She exhaled. "We're taking small steps."

"Seattle two days in a row? I thought you hated the city."

She rolled her eyes. "Then why do you keep telling me to move there?"

"Because I want what's best for you." Claire rubbed the cold from her left arm and looked toward the horizon. "Go to the city. Make a day of it."

She sighed. "Mom, you could go to town, too. Maybe see Luke or your friends at the library."

The older woman smiled. "Worry about your romances, Eliza Edwards. The stakes are higher in your camp." She waved at Skye through the backseat window and walked toward the farmhouse.

Blowing her bangs out of her eyes, Eliza climbed in the driver's seat, put her hat out of Skye's cheesy reach, and tucked the floral order form into the center console. Claire's warning lingered in her thoughts. *Should I keep Julien and Skye apart? That's impossible on the farm.* She glanced at Julien and wondered if he overheard Claire's admonishment. *The stakes are always high when people start thinking with their hearts.*

"Mommy."

Skye's high-pitched voice interrupted her thoughts. She put the vehicle in gear and eased forward.

"Why doesn't Granny like Julien?"

Eliza glanced at him, wondering if he recognized the loyalty behind Claire's gruff comments.

Laughing, he turned to Skye. "Oh, your granny likes me well enough, but she's right. I need a haircut. Maybe I'll get one in Seattle, and we can be friends."

Skye shook her head and stared out the window as potato fields gave way to the county road. "I don't have any friends. I wouldn't mind if they had shaggy hair."

Tears filled Eliza's eyes. She kept her hands on the wheel and merged with traffic headed toward the interstate. "You have friends, Skye. You like to play hide and seek with the Thompsons."

"But they don't come over very much."

She wiped away the wetness before anyone could see it. "When you go back to elementary school next year, you'll have so many friends you won't remember their names." She used the rearview mirror to see if her reassurance worked.

Skye stared out the side window, watching the parade of cars.

Why do the hardest conversations happen in the car?

Skye started singing to herself.

After the third chorus, Eliza glanced at Julien. "Maybe I should re-enroll her. I assumed she would have enough enrichment spending time with Claire and the animals."

"What does her therapist say?"

"The sessions focus on losing Erik and helping her process her emotions. We haven't touched on forming new relationships." A digital sign advertised the travel time to Seattle. Beyond the onramp, drivers sped toward southern destinations. *Could I ever leave Washington?*

"Maybe it's a good sign she's looking for friends."

Everything's a good sign when you're worried about your kids. She managed a weak smile, put on her turn signal, and pressed the accelerator. "You're right. She's a good kid. She won't have any trouble."

"People drive differently up here."

She eased off the accelerator. "Too fast?"

He laughed. "People speed down south, but they rarely give away their intentions." He settled into the front seat. "Louisiana's a strange mishmash of cultures, but you might like to visit."

"Isn't every state?"

He shrugged. "If you have time to sit and talk, you'll learn a lot about your neighbors and parish officials."

"Assuming you're a local."

He sipped his coffee and peered through the condensation forming on the inside of the window. "You laughed at my gothic charm, but the people in my state stretch the things they have to make life work. The trick is to keep yourself from getting stretched too thin."

"I'm not easily broken. The farm's proximity to Seattle is a blessing and a curse, but while Skye's young, I want her to have wide-open spaces." She checked the rearview mirror and saw the mountains receding as she drove toward the city. *I want to let her be little.*

Skye squished her face against the window, straining against the confines of her booster seat. Heart-shaped nose prints littered the glass.

"Most of Louisiana's countryside," he said. "I loved growing up there."

"What if she winds up craving the city?" She frowned, realizing she articulated her fear aloud.

"You can't give her everything without losing yourself."

She jerked back her chin and straightened in the driver's seat. "Don't be ridiculous."

He laughed. "Why not? I have nothing left."

What does that statement mean? She cleared her throat, worried Skye would overhear something too advanced for her age. *Maybe I haven't taken his injuries seriously enough. He's not invincible.* "I want her to have choices."

He nodded and toyed with the radio.

Skagit County traffic swelled into the outer boroughs of Seattle, slowing progress to a crawl. Commuters flooded the interstate at every onramp. "Damn," she said. "I thought we left early enough to beat this congestion."

"Mommy, don't say 'damn.' It's a bad word."

She took a deep breath and met Skye's gaze in the rearview mirror. "You're right, Sweet Pea. I'm frustrated and couldn't think of a better word."

"Take the next exit," Julien said.

She frowned. "We're only in Snohomish."

He held up his phone and demonstrated the source of his intelligence. "App says it's faster to jump over to Highway 9. Probably save you twenty minutes."

She pursed her lips and glanced at him. "You don't even know where we're going."

He pointed to the order form tucked into the center console. "Powers of observation. Plus, the app doesn't lie. We can sit in traffic or you can follow the country boy's turn-by-turn directions."

Sighing, she flipped on her turn signal.

"Nothing wrong with having a co-pilot," he said.

Her mouth skewed into a smile before she could stop it. "As long as we don't get lost."

Julien and Skye took turns singing to the radio.

He has a nice voice. She put the truck in Park in

209

front of a long tunnel of pacific dogwood trees. Beyond them, a white, clapboard church rose above a neighborhood of compact two-story houses. The green tunnel of trees emphasized the openness of the remaining church grounds and the site's wide, reflective pond. "In the early springtime, the dogwood canopy creates a tunnel of tiny white and pale pink blooms," she said. "The branches grow in horizontal layers like they're climbing into the clouds. It's a beautiful shot for a wedding." A gust of wind shook the trees and dropped a cascade of water on the dewy grass. "Right now, they drip water on everyone who passes beneath them."

"Seems like poor planning." He climbed out of the van.

"It's the Pacific Northwest. People are used to getting wet."

"Doesn't mean you have to pile it on higher and deeper."

I must have offended him. "I've always liked those trees." She put her hands on her hips and stretched her back. "They're simple but powerful. The bark used to be a medicine for many ailments."

"Like what?"

"Headaches. Fatigue. People made tonics from the root to increase strength and stimulate appetites."

He shaded his eyes and looked up. "I doubt the church wants to dig up their canopy to brew a cup of tea." He shook his head and turned his back on the trees. "They're pretty enough."

"Some people use religion to heal." She smiled. "Some people use love."

"Some use hard-headed determination."

"Well, I have plenty of determination, too." She opened the door to the backseat and lifted Skye to the ground. "Did the drive make you sleepy?"

"Never!" Skye grabbed a low-lying branch and hung from the smooth bark. "Mommy, can I climb up the stairs in the bell tower?"

She glanced at the pointed steeple and the waiting bells. "Sure, Sweet Pea, but don't go anywhere else without me."

The girl ran up the front steps and pulled open one of the wide double doors.

"She knows where she's going?" he asked.

"I went to school with Reverend Jonathan Mark. She's been here many times. We supply most of the altar decorations, and he refers brides to our shop if they choose to get married during the winter months." She opened the back door of the van and withdrew a garland. "Do you think you can carry this garland and navigate the front steps?"

He nodded and accepted the weight of the foliage. "I'm fine as long as I can see where I'm going. Don't worry about me."

It's my job to worry about you. She picked up the other arrangement and led him up the steps. Transferring the garland to one arm, she held open the door with her butt and kicked the doorstop in place.

He winked and entered the sanctuary. "Good job using your assets."

Jonathan walked out of the church office and greeted them in the nave.

His casual pants and blazer mimicked a businessman's attire, but the scarf around his neck gleamed with embroidered religious symbols.

"Skye is halfway to heaven by now," he said.

She grinned. "My apologies to the pigeons."

Laughing, he turned to Julien. "I'm Jonathan Mark. It's a pleasure to meet you."

"Julien Kroger." He lifted the bundle of greenery in his arms. "Where does this go?"

"Follow me." Jonathan led them to the front of the church and pointed to two railings bracketing the altar.

She lowered the garland onto the right side and gestured for Julien to take the left. Familiar with the church's proportions, she stood back and examined the garlands against the glow of stained glass. "I think the foliage is a perfect fit."

Julien set down the garland he held. "I'll go get the rest of the greenery."

Turning, she watched him make his way down the aisle.

"New boyfriend?" Jonathan asked.

She shook her head. "New foreman."

"You've never had your foreman help deliver things in the past." He cleared his throat. "Or kept your gaze glued to his backside."

Coughing, she wondered if she should do a better job of hiding her feelings. *Claire and Jonathan care for me, but other people might pass judgment on our burgeoning relationship.* She exhaled and met Jonathan's gaze. "I confess Julien's turning into more than a foreman."

He smiled. " 'Count it all joy, my brothers, when you meet trials of various kinds, for you know that the testing of your faith produces steadfastness.' "

She raised her eyebrows. "I liked it better when you quoted rock lyrics."

Shrugging, he picked up a piece of greenery from the carpet and winked. "Sometimes they overlap."

She shook her head. "We have a long way to go before I'm worried about Julien's faith. He's more interested in music than joining a congregation."

"We welcome anyone to the pews, but having that conversation."

She shrugged. "Gabe wasn't much of a talker."

"And you weren't much of a looker."

She met her old friend's gaze.

He smiled.

Skye bounded into the sanctuary. Her wind-whipped hair haloed her flushed cheeks, and she struggled to catch her breath. "Did you time me?"

"Nope, Sweet Pea. But you were fast."

Jonathan turned to the girl. "Would you like to hear the bells?"

She shook her head. "My little friends don't like church bells. They're too loud."

Eliza glanced at Jonathan, ready to apologize for the gaps in Skye's religious education.

He shrugged. "We believe a lot of things before we're wise enough to see what's in front of our face." He looked over his shoulder, met her gaze, and raised his eyebrows.

She coughed and averted her gaze.

"We'll play the bells another day," Jonathan said.

Julien approached holding the remaining garlands.

Rushing to relieve the load, she grabbed the nearest garland. "You could have taken more trips."

He laughed. "They're nothing but a bit of greenery."

She bit her lip. "I worked hard on that bit of

greenery."

The side of his mouth ticked up in a smile. "They smell good." He dropped his voice and winked. "Almost as good as you."

She felt like she won the consolation prize at the county fair, but she preferred to flirt with Julien in private. She turned toward the front of the church. "Rachel wanted to add eucalyptus."

"I guess eucalyptus would smell good, too."

She looked over her shoulder. "Whose side are you on?"

He looked at her breasts and raised his eyebrows.

Heat flushed her cheeks. *Right. Now when lightning strikes the church, we'll be three for three on religious demerits.* She cleared her throat. "Let's tie the garlands to the railings. Skye, do you want to help me with the twist ties?"

"Yes!"

She and Julien split the work and secured the foliage to the railings and ledges surrounding the altar. With the work completed, she turned to Skye. "Do you want to stop at the market to see Ms. Jessica?"

"Yes!"

Julien picked up the loose ties and dropped them in his pocket. "Who's Jessica?"

"A florist."

He laughed. "Does she always get excited about visiting florists?"

"Jessica also has a white shop cat that does tricks."

He winked. "I like cats."

You're in a church, Eliza. Get your mind out of the gutter. "Okay. It's time to go. Now."

Skye raced back to the double doors. "Can we get

ice cream, too?"

"Darlin', it's almost freezing outside," he said.

The girl stared, mouth agape.

"What's your favorite flavor?" Eliza asked.

"Buttered pecan," he said.

"Nuts?" She frowned.

"Pecans and brown sugar. A little salt." He turned to Skye. "You'd love it."

"I like strawberry."

He shook his head. "Figures. You're too young to know better."

She put her hands on her hips. "I'm six years old!"

"Exactly!" he replied.

Eliza watched them banter as they made their way down the church steps. Skye slowed her pace to match Julien's measured progress, and Eliza's heart swelled at the display of empathy. *Between Claire and me, we must do something right.*

Jonathan came to her side. "She seems taken with your new foreman."

"He humors her a lot." She smiled. "Defends her chickens."

Using the sole of his black sneakers, he brushed a brown leaf off the step. "We all need a little humor in our lives."

She looked beyond his clerical outfit and saw the friend she cherished. "What about love?"

" 'And now these three remain: faith, hope, and love. But the greatest of these is love.' "

"Did I love Erik?" She bit her lip, fearing his response.

"I'm sure you did, but people change, and their love has to change with them. It's not a finite resource,

Eliza. The heart swells." He put his arm around her shoulders.

Relaxing in the company of her friend, she smiled.

"Just look at your daughter. She's proof you're capable of achieving great things."

"Maybe." She exhaled and watched Julien finish the steps. He followed Skye through the canopy of dripping dogwood trees. "I'm not ready for love, but something exists between us. The thought of getting close to another man makes me uneasy. What am I getting wrong? Does Skye have what she needs?" She sighed. "I thought Claire and I could love her enough to make up for losing her father."

Jonathan turned her and held both her shoulders.

His grip felt light and easy. She could shrug and walk away from the conversation without incurring judgment, but she lifted her head and met his gaze.

"Nothing can replace Skye's memories of Erik," he said.

She relaxed her shoulders, grateful her friendship with this man endured. She loved him like the brother she never had. "I've never gotten over my father's suicide." The whispered confession brought tears to her eyes.

He released her shoulders and produced a handkerchief. "Nobody should set a deadline to process their grief."

"My dad's choices hurt me." She dabbed at her eyes. "This thing with Julien feels like an indulgence, but I'm so worried about making the wrong choices. I'm worried about getting close to him and holding Skye while we watch him walk away." She stuffed the handkerchief in her back pocket. "I'll send you a replacement."

He laughed. "No need. I order them by the hundred."

She smiled.

"That's better. You've been smiling all morning. Julien must do something right."

She bit her lip. *That's because I put away my projects and spent the night indulging in carnal thoughts.* Compartmentalizing her thoughts, she focused on Jonathan's counsel. "Am I doing the right thing by making room in my life for more drama?"

He rubbed his chin. "Your father made a bad decision, but you're strong enough to overcome it. Erik didn't choose to end his own life and deprive Skye of a father. Don't carry the weight of the world on your shoulders." He released his chin and pointed his finger toward the sky. "We have other people to do that."

She nodded and watched Julien and Skye play hide and seek near the reflecting pond.

"It's too late to join the nunnery," he added.

She smiled, wondering what Skye would make of cloistered nuns. "I know."

"If you're in the mood for penance, the next time you're in town you can drop off a load of plants for the flower beds."

She laughed and eyed the mulch-covered dirt. "I'll start some seeds. Lewisia's pink, red, and white flowers are pretty. The evergreen foliage is a great winter accent. What about lupines?"

He exhaled and stared at the mulch. "You're speaking a foreign language. Hydrangeas?'"

She shook her head. "Not local."

Laughing, he shook his head and looked at her.

"Sometimes local gets stale. Where does your foreman call home?"

"Louisiana," she said.

He shrugged. "I would have guessed Texas."

She nodded, watching Skye try to sneak up on Julien. "He worked there for a while."

"People can adapt to new situations. So can plants."

She pinned her old friend with a steady gaze. "How long did the last hydrangeas last?"

He blushed. "Hard to know. We dug them up and donated them to a nursing home. The social committee said people find it rewarding to watch plants grow."

Laughing, she waved and descended the steps. "I'll put together a list of plants. Next time, take up a collection, Reverend Mark. It's more efficient than taking up the roots."

She drove Julien and Skye to the city center and parallel parked on a side street leading to Pike Place Market. Crowds thronged the public market overlooking the Elliott Bay waterfront. The mix of tourists and locals clamored for whiffs of inspiration from the farmers, crafters, and local merchants occupying the stalls.

To avoid the pilgrims, she led Julien and Skye to the shipping and receiving dock, waved a vendor badge at security, and led her entourage through the concrete halls. At the backdoor of Jessica's shop, she cracked the door and confirmed the florist shop was almost empty.

Jessica turned, her smile blooming when she made eye contact. She waved hello.

"We'll wait," Eliza said.

The florist nodded and adjusted her colorful framed

glasses. She completed the sale and opened the backdoor door to admit the group to the colorful stall. "What a lovely surprise!" She kissed Eliza's cheek and squeezed Skye into a side hug. "You've gotten so big! You'll be taller than Nathan before too long."

Skye looked around the shop, her smile wide. "Is Nathan here?"

"Nope, he's at school today."

She pouted. "What about Madam Windchill Frosty Claws?"

Jessica bowed. "She's waiting on her tree."

Skye bounded to an elaborate carpet throne where a longhaired white Persian cat presided over the shop.

Sensing an admirer, the cat sniffed Skye's fingers and stretched, releasing a yawn.

Skye picked up a jar of treats and doled out several pieces.

The cat stood on two feet and pawed at the air.

Skye laughed. "Are you doing a dance?"

"Meow." The white ballerina hopped on her rear legs in a jittery circle.

"That's quite a routine," Julien said.

Jessica smiled. "Madam came from a local celebrity called the Cat Man."

"Did he teach the cat those tricks?"

She laughed and shook her head. "He did an amazing job socializing her, but she figured out that routine. She's very treat-motivated."

He scratched his cheek where the shadow of afternoon stubble appeared. "How do you keep her from getting fat?"

"Madam's gotten very selective about her audience." Her voice softened, and she turned to Eliza.

"Her kidneys are failing. She's close to retirement."

"Oh no!" Eliza covered her mouth. "Please don't tell Skye she's sick."

Nodding, Jessica turned and adjusted the flowers near the credit card reader. "Nathan is devastated. He keeps asking me to keep her at home."

Skye stroked the longhaired cat, nuzzled her soft white fur, and whispered in her ear.

The cat stretched and licked her lips.

All three adults watched the pair.

Skye's suffered enough loss. Maybe we shouldn't have gotten her those pets.

"Probably telling her about her adventures with the *nisse*," Julien said.

His playful comment drained the tension from the moment.

"Madam Windchill probably knows all about the little people. I'm sure they're delicious."

Jessica laughed and extended a hand.

"Julien," he said.

"Jessica. Welcome to Seattle."

He laughed. "I must stand out."

"Your accent gives you away." Turning, she winked at Eliza. "So much for buying local."

"Julien is the foreman at the farm."

Jessica pushed her glasses back to the bridge of her nose. "What did you do, advertise at the gym?"

Julien laughed at the compliment.

Eliza blushed.

"Why don't you come out to the island for dinner tonight?" Jessica continued. "Skye and Nathan can play while we catch up. This time of year, we hardly have any guests at the inn."

"Dinner would be great." She stilled and turned to Julien. "But it will turn our one-hour drive into two hours and forty minutes."

He shrugged. "I have nothing but time."

"And biceps," Jessica said.

Eliza tried not to laugh at the blush coloring Julien's cheeks. "We came for business, too. I need lavender and white muscari if you have them."

Jessica nodded and removed bundles of purple lavender and dense spikes with urn-shaped white flowers from the cooler. She offered to hold the stock until they reconvened for dinner.

"They looked like a bunch of grapes," he said.

Jessica frowned.

"Lovely grapes."

Eliza smiled. "Don't worry, Julien. She's not immune to your charms." *She has the habit of admiring...stock of all kinds, even when her cooler at home is full to the brim with the type of man we all thought we would marry.* She frowned. *Not that I would ever marry Clark. His charm fuels the inn, but it's too practiced.* She turned to Skye. "Are you ready for lunch and ice cream?"

"Ice cream!"

Skye's shriek startled the cat. Madam Windchill retreated to the highest level of her throne.

Eliza led the way to a cluster of food stalls. In the middle of the week, office workers in business casual stood in line to place orders. She wondered if she could do that for Skye. *I could do anything for her.* She smiled. *As long as I can turn a profit, I don't have to swap my boots for sensible flats.*

Skye scarfed down a plate of French fries and a

chicken wrap. She honored her dedication to strawberry ice cream and threaded her way through the crowd of visitors while holding a dripping cone.

Eliza and Julien lagged behind her.

"Does she ever get lost?" he asked.

"Not really. She knows to stay within eye contact."

"I would be nervous to let her roam in such a busy place. It's not your farm."

She adjusted her pace to match his gait and checked on Skye's whereabouts. "I can see her." At the end of the market hall, she corralled Skye and led her to the truck. Wetting a napkin, she wiped away the most egregious ice cream drips on her daughter's face.

"I'm not tired," Skye said.

Eliza nodded, watching her daughter's eyes droop. She buckled the girl into the booster seat, climbed into the driver's seat, and navigated to a large greenhouse.

Julien glanced at Skye and kept quiet.

She smiled, thankful as Skye drifted off to sleep.

The greenhouse's large parking lot offered plenty of shade. Glancing in the rearview mirror to confirm Skye slept, she saw her daughter's head loll to the side. A bead of pink-tinged drool beaded at the corner of her open mouth.

Julien followed her gaze. "I can stay in the truck with her."

"Are you sure?" she asked.

"Unless you want me to get the flowers? Do you have a list?"

She considered his reaction to the muscari, shook her head, and debated her options. *He's been nothing but patient with Skye.* She decided to go with her gut. "No, you stay with her. If she hopes to keep up with

Nathan, she needs a nap." Half an hour later, she returned and found both of them fast asleep. Hating to open the hatch, she reminded herself business needs underwrote the jaunt to Seattle. She climbed into the driver's seat and started the engine.

He blinked, his sleepy gaze struggling to focus. "Where to next?"

"Whidbey Island."

He yawned. "Do you need directions?"

"No." She smiled. "They live on acreage Jessica inherited from her grandmother. I've known my way to Whidbey Island since I was a kid." *There's something special about spending time on land you own. Once you commit to stewardship, you never forget the pride of a job well done.* "I could find my way there in the dark."

Chapter Twelve

Urban traffic patterns confirmed how much Julien disliked city life. He enjoyed listening to Eliza narrate the scenery and describe the island, but his muscles itched to get out of the truck and stretch.

"The island is Puget Sound's Largest Artists' Colony. The northern end services a large Naval Air Station, but Jessica and Clark run a bed and breakfast on the southern end. It's a combination B&B and flower farm. He manages the cabins and horses. She runs the florist shop in town."

"More horses." He tapped his fingers against his knee and felt the rim of the sock shielding his skin from the prosthesis.

"We used to compete against each other as kids."

"Who won?" he asked.

She wetted her lips. "I guess Jessica won. It's a big island."

He cleared his throat and glanced at the slate waters of the sound. "I like your view of the mountains."

The subtle lines by her eyes softened as she smiled.

He wanted to take her hand, but he shifted in the seat, determined not to interrupt the drive.

"The island's close to thirty miles long, but there are no bridges to the city. Well, one bridge goes over Deception Pass. We'll use it on the way home, but since we're already in Seattle, we'll take the car ferry between Mukilteo and Clinton." She cleared her throat. "Have you ever been on one?"

He rubbed his cheek and remembered why he hated shaving. *I wonder if she minds a five o'clock shadow.* "Maybe once. In Gretna. When I was a kid."

"If we can avoid the rush hour, this ferry trip is about twenty minutes."

"How bad is rush hour on a boat?"

She rolled her eyes. "The wait to get on the ferry can be two hours long."

He coughed. "Floor it."

She laughed. "You don't like traffic?"

"Do you?"

She shook her head and followed the signs for the Suquamish ferry vehicle tollbooth.

He examined the large ferry waiting at the dock. It dwarfed the vessel he expected. Two car decks and two passenger decks loomed over Puget Sound. Passengers stood on a sun deck holding cups of hot coffee and wind-whipped newspapers.

The car ahead of them moved toward the ferry.

Eliza rolled down the window to greet the ticket seller. "Can we have a spot by an elevator?"

The man nodded and handed her a receipt.

She rolled up the window.

No wonder life moves so quickly out here. Back home, that ticket would have come with a few rounds of "How's ya mama and them?" He cleared his throat. "I could have managed with a regular spot."

"But why would you?"

"Why not? Tomorrow, you'll be wanting to borrow my handicapped placard."

She raised her eyebrows. "Tempting."

Skye woke up, a low moan escaping her lips.

Eliza made soothing sounds to ease the transition.

Within seconds, the girl oriented herself. "I don't like the song on the radio. Can I have a cookie?"

He cringed. *She's a sweet kid, but man, she's work. Does Brandon know what's coming his way? We're too close in age for him to remember the terror of a little kid.* He grinned. *Hell, I was probably twice as much work as Skye.*

"Are we there yet?" Skye asked

She stretched the words into a wail. He rubbed his ear.

Eliza glanced in the rearview mirror. "Are we driving onto a boat?"

The girl rubbed her eyes. "Yes."

"Does Nathan live on a boat?"

Skye crossed her arms. "Seriously?"

He struggled not to laugh. *She's been spending too much time with Michelle.*

Instead of reprimanding the girl, Eliza rolled her eyes. "I don't know where she gets that sarcasm." She parked the truck within three inches of the next car and put it in Park. "Do you two want to get out?"

"Yes!" Skye said.

Eliza tucked her hair behind her ears. "It's not fair to ask her to ride around in the truck all day and be a perfect angel. Sometimes I have to choose what's worth the fight."

He followed them to the elevator, his thoughts as scattered as the shifting bay breeze. *That's the problem with my life. I've never known what's worth the fight.* He sighed. *Hell, losing my leg was the first time I had to fight. I almost lost.*

Skye took her mother's hand and led the way to the sun deck. "I want hot chocolate."

Eliza produced an apple.

The child's gaze narrowed.

Dropping her chin, Elisa raised her eyebrows and stared at the girl.

Skye blew her mother a kiss.

They've been playing these games for a long time, but is there room for me? Looking away from the pair, he took in the undulating views of the Sound. The crisp crunch of an apple made him smile. *One point for Mom.*

He spent the rest of the windswept voyage scanning the waters of Puget Sound for marine life. A fat seagull monitored him but came up short as the ferry neared Whidbey Island. The cluster of buildings resolved into two distinct towns. One group of buildings occupied a high bluff, and the other waited at sea level. A few older structures clung to the coast near the north end of the ferry dock, but the remainder of the island looked wild.

Eliza pointed to a cluster of shingled buildings. "That's Old Clinton."

"Is that where we're headed?"

"No, we're headed to the northern part of the island. Swantown Lake is a few miles beyond Oak Harbor."

An amplified voice encouraged all passengers to return to their vehicles.

Back in the truck, Eliza disembarked on the island and drove north.

He craned his neck to take in the landscape. The shoreline gave way to a wide table of pastureland. Lines of fir trees dotted the fields and divided the communities. The truck passed an aged golf and community club anchoring a cluster of businesses. *Some things don't change.*

A wide estuary of marshes and open water claimed the horizon.

Eliza slowed the truck. "Settlers drained the marsh and farmed it. Jessica told me a local group is working to return the land to its natural state. Joseph Whidbey State Park is up the coast. I think the long-term goal is to extend the park far enough to include the lake."

He shook his head. "We're battling to save the marshes back home. A sweet spot exists between compaction and saltwater intrusion. Unless you're working on a geologic scale, finding that spot is dumb luck. I can't imagine engineering it." A sign for Swantown B&B came into view.

She turned on a gravel road.

He considered Jessica's proximity to the park and the country club. *How does rural land exist so close to a downtown environment? We have acres of pavement or acres of land back home. The extremes don't mix.* "Does this location come with prohibitions and uptight state regulations?"

"I don't know. Proximity to the open land might be a selling point. Jessica and her husband are very involved with the island community."

"I bet they have to be involved to make it work." The road turned and revealed an A-frame building anchoring four smaller cottages with private courtyards. He scanned the cars parked near each cottage. *Jessica lied about their occupancy rate.* He looked at the picturesque lake and whistled. *I'm not surprised they're full.*

Eliza put the truck in Park. "Jessica's grandfather built the horse stable behind the tree line. The guests like to take trail rides or borrow canoes. They come for simple pleasures."

He shook his head and unbuckled his seatbelt. "I can't imagine anything worse than counting the flies between two plodding horses."

She laughed and unlocked her doors. "I think you're supposed to focus on the scenery."

He raised his eyebrows. "I've admired the view all day."

She blushed. "Okay. Everybody out of the truck."

He grabbed the overhead handle and shifted his weight until his foot absorbed the impact of the height difference. He distributed his weight to the prosthesis and stretched his back.

Eliza unbuckled her daughter.

The girl ran around the truck and planted her feet in front of him. "Can you ride horses?"

"Yes. Can you?"

She shook her head and glanced at her mother. "I want to learn."

I'm not about to get on a horse in front of Eliza's friends. "Maybe you and your friend…Nathan…can talk your moms into a trail ride."

Skye kicked the ground.

He grinned at the adopted expression. *How many times have I seen Eliza do that?*

"Mom won't let me," she said.

He glanced over the hood of the truck.

Eliza met his gaze.

He smiled at Skye. "Well, it's her call."

"Sweet Pea, it's already four o'clock." Eliza came around the truck. "The sun will set, and we'll miss dinner if we take out the horses."

Skye crossed her arms. Her chin quivered.

Will she cry?

"Next time," Eliza said. "I'm sure Jessica has a docile horse you can ride."

The girl's gaze widened. "Seriously? Next time we can do it?"

"Sure. If the horse bolts, you're old enough to hang on."

"Yes!" She pumped her fist in the air.

The front door of the A-frame opened, and a ginger-haired ball of energy tumbled from the building. The boy shouted Skye's name and ran toward the group.

Skye received her friend with a beaming smile and a chest-smashing hug.

He smiled. *Neither of the munchkins know what to do with their arms.*

Eliza dropped her voice. "They're getting married when they're older. Paleontologists. Two dogs. A red car. They have it all planned out."

"They're ahead of the rest of us." He saw the conspiratorial look fall from Eliza's face.

She stared at the low-lit marsh. "I thought I had it all figured out when I was their age, too."

He squeezed her hand. "You've been wrestling with something all day."

"No, I haven't."

He wiped a tear from the corner of her eye. "Must be the pollen."

She looked up, took a deep breath, and returned the

squeeze. "Thanks."

Skye pulled her friend to his side. "This is Julien. He's a pirate."

"Cool!" the boy said.

Julien dropped Eliza's hand, but he leaned close to whisper in her ear. "Should I fight this pirate thing?"

"Does it offend you?"

He shook his head.

She smiled. "I would use the notion to your advantage."

He faced the kids. "Argh!"

The children shrieked with laughter.

"Well, I'm out of practice," he said.

Nathan stopped laughing, braced his hands on his knees, and grinned. "C'mon, Skye, let's make a treasure map." He reached for her hand and pulled her toward the building.

A middle-aged man stepped over the threshold, his salt-and-pepper hair cut short. He wore a down vest against the chill of the wind and greeted Eliza with a kiss on the cheek.

Julien reminded himself he had no right or reason to be jealous.

Eliza grabbed the man's arm with both hands and smiled.

He looked at the ground, as nonchalant as his twitching muscles would allow. *Knocking the man to the ground would be rude, but I could definitely take him.*

"This is Jessica's husband, Clark," she said.

Julien looked up and offered his hand. "Pleasure to meet you."

Clark smiled and shook his hand. "So glad you

guys could come out." He led the group into the main building. "Let's get inside before the temperature drops any farther."

The common room's spacious interior and oversized furniture could easily accommodate thirty guests. Farmhouse tables and multiple arrangements of couches and upholstered chairs flanked a gas fireplace. A wall of books and board games conveyed a homey feeling, but the abandoned jackets and draped purses signaled the guests felt at ease. A pair of sliding doors separated the warm living room from an expansive wooden deck. Beyond the doors, a fire pit blazed amid a circle of chairs, and several couples sat close together in the pink-tinged, afternoon light.

He stopped short of the outdoor amenity and gestured to a bar-height table with views of the lake and the marsh. A bowl of spiced nuts waited on the table, and savory smells wafted from a kitchen large enough to feed a crowd. "Help yourself and get comfortable before you face our guests. They've been sampling wine flights all afternoon."

Julien laughed and slid onto a barstool. *Clark reigns over the domain like a disciplined proprietor, dispensing hospitality while he keeps watch over the proceedings.* He sampled the nuts. *It's his livelihood.*

Nathan and Skye ignored the subtleties of manners, commandeered a card table, and scattered a box of crayons to draw their map.

Clark nodded.

Julien popped a nut in his mouth. *It's also his home.*

Eliza left his side and peered into the large kitchen. "Smells good!" she said.

Two women returned her greeting. They tended a variety of pots and chopped mounds of vegetables.

"Jessica back there?" she asked.

The women shook their heads.

She scanned the outside deck, turned back to the room, and flashed a shallow smile. "I guess Jessica's running late."

Clark took up his position behind the bar. "She went into town for more supplies."

Eliza's shoulders drooped. "I hope we didn't inconvenience you."

He laughed. "We're serving dinner for fifteen tonight. Three more guests are hardly an inconvenience. Plus, you're not guests, you're friends." He spread his hands on the polished wood. "What will you have to drink?"

"White wine." Eliza smiled.

He felt more comfortable holding a glass than inspiring questioning looks. "Do you have iced tea?"

"You don't drink?"

Julien raised his eyebrows. His mother, a consummate hostess, would have recognized the lure of a juicy story, but saved her questions for a private moment. Clark had skipped the niceties and confronted the issue head-on. *So much for polite conversation.* He met the man's curious stare. "I stopped after an industrial accident claimed the lower part of my leg."

"Was alcohol a factor?"

"No, but I had a hard time during the recovery." He stared at the innkeeper and let the statement settle. *Am I a coward to throw out that detail and let it sit?* He rolled his shoulders and took a deep breath, chastising himself for caring about his reputation. *Asking for help shouldn't be a big deal.* He faced Clark. "I could have done better."

The man nodded. "Tea it is."

"Thanks." *Maybe I won't have to take him out after all.*

A couple came inside. The woman wore furry earmuffs.

Removing them, she looped the cord around her neck like a hunting trophy.

Clark greeted the pair, served Eliza and Julien their drinks, and withdrew two more glasses. "How was your day?"

"Great hiking! We saw the old wooden posts at the end of the trail, but I can't imagine such a beautiful area covered with agriculture. Who wants to see dikes, ditches, and tide-gates?" She wrinkled her nose. "Can you imagine picnicking next to an industrial pump?"

He held his thoughts about the relative necessities of picnicking and agriculture.

Their host nodded, poured two glasses of wine, and placed white cocktail napkins on the bar. "The B&B sits on the site of an old dairy farm. When the farm went under in the 1970s, my wife's family bought the property for a retirement home. For the last several decades, local landowners have worked together to restore the lake to a more natural state. My wife, Jessica, is leading the charge."

The couple sipped their wine and nodded.

"This is Julien and our good friend, Eliza. Eliza owns a flower farm in Skagit County."

The woman with the earmuffs squealed. "Oh, how romantic!"

Eliza nodded and sipped her wine.

Julien watched her gaze drift toward the windows. *That's uncharacteristic. I thought for sure she would capitalize on Clark's introduction.*

"They specialize in native varietals." Clark cleared his throat.

Eliza remained silent.

The guest downed her wine and stroked the earmuffs hanging around her neck. "What's a native varietal?"

Eliza's eyes widened, and she choked on her wine. Turning to face the woman, she smiled, but the gesture failed to reach her eyes. "Hartley Farms is lovely in the spring. Come to the town's tulip festival and come see us."

"I'd love to do that!" The woman pulled out her phone and tapped the screen. Holding the phone aloft, she pointed to the farm's social media account. "These photographs are gorgeous!"

Julien wrestled with Eliza's deflection, wondering if exhaustion explained her succinct remarks or she had something on her mind. *It's not pollen.* He turned to Clark, giving her space in case she needed it. "How about a tour?"

Clark led him toward the sliding glass doors. "Come out with me, Nathan and Skye. Bring your map."

"Yes! Let's go find the treasure."

"Eliza?" Clark asked.

She unfolded her legs. "I'm coming."

Julien trailed his thumb down the curve of her spine. "I'm sure you've seen every nook and cranny," he said. "Take a break, sip your wine, and wait for your friend."

She smiled but rose and walked to the deck. "Some things are worth seeing repeatedly."

He returned her smile. *I'm beginning to understand that fact.*

Skye and Nathan raced around the deck but steered clear of the fire pit and precarious wine glasses.

At the edge of the deck, Clark held court and recounted the site's history.

Julien listened to the broad orientation and felt Eliza's quiet presence behind him. He relaxed and enjoyed the moment of rest.

A black-tipped snow goose called to its mate, wings flapping above the water.

Shading his eyes, he struggled to identify the other animals floating on the lake.

Clark followed his gaze and grinned. "Tundra swans and trumpeter swans. The island is a rich wintering ground for migratory waterfowl. If we stay outside long enough, we might see egrets and bald eagles."

"We have an eagle on the farm." Skye stopped spinning in circles and braced her hands on her knees. "I found a feather."

"Cool!" Nathan said.

"Julien said it wouldn't eat my chickens."

"Nope, I counted them. All safe and sound." He glanced at Eliza and caught the ghost of a fleeting smile.

Nathan pointed to his map. An irregular, large, blue circle anchored the center. "Look, here's the lake. And these dashed lines are the paths. We have to count our steps to find the treasure."

"I can count to two hundred," Skye said.

He stared. "You cannot."

She stamped a foot. "Yes, I can!"

Eliza stepped forward. "Sweet Pea, go show Nathan how you can count off two hundred paces."

Sticking out her tongue, the girl took off running toward the lake. Her breathless yells carried back to the house. "One. Two. Three. Four…"

Nathan followed, arms and legs pumping like pistons.

"Do you want a walking tour?" Clark asked.

He considered the appeal of walking the land against the appeal of sitting on the deck next to Eliza and the roaring fire. He shook his head.

The innkeeper laughed. "Excuse me. I'll go tend the fire and check on my guests."

Alone for the first time all day, he and Eliza stood on the deck. He watched the geese scatter before the children's advance.

A swarm of honking and fluttering fowl rose in the air.

The children changed course and chased the animals. Skye bent at the waist and drew deep, replenishing breaths. Nathan challenged her, his voice carrying over the landscape. The pair gave chase once again.

"They don't have a chance," Eliza said.

He nodded. "I had a great day tagging along with the two of you."

She settled into a weathered, cedar chair. "Me, too, but I'm beat."

"I noticed." He chose the chair next to hers and sipped his tea. Beyond the marsh, the sunset brought a pink tinge to the sky and the reflection on the lake. *Why had today been great? We rode around, did errands, and met their friends. Eliza's capability feels easy and approachable. She doesn't need me to stay, but she's open to the possibility.* He shifted in his seat and considered the six-year-old complication running through the tall grass like a crazed bobcat. Her presence complicated his ability to come and go on a whim. *How long can I pass through before my departure is the thing they remember the most?* "I'll never run and chase Skye."

Eliza took a sip of her wine. "No, you probably won't."

"Does that reality bother you?"

"Does it bother you?" she asked.

I didn't plan to end up here. I've learned to let go of my expectations, but I need to think long and hard before settling in for a spell. Unsure how to answer Eliza's question, he chose on the absolutes of history. "I had a weird feeling when I woke up in the hospital in Texas. A bunch of people stood around the bed. My mom and dad. My brother and my girlfriend."

She raised her eyebrows.

He nodded. *I'll get to that part about the girlfriend.* "Everybody kept looking at my leg, and I didn't grasp what happened after the equipment fell. The doctor came in and broke the news. Instead of taking it like a man, I cried and kicked everybody out of the room."

"Men are allowed to cry." She frowned.

The gesture deepened the lines near her eyes, and he wanted to smooth away the added stress. "Not in my family. I didn't trust the people I knew to understand the thoughts going through my head. When the tears subsided, the nurses came and went without speaking. I expected pain, but I couldn't feel anything." He took a deep breath and stared at the lake. "The hospital monitors beeped and marked the time, but it was two in the morning before I gathered enough courage to pull back the blankets and accept the sight of blood seeping through the bandages. For a minute or two, I realized I was lucky to be alive."

"Just a minute?"

He met her gaze. "I got mad. My whole life had been easy until that point."

"Losing your limb with no warning must have shocked you," she said. "You didn't have time to prepare or make plans. That's the worst adrenaline letdown."

He picked up her hand and held it, but he kept his gaze on the view. "I spent the whole summer learning to walk again, as stubborn and ornery as a mule. The physical therapist fitted me with the prosthetic leg, and I started on a walker. Then a push walker, crutches, and finally a cane." He shook his head. "I never thought a cane would feel like an achievement, but my therapist was a good ol' boy from Alabama. Sterling knew better than to take 'no' for an answer." Looking at her, he caught the hint of a smile.

She kept her hand in his, but she shifted in the chair and tucked up her legs.

Sighing, he rubbed the back of her hand and let the rhythm of idle comfort center him. "Months passed, but I couldn't stand or walk for over twenty minutes before the pain drove me into a wheelchair. After the rage faded, depression settled in, and I shut out everybody from my thoughts. The quiet treatment didn't fool Sterling. He helped me stretch and regain my strength with the patience of someone who has seen pain. We spent a lot of time sitting on medicine balls and tossing soccer balls while we argued about football."

"Did it help?"

"Yeah, I needed a friend as much as I needed a therapist."

"What happened to your girlfriend?"

He took a deep breath and released her hand. "She walked away and got engaged to my brother."

Eliza's gaze widened, and her cheeks flushed.

Yeah, I had that reaction, too, but Caroline had no idea what it meant to pull yourself up and recover from pain. Sterling did, and you do too.

"Are you still hung up on her?" she asked.

Julien shook his head. "I figure she always wanted to be a Kroger. She saw an opportunity for an upgrade and made her move."

She exhaled and picked up his hand. "I think you dodged a bullet."

He shifted in the cedar chair, content to let her set the rhythm of the conversation.

She glanced at his leg. "What caused the accident?"

"An improperly secured load." The technical description felt blameless. *Stupidity?*

"What does that mean?"

She untucked her legs and crossed them in front of her.

The lithe, unconscious gesture amused him. *Leg or no leg, I'm getting too old to sit that way.* He smiled, withdrew his hand, and rested it on her knee. "A piece of heavy machinery crushed my muscles and shattered the bones in my leg. I didn't see the equipment moving when I walked under it." The events of the day played like a movie in his mind. He had repeated the story to so many lawyers and scene investigators that he wondered if his mind settled on the shortest narrative. *Were there details that I missed?* He shook his head. "Somebody should have locked out the area, but I'm ultimately responsible for wandering into the travel path. I put myself in the worst possible spot."

"Couldn't you hear the commotion?"

"Rigs are noisy. Most of the time, we wore hearing protection. One more groaning machine wouldn't have made a difference in my awareness." He took a sip of tea and realized the glass was empty. "A toolpusher named Heath stayed by my side until the paramedics arrived for the evacuation. I didn't realize it at the time, but Heath ripped off his bandana and made a tourniquet to stem the blood loss. I always carry one now.

"I wasn't fast enough to get out of the way. I wasn't good enough for Caroline. I wasn't old enough to run the farm. At the time, I felt like I was everybody's second choice, and who wants to go through life feeling like they're second best?" He risked looking at her.

She rolled her eyes. "Don't be ridiculous."

Her casual dismissal made him laugh, but the pain of the accident sent him to his lowest point, and he wanted her to understand that reality. "To answer your question, I don't drink because there were nights when second best wasn't good enough, and I thought about ending my life. It might be better for you and Skye if I leave."

She turned up his palm and traced his lifelines.

The soft scrape of her nail drew his gaze.

"Why did you agree to be my foreman?"

He took a deep breath and looked up. "I recognized your look of desperation. For a while, I saw it every day when I looked in the mirror."

She frowned. "I wasn't desperate."

He smiled. "You were open to the possibility of help."

She rolled her eyes and tossed his hand back to his lap.

The playful gesture felt at odds with the severity of his confession. *I laid out my failings, and she didn't blink an eye. How much worse could it get?* "Why aren't you shying away? I admitted I thought about killing myself."

She straightened in the chair. "But you didn't do it."

"No, I didn't," he said.

She looked away.

He watched her brush a speck of wind-borne dust from her eye. *Or was it a tear?*

"My father shot himself in the middle of the river by Hartley Farms. The coast guard recovered his body at low tide." She exhaled. "It was five years ago."

Feeling selfish, he bit the inside of his lip and wondered if he should have known. "I'm sorry, Eliza."

She finished her wine and set her glass on the table. "If you spent any time in town, you'd hear the story." She turned to face him. "Don't look so shocked. I appreciate what it means to feel like you're second best. I respect the fact that after all the crap you experienced, you looked in the mirror and kept moving forward. It's the most important thing any of us can do." Her gaze softened. "This attraction between us is hard for me.

The pain of being vulnerable again is hard. Skye has to be my priority. She took to you like a duck to water, but she's not mature enough to separate family life from the workings of the farm. I have to put her wellbeing ahead of the things I want."

Eliza's pragmatic confession made sense, but he wanted her to see the possibilities of more people and more love on the farm. "I don't want to compete with Skye, but I want to be with you. And by "be," I mean in the carnal sense."

She grinned. "If we met at a college bar, I wouldn't have thought twice about leaving with you."

Laughter seemed like the best response. "I've half a mind to give Clark my credit card so I can carry you upstairs and take you up on that offer."

"Do it."

He inhaled. "Don't tempt me, woman."

She laughed. "Chicken."

"I don't want to add to your worries." The confession covered all his doubts.

She smiled. "I can handle more than you think, but don't feel like you're the only person with baggage. If I hadn't needed help, would you have approached me at the hardware store? If we had met on a blind date, would we have made it this far?"

"Hard to say. I spent last summer proving myself with the ladies." He took a deep breath and grinned. "Then again, none of them looked as good as you do in a pair of jeans. About that room?" Her laughter sounded as sweet and pure as summer sunshine.

The sound caught the attention of every person on the deck. They stopped drinking and paused their conversations, caught up in the moment when Eliza's weariness took second stage to the sound of heartfelt amusement.

The children stopped their games and came running. Skye skidded across the decking and wrapped her arms around her mother's muscled arm. "I'm hungry!"

Eliza smiled and rose to her feet. "I'm sure you are, Sweet Pea." She clutched her child to her side and faced the wind and the light reflecting from the distant water. "We accomplished a lot of errands today."

Clark emerged from the sliding doors and rang an old bell made of thick metal. The muted ring echoed from the trees bordering the bed and breakfast. "Dinner is ready!"

The couples clustered around the fire pit gathered their empty wine glasses and their discarded outerwear.

Jessica stepped around Clark, held out her hands, and embraced Eliza. "I'm so glad you made time to come out. We've missed seeing you."

Eliza leaned into a side hug and continued rubbing her daughter's back. "Skye's been lonely."

Jessica nodded and met Julien's gaze. "That can happen."

He tipped his chin to acknowledge receiving her message. *I'll do my best.*

The cooks carried large platters of food to a buffet.

Clark pointed to the offerings. "Everyone, fill your plates and claim your seats."

The children eyed the display of food and wrinkled their noses.

He laughed, imagining their pained expressions as they sampled the rich fare.

A cook appeared with sliders and sweet potato

fries.

"Yes!" Nathan said.

Eliza claimed the seat beside him. Her thigh brushed against his, and he relished the point of contact. *So much for scaring her off.* Lifting a spoon to his mouth, he sampled the seafood stew made with fish and shellfish. The tomato-based broth held hunks of white fish and chunks of vegetables, but the buttery flavor tasted nothing like the rich seafood gumbo he grew up eating. "It's different, but good," he said. "What is it?"

"Cioppino," Eliza said.

He nodded.

"What's the news in Skagit County?" Jessica asked.

Eliza's focus shifted to her friend. "Nothing too much. Someone made an offer on the farm yesterday. Claire probably would have sold the land if she still had power of attorney over the family assets."

Jessica raised her eyebrows. "How much did they offer?"

"Does it matter?"

Clark paused with the salad tongs in his hands. "Everyone has a price."

A guest lowered his fork and leaned forward. "Would you sell the B&B?"

"Absolutely not." Clark dropped the tongs in the bowl.

Several of the diners chuckled and raised their glasses to the innkeeper's double standard.

"The value of the land isn't my only consideration." Eliza put down her fork. "That's my family farm. Or what's left of it. It's not for sale. If the developers show up again, I'll have Julien mock up a

No Trespassing sign."

Jessica eyed his forearms. "That could be effective."

Her appraisal lasted longer than he expected. He raised his eyebrows.

She sipped her wine and refocused on her friend.

"If that doesn't work, I'll have the sheriff run them off." Eliza crossed her arms.

"What were their names?" Clark asked.

She turned and looked at him. "Do you remember?"

He nodded and scanned the assembled guests. "Here?"

"Why not?" She shrugged. "I have no intention of selling."

He put down his fork. "Nicole and Steven Warly."

One guest whistled. "Fake tans and shiny teeth?"

The evening's lighthearted conversation sank into muddy waters. Struggling to hide his frustration, he turned to the man who whistled. "You know them?"

"Not personally."

The man's plaid flannel shirt looked country, but hairspray held the part in his combed white hair.

"They're property developers from California. They made a lot of money carving Palm Oasis Ranch out of the farmland between Bakersfield and Los Angeles. Made progress on an exurb south of Seattle, but the established residents commissioned a traffic study and ran them out of town. Looks like they didn't travel far if they're sniffing around Skagit County."

"An exurb?" The word felt gritty and disgusting in his mouth.

"A haven for yuppies!" said an older guest from

the end of the long table. "Everything is shiny and bright in a planned-unit development. It's a safe, little enclave of homogeneous wealth."

His wife leaned close. "I thought your hearing aids had low batteries!"

He grunted and rubbed his ear. "Found a way to change them."

"I don't think Skagit is ripe for an...exurb." Eliza put her napkin on the table. "At Hartley Farms, we only have twenty acres."

"Maybe they want a vacation house," Jessica said. "It's such a pretty piece of property. I can see someone playing gentleman farmer on the weekends."

Eliza crossed her hands over her chest. "How about someone growing flowers and running a floral design business?"

Jessica rose to fill Eliza's wineglass. "Also a good choice."

She shook her head and put her hand over the vessel. "I need to drive."

The two women locked gazes.

"Let Julien drive," Jessica said.

Eliza's expression lit up.

He watched her contemplate the pleasure of letting go of her obligations. *I'd do a lot to bring a flash of pleasure to that woman's face.*

Then her face fell. "Julien can't drive the truck."

Jessica frowned. "Why? Is it a stick?"

The absurdity of the question made him laugh. "Ma'am, I know how to drive a manual transmission, but I only have one working leg. I can't drive standard vehicles without a pedal modification."

She blushed and sipped her water.

Clark's cough filled the silence.

"It doesn't matter." Eliza pushed back from the table. "I don't mind driving, but the drive is long. We should hit the road soon."

Her visible disappointment seared his heart. He thought about offering to spend the night on the island, but Skye needed routine, and too many questions and unspoken expectations remained between him and Eliza.

The guest with the hearing aid cleared his throat. "Skagit County has a lot of farmland."

Eliza nodded. "Agriculture is our number one industry. Skagit farmers manage about 90,000 acres of land. The next biggest draw would be tulips."

"No offense," the man in plaid said, "but the Warlys aren't interested in flowers. Scale is the only thing that matters to them. Any big farms or companies go out of business in the county?"

She shook her head, but then her gaze narrowed.

Julien watched her features shift and wondered if she was reconciling the man's question with her knowledge of the area.

Her mouth settled into a grim line, and she exhaled. "Smith Specialty Potatoes might have the biggest tract in the county."

He winced. *Shit. That's too close to home.*

The guest nodded and smoothed his white hair. "I would ask the potato farmers if they've had a visit from Mr. Warly and his trim-fit wife. Ask their neighbors, too. I bet the Smith family and their kin are planning to vacation in warmer climates as soon as the check clears."

Eliza drummed her fingers on the table. "I'll plant

a hedge."

Jessica laughed. "Dollars might not sway you, but traffic and national coffee shops might do it. This deal could be good for your business. Move the barn closer to the highway and let Serah and Michelle run the florist shop with a walk-in counter."

She scooted back her chair. "That's not what I want."

"A buyout could be an unexpected blessing," Jessica said.

Eliza stood. "I'll call the Smiths tomorrow. I can't imagine them selling out."

Jessica sipped her wine and looked at Eliza over the rim. "But what if they did?"

Eliza squared her shoulders. "Then I'll cope. Or I'll fight back." She frowned. "When my father sold the land, he included buyback options in the contract."

Jessica shook her head. "You don't have that cash."

He stood and put his hand on the small of her back. "It's your farm, Eliza. You're under no obligation to sell it."

She turned to him and smiled. "Thank you."

A long time has passed since I felt like I got something right.

The kids pushed aside their plates, grabbed markers from a nearby shelf, and scribbled on the paper tablecloth.

"Skye, it's time to go," Eliza said.

"But I haven't had dessert yet."

"You can eat your cookie in the truck."

"Really?" The girl's mouth hung open.

Eliza nodded.

"Bye, Nathan!" She hugged the little boy with one arm.

Julien laughed. The girl's casual gesture offered little in the way of regrets. "She's a cheap date."

Eliza looked at Skye and smiled. "Ice cream *and* cookies in one day. She's in heaven."

Feeling tension in her back relax, he dropped his hand and met Clark's gaze. "Thanks for dinner."

"You're welcome back anytime."

The headlights on Eliza's truck illuminated the dark island roads. She crossed the bridge over Desolation Pass and let Skye devour her cookie. "What was your favorite part of the day, Sweet Pea?"

"Seeing Nathan." Skye yawned. "Maybe he can come to visit us next."

"I'll ask his mom," she said.

After five minutes of silence, Julien glanced in the back seat and saw Skye's head leaning against the supports of her booster seat. He looked at Eliza and smiled. "She's out."

Eliza nodded. "I'm glad she saw her friend and burned off some energy."

"They seem like a nice family." He let his comment hang above the rumble of the engine, the blowing heater fans, and the road noises seeping through the weather stripping. *Even if they're not looking out for your interests.*

She sighed. "I've known Jessica for long time, but sometimes I feel like she doesn't understand me at all."

"People have a habit of changing."

She turned the steering wheel. "I appreciate you sticking up for me."

"You said you weren't interested." He turned his

face toward the cold comfort of the night and heard his voice reflect off the cold window glass. "That's an easy line to respect."

She drove north. As the road left the coast, the steady blur of traffic diminished. "The Warlys might be the first wave of speculators, but it's only a matter of time before someone cinches the opportunity and destroys our way of life. Developers could piece together a dozen farms and assemble the type of development that dinner guest suggested. Sweetbriar Nursery has listed its parcels for months. They're advertising the collection as a turnkey nursery with one hundred and fifty acres of land, offices, barns, greenhouses, and hoop houses. They have everything a greenhorn would need to grow woody ornamentals, trees, conifers, and native varieties. They've entertained a few wholesale bites, but my hunch is they're holding out for more than the land and inventory. That name comes with a lot of recognition and goodwill. What if the Warlys get there first?"

He heard the speculation in her voice shift to worry. "What's the price for Sweetbriar Nursery?"

She glanced at him. "Are you in the market?"

He shook his head. "I'm curious if the tanned duo offered you a fair price."

"Four-and-a-half million dollars."

He did the calculations in his head. "They're not shorting you for twenty acres. Add in the house and seven seventy-five is a reasonable price."

"Nobody is snapping up Sweetbriar."

"Doesn't matter if they're holding out. You're worried about your neighbors. A thousand acres of potatoes creeps toward thirty million dollars. If your friends are right about their intentions, these property developers aren't playing with pocket money."

"I don't care what type of financing they secured. My farm matters to me, but my neighbors matter, too. I don't want a big check to make my decisions."

He crossed his arms and stared at the moonlit structures. "Compared to your farm, my family runs big agriculture. It's your land, but I have no idea how to grapple with the county impacts. When I stand on my mama's front porch, I see cane to the river road. We're an island of productivity." He smiled. "Still, I wouldn't want to go up against you in the court of public opinion."

"Have I been in a mood?"

He weighed his approach. "Did I keep you up too late last night?"

She grinned and shook her head. "I slept like a rock."

"Speaking of hard as a rock…"

She changed lanes and skirted a slow-moving vehicle. "You think the Warlys will come back?"

I'd like to get you home and bedded without further conversation. Maybe we both want to sleep well tonight. "Most likely. And those negative reviews you've been worried about? Not a coincidence."

"But some of those reviews are months old!"

"In my experience, people play the long game when improving their circumstances." He stared at the blinking taillights of intermittent traffic. *Caroline did.*

"They thought you were my husband."

At the amusement in her tone, he smiled. "I've been called much worse."

She laughed and drummed the steering wheel.

"The Smiths would have told the Warlys about Erik's death. Have they even talked to the locals? The whole thing doesn't make sense. Why do they need my acreage?"

"It's a pretty piece of land. I'd buy it."

She slowed for the access road. "It's not for sale."

"I've caught on to that fact." He considered the dark alley and imagined an onslaught of multistory houses and narrow lots. *Families need a place to live, but Brandon would have an absolute fit if some developer threatened his sugarcane. Doesn't matter if Mama called us the "heir and the spare," the sugarcane has always belonged to him.*

The gate loomed, and she came to a stop.

He hopped out of the truck to open the gate. The cold air sharpened his thoughts. He climbed back inside the truck. "They've got a little saying in Cajun country. *Lâche pas la patate.*"

"Translation?"

"Don't drop the potato."

She rested her arms on the steering wheel. "I'm not tracking."

He shifted in the seat to measure her interest in Louisiana colloquialisms. "It means don't give up when you're going through a rough time. In your case, don't give up on the Smiths and your vision of life out here. There might be a way to get through all this crap without feeling threatened by the possibilities of what's coming."

She put the truck in gear. "What if they've already signed a sales contract?"

"Then at least you'll know what you're up against."

She nodded and continued driving.

The gravel road crunched beneath the tires.

At the barn, she put the truck in Park, pulled the key from the ignition, and climbed down from the cab.

He exited the vehicle and waited near the tailgate where the bright security lights highlighted fluttering moths and buzzing insects. When Eliza walked past him, he reached for her hand. "I know this farm is your livelihood, but don't let the unknown keep you up all night. A million possible outcomes exist, but you need sleep."

She stared at the moonlit fields. "How many outcomes do I win?"

He smiled. "You might eventually find yourself staring down the back of a coffee shop."

"I don't even like espresso." She pulled free her hand and wrinkled her nose. "Jessica knows that, too."

He smiled. "I care about more than your coffee preferences. I'll do my best to help you."

"Please don't offer me money." She gripped his forearm.

Watching her withdraw her touch like she touched a hot skillet, he laughed and slid his hands in his back pockets. "I have cash, but not thirty million."

"Good. I don't want your money." She crossed her arms. "I can figure out this situation on my own."

"Thank goodness." He tugged free her arm and linked hands. "I'm not keen on digging up acres and acres of potatoes."

She sighed. "I want to grow flowers and keep my family intact. I thought Skye would grow up surrounded by the beauty and the mountains I love. I never anticipated a multiplex could block her view."

"Use the life insurance money and exercise your buyback options. Let Warly know you'll sit tight and fight for your servitude rights in court. The threat of an expensive legal battle might be enough to run him off."

"I let Erik handle this side of the business." She sighed.

He squeezed her hand. "Why? You have a good head on your shoulders. You work hard."

She pulled against his grasp. "Not hard enough. I don't have any patience for laws and regulations. I'm good at working with the plants."

He turned her palm up, tracing the calluses and wondering how to help her see the possibilities within her grasp. "You can expand beyond cut flowers, Eliza. You've had your eye on more land. This neighborly threat could be the kick in the pants you need." He looked up and met her gaze. "What about your children's book? You already sell bulbs. Expand your offerings. Sell your varietal seeds to the general public."

"I only sell bulbs in limited quantities. Seeds would be a lot more work."

He grinned. "So you've thought of it."

She pulled free her hand and ran it through her hair. "I love to imagine my flowers blooming across the country, but I'm not sure I can summon enough enthusiasm for the logistics of an online store. Packaging, processing, and FDA compliance increase with scale. Right now, I can barely manage the heartache of negative online reviews."

"Those reviews aren't real."

She frowned and stared. "They still hurt."

He wanted to fold her into his arms, but he worried

the intimate gesture would send Claire careening out of the farmhouse like a cotillion chaperone. He scratched the nascent bristles on his cheek. "Think about the range of options and find the solution that feels right. You don't have to make any decisions tonight."

She opened her mouth.

What the hell. Leaning forward, he kissed away her objections and let the quiet pressure of his lips soothe her concerns. "On second thought, come back to the cottage and talk shop. We'll call it a 'strategy session'."

She ran a thumb along the back of his neck, shook her head, and pulled out of his embrace. "It's late. I won't be any good at…work."

He adjusted his pants. "Just so we're clear, I wasn't really talking about work."

She laughed. "Also, I need to get Skye into bed."

He glanced at the girl, passed out cold in the backseat. *I completely forgot about the kid.* The moonlit mountains shone in the distance. He opened the rear door and admitted the chatter of night insects. *How does Eliza juggle so many responsibilities?*

"I appreciate you sticking up for me at dinner." She reached into the truck and extracted Skye from the straps of her booster seat.

"It's your fight, Eliza. But I want to see you win."

"Why?"

He thought about the question. "If I was in your shoes, I'd be mad as hell."

She nestled Skye's head against her shoulder. "How far would that anger get you?"

"Not far enough." He exhaled and nodded to say goodnight. Letting himself into the cottage, he leaned against the doorframe and surveyed his life. The cold furnishings held little appeal, but Eliza's presence in his life warmed his heart. He thought of her kisses and wished their outing ended on a happier note. *She accepts the facts of my injury with the practicality of a farmer who knows a person can work from sunup to sundown and still have no say in the outcome. She works hard, but why is it so difficult for her to fight for herself?* He shook his head. *I required thousands of pounds of falling metal to learn the same lesson.* He pulled out his cell phone and tapped his brother's name.

"*Mon frère.* What's up, French Fry?"

He smiled at the old nickname. "Living the dream."

"Your GPS hasn't moved in a few days."

He grunted. "Don't you have better things to do than monitor my location?"

"My only brother bought a new motorcycle and disappeared the next day. We've had three postcards and a box of beef jerky."

"It was good beef jerky."

"Come home and get some *boudin*."

He scanned the dark interior of the cottage. "I'm not there yet."

Brandon took a deep breath. "How're the pansies?"

"It's a farm. Plenty of work remains."

"Did that heavy object fall on your head? You already have a farm."

He rolled his eyes. "The farm's always been yours."

Brandon cleared his throat. "Brothers should work together. I have reps from the USDA demoing irrigation programs and soil health. Who knew cover crops and a few acres of soybeans would make the five o'clock news? We've reduced tillage, and the ratoon fields are turning into a regular field trip for local school kids. I could use an extra hand."

"I could use an extra foot." He waited for his brother's easy laughter, but Brandon's silence confirmed his suspicions. *He thinks of me as a responsibility*. He cleared his throat to dislodge the swell of emotions. "I'm staying at Hartley Farms for the near future. Try not to worry about it."

"Come on, man. It's almost Easter. Come home and see your mama."

He glanced at the dark, expectant fields. "I'll send her flowers."

"That won't be enough. You're her favorite son."

The platitude almost made him laugh. "We both know that's a lie."

"Julien…"

"Give my best to Caroline." He ended the call.

Chapter Thirteen

Eliza carried Skye to the bathroom, soothed her quiet questions, and tucked her into bed. Closing her door, she saw Claire's light go off. The house settled with the sound of creaking wood, and she took a deep breath. *I need to go research the Warlys, email the town council members, and check on the progress of the flower arrangements.* Closing her eyes, she leaned against the hall wall and smiled. *What I want to do is to take up Julien on his offer and lose myself in mind-blowing sex.*

The acknowledgement grew in her thoughts as she returned to the bathroom and started a shower. She shaved her legs and thought about Julien's large, tanned hands and the hard press of his arousal when their lips and their bodies met. The cascade of steaming water and the slick soap bubbles felt amazing on her skin, but not as amazing as the touch of a man. She thought about Julien's cocky smile and the ripple of muscles beneath his work shirts.

Turning off the water, she listened to the dripping faucet and let the steam swirl around her overheated body. *"Just think about the range of options and find the solution that feels right,"* he said. *Ha! I don't see him putting any skin in the game.* She wiped clean the mirror and stared at her reflection. *I can make one decision. What's the worst he can do? Slam the door in my face?* She grabbed the hair dryer and cranked up the heat. Ten minutes later, she left the house in jeans and a coat. Seeing Claire's light pop on, she shook her head, strode toward the cottage, and knocked on Julien's door.

He answered the door wearing a pair of sweatpants.

"Good, you're still up." She breezed through the entryway and admired his defined torso and the powerful swell of his shoulders. "Thanks for the coaching tonight, but you're hung up on life before and after your injury."

He closed the door and crossed his arms. "How so?"

She circled him, maintaining enough distance to enjoy the smell of soap and a subtle musk but resisting the allure of touching his skin. "You're using your injury as an excuse. How long would you have spent working on that rig?"

"A few years?"

"I don't think so. Would you have married your girlfriend?"

"Probably." He scratched his cheek.

She felt like slapping his ass but kept her hand pinned to her side. "So, why didn't you do it?"

He dropped his hand. "It didn't feel right."

Exhaling, she gave him credit for stalling. "The way I see it, that accident saved you from a lot of heartache and regrets. It's a shitty way to turn around your life, but I'm pretty sure you were headed in the wrong direction. You never had to fight for anything. The accident made you fight for yourself, but you're not done yet."

"That's one way of looking at it."

She ran her hand along his chest. Her nerves magnified the sensation, and the heat of his skin scalded her fingertips. *How can he generate so much heat against the cold?* "Let me see it."

His eyes widened.

"You have to keep fighting, Julien. One step at a time. Let me see the leg."

He stilled her hand. "I'm not sure what they teach you in Washington, but legs are not integral parts of human intercourse."

The clinical term threw her off guard, and she faltered. "What's the most difficult part?"

"Balance."

That's it? "So, no sex in the shower?"

He pulled her hand lower, turning her body until he had access to her neck. "Not likely."

"Was it awkward the first time?"

He kissed the soft curve of her neck.

The reassuring gesture warmed her heart.

His lips traveled north.

She felt the scrape of his teeth. "Again." Her whispered plea masked the need building in her core.

He pulled her closer and brushed his rough stubble against her cheek. "Isn't all sex awkward the first time? I learned to laugh about it. Well, first, I found some space, and then I cried. Nothing feels less satisfying than two curious people who only want to scratch an itch."

Her protective streak kicked in, and she pulled away. "She didn't ask for your phone number?"

He tightened his hold. "I wouldn't have given it to her."

Feeling his hand flex against her hip, she looked up

and felt she had one more chance to walk away. Within the shadows of the cottage, his warm brown eyes deepened into decadent black. She drifted her hand farther down his skin, tracing the hollows where his abdominal muscles disappeared beneath his sweatpants. "I already know where you live."

"For now," he said.

Nodding, she accepted the conditional boundary. "For now is good enough." He held her gaze long enough to make her wonder if he had second thoughts.

Then he released her and braced his arm against the doorframe to remove his sweatpants.

She followed his movements, watching his muscles flex before he straightened, waiting for her reaction. His arousal caught her gaze, but she forced herself to look at the muscles swelling his thigh, the bland smoothness of the prosthetic sock, and the high-tech hardware attached to the end of his leg. Then she went back to his cock. "No big deal."

He laughed. "Hell of an aphrodisiac."

Intent on showing him she was well past the point of needing an aphrodisiac, she smiled and led him toward the couch, tossing her coat over the back of a chair.

He followed her lead.

With little effort, she pushed him down to the rough fabric, his warm brown eyes staring up, waiting for her to make the next move. The offering erased the last of her reservations. She straddled him and centered her hips against his arousal, claiming his lips and letting her senses drift between the centers of heat.

His hands rose to grasp her ass, and he picked up the pace of the kiss, sliding his tongue beneath her lips and angling his head.

She opened to receive him and matched his pace.

He grabbed her hips, pulled her flush to anchor her movements, and then swore and broke the kiss. He tugged off her shirt and exposed her breasts. "Fair is fair."

The cold air brought her nipples to attention. She drew a breath, thinking his skin tasted of salt and the fresh green scent of cedar. Grabbing his hand from her hip, she brought the heat to her breast and arched into his touch.

"You're beautiful," he said.

The compliment cracked the haze of lust driving her forward. She leaned forward and kissed his neck. "We've got one problem."

He stilled. "What is it?"

"I don't have any protection."

He laughed and told her to check his duffle bag.

She climbed off and rooted through the pile of masculine items, ignoring the smells and her curiosity until she found a foil packet. Holding the condom in the air like a prize, she stripped off her pants and scrambled back to his lap.

He took the condom from her hands and set it aside.

His lazy kiss told her he was more interested in reestablishing her position than racing toward the finish line. She grinned and rose to her knees to trace the hard planes of his abdomen. The muscles fascinated her, but she leaned forward and teased her nipples with the soft give of his chest hair. Feeling him inhale, she grinned and wondered how long his patience would last. She explored his body and let the heated slide of their skin swell into a simmering heat. *I could spend all night exploring his body*. Pulling back, she met his gaze.

He drew her nipple into his mouth. Sucking and teasing the sensitive peak, his hands supported her weight and parted her folds, one thumb slipping past the remaining fabric to stroke her clit.

A soft musk rose between them. She closed her eyes and let the firm pressure of his touch tease and heighten her arousal. Wrapping her fingers around his length, she found the slippery head and stroked his length.

He sucked in his breath.

The reaction thrilled her. She braced her weight on his shoulders and met his gaze. "Whose move is it now?"

He raised his eyebrows, shifted his grip, and slid the soft pressure of his thumb past her folds.

"Yes."

He pulled up and amplified the pressure.

"More." She closed her eyes and shifted her hips, searching for the pressure she craved.

Drawing out her moisture, he found her clit with his thumb.

The sensuous circles anchored her attention. She focused on the pressure and let her pounding heart and quick breaths run wild.

He increased the pressure.

Gasping, she arched into his touch. "You win."

He kept up the pace. "This is a win-win game in my book."

She nodded, willing to agree to anything he said while he chased her release. The pressure and heat in her core built, leaving her wound and desperate for satisfaction.

"Let me see you come."

His soft command pushed her higher. She reached for his hair and the matching pleasure of his kiss.

He tipped his chin and submitted, claiming her lips.

"Julien, I want more."

He laughed and kept his pace at the entrance to her sex. "Hardheaded woman."

She rocked back and straddled his thighs. Her chest rose and fell with shallow breaths. She replicated his touch, stealing his momentum and every ounce of his attention.

Narrowing his gaze, he swore, pumped his sex, and reached for the condom. "I take it back. You do you."

Amusement mixed with pleasure. She closed her eyes, remembering the reassurance of his strength and the pleasure of his touch. Tension coiled in her center. *This man won't let me fall until I'm ready to go all in.*

He grabbed her hips and guided her down.

Poised against her entrance, the heat of his cock promised fulfillment. She opened her eyes and met his gaze. "I want all of you."

He nodded and tightened, possession straining his features.

Welcoming his heat into her body, she lowered herself over his length, and the hot stretch of his presence captured her senses. When he reclaimed his grip, she shifted her body, rolled her hips, and found the pressure she needed, rising and falling to set the pace of her pleasure.

"More." He grunted, rising to meet her.

As his hips thrust to match her rhythm, her breath quickened. Skin slapped against skin as she rode him and the pressure building in her core. Gasping, the pleasure flashed into the blinding heat of a brand. "Fuck!" She found her release and felt his body shudder within her. Dropping her head to his shoulder, she smiled as echoes of satisfaction rippled through her system. *I think the whole farm heard us.*

He trailed his fingers along her back. "You were right to call me out."

She lifted her head and blinked away the urges to close her eyes and sleep. Cool air rushed to fill the space between their bodies. She lifted her hips and paused while he grabbed the condom. Then she climbed off his lap and settled beside him, her head heavy enough she rested it against the back of the couch. *They'll find me naked and sprawled across the couch if I don't get up.* "How so?"

Turning, he looked at her. "I was stalling in Texas."

She blinked and focused on his face. Staying awake was a struggle and gave her a reason to bite her lip. *I should have kept my mouth shut and jumped him.* Instead of toying with the man's hair or running her fingers along his cooling skin, she sat up, tucked her chin on top of her legs, banded her arms around her legs, and confronted his statement. "I know losing your leg was terrible, but the loss forced you to make decisions."

"Please don't call it a 'silver lining'."

She smiled at the wariness wrinkling his suntanned face. "How about a kick in the ass?"

He rubbed his brow and looked at the ceiling. "You know, all three of us grew up together, but everything fell into place for them."

"You felt left out. That must have hurt."

"The accident was a catalyst, but I don't know where I'm going. I never knew what I wanted to be when I grew up. I was working on that rig because I didn't know what to do with my life. I didn't want to be at home. I didn't want to be in business school."

She nodded. "You're good with numbers."

"Arithmetic isn't enough to forge a career."

Or a relationship. She risked reaching for his arm and running a thumb along his cooling skin. "Maybe you need to ignore your family's success to figure out what you want to do with your life. You'll work harder in life without it."

He cocked his head. "How so?"

"My father's decisions taught me about the burden of a legacy. I've tried to prove to everyone I know that I won't crack under pressure, and I won't become him. Public knowledge of his death holds me accountable, but I'm growing flowers because they make me happy. If I work hard enough, I think I can support my daughter. You need to find that balance in your life."

He tugged her close and closed the gap between them. "That's not a bad idea. Do you have any spare inspiration lying around this farm?"

"Fresh out."

He laughed. "Turnkey business plans?"

She smiled. "I have rolls of paper and color-coded sticky notes, but those plans aren't your jam."

"You're right." He laughed, stroking her arm. "Those are your dreams."

"Or not." Doubt eroded her confidence. "I should choose."

He nodded. "I'm not the only one finding footing

in a new life. I appreciate what you're saying, but I need to do more than pick a direction and go all-in."

She settled beneath the weight of his arm and let her thoughts smolder. The quiet intimacy of the cottage gave her courage. "You're not second best to me. You work hard, and you have a knack for business. You're welcome to stay as long as you can."

"It might not be that long." He shifted on the couch. "I'm not looking to put down roots."

How can you build a new life without putting down roots? She yawned. "I don't care. You look good, and you're easy to have around."

He laughed. "That's the sex talking."

She opened her eyes. "Do you practice deflecting compliments?"

He trailed his fingers along the slope of her arm and stroked the side of her breast. "Chalk up the habit to Southern charm."

She submitted to the pleasure of his touch. "Next time I'll be more specific with my HR requests. 'Capable man, good in bed, less complicated.' "

"Less complicated than what?"

She yawned. "Don't ask me to think right now."

His hand stilled. "If your husband were still alive, you wouldn't have given me a second glance."

"You're right." She kept the rest of her thoughts to herself. *I wouldn't have seen you from my place in the kitchen. I wouldn't have had the chance to look at you, much less consider acting on the attraction.* "I made my vows, but this desire doesn't feel like breaking them."

"You said I'm hung up on my leg, but I'm not."

His rich voice jogged her from the beginnings of sleep, and she watched him run a hand along the prosthesis. The connection made its presence more real. She wondered how much time the device required.

"I think of the prosthesis like a tool. For the most part, I ignore the hardware and take it for granted. Then I do something stupid and realize I've lost a few capabilities and feelings." He ran a hand through his hair. "I hate being dependent on something."

"That's the part you hate?"

"Well, I wouldn't mind if the world got over it as well. When I enter a room wearing a pair of shorts, I hear a moment of silence."

"Maybe they're admiring your muscles. Most people probably think you were a soldier."

He closed his eyes. "Surviving an industrial accident doesn't make a man feel proud of his service. The city doesn't host ticker-tape parades for unlucky bastards."

She toyed with the idea of initiating round two but knew her obligations waited. Yet, she could not bring herself to leave him weary and dejected. "That difference never would have occurred to me. I assumed you would find camaraderie with another survivor."

"A difference exists between serving your country and running away from your problems." He sat up and reached for her. "For all my whining about being second best, I'm still pretty damn good."

She laughed and rose to her feet. "Just not as good as you used to be?"

He glanced toward the dark windows. "My limb is extra sensitive. The liner helps, but it also distracts me." He shrugged. "When a specific position doesn't work, I laugh and move on."

She bit her lip. "That's diplomatic."

"Nah, diplomacy is blaming old age and limited flexibility on the amputation." Looking at her, he grabbed her hand and kissed her fingers. "I can tell you a thousand tall fish tales about my college years. You'll believe every one of them."

Torn between the warmth of his lips and the mischievous glint in his eyes, she frowned. "Why is that?"

"Because you can only assume I was better back then."

She pulled free her hand. "I thought you were with Caroline in college?"

He shrugged. "We took breaks."

She laughed. "Whose idea was that?"

"Hers."

The regret in his statement almost broke her heart. *Does she know how much damage she inflicted?* Shaking her head, she reached for her clothes. "I think you dodged a bullet."

He nodded. "She dumped the broken goods."

One leg inside her jeans, she stopped and considered the man who gave her so much pleasure. "Julien, you're far from broken."

He rose to his feet. "I'm not so sure. Admitting my flaws seems like a hell of a good defense against your high expectations."

She turned away and shimmied into her pants. *I've seen him hard at work, absorbed by a task. I've seen him tending to Skye and her ridiculous chickens. He'll be dynamite when he wraps his head around the changes in his life and finally moves on from that accident.* Yet, instead of being brave enough to say those things and risk his rejection, she faced him. "You don't need to worry about my expectations."

He cupped her elbow. "You said we have to maintain the line between business and pleasure."

The possessive gesture brought a smile to her face. "It can be a thin line."

Dropping her arm, he wound her hair around his finger. "That's good. Physical therapy gave me plenty of practice walking the line. Stay a little longer. We can work on my...stretches."

"Does that approach work with the ladies?"

He smiled and tugged her hair. "Right now, I only care about you."

She scanned his wide chest and the smoldering desire in his gaze. *How can he stand there, so vulnerable one minute and so guarded the next? I'd spend all night with him if I could sleep past dawn.* She pulled free and kissed him goodnight, knowing the warmth of his lips would stay with her as she dashed across the moonlit yard. "Sleep well, Julien. I'll see you at six."

He sighed. "I'll walk you out."

"Don't be ridiculous," she said without thinking. "I know every inch of my farm."

He took a deep breath and looked at her. "Yes, ma'am."

Realizing she went too far, she closed the distance. "Wait, that didn't come out right."

He sighed. "No, it didn't. It sounded a hell of a lot like putting me in my place."

Hearing the offense in his voice, she looked at the carpet. "I have a hard time letting go of control."

"I'm catching on to that fact."

She smiled and met his gaze. "Gabe and I never

had this…problem."

He bit her ear. "I'd be open to calling it 'special treatment'."

The hint of forgiveness and innuendo in his voice gave her hope, but she pulled back. "Rain check?"

Nodding, he straightened and released a yawn. "Don't worry about it, boss. I'll see you bright and early." He walked toward the bedroom.

Left standing in the cottage she owned, she sighed. *The old couch bore our explorations, but how many one-night stands lead to something else?* Opening the front door, she walked down the cottage steps. The cold wind replaced the memory of his lips, and she acknowledged her visit strayed past the limits of physical indulgence. *I want him to stay.* The thought unnerved her. She tucked her head against the wind. *What would have happened if I'd stayed until dawn?*

****

The next morning, Eliza stood at a card table in the greenhouse and glared at a jumble of spare irrigation parts. At some point, Gabe dumped a mess of black components in a catchall box. The resulting tangle of polyethylene tubing defied her powers of logic. Swearing, she struggled to stay focused and make sense of the mess. *I have to leak-test this kit.*

Julien opened the door to the greenhouse. "Can I help?"

She nodded, not trusting herself to speak without cursing Gabe or her stupidity. *One impulsive night and everything's awkward between us.*

He returned with a chair.

She made room and attempted to explain the mess spread on the table.

"Let's tease apart the components one by one," he said. "Everything must come to an end."

An end? She drew a deep breath. *I thought we were just getting started.* The intimacy of the late night blurred her focus, but she refused to give up on the irrigation lines. Tubes bunched in her hands, but his companionable silence and diligent patience kept her from swearing. *Untangling this mess has to be easier than untangling my life.* She stopped to watch his steady progress. Instead of worrying about the primary tangle, he removed bits and pieces of hardware and sorted them into piles of barbed tees, elbows, stakes, and plugs. He appeared as relaxed as a day-tripper, the hint of a smile flashing beneath his worn baseball cap. *Why do I feel like tearing out my hair?* She dropped her jumble and threw up her hands. "This tubing is way too springy. I'll have to stake it every foot to keep it in place."

He looked up. "It needs time to relax. Do you have a heat lamp?"

"What?"

"The tubing is malleable. If you get it hot, it'll relax." He winked.

Her skin warmed, and she felt foolish. "It's seven in the morning. You promised to walk the line."

Holding up his hands, he grinned. "What did I say?"

She raised her eyebrows, amused at the sexual innuendo, but frustrated with the task at hand. "If you get it hot, it'll relax?"

He picked up a coil of tubing. "Time-honored method."

Nothing about last night felt 'time-honored'. It felt

like velvet-clad steel, and I slept like a rock before I realized what I did. The crunch of tires on gravel interrupted her thoughts. She looked toward the door of the greenhouse.

"You expecting visitors?" he asked.

She shook her head.

He stood and stretched his back. "Well, let's see who came to call."

"You don't have to get up."

He laughed. "Oh. I want to."

She brushed the dirt off her dark blue jeans. "I think we made a mistake."

"One? I was willing to make several of them."

"Julien!" She rubbed her eyebrows. *I don't have time for games.*

"Come on, Eliza." He handed over her wide-brimmed hat. "The day's just getting started."

Stepping out of the greenhouse, she blinked against the bright winter light, pulled her hat low, and examined the shiny black SUV idling in the yard. The vehicle's doors remained closed.

Claire peeked through the farmhouse's front curtains.

Eliza shook her head.

"That's the Warlys' vehicle." Julien hooked his thumbs in his belt loops.

"The least they could do is cut the engine." She wrinkled her nose. "Their exhaust is fouling my air."

"Maybe they're too scared to get out."

Liking the idea of big city property developers warming their hands and rehearsing their plans, she grinned. "I'm not a scary person."

He laughed. "You've had me shaking in my boots

since I got here."

She glanced at his expensive leather boots. "I doubt it."

The SUV driver's side door opened, and a man in ironed jeans and a pressed shirt climbed out of the vehicle. He glanced at Julien.

The man turned his bright white smile on her. *At least Mr. Warly is a quick study.* She folded her arms, faced the developers, and took a deep breath. "Can I help you?"

"Are you Mrs. Edwards?"

She nodded.

The man walked closer, extending a hand. "Steven Warly. It's a pleasure to meet you. Hartley Farms is gorgeous, even in the dead of winter." He tipped his head and winked. "As are you."

Julien whistled, the sound low and mocking. "Smooth."

His Southern drawl imbued the word with warnings and menace, but she wondered if Warly noted the threat.

He cleared his throat. "Mr. Kroger."

Julien smiled. "Done your homework this time?"

"Excuse me?" Warly swallowed.

"The last time we spoke, I don't believe I gave you my name."

Eliza grinned. Warly's tight, dismissive smile spoke volumes.

The passenger SUV door opened, and a woman in a metallic pink puffer jacket and fur-trimmed boots climbed down from the seat. Her expensive blonde highlights and shimmering lipstick set off her uniform tan, like a Barbie from the late 1990s.

Warly beamed. "This is my wife, Nicole."

Nicole scampered toward the group.

Eliza wondered if her jeans were too tight, but she nodded at the woman and accepted her perky handshake.

"Why don't we go inside?" Warly gestured toward the farmhouse.

"How about not?" Ignoring Claire's teachings on hospitality, she crossed her arms. "I understand you expressed an interest in purchasing Hartley Farms. Unfortunately for you, the farm is not for sale."

Warly cocked his head. "Did Mr. Kroger present our offer?"

"Your offer doesn't matter," she said.

"Ms. Edwards, I hope you understand I have nothing but admiration for what you've accomplished on your own. Nicole and I admire the beautiful setting." Scanning the trees by the river, he smiled and faced her. "We want to relieve you of your daily burdens, but I promise we'll continue the authenticity of this haven as our private residence."

"Mr. Warly, this is my private residence." She ground out the words.

Nicole cradled her stomach. "But we're expecting!"

"Congratulations." She kept her gaze on Warly.

The man rocked back on his heels.

He looks as pleased as a banker on bonus day, but I've had enough of these pretenses. Removing her hat, she scratched her head like she had a hard time making two plus two equal four. "Sir, how many children are you expecting?"

Julien laughed.

"Excuse me?" Warly asked.

"Smith Specialty Potatoes comprises more than a thousand acres. I understand you're interested in raising your children there as well."

The developers glanced at each other.

"Surely the neighboring farm can meet your... aspirations for a large family."

Nicole rolled her eyes. "That farm's flat and shapeless. We need your trees."

She nodded. *Leave it to the woman to be a straight shooter.* "Ms. Warly, my answer remains the same. I don't want to see a housing development next door to my flower farm, but the Smith family has every right to manage their assets as they see fit. Hartley Farms is not for sale. I'll plant a hedge and ignore the suburban paradise next door."

Warly narrowed his gaze. "One million."

"Not for sale." She turned her back on the power couple. "Have a good day."

Warly cleared his throat. "We can make your life very difficult."

She paused and looked over her shoulder.

Julien stepped toward the man.

She reached out and touched his arm. The vibrations of his tightly coiled muscles reassured her, but so did his restraint. *Watching him go head to head with Warly might be fun, but Skye's probably peeking through the curtains. She does not need to see Julien deck the over-starched developer.* She faced Warly. "Excuse me?"

"You access your farm through a servitude across the Smith spread. I'm about to own the Smith spread. I will move the servitude. I will make your point of access so convoluted and time-consuming that your business logistics become a nightmare. The farm will fold, and you'll lose everything."

She felt her heartbeat accelerate. "That doesn't seem legal."

Nicole smiled. "Statutes allow property owners to move a servitude."

She glanced at the frosted-pink woman. "I appreciate your interest in abiding by the law. I'll phone my lawyer and give him a head's up about that threat." She cleared her throat. "Please leave. You're trespassing."

"We'll make your land the center of a community park." Nicole spread wide her arms. "The trees and the river access will be a beautiful backdrop for the community center and the organic gardens. Imagine a playground and a walking trail right next to the kale. Kale?" She dropped her arms and raised her eyebrows. "The park will be lovely. Maybe you could stay on and help run the facility on a salary?"

She kicked the dirt. *I'd rather grow potatoes.* Looking up, she exhaled. "Ms. Warly, that's a pretty picture, but it won't be on my land."

The woman rolled her eyes and picked at her manicure. "Too bad your father didn't hold onto more of the land."

She narrowed her gaze. "Well, that's true. He made a series of mistakes, but he left me first right of refusal and the option to buy back the land he sold."

The two developers stared at each other.

She watched their artificially smooth faces struggle to frown. "Oh, did your city attorney fail to mention that? Go read the old purchase contracts. The tract is a series of parcels. My father made the same mistakes year after year. Until I decline the right to exercise my options, Smith can't enter into formal agreements with you."

Nicole sneered. "You don't have the money."

"No, but right now you're high on my spite list." Determination emboldened her. "I have a dozen business plans to implement, my husband's life insurance payout, and I'm willing to use the land I have as collateral. Maybe I should chip away at your little dream to claim my own."

Warly cleared his throat. "Litigation can be very time consuming and expensive. You wouldn't want to tie up your resources in a prolonged legal battle."

A flock of geese rose from the field and exchanged calls. She donned her hat. "Is that another threat? I can't keep count."

"No, it's a promise." Warly cleared his throat. "I'm giving you a graceful exit. A pretty lady like you could re-establish herself in Seattle in no time. We'll have lots of publicity events in the future. There will be big media spreads in local publications, VIP meet and greets and open houses. I could promise you exclusive rights to the floral arrangements. An association with my company would be a big PR boost for your business."

She rolled her eyes. "I don't need a boost."

"Don't you?" He sneered. "Seems like your public reviews have gone downhill."

"And you wouldn't know anything about that?" she asked.

The man raised his eyebrows. "Pinning down anonymous reviews is difficult."

"I have a very clear impression of how you do business. I'll spread the word in Mount Vernon." She pointed toward the gate. "In the meantime, get off my land, or I will call the sheriff."

The developer opened his mouth.

Julien took a step forward. "Ms. Edwards said it's time to go."

Nicole sighed and stomped her foot. "Come on, Steven. We don't have time for this shit." Turning, she pranced to the idling SUV.

"Better listen to your missus." Julien smiled.

The developer glanced at Julien's injured leg and raised his eyebrows.

"Oh, you'd be surprised what I can do with one leg."

She stifled her laughter, but the tension and adrenaline of the encounter weakened her reserves. The sound slipped out, and she clapped a hand over her mouth.

Julien winked.

Pulling down her hat, she returned to the propagation greenhouse. *I trust Julien to stand his ground.* Within minutes, she heard the SUV retreat on the gravel drive and released the tension in her shoulders. Each of Warly's threats hit home, and her show of bravado consumed everything she had, but Julien's steadfast support bolstered her courage. *I faced Warly once, and I can do it again.*

Chapter Fourteen

Julien stood in the driveway, watching the SUV depart with unnecessary speed. *We'll see how long your dreams of ownership last.* He returned to the greenhouse. "They're gone."

Eliza looked up and met his gaze. "Thank you."

The fine sheen of sweat on her forehead and her quick glances toward the driveway raised a flag of protectiveness he thought he buried. He considered what to add to his report to soothe her nerves. *I'm proud of you for staring them down? I know a lot of men and women who would have buckled under that pressure?*

Skye bounded into the warm space. "Who was that? She was pretty!"

Eliza rubbed her temples. "Honey, not all that glitters is gold. Or pink."

"Can I have a jacket like that?" Skye widened her gaze. "But with feathers?"

Eliza dropped into a crouch and tugged the edge of her daughter's dark purple pea coat. "I think yours is warmer," she said. "Let me check. Are you warm and cozy?"

Skye nuzzled into the hollow below Eliza's chin, pressing a wet kiss against her neck. "I could be cozy in pink too."

Laughing, she hugged her daughter. "You're

growing big and strong. Next year, when you're seven years old, we'll buy a pink coat."

"Can I have pink boots too?"

She tapped Skye's footwear. Pink and purple unicorns covered the hand-lasted rubber. "I'm not sure that company makes pinker boots."

"More pink. Pretty please?"

She ruffled Skye's hair and stood. "You're silly, Sweet Pea."

Realizing he stared, he shook his head. Turning his gaze to the pile of irrigation parts, he busied his hands to disguise his thoughts. *She's lean and committed to local blooms, but if it made Skye happy, she would dress her in mountains of pink lace. I can't imagine Caroline carrying on with that devotion.* He picked up a dense tangle of parts. *Hell, maybe I'm not giving Caroline enough credit. Don't all women love pink?* He thought of the arrangements in Eliza's book and the poem of the winter rose. *Eliza loves every hue.*

Skye picked up and discarded a series of irrigation parts.

"Where's Granny?" Eliza asked.

"On the phone. She sent me outside to play."

Eliza partitioned a pile of tubing and handed it to the girl.

Occupied by the puzzle, Skye sang a nonsense song.

She seems to have no problem with Skye's free-range tendencies. Given her recent visitors, I'm surprised she's not keeping the girl close at hand.

Five minutes later, Skye whined and ignored the list of chores Eliza proposed.

Eliza put her hands on her hips and inhaled. "Do

you want to make a present for Granny?"

"Yes!" Skye's fist shot into the air.

"Let's go to the barn for seeds and pretty tulle. You can tie up little sachets of flower seeds, and Granny can give them to her friends."

Skye planted her feet. "What about Julien?"

"He's working."

The girl frowned.

"He can help us pick the colors." She glanced at the door and bit her lip. "I like the company."

Realizing how much the Warlys' threats fazed her, he put down the irrigation components and followed the pair out of the greenhouse. *She's skittish as a horse. I don't mind being the protection if that puts her at ease.* A text message from Brandon slowed his progress.

Finally entering the barn, he winced at the sound of Eliza and the teenage assistants fawning over Skye. Discarded centerpieces stood sentinel on the worktable. The trio of chattering magpies ignored him, and Skye beamed. Keeping one ear trained on the ambient noise, he leaned against a sturdy wooden post and stood guard.

Eliza pulled out seed bins, tulle, and ribbon. "How many sachets should we make?"

"Like fifteen million," Skye said.

Laughing, Michelle handed her boss a pair of scissors. She glanced at him. "Who came by to visit?"

He jerked his head toward Eliza and ignored the question.

"The brand new black SUV?" Michelle asked.

Skye put down her project supplies. "The pink lady wants to buy our farm."

He grinned. *So she has been listening.*

Michelle pumped a fist in the air. "Maybe we'll get a coffee shop."

"Aren't there like ten of them in Mount Vernon?" Serah asked.

Michelle shook her head. "They're all scattered around I-5."

"Skagit County has other strengths." Eliza braced her hands on the worktable. "We don't need fast-casual on every corner."

"Like fast food?" Serah asked.

Frowning, Eliza left the table and stared at the wall of ribbon spools. She pulled down a gauzy, light pink ribbon and snipped off a length. "Yeah. Whatever."

Serah fluffed the arrangements. "An uptick in traffic would be good for a florist business. I mean, for any business."

Eliza turned from the wall and gestured toward the glass vases and circles of green florist foam spread across the table. "Why do people keep telling me what would be good for my business? We're making it work." She frowned and rubbed the ribbon between her fingers. "We won't finish the wedding arrangements unless we put in the hours."

Serah turned an arrangement. "We'll be done by the end of the day."

Looking up, she met his gaze. "Great. Let's get to work."

He shrugged and turned to leave. *You're the boss.*

"I'm sorry," Eliza said to her assistants. "I'm figuring out how to manage everything that's happening. We'll deliver Saturday morning. Are you both available to help with deliveries?"

"I have plans on Saturday," Michelle said. "It's

Valentine's Day."

Eliza raised her eyebrows. "I'm aware of that fact."

He heard the tension in her voice, stopped walking, and turned to intervene.

Swallowing, Michelle glanced at him. "What about enlisting your new foreman?"

"All four of us can fit in the truck," Eliza said.

"Me, too." Skye jumped in place. "I want to go too!"

"Not this time, Sweet Pea. You get to stay with Granny." She handed the sachet materials to her daughter. "Come on, let's go back to the greenhouse with Julien."

Skye held up a spool. "Pink tulle!"

"And Salmon. Coral. Dusty Rose."

Skye chanted the names of the colors and skipped past him toward the greenhouse.

He followed suit with Eliza by his side and helped her make space on the card table. "This arrangement is quite an array of... pink."

Eliza exhaled. "We aim to please."

He grinned.

Ignoring the joke, she showed Skye how to cut out neat squares of netting, place seeds in the center of the fabric, and tie the bag with a piece of ribbon. "Julien and I can help you with the bows."

"All thumbs," he said.

Eliza looked up.

He winked and watched a slow smile warm her features.

She cleared her throat and guided Skye's hands.

That's my girl.

"Okay, I can help you with the bows while Julien

wrestles the irrigation equipment. He seems to have a knack for solving problems."

Skye clapped and went to work. She cut fabric and counted out twenty seeds for the first sachet, her mouth forming each number.

Walking toward the door, he paused and looked at Eliza and her daughter laying out the craft supplies. "Seeds can be big business. Have you given any thought to selling your favorite varietals?"

Eliza kept her head down. "I heard you last night, Julien."

"Well, I'm glad I made an impact."

Looking up, she met his gaze. "Later?"

He winked. "You're the boss."

Sighing, she picked up a handful of seeds and let the material run through her fingers. "Flowers aren't cut and dry like vegetables. Cultivating interesting blooms requires art and science."

"Of course it does." He researched local production over his morning coffee. Six vegetable seed companies maintained headquarters in Skagit County. *Cabbage, table beets, and spinach seeds can't be any different than petunias*—he swallowed—*or fluffy scabiosa.*

"I leave flowers on the best-producing plants. When the blooms fade at the close of the season, I cut off the pods or seed heads and store them in a paper collection bag. By trading with the collective and local growers, I've built up a personal collection."

He cocked his head. "That's a manual process."

She nodded. "On the other hand, you're right."

"Always nice to hear."

She rolled her eyes. "The tulips, narcissus, and spring-flowering bulbs went live in September, and they sold out in one day."

Scratching his thumbnail, he hid a grin. *My mama taught me to let people find their way home. Sure as hell, she wasn't talking about me.* He looked up. "So if you wanted to expand your commercial presence, the sales infrastructure exists. Keep you-know-who entertained in the courts and start with a couple of varietals. Seed production could help expand your business, provide financial stability, and reclaim the land you want."

Skye stopped singing an off-key cartoon ballad. "What land?"

Eliza blew her hair from her eyes. "A perfect solution, but I have my hands full. Are you sticking around to manage these operations?"

He scratched his chin. "How much can go wrong with little bags of seeds? Hire a few more high school students to fill orders and to drop packages in the mail."

"Oh, why didn't I think of that?" She put down the tulle. "Let's see. I need pickers, separators, and processors. I can't keep commercial quantities of seeds in my kitchen refrigerator, so I need proper temperature and humidity storage. Have you ever run a seed germination test? Nobody buys commercial seeds without the results. Last winter, I had an outbreak of downy mildew and lost over fifty flats, which was about 13,000 plants."

He swallowed. "That's a lot?"

"Around one dollar per stem. You don't have to be good at math to calculate the loss."

A flock of geese flew overhead, clacking and calling. In the ensuing silence, the eagle's high-pitched whistle pierced the air. Looking up, he saw the silhouette of the bird pass over the greenhouse. *Ok, so a few logistical problems exist, but I can manage them.*

"My chickens!" Skye ran outside.

Eliza looked at the door.

He waited to see if she would finish the work at hand or trail her daughter.

She picked up the tubing.

"You named challenges," he said, "but solutions to these problems exist. Give me another reason you shouldn't leverage your reputation and expand into the seed business."

She exhaled. "I don't know if I can supply blooms and seeds in sufficient quantities to meet commercial demands. If I advertise new products and fail to deliver them, I'll harm my existing business. I appreciate the suggestion, but the idea feels too risky right now. You're enough to handle."

"Then I'll leave."

She blew her hair out of her eyes. "Julien, that was a joke."

He dropped a load of fittings into a plastic bag and labeled the bag. "Expansion fields would allow you to risk a larger planting and sell the seeds the following year. You'd be selling a known product."

"Tastes are fickle. I spend hours keeping my eye on blogs and industry chatter."

"Be the taste-maker." He captured her hand and rubbed the sensitive flesh of her palm to still her uneasiness. "Then set up pre-orders or a futures market. The Dutch tried it."

She pulled free her hand. "The Dutch market collapsed in the seventeenth century."

He tucked his hands in his pockets. "As I

understand it, the tulip market didn't collapse. The Dutch parliament turned the futures contracts into options and made the purchase contracts much more favorable for the buyers."

She blinked. "How do you know all that?"

"Darlin', the Internet made it to Louisiana."

She rolled her eyes. "You should have gone to business school."

"Agreed. I'll help you write up the plan."

She shook her head. "I want to sell flowers, bring people joy, and preserve my land. What if the new fields don't sprout? What if I'm running tight margins and fighting the bank over a mortgage payment that's draining my reserves?"

He shrugged. "Then you default."

"And ruin the shreds of my reputation." She shook her head. "If only life were that easy."

Bracing his hands on the table, he swore. "As God is my witness, Scarlett O'Hara. If you don't take this risk, what happens?" He jabbed the wood. "You spend the rest of your life driving circles around Warly-town? You regret the chance you never…"

An ear-piercing scream split the air.

Bolting from the greenhouse, he scanned the winter wonderland and spotted Serah and Michelle clustered near Skye.

As Eliza outpaced him, her hat flew off and landed on the frozen ground. Parting the group, she folded her daughter in her arms and surreptitiously inspected the child for injuries. "What happened? Are you hurt?"

"Luke dropped off Julien's motorcycle while you guys were in Seattle," Serah said.

The child's sobs intensified.

"I covered it with a tarp, but Skye must have pulled off the cover and seen the bike. When we heard her scream, we ran out and found her curled up in a ball."

Eliza cradled her child. "It is okay, Sweet Pea. It's not daddy's motorcycle."

"But. But." Skye shuddered. "But it's Julien's motorcycle."

"I know, love." She turned to her assistants. "Please, go get Claire."

Both sisters nodded and hurried toward the main house.

Lingering at the periphery of the encounter, he stepped forward and stopped, unsure of the best way to approach the pair. *What does Eliza want me to do?*

"Look, sweetie. Julien's right there." She beckoned him closer. "He's okay."

Skye widened her bright blue eyes.

He crouched on his good knee. "I'm still here."

She nodded.

Her movements were as slow and timid as a mouse. He tucked her pale braid behind her ear. "You don't like my old motorcycle?"

Lip pouting, she shook her head.

"Your daddy was in a motorcycle accident?"

"He died!"

Her plaintive wail almost broke his heart. "I know, Skye. I'm so sorry. I didn't know Mr. Luke was bringing my motorcycle to the farm. Would it help you if I covered it up?"

Nodding, she wiped her tears.

He exhaled and met Eliza's gaze. "I'm sorry."

She looked away. "I should have known better."

Claire came running to the barn.

The assistants trailed her, and the front door flapped in the cold, winter wind.

The woman glared at him and wrapped her good arm around her granddaughter. "Oh! Sweet Pea! What a scare."

He crossed his arms. *Indeed. A little more pressure and I might have broken Skye's spirit for good.* He surveyed the crowd of adults focused on the child. *It might take a village, but for better or for worse, they have one.* Realizing he was crouched in the middle of the village square, he stood. *Shit, what am I doing here?*

Claire rubbed her granddaughter's back. "Come inside the house, Sweet Pea. I have fresh, hot cookies."

Skye nodded, leaned on her grandmother, and followed her toward the farmhouse.

Eliza and the assistants remained in the yard.

Left to his devices, he inspected his motorcycle and threw the tarp back over it. He returned to the group and found Eliza interrogating her two assistants.

"Were either of you here when Luke dropped off the motorcycle?" she asked.

Serah looked at her sister.

Michelle shrugged.

"We thought you knew it was here," Serah said.

Eliza put her hands on her hips. "How would I have known that?"

She frowned. "Claire told us to watch out for the delivery."

Julien whistled. *Damn, girl, never throw your opponent's mama under the bus.*

Eliza stared at the farmhouse.

Leaning against the side of the barn, the indistinct

shape of the motorcycle looked like more than a coincidence. He cleared his throat. "Convenient day to bake cookies."

"Claire doesn't like you," Eliza said.

"Ya think?"

"I'm sorry." Serah rubbed her forehead. "Did we do something wrong? Were we supposed to call you?"

Eliza closed her eyes and pinched her lips. Exhaling, she looked at the teenagers. "No, please go work on the centerpieces. I appreciate your help with Skye." She swallowed. "I know how much she enjoys her time with you."

The sisters looked at each other, nodded, and left.

Hooking a thumb in his pocket, he stood next to Eliza and waited.

She picked up her hat and brushed off the dust. "I'll deal with Claire later, but first things first. I need to make another appointment with Skye's therapist. That motorcycle might have been enough to trigger her nightmares."

"What do you think the therapist will say?"

"That we can't isolate her from society. That she's bound to see another motorcycle"—she looked at him—"This bike belonging to you didn't help matters."

"Anyone's bike could have set her off." The words felt hollow, but he understood Eliza's fears and reached for the distance of a temporary visitor. Then he recalled Skye's tear-stained face. "How much does Skye know about what happened to your husband?"

Eliza looked at the distant mountains. "Very little. He crashed his bike, and her world changed in an instant. That's all she needs to know."

He nodded. *But what about you? What ghosts are*

you carrying? "Was it quick?"

She shook her head. "Skye won't be the only one with nightmares tonight. Erik never should have been on the road." She sighed. "The weather was beautiful. Erik and his friend, Devon, stopped to admire the views of Mount Shuksan. They ate lunch overlooking Mount Baker. The peak is a thermally active crater, like Mount Saint Helens. Erik always said the peak reminded him of his home near Beerenberg. He appreciated the latent energy lurking beneath the snow-covered peaks, like a boogeyman, waiting to pounce."

"Your ex liked to be put in his place?"

She smiled. "No. He liked the idea of a stronger force waiting somewhere out there."

Julien shook his head. *Or did he like to keep the stronger force locked up in the kitchen? Does a fairy tale become a nightmare when it jails you in a cell?* He cleared his throat and saved his arguments for another day. "It must be quite a view."

"The view is breathtaking, but Erik never anticipated the mountain would be the last thing he saw. His friend, Devon, lost control on a turn, flipped his motorcycle, and landed against a side embankment. Erik hit the downed bike and landed next to his friend."

"They both survived the initial collision?"

She nodded and stared at the distant mountains. "They had on all the right protective gear, but Erik hit the bank hard and injured his spine. By the time the police contacted me, emergency services had flown him to the trauma center in Bellingham." She turned and faced him. "I sat by his side until he died."

"I can't imagine," he said.

She stamped her boots in the cold air. "I'm proud

he was an organ donor, but the medical staff swarmed the room and ushered me out. I had so much left to say."

"They didn't give you time to say goodbye?"

"What's the point?" She shook her head and rubbed her arms. "His corneas went to a mother in Spokane. His heart saved a man who lingered on the transplant list for three years. I was still crying when the hospital staff flew his lungs to California and prolonged the life of a man with cystic fibrosis."

He pulled free her hand and linked their fingers. "Most silver linings come with a hint of tarnish."

She stared at their hands. "Dying was never part of our plan, but I wish it had been even quicker. I wish he had never suffered." She looked up.

Her eyes were dry and clear.

"Julien, I told him to leave for the day. We'd been fighting about the farm, and we wanted to go in different directions. He had a habit of making decisions on his own, but then people deferred to those decisions. I felt like I was losing my place on my home turf, and I didn't want to bury myself in the kitchen. Why didn't they give me time to apologize for making him go?"

"You told him to take the trip?"

Nodding, she bit her lip.

He brushed her hair out of her face and focused on her jade green eyes. *You're not the villain or the victim of this story. I've never met a stronger or more capable woman than the one who's keeping me at arm's length.* "Did he get on the bike?"

She sighed.

"Did he hold down the clutch lever and push the start button?"

She blinked. "I guess, but..."

"Then you didn't make the man do anything. I'm sure he fully intended to come back after you'd both cooled off. I can't apologize for living through my accident, and you can't let survivor's guilt eat you up."

She pulled free her hand and wiped away a tear.

"Nobody should have to apologize for living," he said. "Is this the reason you keep telling me to walk the line? You're worried about Skye, but you're worried about pushing me away?"

"Sometimes I'm just"—she inhaled—"too much for people. I don't know if I can pick up the pieces again after you leave."

The specter of his departure never felt less certain. "You need to separate your decisions, Eliza. I have no interest in taking control of your operations, but I want you to consider which one of those pretty, rolled-up plans will help you expand."

"Why?"

Her furrowed brows almost looked cute. He raked a hand through his hair. "So you're not so stressed out? So I can leave you in a better place than I found you?"

"Sticking to the operations I know I can control feels so much easier."

He wiped the tears from her cheeks. "You're making excuses." He felt her stiffen, but he pulled her close and wrapped his arms around her slender frame. "I understand your fears, but you're strong. Don't let your fears or your memories shackle you from living. I don't know what I'm doing here, but I'll feel a hell of a lot better about the risks if we agree to take it day by day."

She settled against his chest. "I can do that."

Dropping his head, he pressed a soft kiss against her hair. *How long can I do what's best for her and ignore what I need?*

She looked up, her eyes reflecting the winter light.

He stroked her cheek and considered the purple shadows below her eyes. *You're so beautiful, even when you're doing your best to hide your wounded pride.* Pressing his chapped lips against hers, he felt the warmth of her kiss and the salty sting of her tears. "What do you want me to do with the bike?"

"Get rid of it."

The stark command stole his breath. "Eliza, that's my only ticket off the farm."

She closed her eyes, and the wind swallowed her sigh. "Of course it is." Stepping back, she brushed off her clothes and righted her hat.

He watched her collect the shards of her pride. Without her warm embrace, his body cooled, and he hated the absence. Swearing, he closed the distance. The hard stop pained him, but he held onto the lifeline. "I can take the motorcycle to the sapling greenhouse and make sure it's out of sight."

"That would be fine." She pulled her hat low and kicked the gravel. Eddies of dust drifted along the drive. "Do whatever you see fit, as long as Skye doesn't see it." She entered the greenhouse, and the hinges groaned in the wind.

He made a note to oil the hinges, but the soft, dusty panes of the structure swallowed her silhouette. Staring at the ground, he convinced himself he enjoyed their connection, but amid the bright lights of the hardware shop, he had overreacted to a woman in need. *I promised her hard work and honesty. What did she promise me in return? A fair wage. Nobody said anything about emotions and regrets.* The wind cut through his jacket. He shook his head. *To make the situation easier, I should walk away first.*

Chapter Fifteen

By twilight, Eliza's boots felt heavy. She climbed the farmhouse steps, plopped her hat on the porch bench, and sat to remove her leather tool belt. The boots came last. She stared at the worn leather and wondered how many days she had before the seams ripped.

Claire cracked open the front door and peered at the farm buildings. "Is he gone yet?"

"Nope." She hung her head and avoided her mother's gaze. *If today's a day for big feelings, I'm mad enough to spit, but I'm too exhausted to scream.* "Try harder next time."

"A decent man would take stock of the situation and hit the road."

She raised her head. "Who gets to roll out the welcome mat, Mom?"

Claire pursed her lips. "Your daddy made sure the farm belongs to you."

"Then let me run the staff." She stood. "And let me decide when to fold."

"Is this how you intend to *run the staff*? What will your daughter think?"

She widened her gaze and held a hand to her chest. "Who called Luke and asked him to deliver the motorcycle? Who made sure a plate of fresh cookies waited to soothe Skye's pain? You want to say something to me?" She tapped her chest and raised her eyebrows. "Say it. Don't use Skye as an intermediary."

Her mother stared. "He will leave the two of you heartbroken."

"I doubt it," she said. "He made his position clear from the start. If you've already locked away your heart, nobody can break it."

Claire frowned.

Do you think we'll spend our last days together? Bitter and alone? She sighed. *I don't want that fate for either of us.*

"Keep him focused on the repairs. He doesn't need to spend so much time with Skye."

Eliza rolled her shoulders and cupped her chin, wondering how to soften the conversation without letting her mother off the hook. "One visit to Seattle is hardly *time*. Skye's used to people coming and going during the summer months. I can't screen a man out of my life because she likes being around him."

"She likes everyone." Claire dropped her chin. "That doesn't mean everyone should spend the night."

She rubbed her eyebrows. "That's ripe. You and dad built the cottage for a reason. Should I increase Julien's salary and ask him to bunk in town?" Dropping her hand, she met her mother's gaze. "We'll be SOL when summer comes, and we can't afford to pay market rates or offer room and board."

Claire opened her mouth.

To halt the argument, she raised her hand. "Please stop undermining me. I know you want me to move to town, but picking on Julien won't help. The things he and I do behind closed doors have no impact on my life choices."

Claire rolled her eyes. "You're fooling yourself."

Am I? She swallowed. "I can't say thank you enough for being here, but I don't like you much at the moment." She rose. "I don't want you to trigger Skye on purpose. The games aren't fair to her."

Claire clutched her weak arm and pulled her sweater tight against the wind. "She's napping. She'll be over the drama by the time dinner rolls around. I made her favorite meal."

"No, she won't." Her voice cracked, and tears pricked her eyes. "She'll smile and chatter until the lights go off. When loneliness creeps in, she'll cry herself to sleep or creep into my bed. She'll wake up terrified from nightmares she doesn't understand." Knowing she would always be there for Skye, she sighed. "It was a lousy thing to do, Mom. If I didn't know you better, I'd say it was borderline cruel."

Claire bit her lip, her gaze locked on the fallow land. Taking a deep breath, she exhaled and met Eliza's gaze. "I'm sorry. I thought the drama might scare off Julien. Skye should always come first."

She nodded and moved toward the living room.

"The Warlys came by yesterday, too," Claire said.

She froze. "How long did they stay?"

"Maybe five minutes. I told them you weren't home."

"They're persistent."

Claire shook her head. "They think you're vulnerable."

She locked gazes with her mother. Decades of unexpected consequences fortified a shared understanding of life. "It won't work."

Claire raised her eyebrows.

She took a deep breath and squared her shoulders.

"They've got a lot to learn about us." She reached for her sneakers. "I'm going up the road to pick up ice cream. We'll need the treat when we're all up at two in the morning."

"Skye likes mint chocolate chip," Claire said.

She accepted the peace offering. "Nope. She's moved on to strawberry."

Claire blew out her breath. "I can't keep up."

Smiling, she squeezed her mother's hand. "You don't have to worry about all the details, Mom. If you'll trust me, we can work together."

"I want to see my girls in a good place. My relationship with your father led to a lot of heartache and disappointments. I don't want that type of life for you. I don't want you to feel you have to shoulder the worries alone."

"Don't worry about me." She dropped her mother's hand. "I've managed everything life's thrown at me. The upsets hurt, but nobody on this farm is irreplaceable. Gabe left and Julien came along. I'm bending the rules to scratch an itch, but he already told us he's not staying. Other workers will come along."

"That's so unstable."

She smiled, hiding her fears and her agreement behind a brave and defiant facade. *What other choice do I have?* She walked away from everything she held dear and climbed in the old truck. *When do I get to breathe?*

Driving down the county road centered her nerves. Her fuel gauge ran low, but she popped in her hands-free earpiece.

Jessica answered on the third ring. "Hey!"

She kept two hands on the wheel. "Hey. Your

muscari is holding up."

"I worried the blooms would wilt."

She scanned the remnants of snow in the roadside fields. "Not in this weather." She cleared her throat and yielded at an intersection. "You were right about the Warlys."

"That's a pity. They came back?"

"They increased their offer."

"How much?" Jessica's voice hovered above a whisper.

She put on her turn signal and turned at the entrance to Smith Specialty Potatoes. The dirt and gravel access road never felt like a luxury until the Warlys threatened to take it away. Tall brown corn stalks bordered the rows of potatoes. *I barely remember seeing horses in these fields, but Julien's right. If we plan to survive on our terms, I have to figure out a way to fill these fields with flowers.*

"How much was the offer?" Jessica asked.

"One million."

Jessica whistled. "They're serious."

"So am I." She took a deep breath. "Jessica, I don't want to move the barn closer to the highway and let Serah and Michelle run a florist shop. I don't want to play farmer while I sip white wine and drive an ATV wearing a pair of boat shoes. Those are other people's fantasies. That's not who I am."

"I'm sorry. It was a lousy thing to say. You've always been a loyal friend."

She slowed for the gate to Hartley Farms. "Apology accepted. I don't want these property developers to become a lingering issue or to force me to take unnecessary risks. I'll barely have time to think when the weather warms up. I need to make changes, but the changes have to be at my pace."

"So what do you need?"

She smiled at her friend's eagerness to help. "The name of a good contract lawyer."

"You don't have a lawyer? At all?"

"I need a big, scary lawyer. Someone outside of Mount Vernon who doesn't blink at million-dollar valuations. Someone who will intimidate the Smiths and the Warlys into realizing the value of my rights."

"Oh, I know the person. He always orders white bouquets for his office."

"Why?" she asked.

"When people enter his office, he wants them to know two choices exist."

Eliza smiled. "A wedding or a funeral."

"Exactly! You can't go wrong with white."

She rolled her eyes. "No, but you sure as hell can get bored."

Jessica laughed. "So what about the developers?"

She looked at the cluster of buildings and the dense line of trees separating her fields from the Smith family's acreage. Taking a deep breath, she wondered if she could isolate her decisions from the people who beautified the land. "I don't know yet, but doing nothing no longer seems like an option."

Chapter Sixteen

The sun hovered in the late afternoon sky when Julien saw Eliza stop the truck and close the farm gate. He relaxed, feeling the tension in his shoulders release. Her hasty departure left him anxious. He folded the tarp covering his motorcycle and secured the plastic to the seat of the bike. *I should have done this move earlier, but the boss lady expanded my job description to head of security, and those two assistants of hers don't stay still.* He grabbed the handlebars of the motorcycle and prepared to stow the machine out of sight.

Michelle emerged from the barn. "Do you need help?"

He shook his head and pushed the bike forward.

"I feel b-bad." She swallowed. "When you all returned from your day trip, I should have mentioned the delivery."

Glancing at the approaching truck, he wondered if he should stall until Eliza could manage the conversation. *What does Michelle want to say to me?* He put down the kickstand, crossed his arms, and faced the teenager. "By the time we returned, you must have been long gone."

She looked up. "Did Eliza say something? Am I not working enough hours?"

"I assumed you and Serah worked nine to five. If I'm wrong, I apologize. I haven't been onsite long enough to know the rhythm of this place."

The assistant shook her head. "Nothing's been normal since Erik died."

He lifted the kickstand and grabbed the handlebars. "You want to walk with me?"

Michelle nodded.

"He ran a tight ship?" She lingered behind him, frustratingly out of his peripheral vision.

"He treated the farm like a tiny kingdom. I mean, he wanted the land to do well, but he made our life fun with his folklore and magical stories." She jogged to catch up. "Skye adored him."

He imagined younger versions of Michelle and her sister following the man around, their eyes round with puppy love. "And Eliza?"

"She wasn't out here as much. She'd come out to plan arrangements, but if Skye fussed, she would take her back inside to nurse or settle for a nap. I feel like Serah and I worked for him."

Or you're jealous of your pseudo baby sister. "Well, Eliza seems like a fair boss."

Michelle shook her head. "I don't know how two different people stayed married to each other. She has firm opinions on how to run the farm."

"Wouldn't you?"

"Oh yeah. I would love to open a flower shop." She kept pace. "I'd use the collective as a resource, but I would bring in exotics and spice up things. A little more glam from the city, a little less chic field-rose."

He blew out his breath. *Ownership and pride go hand-in-hand. Eliza's vision matters the most on her land.* He scanned the fallow acres waiting for spring. "Those ideas might be winners, but respect Eliza's aesthetic. Learn everything you can from Hartley Farms before you move on."

"Mr. Warly said the same thing."

He swallowed, knowing the covered distance kept the conversation private. "Mr. Warly?"

She cocked her head. "You know, the developer?"

Slowing her words, she took him for a simpleton, but his family perfected the art of drawn-out stories. *I prefer to cut to the chase.* "How do you know him?"

"He stopped by yesterday. I told him Eliza went to Seattle to make deliveries, but he stayed for a few minutes." She smiled. "He liked my sketches."

Great. Let's add pedophile to the list of the man's crimes. "You should tell Eliza when someone visits the farm."

"Sure, but I told Claire." She shrugged. "That's like the same thing, isn't it?"

It isn't. He shook his head and tackled one problem at a time. "What did Claire say?"

"It's a free country. As long as men know the right time to get lost, they can come and go as they please."

He choked back his laugher. *Did the old bird know her lines would travel back to me?* "The next time someone visits the farm unannounced, tell Eliza. She should know."

She rolled her eyes. "Why? The last time I suggested the benefits of having new neighbors, she threw up her hands."

"That's not the help she needs." He adjusted his grip on the bike and listened to the wind rippling the trees at the border of the field. "Focus on Eliza's priorities instead of your opinions. That's what she pays you to do."

"Did I do something wrong?" Michelle lowered her voice. "I don't want her to fire me. I like this job and the designs I'm adding to my portfolio."

"I'm glad to hear it, but if you see the Warlys onsite, they're trespassing, and you should tell Eliza." He cleared his throat. "If she's not here, call the police."

"What if I tell you instead?"

"The farm belongs to Eliza." He sharpened his pitch. "Don't keep secrets from your boss."

She stopped walking. "Eliza would have turned in Gabe."

Looking over his shoulder, he saw Eliza through the truck's dusty windshield. He thought about the ways she humored Skye and deferred to her mother. "Eliza's not black and white. I think she would have given Gabe a chance to set things straight or move on."

Michelle shook her head. "You have a lot to learn."

"I'm not disputing that fact. Go tell her the same things you told me."

"B-but"—Michelle cleared her throat—"can't you tell her?"

He shook his head and left Michelle standing at the edge of the field. Outside the distant greenhouse, he threw the tarp over the bike and peered inside the dusty windows. Nude rose bushes and leafless saplings promised spring greens, but they lacked the glow of Eliza's attention. *The farm belongs to Eliza, but rows of seed flowers would give her the income she needs. Erik pushed her toward a nursery, and look how that turned out. She has to decide what happens next. The only things I can do are stick around and help get her started.* He returned to the drive and spotted Skye standing on the steps of the farmhouse with a chicken under each arm. He approached the girl, as lazy as an old farm hound.

She kept her gaze on the ground.

Lowering his body to the dusty step, he pulled his coat tight against the cold. "My motorcycle gave you a scare. I'm sorry."

Skye took a seat beside him but kept her gaze on the packed dirt. "Do you know when you will die?"

He coughed and slapped his chest. *Maybe I should have studied up on kids.*

She peered at him. "Will Granny Claire die first because she's old?"

"Darlin', I don't know the answers to those questions. Dying's not something most people plan to do. Your daddy didn't plan to die and leave you alone."

"I'm not alone." She released the chickens to peck at her feet. "Everyone on the farm helps take care of me, even you."

He stared, understanding the truth behind her statement. *I wondered if bouncing between Eliza and Claire took a toll, but this kid knows love. Hell, even I care for her, if that matters.* He sighed. *Is this conversation a coping mechanism or a sign of emerging trouble?* Searching for a way to ground the conversation, he thought about the things she enjoyed the most. "You like to believe in magic?"

She scooted to the edge of the step.

He lifted an eyelash from her cheek. "My mama always told me to make a wish on an eyelash and let the wind carry away your pain."

"Where does it go?"

He rubbed his chin. "I dunno."

"Did your wishes ever come true?"

"Some of my wishes came true." He thought of the things he wanted as a boy, like the resources to buy his whims and the freedom to control his world. The simple construct made him smile. *Big dreams for a kid who knows he can always come home. New dreams require a home of their own.*

She stared at the eyelash on his finger. "I wish that no one else in my family will ever die. I know Granny Claire is sick and old people die, but I don't want her to die yet. You either. We could stay here forever and protect the land, like the *nisse*."

He smiled, appreciating the generosity of young hearts. *At least someone cares.* "I can't make any promises about those wishes, but feeling strong and alive is important. Even when you're not sure about life, people like your mom and your Granny can help you make sense of the world. They can help you figure out the things you don't know."

Looking up, she cocked her head. "When you lost your leg, is that what you did? You talked to your mom?"

Ignoring his complicated relationship with his mother, he decided not to correct the girl's statement about the state of his leg. *My leg's not lost, it's gone, and so are those old, generic dreams.* "You know the thing I miss most about my leg?"

"Hopping?"

He laughed. "I haven't attempted hopping yet."

Her nose twitched, and she offered a slow smile. "What?"

"My family grows a plant called sugar cane. We mill it into table sugar that sweetens your cookies and makes pink lemonade." She focused on him with the dedication of a connoisseur. "After we harvest and process the cane, we store refined sugar in big empty barns where it looks like mountains of snow. When I was a kid, I used to slide down those mountains on a piece of cardboard. I'm not sure I should do that anymore, but man, it was fun."

"Because you're not a kid?"

Julien smiled. *At least she's no longer calling me a pirate.* "If I fell, I'd have a hard time saving myself. To avoid looking like a pancake, I take care of myself and minimize my risks." He tapped his head. "I'm getting smarter."

"You could wear a helmet."

"I could," he said.

She frowned. "But you still might end up dead."

"I might, but now I find other fun things to do."

"Like riding your motorcycle?"

He nodded, pleased the word itself was not a trigger. "Lots of people ride motorcycles, climb trees, and take minor risks. Clever people learn to believe in themselves and know their limits."

"Everything dies." She sighed. "The flowers die. The bugs die when Claire squishes them." She stroked the bright plumage of a hen pecking at her feet. "I don't like it when things die."

"You can't avoid death, but you can do a lot of things to avoid it."

Looking up, she nodded. "Like wearing a helmet."

He grinned. "You have two sturdy legs. When you get a little older, I think you could slide down those sugar mountains I mentioned."

She smiled. "We have real mountains."

He looked at the snow-covered ridges. "I want you to climb them, too."

"Would you come with me?"

Glancing down, he saw her hopeful gaze. "I'm willing to try it."

"I'll wait for you." She grinned. "We can take a lot of breaks."

"I would like that." Rising, he brushed the dust from his pants. *Damn, I did well on this little heart-to-heart. I'll be prime uncle material.*

"My therapist read me a book about a dead cat. Do you think the cat in the book will go to heaven or sink into the earth?"

Not so fast. Rubbing his eyes, he considered the benefits of a stiff drink. "What do you think?"

"I don't know." She stood and stretched her arms high above her head. "Maybe in between?"

He nodded. "Tough to know."

Eliza emerged from the doorway and met his gaze.

Her cheeks looked streaked with sweat or dried tears. Torn between the pair, he stood immobilized.

"Go clean up, Sweet Pea. I picked up some strawberry ice cream from the farm stand."

Skye flung her arms around her mother's legs. "Is it all for me?"

She rubbed her daughter's back. "Maybe you could share some of it."

The girl cocked her head and looked at him. "Julien, do you want ice cream right now?"

Eliza laughed and patted her daughter's bottom. "After dinner." She ushered her into the house. "Go get cleaned up."

He cleared his throat. "I didn't mean to get into all

that stuff about death."

"I'm pretty sure the minute you sat, she had you pinned. Kids like to talk about death. Her therapist said the concept is the first big idea Skye's age group grasps."

"Did I say anything wrong?"

She shook her head. "Skye understands her father's body doesn't work anymore. That's what it means to her to be dead. Maybe she looks at you and sees other possibilities, but I don't think answering her questions hurts anything."

Pulling off his baseball cap, he ran a hand through his hair. "So I'm slightly dead? That's not the image of health and vitality I strive to project."

She laughed.

He climbed the steps and rubbed the watermarks from her cheek. "I'm no good at making promises. I can't promise to stay here, and I can't promise to live forever."

Leaning into his touch, she smiled. "One of those promises is easier than the other."

He smiled. "It has nothing to do with you or your beautiful family."

She straightened and pulled back. "So you're still not committed to staying?"

"What if I promised to get you through the spring?" he asked.

Exhaling, she cocked her head. "What if you take life day-by-day and avoid setting limits?"

He shook his head. "I'm damaged goods."

She turned from him. "Why would you say that?"

"A brief history of failure and catastrophe."

Bracing her hands on the railing, she sighed.

"Accidents happen."

He thought of the times his mother prioritized Brandon's ideas and the pain of watching his brother walk down the aisle. Half his brain touted Eliza's loyalty, but the other half acknowledged he barely knew her. "Life has consequences. I don't want to hurt you or Skye."

She cleared her throat. "Well, I can't say you didn't warn me."

"What does that mean?"

She left the railing, unfastened his jacket, and dragged her hands along his stomach.

The cold air and the heat of her touch took away his breath.

"It means I'll use you and let you walk away," she said.

He nodded, struggling to focus on the conversation "And if something better comes along? No hard feelings?"

Her hand dropped lower. "I doubt if that's the way this attraction will end."

"Ridiculous woman." He kissed her in full sight of the farm. She melted beneath his touch, but he tore his mouth from her sweet taste. Shaking his head, he dreaded upsetting their momentum. "You have a problem."

She gripped his jacket. "I've gathered that. Beneath that charm, you're stubborn and hard-headed."

"Point taken, but you have more problems. Warly was here yesterday."

Her gaze sharpened, and she released his jacket. "Claire mentioned the visit."

"Michelle spoke to him."

She frowned. "What would Michelle have to say to the man?"

He shrugged. "When you find out, she's worried you'll fire her."

Rolling her eyes, she sighed. "Only if she keeps changing my designs."

He took a deep breath. "Does she ever make improvements?"

"Sometimes."

She looked like the admission galled her.

Shaking her head, she took his hand and pulled him toward the door. "Come eat dinner with us."

He resisted. "Claire will bring me a dish."

"The food is better hot." She tugged his hand again.

Laughing, he let her momentum pull him forward. "The two of you send out plenty of sparks. I don't want to get caught in the crossfire."

"Oh, I'll be sugar and spice until Skye goes to bed." She smiled. "My mom and I have a few things to iron out, but you can make your escape during story time."

He raised her hand and kissed it. "My mama's nearsighted, but she taught me you get more flies with honey than with vinegar."

Laughing, she dropped his hand, opened the door, and looked over her shoulder. "I'm not here to catch flies, Julien. I'm here to get things done."

Grinning, he crossed the threshold of the farmhouse.

Claire took one look at him and shook her head. "Take off your boots."

Trying not to feel conspicuous, he sat on the couch

and pulled off his left boot.

The occupants of the room remained silent.

Their wordless observations felt eerie, but he had years to adjust to his new normal. Hitching up his right pant leg, he removed his sturdy leather boot from the prosthesis. The technology rested on the shiny, wood floors, alien and at odds with the warmth of the room. Wondering what expressions he would encounter, he took a deep breath and looked up.

Eliza smiled.

The woman has already seen me naked.

Claire nodded.

Well, she got what she wanted. I took off my damn boots in the house.

Skye pointed at the chunk of metal below his knee. "Your leg is green!"

He laughed. "Is that better than a green thumb?"

Eliza folded down her daughter's pointer finger. "Pointing at people is rude. If you have questions about Julien's leg, ask him."

Skye made a beeline for the prosthesis. "How does it feel?"

"Like a padded stick."

Her laughter filled the room. "Cool! Like a peg leg!"

"I'm sorry." Eliza mouthed the apology.

He shrugged.

"How do you get it into the boot? Do you have other shoes?" She bounced in place. "Can you wear flip-flops? I like flip-flops."

She fired off questions without restraint, her sentences running together like the swirl of an ice cream maker. "I've never tried flip-flops. I wore tennis shoes during therapy. Boots are heavier and have a larger heel. When I told my physical therapist I wanted to wear boots, he matched my prosthesis to the shoes."

"My mom has high heels."

Meeting Eliza's gaze, he grinned. "I bet she does."

"Sometimes she lets me wear them," Skye said.

He focused on the girl. "I'm sure you both look good in dancing shoes."

"I can go get them." Skye rushed toward the stairs.

"After dinner," Claire and Eliza said at the same time.

Skye pouted. "You'll make me go to bed after dinner."

Laughing, Eliza crossed her fingers. "I promise you can get the shoes after dinner."

Skye eyed the adults with the suspicion of a cornered cat.

The girl yawned. "I'm hungry."

He made his way to the table and dropped into a seat. "Looks good."

"Roasted root vegetables and homemade lasagna," Claire said.

He stabbed a tender beet and made a show of smiling and savoring it. "Delicious."

Eliza eyed Skye's plate.

The girl pushed a beet in circles, wrinkled her nose, and shoved it in her mouth.

"Eat a few more, Sweet Pea. It'll turn your poop pink."

He choked on his water. *Man, I have a lot to learn.* Lifting lasagna to his mouth, he thought about mentioning the merits of asparagus.

"Pink?" Skye asked.

Eliza winked at her daughter. "Extremely pink. Hot pink."

A knock at the door interrupted the meal.

Eliza put down her napkin and stood. "If that's Warly, I swear I will call the sheriff."

Claire raised her eyebrows. "Maybe he increased his offer."

Skye eyed a beet on her fork.

Scooting his chair closer to the girl, he tugged on her braids. "Warly's uglier than your pigs."

The child widened her gaze and pushed her chair back from the table. "Really?"

He realized he needed a stronger deterrent. "Smells like a dirty chicken."

She squinted. "Chickens are clean!"

Eliza opened the front door and spoke to the backlit visitor. Stepping back, she admitted the guest to the foyer.

He looked up from his conversation and squinted. "Shit."

"Mommy! Julien said a bad word."

Eliza sighed and gestured to the visitor. "This is Brandon, Julien's brother."

Claire rose. "I'll get another plate."

He put down his napkin and stood. "That won't be necessary." Making his way to the foyer, he shook his brother's hand and jerked his chin toward the door. *What are you doing here? Checking up on me? Has something happened to Mom and Dad?*

Brandon eyed the fire in the living room. "You didn't warn me about the cold."

He exhaled. *Nobody's dead.* Grabbing his boots and his hat, he gripped his brother's arm and turned him around. "You didn't ask."

Standing face-to-face on the front porch, he scanned Brandon for signs of wear and tear. The crisp edges of a haircut kept his black hair in line, but the shadow of a beard meant his brother traveled hard. He shook his head at the man's presumptuous decision to show up unannounced. "You're wasting your time."

Brandon rubbed his arms. "Can't we go back inside?"

"Oh? Did you come to visit? Come on. Let's go crack open a few beers and shoot the breeze."

Brandon frowned. "Not exactly."

"I didn't think so." He muttered about the arrogance of older brothers, sat on the step, and pulled on his boots. Grabbing the handrail, he stood and walked down the stairs. "Follow me." After a moment of silence, he heard Brandon comply and smiled. An economy rental car sat in the driveway. He laughed and looked at his brother. "Didn't want to spring for a midsize?"

"What's the point? Shouldn't the rental come with snow tires?"

Shaking his head, he crammed his hat in his back pocket. "Washington is different, but it feels a hell of a lot closer to home than the desert."

Brandon looked at the moonlit mountains. "You're a far cry from a cane field."

"It's still a farm. Same desperation. Different crop."

Turning, Brandon met his gaze. "Is that why you're here? She's desperate?"

He shook his head and opened the front door of the cottage. "With the right help, Eliza's more than capable of running the place. A busybody pushed us together, but she has no problem showing me the exit."

"Maybe you should listen."

I don't want to leave. Opening the fridge, he withdrew Gabe's beer and tossed it to his brother.

Brandon caught the beer and examined the silver can.

The disdain wrinkling his forehead made him laugh, but he watched Brandon pop the tab, sink onto the old couch, and sip the beer.

"Nice place." Brandon waved a hand toward the dark recesses of the cottage.

He shrugged. "It's basic."

"Buy curtains."

Laughing, he leaned against the kitchen counter. "Go home and run your empire."

Brandon rubbed his stubble. "I told you there's plenty of work for the two of us."

"I don't want to take orders from my big brother. You were always Mama's favorite. Now you're Caroline's favorite, too. That combination's a special misery."

Brandon sipped the beer. "You came to the wedding."

"Yeah. Family members do things like that."

Meeting his gaze, Brandon rested the can on his knee. "I didn't think you'd show."

He raised his eyebrows. "I didn't think you'd marry my ex-girlfriend."

Brandon saluted him with the beer. "Is that why you ran away?"

"I didn't run away." He rolled his shoulders and realized how far he had come. "I'm finding myself."

Brandon laughed. "You have a million dollars in the bank, and you're living like a day laborer. I think we lost you."

He crossed his arms. "When did you turn into such a snob?"

"When did you stop chasing tail and holding court 'til three in the morning?"

"When a team of surgeons cut off my goddamn leg." The wind whistled through cracks in the window putty. He shook his head, wondering when he would find time to fix it.

Brandon stood and wandered around the living room. Picking up a magazine, he scanned the cover, rolled his eyes, and tossed the wrinkled paper back on the table. "Losing a leg hasn't stopped you." He met his gaze. "Go scratch an itch in Vegas. It's less complicated."

He smiled. "Tried that. Didn't work."

"And this setup works?"

"For now." He thought of the dormant fields and the woman whose smile and pert ass teased his thoughts from the tedium of manual labor. Days in the south passed when he wondered if he had the willpower to get out of bed. A thousand novelties lured him back to life, but he feared the darkness where the road ended. Eliza acknowledged that fear without mocking it. She gave him the confidence to come to her aid and believe in her dreams. *I thought I needed manicures and blonde hair, but I'm sold on a tight pair of jeans and hardheaded determination.* He thought about the glimpse of a smile hiding beneath her hat or the worn tool belt slung around her hips. Her beauty came through strength and endurance.

"You'll break her heart when you leave," Brandon said.

He shook his head. "She knows I'm not staying past spring." The lie tasted bitter.

"I don't care what excuses you use. When I walked into the house, you were eating dinner with three generations of women."

Gripping the edge of the counter, he shifted his weight. "Claire doesn't even like me."

"And the girl?" Brandon raised his eyebrows.

He smiled. "She thinks I'm a pirate."

Brandon laughed. "You're right. I shouldn't have come. I should have sent your mama."

"She wouldn't have made it past the airport back home." He snorted. "That woman's lived in the same parish her entire life."

"She and Dad talked about one of those riverboat cruises."

He raised his eyebrows. "Good. They should go."

Brandon sat, dropped his head to the back of the couch and stared at the ceiling. "Is that what I have to look forward to? Canned entertainment and a geezer pissing contest?"

"How about raising a family and contributing to the world?" The words tumbled from his mouth before he thought about them. *Those possibilities never felt as appealing as they did right now.*

Brandon turned his head and smiled. "The baby's a boy."

He envisioned a tiny, toddling Brandon ruling the family farm. "Why are you here?"

"To bring you home before you do something stupid."

321

He raised his eyebrows and let the lie settle.

Brandon exhaled. "Fine. I need you to come home."

"Why?" He recognized the truth, but Brandon could run the crews blindfolded.

"I can't sleep, Mama's praying all hours, and Caroline's building a nursery fit for Bonaparte. The rum. The cane. It's too much to handle on my own." He rubbed his hands over his face. "I can't wake up each morning and check my phone, wondering if you've crashed out on the side of a highway or taken too many pain pills in a dingy hotel room."

Shaking his head, he reached for a glass, looked over his shoulder, and met his brother's gaze. "Give me credit, Brandon. I wouldn't risk waking up."

Brandon blinked. "Come home, brother."

He filled the glass with water. "I'm not ready."

"Will you ever be ready?"

Straightening, he walked to the living room, sank into the recliner, and downed the drink. "Probably not." The truth tasted as sweet as the clear, cold water.

"Our family has been on that land since 1789."

He laughed. "You're still there, and things have gotten a hell of a lot better since the 18th century. Life evolved, and you're doing a fine job of keeping up the momentum. You have what you wanted out of life. Enjoy it."

Brandon cocked his head. "Will you ever forgive me for marrying Caroline?"

He set the glass on the table, the knock of glass on wood as sharp as a gunshot. "What kind of woman switches from one brother to another? Doesn't her attitude bother you?"

Brandon cleared his throat. "You never loved her."

"Bullshit." Disgust roiled his stomach, and he closed his eyes. "I gave her everything I had."

"You signed up for twenty-eight-day rotations and left her in a luxury apartment." Brandon's voice rose in defense of his wife. "Don't lecture me about enjoying what I have."

He looked up. "She didn't care when I was home. She spent most of her time at the salon before charity board meetings."

Brandon nodded. "She has a big heart."

He avoided his brother's gaze and stared at the window blinds. *Brandon's blind. Caroline wants prestige and her name in the local paper. I never saw her slogging through a task list for a passionate cause. I never saw her deny herself pleasure for someone else's benefit. Eliza's heart would dwarf her charity endeavors.*

"I didn't realize I had to choose between the two of you," Brandon said.

He met his brother's gaze and released the tension in his jaw. "At least you had the choice. I woke up and had nothing."

"We were all there." Brandon crossed his arms. "You were our priority."

"Yeah." He smiled. "I appreciate what family obligations compelled you to do."

Clearing his throat, Brandon stood. "We can carve up the acreage."

"I can take care of myself, brother. Go back to your kingdom."

"You don't have roots out here. Nothing can stabilize you against a storm."

He considered the unplanted fields and the latent promise of new seeds germinating in the greenhouse. He promised to stay until spring, but the allure of Eliza's strength and beauty eroded his determination. "I've learned to do without levees."

Brandon closed his eyes. "Can I sleep on the couch?"

His brother's tone admitted defeat. "Yep, but you're going home tomorrow."

Brandon sighed. "Caroline told me you wouldn't return."

Laughing, he shook his head. "She always could judge the tide."

Brandon scanned the living room. "Do you love this woman?"

The emotion carried so many implications. *Do I know how to love a woman?* He thought of Eliza's jade-green eyes and the way she tucked her hair behind her ears. The simple gestures were like glimpses of vulnerability beneath the thorns she developed to run this land. Meeting her felt like stumbling into the sunlight, but instead of blinding him, she tempered his impulses with the ethics of growing a steady crop. Working from sunup to sunset, she sacrificed her comfort for the people she loved. Her loyalty gave him hope. Believing she could stand at his side without considering him second best, he met his brother's gaze. "Yes, but I'm not sure I deserve her."

Chapter Seventeen

Eliza awoke before sunrise and longed for Julien's warmth and calming presence. *He's leaving.* She bit her lip, struggling to hold back tears. First light peeked over the mountains, but thick, gray clouds promised snow. Throwing back the covers, she suppressed the memory of his departure, dressed, and made her way to the barn.

The dark windows of the cottage drew her gaze. *He works hard and has a knack for business, but when I'm standing beside him, I feel confident. My feelings for him don't matter. He said spring, but he and his brother probably popped a few beers and booked his flight back to the spooky swamp.*

She let herself into the barn and flipped on the lights. Solitude amplified the sounds of nesting barn animals and the steady hum of the coolers. As sunrise came and went, she corrected arrangements and added blooms to centerpieces. The decisions calmed her nerves. Itemizing the wedding decorations, she checked the stock needed to craft the remaining bouquets. A rose caught her attention. Teasing the petals into a wider bloom, she sighed. *I can do this work alone.*

Skye bounded into the barn wearing her nightclothes, insulated boots, and a half-buttoned pea coat. Her nightgown flapped below the warm outer layer and kept time with her bouncing braids.

Squished flat by a knitted hat with traditional

Norwegian crosses, the braids reminded her to enjoy her blessings. *At least Claire put a hat on her*. She set aside her work and lifted Skye for a hug. "Did you sleep well?"

Rubbing her eyes, Skye nodded. "Mmm-hmm."

Setting the girl on the big worktable, she kissed the top of her head. "No nightmares?"

Skye shook her braids and nuzzled into the warmth of her chest. "Granny told me to tell you she made coffee." She yawned. "She'll make breakfast, too."

She ignored the coffee machine sizzling in the corner. "That's kind."

"And I need to feed the animals and collect the eggs."

Crossing her arms, she nodded. "Yep."

Skye peered through long lashes. "And Julien's probably going home today."

The acknowledgement seared. Closing her eyes for a moment, she forced a smile, removed Skye's hat, and smoothed her bed-tousled braids. "How does that make you feel?"

"Sad." She pouted.

"He's a nice man," she said.

Skye frowned. "He said he would take me hiking."

"And if he doesn't?"

She frowned and stuck out her lip. "Then he's a liar!"

"I don't think he intended to lie. Sometimes people make promises they can't keep." She tugged the girl's braid. "I'll take you hiking, Sweet Pea. I'll always take care of you."

Tilting her head, Skye eyed the arrangements. "Can I stay in the barn all day and help you with the flowers?"

The youthful request deflected the intensity of her promise. Inventorying the remaining work, she shook her head. "Not today. Michelle, Serah, and I have a lot of tasks left. How about helping me plant seeds? I think Granny might make biscuits."

Skye crossed her arms. "I don't want biscuits."

"Muffins?"

"Pancakes." Skye raised her eyebrows.

She nodded. "With blueberries?"

The girl licked her lips and grinned.

Setting out a series of trays, she filled the cells with light-textured potting soil designed to let seeds breathe. Tiny black seeds pooled in her hand. Imagining the sherbet-hued blooms of Iceland poppies, she made a fist. *Julien won't be here to see the blooms.*

Skye poked her fingers into the soil. "What type of seeds?"

"Poppies," she said.

"Like on the bagels?"

She smiled. "Pretty much."

"When do we plant sweet peas for the outdoor tunnel?" Turning to her stomach, she slid off the worktable. "The *nisse* loves the tunnel!"

She ruffled Skye's hair. "I think you love the tunnel too."

The barn doors opened.

Raising her gaze, she prepared to greet Serah and Michelle, but the siblings striding into the barn looked nothing like teenagers. The men moved with similar confidence, but she recognized the quirk of Julien's gait. *Anybody would know they're brothers.*

Brandon stomped his feet and breathed warmth

into his hands. He scanned the interior of the barn and nodded. "Mornin'."

Julien stopped short of the worktable and met her gaze. "You were up early."

She wiped her hands and drew Skye against her chest. *When he says he's leaving, I can act dignified. I owe myself that memory.* Doubting her ability, she released Skye. "Go feed the chickens and pigs. Find your basket and collect the eggs for blueberry pancakes. When you're done, you can help me with the seeds."

Skye stared at Brandon. "The animals aren't hungry yet."

"Unattended chickens get eaten." She raised her eyebrows and hoped the possibility of losing her pets to the stockpot would motivate the girl.

Skye cocked her head. "You're so mean."

Prepared for the tempestuous switch, she smiled. "I'm not mean. I'm your mother." *I'm also doing everything I can to ensure you learn the value of caring for yourself. Right now, that means giving myself space to fail.* She thought of Claire in the hospital. Amid the clinical beeps and scratchy white sheets of the hospital, she issued orders until the pain medication wore off and she needed rest. *Mothers learn when to make a stand.*

Sticking out her tongue, Skye ran toward the soft clucks and rooting sounds of her pets.

She faced the men, prepared to hear their announcement. "Getting an early start?"

"The fish won't wait around for warmth," Brandon said.

Julien opened a storage closet. "I told him you probably don't have any gear lying around."

They're going fishing? Shaking her head at the

absurdity of men, she exhaled and pointed toward a little-used storage closet. "Look in there." Listening to them root through the ancient fly-fishing outfits, she tried not to care about the outcome of their decisions. "How long are you staying?"

Julien poked his head out of the closet. "Brandon's flight is at three."

Closing her eyes, she took a deep breath and waited for the second half of his announcement.

Stepping into the aisle, the men held up waders and compared lengths.

Wouldn't he be packing if he intended to leave? Making plans to ship the bike? She turned toward a flower arrangement and allowed herself to breathe. "When you're in the water, look for clipped adipose fins. You can keep hatchery steelhead, but if you hook a wild fish, catch and release it."

Julien nodded. "Do we need fishing licenses?"

"You also need catch records. Before the fisheries police show up, I'll call Luke's hardware store and get you squared away."

Brandon laughed. "I wouldn't want my baby brother to get arrested."

Julien snorted and glanced at her. "Ask Luke about welding equipment."

Avoiding his gaze, she nodded.

He sat on a bale of hay and slipped on the waders. "I have an enormous advantage. I won't feel the cold."

Brandon laughed and tightened his straps. "Don't over-sell yourself. You'll still come up empty-handed."

Shaking his head, Julien pulled up the thick fabric. "I've seen an eagle hanging around the farm. It's prime fishing ground."

The banter soothed her nerves. She let routine tasks and the brothers' activity convince her the day held promise. "If you clean the fish, you might talk Claire into cooking them."

Julien slapped his brother's back and strode toward the open doors. "Now we're talking."

"Can I come?" Skye popped up from the chicken coop.

"Not this time, Darlin'," Julien said. "First, let me get a feel for the water."

Brandon laughed. "He knows he'll land flat on his face."

She smiled. "I'll take you fishing, Sweet Pea."

"But I want to go with Julien!"

Maybe her blood sugar is low. "Next time, I promise. Come help me with the seeds. You're due for pancakes and syrup."

Nodding, Skye watched Julien and his brother walk toward the river. "It's still not fair."

"Life isn't always fair." She focused on her daughter's needs. *He might not fly out today, but he warned me he's not staying. What does spring mean to a six-year-old?* "What color Sweet Pea blooms do you want to plant?"

Skye turned away from the river. "Pink!"

"What about purples and blues?" she asked.

Skye crossed her arms. "Pink."

"White? Orange? Cream?" The simple pleasure of egging on her daughter gave her reason to smile.

The girl took a deep breath.

She opened a new paper bag and stirred the seeds. "Oh, you're in luck. A whole bag of pink seeds!"

Skye clapped. Twenty minutes later, she went to

the house for breakfast.

Eliza exhaled. *I'm grateful for what I have.*

Serah and Michelle arrived, placed their purses and insulated coffee cups on the work surface, and eyed the arrangements.

"How do they look?" Michelle asked.

"Pretty good. You followed my designs, but I added a few more blooms. We should always try to over-deliver."

Michele frowned. "If money's tight, the bride shouldn't have ordered blush and cream roses."

Have you ever priced a mid-winter succulent? Instead of goading the teenager, she focused on praising her and her sister. "You two did a good job mixing in the filler. The tulips, hydrangea, and freesia add bulk."

Michelle turned an arrangement and cocked her head. "We could try more greenery."

Nodding, Eliza reached for a stem. "She specifically asked for Dusty Miller. She wants a rustic, pretty style."

Michelle grimaced. "People have different definitions of 'pretty'."

Swallowing, Serah reached for the Dusty Miller's downy leaves.

Eliza nodded. "That's true, but the woman walking down the aisle gets the final say."

Michelle crossed her arms. "Some people enjoy collaboration."

She looked up, unsurprised to encounter such resistance. "Some people enjoy repeat business."

The teenagers looked at each other.

She spread her fingers against the worn wood. "I understand Mr. Warly paid a visit."

331

Michelle swallowed.

Serah raised her eyebrows, turned from her sister, and pulled an incomplete arrangement from the cooler.

"Please don't speak to Warly again," Eliza said.

Michelle cocked her head. "This is a free country."

"That's true, but you're working on my farm. I don't like him or his plans for Skagit County. He understands he's unwelcome here, and any additional visits mean he's trespassing."

She wrinkled her nose. "You and Julien sound like a pair of parrots."

"Well, at least someone has my back."

Serah cleared her throat. "I saw Julien head down to the river with another man."

"His brother." She appreciated the teenager's peace offering. "They're fishing before Brandon returns to Louisiana."

Michelle snorted. "That's a bit of a double standard. Isn't he an employee?"

"As soon as you clock out, you're welcome to go fishing." She raised her head and met the teenager's gaze. *Challenging authority might be a teenage tradition, but she never felt the assault before her charges grew up.*

Michelle lifted a bloom and wrinkled her nose. "Fishing's the last thing I want to do."

"Good, then let's work on the bouquets." She struggled to suppress a grin.

The air warmed, and morning sunlight gave way to the brilliance of midday. Considering lunch, she scanned the path to the river and spied Julien and his brother carrying a haul of steelhead. She remembered her father cresting the edge of the levee with a string of silver-backed salmon, and her gaze softened. "Daddy loved to fish." Pulling a wide tarp from the closet, she unfurled the fabric on the ground outside the barn.

The men laid their catch on the tarp.

Serah came outside and raised her phone. "Let's take a picture in front of the barn."

The men stood shoulder-to-shoulder and grinned.

"Good catch." She set up a folding table. "Either of you take a drink?"

Gazes on Serah, they shook their heads and puffed out their chests.

"Well, I'm impressed."

Julien met her gaze and smiled.

Skye tumbled from the farmhouse and inspected the catch. "Why's this one different? Why did you cut that? Do they have more than one heart?" She invaded the men's personal space and peered at a gutted fish. "Ew. Are those eggs?"

Answering her questions, they discarded the offal in a plastic bucket.

A splash of blood landed near Skye's boots, and she jumped back.

"Do you want to hold an eyeball?" Julien offered the sphere on his palm.

"No."

He tossed the eye in a bucket and held up the butchered, bloody end of a fish. "The tail?"

"No!" she screamed and covered her eyes.

He grinned. "Okay. You can man the hose."

From the spool on the side of the barn, Skye tugged free coils of hose.

Eliza surveyed the catch. "You did well."

Brandon nodded. "Thanks for the gear and the

hospitality.

"You're welcome," she said. "Will you stay for lunch?"

He eyed the fish fillets.

Longing whitened his lips, and Eliza considered sweetening the offer.

He shook his head and clapped Julien on the back. "No, ma'am. I'm leaving this mess in your hands."

She scanned the gutted fish and Julien's smile. He looked proud of his catch, but his grin warmed her heart. "That's quite an offering."

Brandon winked. "Well, he's a pile of work, but I'm sure he's worth the effort."

She nodded. *I think he's more than worth the effort.* "Thank you."

"Y'all will have to excuse me." Brandon rolled his shoulders. "If I want to get on a plane, I need to shower and change clothes."

Nodding, she watched him walk toward the cottage.

Julien came to her side. "Hey, what's wrong?"

Forcing a smile, she faced him. "Nothing. I wished he had stayed longer."

He tipped up her chin.

She found it hard to meet his gaze. "You smell like fish."

"You look like you're about to cry," he said.

"I don't cry around other people." She cleared her throat.

"You look like a bug flew in your eye."

She blinked and managed a laugh. "It's possible. I barely had time to know him."

"He'll be back."

Meeting his gaze, she nodded.

Skye freed the hose and sprayed the gutted fish. Water bounced off the tarp and hung suspended in the air, creating a rainbow above the catch. The force of the hose threatened to send the fish sailing.

Julien shook his head and redirected her hand. "Let me pack up the fillets so you can hose off the rest of this gunk."

Grinning, Skye released the hose.

Serah snapped a picture.

Eliza looked at the group, considered the impending mess, and wrinkled her nose. The smell of fish emulsion could linger on the fields for weeks. *I wouldn't change my life for the world.* She grinned. "Make sure the water runs away from the barn. Otherwise, everything will stink."

Laughing, Julien put the fillets in a bucket. "Nah, the cold will keep down the smell."

"It's forty degrees outside," she said.

He met her gaze and winked. "The fish are dead, Eliza."

She rolled her eyes. "Please, try not to get Skye wet." Squaring her shoulders, she walked toward the greenhouse and let the sound of Julien ribbing Skye warm her heart.

****

In the greenhouse, seedling trays rested atop metal stands. Eliza checked the soil's moisture content and imagined the waving color of mature plants in the fields. The rhythm of the work soothed her anxiety. *Farming is a lot like life. The faint of heart struggle, but perseverance yields rewards.* She heard the door swing open.

Julien entered and blinked in the filtered light.

Checking her watch, she realized much of the afternoon passed while she sought refuge and comfort among the plants.

He lingered near the door.

She cleared her throat. "Your brother made it to the airport?"

"Just in time for him to take off." Shaking his head, he walked toward her. "Why don't you let Serah and Michelle do the menial work?"

"They're finishing the bouquets. Besides, these plants carry so much potential. I love watching seeds grow." She smiled and ran the back of her hand along a tender, green leaf. "I'm too selfish to outsource the pleasure."

He rested a hand on her lower back. "All right, why don't you come outside and take a break? Walk me through the summer trials you sketched up."

"I have a lot of work left to do." She reached for a spade.

His thumb kneaded her lower back. "The work never ends."

She nodded and pulled duplicate sprouts from the trays.

Dropping his hand, he mimicked her actions. "I enjoyed fishing with my brother this morning. Taking a break and letting nature set the pace does a body good."

"You'll miss him," she said.

"He'll come back for the fish."

She smiled. *Only if you're still here.* Looking up, she found him staring. She cleared her throat. "I'll fight Warly with everything in my arsenal."

He nodded. "Good."

Good? "That's all you have to say?"

"Walk with me?" he asked.

She planted her feet and focused on the rows of seedlings. "Spending time outside feels like an indulgence. That's how I ended up with plans for fields I don't own. Maybe I'm getting in over my head."

He crossed his arms. "Beauty thrives on this farm."

She bit her lip and turned away.

He stopped her retreat, cupped her face, and pressed a kiss against her lips.

When I thought he was leaving me, my body ached. She resisted and then leaned into his tenderness, wondering how she would spend the next few months navigating between desire and defense.

Pulling back, he met her gaze. "I wouldn't trade your kisses for a thousand blooms."

The unexpected compliment startled her. She smoothed his shirt. "T-that's quite a statement." Clearing her throat, she looked away. "Do you know the stem price for these plants?"

He sighed, pulled off his ball cap, and leaned against the metal stands. "Does it matter? You'll do what you want to do. You turned down Warly."

She nodded.

He crossed his arms. "You don't try to pin me down."

"I told you I want you to stay."

"But you'll let me go in the springtime without another word."

Turning, she fussed with the trays. "Don't make Skye any promises you can't keep."

"C'mon, Eliza. I'm not talking about the kid."

His criticism raised her defenses. "Julien, I have a

job to do. It's no different from working nine to five. She's not a toddler anymore. She'll go back to school in the fall and make a lot of friends. They age out of day-to-day dependence."

"You're ridiculous. As she gets older, she'll need you in different ways."

She inspected her worn nails and heard the wind teasing the joints of the building. "She loved Erik more than me." The lump in her throat loosened, and she swallowed.

"You're still her mama."

Nodding, she dropped her voice to hide her shame. "When he walked into the room, her eyes lit up."

He cupped her elbow. "You're doing a good job, Eliza."

A door slammed in the distance. Startled, she pulled away from his grasp. "Thank you. She's everything to me."

"You're her mother, but you're also a woman. The two aren't mutually exclusive."

She felt the latent heat of his words and the intimacy of the warm space, but her early morning fears lingered near the surface. She rounded the table. "I'm with her as much as possible, but Claire does a better job baking cookies and tending to her needs. I know Skye loves me, but someone has to keep the farm running."

He crossed his arms. "And drum up business for the florist business."

"Exactly."

He followed her path. "Let me help you get back your time."

She narrowed her gaze. "You are helping me."

"I'm talking about more than the work I do." He pushed the trays to the side and tipped up her chin. "Buy the acreage, and I'll help you plant it. If you don't want to risk your capital, draw up a business partnership. I believe in you and what you're doing. If you slow down and take off a day to enjoy the things you love, I won't relegate you to the kitchen."

A glimmer of hope rose from her sea of emotions. She spent her adult life minding account balances and making decisions. *Will partnership give me space to breathe?*

The memory of losing control to Erik sank that ship.

"No, you won't." Determination solidified her statement, and she spun away from the intimacy in his gaze. "You can't buy peace of mind. I'm capable of fending off the bad guys and figuring out this threat on my own. I asked Jessica for the name of a lawyer."

He grabbed her hips, turned her to face him, and held fast. "Good. You'll need representation. That doesn't mean you have to do it on your own."

She pushed against his chest. "Did you come here looking for a fight?"

Tightening his hold, he smiled. "No, I came in here looking for you."

Collapsing in his arms, she sighed. "Well, you found me. Flaws and all."

"What has you all worked up?"

She met his gaze and swallowed. "If I'd been the one to die, everyone would be a lot happier."

He swore and tightened his hold. "Why would you say that?"

"Why not?"

"Because Claire and Skye would be heartbroken without you. You're fierce, Eliza, but life is more than a series of risks and chances. Don't delude yourself. You count, flaws and all."

"I can't do everything." The admission stung. "What happens when I drop the ball?"

"You find a reason to keep going." He tipped up her chin. "You always have that choice. I woke up in the hospital and realized that piece of heavy machinery shattered more than my leg. My body was a mess, my company was keeping me at arm's length, and my girlfriend was making sweet eyes at my big brother."

She frowned. "That's different. You shouldn't have been with her." She tried not to hate a woman who thought she could swap one man for another. "You're better off without her."

"Yeah." He shifted her hips and settled his hands on the small of her back. "I came to the same conclusion."

Looking up, she smiled. "Good."

"But life still hurts." He scratched the stubble on his chin. "I know what doubting your self-worth feels like. I also know what pulling through feels like. You're more than capable of running this farm, Eliza." He kissed her forehead. "You told me I need something to believe in. Well, I believe in you."

Pulling back, she smiled.

He frowned. "I need you to view me as more than someone to warm your bed. I need you to see me as your equal."

I'm not ready for that possibility. Sticking around and keeping me warm is one thing, but asking me to consult him on decisions is a much bigger deal. She blinked. "What happened to spring?"

He dropped his hands. "Brandon went to sleep last night and left me staring at the stars. I thought about the warm, muddy waters back home and the countless days we spent fishing the marsh for speckled trout and redfish."

"You miss Louisiana," she said.

He nodded. "Our boat had a slow motor, but our mom made sure it always held a cooler of ice, a backpack of snacks, and room for big adventures."

The marsh never seemed so far away. She turned to the seedlings. "How sweet."

Laughing, he grabbed her arm and spun her around. "Given a clear forecast, we cast our lines without caring what we pulled into our dingy boat. The fun was in the self-reliance and the fish we displayed like trophies on the dinner table." He fingered a small scar between his thumb and his pointer finger.

She stared at the silvery-white mark.

"A wayward fish hook chewed through my flesh, and I ripped it out. I was too young and naïve to wait for Brandon to clip it. Twenty years later, I realize every decision leaves a mark."

She met his gaze. "So you have a couple of scars."

He laughed. "And you've seen all of them, but here we are. I understand the legacy of scars, but I won't spend my life building a pile of regrets." He reached for her hand. "Screw spring, Eliza. We'll make this work; I'm in for as long as you'll have me."

Seeing the yearning in his gaze, she moved closer and touched the exposed skin at the base of his neck. She sucked in a breath. *He's too good to be true.* Hesitancy and disbelief warred with the sincerity of his offer. "Julien?" Her voice shook.

Capturing her hand, he pulled her fingers to his lips.

His sweet gesture anchored her thoughts to the moment.

He kissed the skin of her palm.

Pulling free her hand, she fiddled with the buttons on his jacket. "How long have you been sober?"

"Almost a year."

She nodded. *He made a commitment. He told me he stopped drinking after the accident. I don't know how many people could make that choice, but what if he gets a better offer?* She bit her lip. "I thought you would go home with your brother."

"He thought so, too."

"Why did you stay?" she asked.

"I realized what drove the desperation I saw in Luke's hardware store."

She frowned. "Archaic enforcement policies?"

Laughing, he tucked her hair behind her ear. "I meant grit and determination. Loyalty. Most people don't think of strength and self-sufficiency as feminine characteristics. When I look at your body, I think you're feminine as hell, but I didn't realize how much I needed your strength."

His words unleashed a spring of hope, but she felt too unsteady to sip the heady flow. That morning, she went from craving his warmth to preparing herself for his departure. *I need time to think through the implications of having him stay.* Buying time, she unhooked the first button of his shirt. "I admire a lot of things about you too."

He stilled her hand. "Are we done talking?"

She unhooked the second button. "I'm done."

"You won't mope around with sad eyes?"

Offended by the thought, she swatted his chest. "I don't mope!"

"And I don't leave in the middle of the night."

Looking him in the eye, she nodded. "Fair enough. You'll stay until we're through?"

"As long as you'll have me." He kissed her.

She yielded, savoring his rhythm until their kiss warmed her cheeks.

He eyed the greenhouse's cold, metal trays. "I'm pretty sure the cottage has a bed."

"Overrated." She reached for his belt.

"Skye might catch us with our pants down."

She checked her watch. "She's napping."

"Your assistants?" he asked.

Laughing and determined to take what she needed, she released her hold, unbuckled her tool belt, and let the worn leather drop to the dirt floor. "My assistants don't have any business in the greenhouse."

He raised his eyebrows.

Unbuttoning her jeans, she slid the denim over her hips and waited for his reaction.

Catching sight of her underwear, he whistled. "Pink."

She stepped out of the scrap of fabric. "It's cold in here, Julien."

Smiling, he closed the distance. "Yes, ma'am."

His hands grasped her hips, and she surrendered to the pleasure of his touch. *He said he needed my strength, but how long can I stand strong?*

****

"Today is the first night of the Winter Art

343

Festival." Twilight settled over the farm while Eliza stood in the kitchen peeling apples.

Claire continued organizing the pantry.

She cleared her throat. "Let's take Skye into Mount Vernon for the festival."

Turning, her mother stared.

"We can get pizza," she said.

Claire raised her eyebrows.

She smiled. "And hot cocoa."

Claire wrinkled her nose. "I make better cocoa."

"But this way, you won't have to do the dishes." She gestured toward the immaculate kitchen. "And Skye will love the festival."

Claire cocked her head. "What about the weekend flower arrangements?"

"What about them?"

"Another late night?" Claire put her good hand on her hip.

She grinned. "We finished them before I sent Serah and Michelle home."

Untying her apron, Claire folded it and placed it on the countertop. "Skye!"

Her mother's volume surprised her, and she laughed.

Skye came into the room wearing socks and soft sweats, her face wrinkled. "What's wrong?"

Eliza smiled. "Nothing, Sweet Pea. Go get your shoes and your coat. We're driving to Mount Vernon to see a light display."

"And getting pizza." Claire raised her eyebrows.

"Yes!" The girl ran toward the pile of outerwear by the front door. Coming to a skidding halt, she pivoted to face the adults. "What about Julien?"

She glanced toward the cottage. "I'll ask him if he wants to tag along."

Nodding, Skye fumbled with her coat.

"So you made that decision?" Claire asked.

She set down the apple peeler. "Yep."

"Do you know what you're doing?"

She shrugged. "Does anybody know what they're doing?"

Claire slid the apples off the edge of the counter and caught them in a plastic container. She snapped on the lid.

The sound echoed.

"Your father thought he did. Look where we ended up."

She met her mother's gaze. "Hopefully, I inherited your sense."

Claire shook her head. "I'm the stubborn woman who stayed with him. I'm not sure which inheritance option worries me the most."

She took the apples from her mother. "I'm not working myself into an early grave."

Claire held her weak arm. "Like I didn't work myself into a stroke?"

The reminder sobered her carefree attitude. She thought about the debilitating setback and the hesitancy she observed in her loving mother. "I should have caught the symptoms earlier."

"You can't be responsible for everyone." Claire sighed.

She nodded. *No, but while Julien is here, I can share the load.* "I'll be right back." She walked down to the cottage and knocked on the door.

Opening the door, he leaned against the frame.

"Just can't get enough?"

She laughed. "Table that thought and come to town with us for pizza."

"You're selling yourself short." He grabbed his coat from the back of the worn armchair.

"If you're staying, you need to buy a warmer coat."

He shrugged into the jacket. "I'm staying."

Smiling, she accepted his hand.

Traffic heading into Mount Vernon reflected the popularity of the festival. "In the summer, the Tulip Festival's street fair generates solid income." Shaking her head, she slowed for taillights. "To duplicate the tourist draw, the city council resurrected an old tradition. Our winter festival has art workshops, local authors, and an art show for the people willing to brave the cold."

"I can think of a variety of ways to keep warm," Julien said.

She met his gaze in the rearview mirror and tried not to smirk.

"It's an old tradition." Claire stared out the passenger window. "When I was a kid, we went ice skating and rode tractors. Times have changed."

Constrained in a booster seat, Skye bounced up and down. "I want to ride a tractor!"

Eliza laughed, parked the truck behind the historic theatre on First Street, and climbed out of the cab. The deep notes of the theatre organ brought back memories of her childhood. Rubbing her ear, she took Skye's hand. "Let's go. They set up lights along the river walk."

"Pizza first?" Julien asked.

She nodded. "Maybe Puccini's has a booth. Let's

go find out."

Skye chattered about pizza toppings until they passed the theater and confronted the beautiful, light-strewn chaos of First Street. Stores twinkled with fairy lights, and people holding cups of steaming cocoa and mulled cider roamed between art booths. A festooned fire truck sat in the middle of the street. Uniformed firefighters guided children up and down the polished steel ladders with promises of iced cookies at the top. Beyond the rig, high school students worked STEM booths. She waved to Serah and Michelle.

The organ finished its song.

Skye took off running.

Julien made a quick grab for the back of her shirt. "Slow down, Darlin'."

Frowning, Skye looked up. "Why?"

He released his hold. "This isn't the farm."

"It's Mount Vernon." Claire clucked her tongue.

"Do me a favor and ask an adult before you go darting off." He shrugged. "All the noise and people make me nervous."

Skye looked at her. "Mom?"

"Julien makes a good point." The blinking spectacular beckoned for attention, but Skye lived in a sheltered ecosystem, and she appreciated his attention. "Let's stick together."

Pointing to the fire truck, Skye raised her eyebrows.

"Go for it." Watching Skye climb the ladder, she took in the winter wonderland with the enthusiasm and delight of a child. *For all their faults and mistakes, I appreciate how my parents gave me the freedom to explore, too.*

"Pizza?" Julien jerked his thumb toward a line outside the restaurant.

"Five minutes." She pointed to a mailbox festooned with ribbon. "We dropped anonymous valentines into the chute. The mail carrier delivered every one, but nobody fessed up to their crushes."

"Nobody?" Julien asked.

She thought of the lipstick she and Jessica applied to make kiss prints. "Well, some people left clues."

"Did the crushes work out?"

Shaking her head, she smiled. "No, but those memories make this town feel like home."

He swung an arm around her shoulder and leaned close to her ear. "I like your mischievous side."

"Do you?" She raised an eyebrow.

Laughing, he swatted her butt.

"Eliza?" a man asked.

She stopped and turned.

Erik's best friend, Devon, strode through the crowd wearing a pair of clean turnouts. He carried a basket of cookies shaped like fire engines.

She figured the heavy gear doubled as a costume and a way to keep warm. Devon's confident stance squared with his attitude toward life. A gentleman and a kind soul, he served as the fire station's ambassador and the town's unofficial spokesperson. After Erik's funeral, he came to the farm and helped, but she knew she needed more than a dedicated friend.

Amid the chaos of the crowd, he wrapped her in a hug and kissed her cheek.

She returned the gesture and reached for a cookie. "Are you diversifying?"

He laughed. "They're for the kids." He nodded at

Claire. "Hello, Mrs. Edwards."

"Devon."

"How's your arm?" he asked.

"Fair enough." She beamed.

He offered her a cookie. "Glad to hear it. You're feisty enough to be our best recruit."

Grinning, she took the cellophane-wrapped treat and dropped it in her coat pocket. "I doubt that, but I'm keeping the cookie."

Devon winked and looked at Julien.

Realizing this meeting could be the first of many introductions, she cleared her throat and wondered whether Devon came over to check on her or to check on the town gossip. "Devon, this is Julien Kroger."

The firefighter nodded. "Luke said you had someone new helping on the farm."

"Gabe left in a hurry." She left the explanation vague and waited to see how Julien handled the introductions.

"I was sorry to hear that news." Devon extended a hand toward Julien. "Pleasure to meet you."

Julien shook the man's hand. "Likewise."

She wanted to laugh at Julien's curt response, but she also wanted to enjoy her evening. *If they met at a football game, they'd be best friends.* "Let's get that pizza."

"Mom!" Skye yelled from the top of the engine.

She and the other three adults looked up.

Devon pointed toward a brass bell and pantomimed a ringing motion.

Skye grinned, and the clanging sound echoed along the street.

He gave her a thumbs-up. "She's a natural. Erik

349

would have gotten a kick out of seeing her up there."

Thinking of the first time she brought Skye to the station house for coloring books and a tour, Eliza nodded. Her wide-eyed daughter sat behind the wheel of a fire truck and absorbed the moment. "When her dad died, she wasn't brave enough to climb ladders."

Devon looked at her. "I'm sorry. The comment slipped out."

"It's okay." She smiled. "You're right. He would have loved seeing her up there."

He wrapped an arm around her shoulder.

She watched Skye climb over the equipment like an eager recruit.

Julien cleared his throat.

Extracting herself from Devon's comforting warmth, she smiled at the possibility of Julien's jealousy. *They're both strong, capable men, but I don't need brotherly love from Julien. I need the heady mix of charm and determination I can get only from him.* She entwined their fingers and squeezed. *If Caroline and I ever meet, I have a few things to say to her, too.*

"Mom!" Skye waved.

Amid the chaos of the festival, she turned toward her daughter and returned her wave.

"It's good to see her smiling," Devon said.

Julien cleared his throat. "She deserves it."

The crowd swallowed the rest of their conversation, but she trusted them enough to chat without coming to blows. "Come on down, Sweet Pea. It's time for pizza." Raising her voice, she hoped the lure of food would bring Skye back to ground level.

Jumping from the third rung, Skye landed on two feet.

"Well, that did the trick." She turned to the men and watched them shake hands again.

"Catch you later," Julien said.

Devon smiled. "It was nice to see you all." He cupped Eliza's elbow and kissed her cheek. "If you need anything, call me."

"I will," she said.

Julien leaned close. His body blocked the wind. "Seems nice enough," he whispered in her ear. "If he touches you again, I'll punch him."

His subdued threat made her laugh. "That man's like my brother."

Leaning back, he raised his eyebrows.

A possessive threat simmered in his deep, brown gaze. Lifting his hand, she kissed his fingers. "Did I kiss him like I kiss you?"

He shook his head. "No."

She dropped his hand. "Remember, actions speak louder than words." She leaned forward and bit his earlobe. "Or I'll find someone else to kiss."

He rubbed the tender flesh. "I've always hated that expression."

She grinned.

Luke approached, carrying a steaming cup of coffee. A dark, micro-fleece vest replaced his daily cargo vest, but the unmistakable glint of metal dog tags remained on his chest. "Fancy seeing you bunch in town."

She turned to Claire, waiting for her mother to take the lead in the conversation.

Claire remained silent.

Seeing no other choice, she blew her hair out of her eyes and took charge of Cupid's arrows. "Luke, why don't you and Claire grab a drink?"

Claire frowned. "I'm not thirsty."

Luke laughed and offered his arm. "Come on, your chicks are in capable hands."

She glared at the man, looked at Julien, and narrowed her gaze.

Julien gave her a three-finger salute. "Safe and sound. Scout's honor."

Sighing, she threw her scarf over her shoulder. "One drink, Luke."

Winking at Eliza, he turned and escorted Claire down the street.

Tugging on her sleeve, Skye gestured to the ice cream booth.

She shook her head. "Pizza first."

Skye pouted. "Granny's more fun."

The comment brought her back to the reality of managing a hungry child on a city street. *Giving in to her demands would be so much easier, but she's worth the effort to get things right.* "That might be the case, but I'm your mom." She took Skye's hand. "Come on, you can have the first slice."

The booth outside Puccini's restaurant offered Neapolitan-style pizzas to the hungry members of the crowd who were too impatient to claim a table. Joining the line with Julien and Skye, she led a debate on the merits of the Mad Greek and the Puttanesca.

Skye stamped a foot. "I want pepperoni!"

Definitely hungry. She tightened her grip on Skye's hand.

Julien laughed and tugged a braid. "I'm surprised you're not a vegetarian."

She stuck out her tongue.

Eliza thought of farm life and gutted fish. "She loves hamburgers and chicken nuggets as much as the next kid."

He smiled. "Kids have a strange definition of loyalty."

Laughing, she met his gaze. "She took to you easily enough."

"It's the peg leg." He winked.

Secure in the warmth of the crowd, she smiled and thought about how quickly Julien claimed a place in her life.

"Eliza?"

She swiveled, prepared to meet another friend, but she came face-to-face with the patriarch of the Smith family. His ruddy cheeks looked chapped from the wind, but he wore a brand-new shearling coat. *I wonder if he removed the tags.* She attempted to summon a neighborly smile, but a litany of questions sprang to mind. *Did you think to warn us? Do years of shared boundaries mean nothing?* Anger and fear lifted bile to the back of her throat. She transferred Skye's hand to Julien, took a deep breath, and settled for a simple greeting. "Hello, Mr. Smith."

Julien crossed his arms over Skye's chest and held her against his body. "The potato farmer?"

The man put his hands in his pockets and grinned. "The biggest tract in the county."

Warly's threats hung over her land like a dense fog, and the fear of losing control accelerated her heartbeat. "I heard that tract is for sale."

Heads swiveled, and conversations stalled. The other people in line zeroed in on her conversation with the portly man.

Smith eyed the crowd. "For the right price, every asset is for sale." He folded his arms.

They looked like pale, moldy sausages.

"My lawyer brought me an opportunity I couldn't refuse," he said.

She rolled her eyes. "Have you even met the purchasers?"

Narrowing his gaze, he stared and chewed his lip. "They're irrelevant to the deal."

She blew her hair out of her eyes. "They're not irrelevant to me." She stepped forward and raised her voice. "I've met them. They're pretentious and dishonest."

The crowd murmured.

"You left Mount Vernon a long time ago. You've forgotten what it's like to live here." She gestured toward a map of the Winter Festival. The logo for Smith Specialty Potatoes occupied prominent space. "I'm surprised you still sponsor the festival."

"Why?" He squinted at the map. "Maintaining a local foothold is good for business."

She put her hands on her hips. "What exactly is your business? Does growing potatoes excite you?"

He raised his eyebrows. "Making money is my business." He rubbed together his fingers. "I see a lot of financial opportunities in the cannabis trade. Burgeoning medical and recreational markets will make me richer than rich."

Residents chattered around her.

She shook her head to block out the noise. "That's the difference between us, Smith. I'm making money to provide for my family and fill my days with joy. You're making money to accumulate wealth."

He uncrossed his arms. "I have many assets."

"How many assets can you manage?" She ground her teeth, feeling the tightness in her jaw. "Will you manage the water runoff from a thousand acres of paved driveways and tidy streets? Foot the cost for the substantial infrastructure upgrades needed to handle added traffic? Franchises will follow the houses."

A woman moaned.

"To support the swell of working-class residents, will you bring affordable housing to Skagit County? Do you have of those skills and assets?"

He backed up and scanned the crowd.

She held up a hand. "No, you don't. You'll take the profits from your land sale and leave your neighbors to clean up the mess."

"It's my land." The man exhaled. "You still hung up on your daddy's accident?" He lowered his voice. "The accident wasn't my fault, Eliza. Don't you take out your grief on me."

Julien shifted.

Confirming Skye's safety, she shook her head and faced Smith. "This conversation has nothing to do with my father's suicide. He spent his life chasing riches, but he was stone-cold sober when he sold you his assets."

"Then why can't I do the same?"

"Because I have twenty acres of potential I'm protecting. I have a daughter who deserves quiet evenings. I want to see geese in my fields, not packs of high school kids trespassing to pick bouquets and take selfies."

A shop owner stepped forward. "Smith, what is Eliza talking about? What have you and your lawyers cooked up?"

The man adjusted his coat. "A planned development on the potato farm. The buyers made a competitive offer. I heard they offered Ms. Edwards a contract, too, but she's too shortsighted and sentimental to consider it."

"Not only did they make me an offer"—she raised her voice to carry her message to the crowd—"but they threatened me and tried to coerce me into accepting it."

The crowd murmured and shifted. Neighbors whispered to each other and sent text messages skittering across town.

Smith scratched his head. "I thought we were on good terms, Eliza."

"We are. When I pass your workers on the servitude, I wave at every single one of them. Did you write a preservation order into the purchase contract?"

Smith paled. "They have to honor the law."

She shook her head, abandoning the hope she reserved for her former neighbor. "Only the letter of the law. If I don't sell out, they threatened to make my access damn inconvenient. Are those the kind of neighbors you'd want?"

Skye slipped from Julien's grasp and pressed her face against Eliza's leg.

She pulled her close and rubbed her back. "Don't worry, Sweet Pea. Mr. Smith and I are having an adult conversation. Nothing bad is happening."

The potato farmer shook his head. "I was sorry to hear about your husband, Eliza, but use common sense. Sell your property, take care of your kid, and enjoy life's upgrades."

"Do the county commissioners know about your deal?" the shop owner asked.

The question saved her from telling Smith exactly what she thought about his proposed upgrades.

"My lawyers said Skagit County would have to change its Comprehensive Plan." Smith coughed. "The changes would kick off a lengthy environmental impact process."

"Oh, it will be lengthy." The shop owner dropped his chin.

Smith frowned. "Unless Eliza sells her dinky flower farm, there won't be any developments. The buyers want to use her land as a community park."

She smiled. "That's too bad. I'm not interested in selling. Maybe *dinky* won't be a future adjective. I've considered expansion plans. Tell your lawyer to expect a call."

He widened his gaze. "Come on, Eliza. You had years to exercise those options."

"The timing wasn't right." She glanced at Julien, knowing he had her back. "Now it is."

Smith stamped a foot and swore. "Your stubborn pride will cost the county a thousand construction jobs."

She shrugged. "Not my problem."

The woman who scoffed at franchises stepped forward. "Skagit County is different. We take care of each other." She narrowed her gaze. "Eliza did the flowers for my father's funeral."

"And my high school graduation."

The man who spoke moved to Seattle, but he faithfully returned for the winter celebration. *At least some people remember their roots.*

Smith twirled his stout finger in the air. "Whoop-dee-doo. This development will enhance Skagit

County's competitiveness and attract new businesses. It will help drive the economic development you're all pretending comes from tulips and hot cocoa sales."

The shop owner laughed. "You're the last person who gets to decide what's best for this town."

The potato farmer turned as red as one of his spuds. Uninterested in drawing attention back to herself, she stifled a laugh.

"I've never met a more ungrateful, pigheaded group of backcountry nitwits in my entire life."

Laughter rippled through a crowd, and locals peppered Smith with questions about the proposed development.

Skye looked up. "What's a nitwit?"

She cupped her daughter's cheek. "A foolish person who forgot how small towns work."

The girl wrinkled her nose. "Can we have pizza now?"

"Sure, Sweet Pea. One slice or two?"

Skye held up two fingers.

Nodding, she turned to Julien for warmth and encouragement. He met her gaze, but she saw distance in his tight-lipped smile and unblinking gaze. *What did I do now?*

Chapter Eighteen

Julien lay in bed, staring at the ceiling and
doubting his next steps. The bouquet resting on the side
table pulled at his heartstrings. Late in the afternoon, he
had commandeered the unneeded stock, added
greenery, and hoped Eliza would appreciate the gesture.
He never found time to give her the bouquet. *What's
the point of grand gestures if nobody sees them?*

He wondered what internal defect let him fall for a
woman he barely knew. She flayed Smith's excuse for
neighborly conduct, but she relegated him to support
staff. *If I'm the only person who's committed to a
partnership, our relationship won't last. I don't know
how long I can survive slow, subservient torture. Spring
will come, but if we're not standing side by side, I will
run out of excuses to stay off that bike.*

A sharp tap against the window interrupted his
thoughts. His pulse spiked, and he sat upright, looking
for an unannounced visitor. Instead of a brunette, wind-
kissed beauty, an eagle stared at him, and the bird's cap
of white feathers glowed beneath the full moon.

Opening its beak, the bird made a low kuk-kuk-
kuk, turned its head, and looked toward the slow waters
of the Skagit.

"Run out of fish? We're not feeding the wildlife,
champ."

The bird raised his talon and knocked the glass.

Cringing, he eased open the window. "You're supposed to steer clear of humans." He looked for a band on the animal's leg but found it bare. "Are you fresh out of a rehabilitation center?"

The bird raised a scaled foot and flexed its forward-facing toes.

He kept his eyed trained on the animal's serious claws. "Point taken."

The eagle shook its head and flexed its six-foot wingspan. Flying to the top of the barn, it screeched.

He scanned the wooden structure for signs of activity. The dark windows reflected moonlight. He looked toward the farmhouse. Someone extinguished the last downstairs light. *Is she thinking of me at all?*

The eagle screeched again.

Hoping the animal would leave, he closed the window and shifted in the cold bed.

A firm knock gave him a reason to smile. *Good evening to you, too, boss.* Burying his regrets, he rolled the liner over the stub of his leg and hoped she would apologize for pushing him aside. He straightened the pin, pushed it into the socket of the prosthesis, and stood, hoping the pair of briefs he wore would not be an issue.

The knock came again.

Impatient woman. He walked to the door, opened it, and smiled. Eliza's downcast expression and twisting hands rerouted his thoughts "Are you okay?"

"I wondered if you were asleep."

He stepped back, allowing her to enter the cottage. "I take longer to get moving than most men."

"I, uh…" She strode past him, but her words died in her throat.

Closing the door, he brushed her long bangs off her forehead.

She curved into his touch.

What happened to her bright smile and pert wave? She's as skittish and needy as a colt. Pulling her close, he wrapped her in his arms and felt her body relax. "You did a good job exposing Smith's plans."

She nodded against his chest.

His briefs hid nothing of his response to her presence. Kissing her lips, he felt her lips soften, but he pulled back before sex erased his misgivings about their relationship. *Side by side.* Drawing a deep breath, he loosened his hold.

She glanced up. "I feel like I need to apologize for something."

He nodded.

"But I don't know what I did wrong." She swallowed and trailed a hand along his chest, stopping at the elastic band. "Now, I really want to apologize."

Smiling, he stepped away and turned toward the anonymity of the cottage. "You took care of your business without my help. I'm proud of you." He sat on the couch and rubbed his temples. "But what happens when you wake up and realize you don't need me? I don't want to feel like a tool left to rust on the shelf."

She sat beside him and reached for his hand. "I needed you to take care of Skye. I needed your strength, so I felt confident enough to tell Smith what I thought about the deal. I was so mad I was shaking! If I had had to worry about Skye, I would have lost my nerve and walked away."

Sighing, he leaned back. "Skye will grow up one day. If you can replace me with another foreman, what good am I? I don't want to stand in your shadow and wonder what I'm worth to you."

She stroked his cheek.

He longed to turn and kiss her palm.

"Your scars are so visible," she said, "but time etched mine deep. I think my life has poisoned me against trusting people and knowing what to expect from them. I'm so accustomed to running this place on my own."

"Have I disappointed you?" He stilled her hand.

She shook her head. "I felt you the entire time you were there, steady and sure at my back. What if I'm not capable of love? What if I push you away like I pushed away Erik?" Pulling her hand from his grasp, she tucked it in her lap.

He picked it up and held it, palm turned toward the ceiling, and he rubbed the tension from her grasp. *She deserves the calluses, but she also deserves the soft, pale skin of her palm.* "Eliza, you're just as capable of love as I am. Nobody doubts your relationship with Skye, but for us to be together, you have to expand your heart and let me in."

She made a fist, stilling the pressure he meant to soothe her. "I'm working on that."

That can be enough, can't it? He sighed. "I hope you know I won't let Smith lay a finger on either of you. You don't have to choose between you and your daughter. I can take care of you both."

Her lips parted, and she leaned in. "I know you can take care of me."

He smiled. "You can't bury this conversation with sex, Eliza."

"I can try."

How many times have I tried and failed? Taking a deep breath, he wondered how hard he should fight for what he needed. *Leaving first might be easier for both of us.* A future of sleepless nights and rehashed glory felt like a shitty outcome, but if he made that choice, memories of her desire-laden sighs might through the darkest nights. "Tomorrow we'll talk?"

She stoked his bicep and smiled. "Tomorrow."

Her sweet scent of lust, honeysuckle, and soap undermined his willpower. *One more taste.* Standing, he pulled her upright and captured her lips while he could. *I can't talk her into loving and trusting me, but I can show her how good she makes me feel.*

She nudged him toward the wall.

He felt the restless energy in her stance. "You want more?"

"I want all of it. All of you."

"Show me." He picked her up and carried her toward the dark bedroom.

"This weight can't be good for your leg."

He laughed and lowered her to the bed. "Don't ask me to carry you up a mountain." Her laughter inspired a hundred pleasurable thoughts, but he looked at the silhouetted bouquet. *What if tomorrow doesn't work out?* He turned on the lamp. "I spent most of the day thinking about you."

"Only most of it?"

Grinning, he pinned her against the bed. "Aren't you paying me to work?"

She raised her eyebrows. "You're off the clock. Tell me all your secrets."

He reached for the bouquet and offered her the blooms.

She examined the flowers but stopped short of accepting them.

A lifetime of feeling second-best stole his breath, but he inhaled. "It's the thought that counts."

"They're lovely."

He pulled out a rose. "Why didn't you use this bloom in the bouquet?"

Cocking her head, she sighed. "Too many imperfections."

"Imperfections? It looks perfect to me."

She rolled her eyes. "Look at the guard petals and the spacing of the thorns."

"I'm looking at it, Eliza. I see most of the same things you do, but I also see the softness of the petals. The pink blush reminds me of your skin." Trailing the petals along her neck, he grinned. "Those imperfect, defensive petals look like armor, but they guard beauty. They're a perfect match for you."

She turned her face toward the bloom. "You're romantic?"

"No, I'm committed."

"Committed."

She whispered the word but avoided his gaze.

"The flower's still beautiful," she said.

He dropped the bloom and braced his weight. "And so are you."

Blinking, she looked up.

"When I was the life of the party, you wouldn't have taken a second look at me."

Lifting a hand, she stroked his cheek. "Oh, I would have looked."

"But would you have taken me seriously?" he asked.

She shook her head.

"Exactly. Fighting for what you deserve forges beauty and strength. When you confronted Smith, you shook in your boots, but you never looked more beautiful."

She smiled.

"I wanted to be by your side, but the gap between us damn near broke my heart."

Grasping his shirt, she pulled him closer. "I'm right where I want to be."

"For right now?" He cocked his head.

She shook her head. "For the future."

He remained silent, feeling her hips pushed against his and watching her gaze soften with lust. *If she's wrong, sex and affection can be enough. I'll be strong enough to make it count.* He shifted his weight and rose to his knees, maneuvering to the side of the bed. Removing the prosthesis and shucking the sleeve without a care for where it landed, he glanced up and found her watching him. He pulled her onto his lap. "I think you're overdressed."

"It was cold outside."

Pushing her coat off her shoulders, he lifted the back of her shirt and ran his palms up her back, pushing the heels of his hands into her corded muscles.

She draped her arms around his neck and arched into his touch.

"You're the strongest woman I've ever met," he said, "and also the softest."

"That says a lot coming from you." She kissed his throat. "You taste like sweat and hard work."

He laughed. "If I'd known you were coming to call, I would have showered."

"Hmm. I like it."

Her quick lick teased the moist heat he craved. He stroked the side of her breast, pulled off her shirt, and let the moonlight share his admiration. "You're beautiful. More beautiful and resilient than any flower."

"So are you." She ran her hand up and down his thighs.

Resisting the urge to flex, he laughed. *Isn't this feedback the Holy Grail? Take me as I am?*

"Handsome, I mean. I love your body and your tanned skin."

Amusement lingered on his lips. "You already have me in bed," he said. "No need to overdo it."

She raised her arms and caressed his face. "Look at me."

Thumbing her nipples, he felt them harden beneath his touch. "Oh, I'm looking plenty."

"Julien?" She swatted his ass.

He met her gaze. "What? I thought we were done talking."

She rolled her eyes. "I'm sure you'd rather have your leg, but your recovery forged new strength, too. Were you this strong before the accident?"

He settled her heat against his erection and felt her legs tighten around his waist. His thoughts shattered into incoherent sentences. Gripping her hips, he slowed her subtle thrusts and the pressure building in his system. "Maybe."

Blinking, she looked up. "Maybe?"

He bent her over his palm and held her weight with one arm, running his free hand from her sternum to the edge of her waistband. Her heated skin felt softer than silk. Leaning forward, he kissed the path laid down by his hand.

She raised her head. "You're dodging the question."

Biting back laughter, he did his best to divert her attention with a kiss. Feeling her lips soften, he claimed success, but she reached for his shoulders and pulled herself upright. The shifting pressure against his cock made him groan. Reminded of how good her sheath felt, he closed his eyes. *Will I survive this woman?*

"I like the way you move." She ran her hand along his abdomen.

Unbuttoning her jeans and slipping his hand past her waistband, he searched for the heat and wetness he craved.

"Are you listening to me?" she asked.

He shook his head and pulled his thumb through her curls, tracing her clit with her moisture. "I thought the listening part was over."

Laughing, she rose on her knees and slid down her jeans to give him better access. "The listening part is never over."

Lacy underwear claimed his attention. He cupped her, wondering if he could rip the delicate fabric from her skin. "Have you been wearing these all night?"

She nodded.

Meeting her gaze, he swallowed. "I'll listen to every word. Strength"—he grabbed her hips—"goes both ways. We're stronger when we're together."

Nodding again, she rubbed her body against his touch.

I'll buy her new underwear. He found a seam and split the fabric.

She gasped.

Smiling, he lifted her ass until he could bury his face in her curls. She tasted better than any rose, as sweet as sun-drenched honeysuckle and heady wine. "You're my intoxication," he whispered against her skin. "I let myself go with you." He teased and tasted her, testing her resolve, while he held her bucking hips. Feeling her muscles tighten, he adjusted his grip, willing to let her go first and to soak up every minute of her pleasure.

"I want to feel you inside of me," she cupped him.

"We'll get to that."

"Now, Julien." She pushed against his shoulders. "I want all of it."

He loosened his grip and lowered her to his lap, ready to feel her hips rock.

She raised her chin.

All of it? Bracing his weight, he lowered his foot to the floor, pulled her to the edge of the bed, and spread her legs until he could see her body laid out, hips curved and breasts thrusting upward. Watching her, he grabbed a condom, centered her hips, and leaned on his arms.

A lazy smile teased her lips.

"I'll give you as much as you can take." Easing into her heat, he closed his eyes and waited. When he felt her hips buck, he grinned, picking up the tempo until she matched him thrust for thrust. They came together, her body tightening around him as he let go.

He rested his weight, spent and thrilled. Exhaling, he rolled to the side, closed his eyes, and reached for her.

She slid from his grasp.

Hard-headed woman. Groggy, he grabbed an ankle

and pulled her back into bed. "Stay the night?"

"I kick."

"Of course, you do." Smiling and confident she would return, he released her. "Well, then you'd better go."

She nodded and slipped into her clothes, padding barefoot toward the front door. Smiling, she pulled on her boots and faced the night.

Cold air rushed into the cottage.

The eagle screamed.

She turned her head toward the barn. "Your friend is back."

He pulled a pillow over his head. "Crazy bird."

"Julien? Do you smell smoke?"

Sitting, he peered through the window and caught the crisp acidity of dry wood smoke drifting on the wind. Memories of a sooty cane field flashed through his mind, and a surge of adrenaline coursed through his body. "Something's on fire." Swearing, he grabbed his clothes and the prosthesis.

Eliza ran down the steps. She looked over her shoulder and returned to the cottage.

He leaned against her shoulder, righted the artificial limb, and followed.

Smoke and fog mingled in the air. He looked at the farmhouse and shook his head. Smoke detectors would have alerted Claire. Flinging open the barn doors, he searched for a point of combustion. Freed from the confines of the building, smoke intensified.

Eliza coughed and waved it away.

He scanned the florist coolers and supplies. A popping noise confirmed his fears. Glancing up, he saw the first lick of flames rising from the hayloft. The destructive heat reached for the freedom of open air. "Get out of here and call the fire department."

She pulled the collar of her shirt over her mouth, nodded, and placed a call.

The eagle screamed.

"Yeah. You warned me." He scanned the coolers, wondering if he could wheel them out of the barn while Eliza relayed the details of the fire to the emergency dispatcher.

She slid her phone in her pocket and grabbed his arm. "Julien, come outside."

"What about your arrangements?" he asked.

"They're not worth the risk."

Drawing his shirt over his mouth, he shook his head. "The roof will take most of the damage. I'll be quick."

She tugged. "I don't care about the stock. Let the firefighters extinguish it. We have plenty of water."

He blinked the smoke from his eyes. "How long until they get here?"

"I don't know. Ten? Fifteen minutes?"

He eyed the hose he used to clean fish. "Your water pressure is shit. You could lose the whole barn."

She nodded and coughed, pulling him away from the thickening smoke.

Weighing the risks, he followed her lead. *This farm is her home.* Standing at her side, he watched the glow of the flames behind the old boards. He put his arm around her shoulder and tried to keep her warm. "It will be a mess."

"I know." She cleared her throat.

The orange glow gilded her features, and he saw a tear slip down her cheek.

"We can rebuild the barn."

She wiped away the tear. "I know."

Light after light in the farmhouse turned on. "Eliza!" Claire came flying down the steps wearing her nightgown. The old woman ran across the frozen ground in bare feet, struggling to catch her breath. "Skye's not in her bed."

Fear rose in his throat like bile. The searing pain threatened to steal his breath.

Eliza jerked from his grasp. "Are you sure?"

Coughing, Claire banged her chest and nodded. Tears leaked from her eyes.

Eliza charged toward the barn.

Lunging, he caught her around the waist. She fought his grasp, bucking, and twisting. Her desperation tested the limits of his strength.

"That's my child!"

He tightened his hold until she stilled and faced him. "I'll go get her."

Her body jerked toward the barn. "I can't ask you to do that."

"You're not asking me to mind the chickens, Eliza. You trusted me to watch your daughter while she slept. Let me stand by your side as a partner. Can't you trust me to rescue her?"

She shook her head. "I can't lose her."

He released her, knowing nothing in the world could stop her.

A beam fell, shaking the ground. A shower of sparks rose in the sky.

Skidding to a stop, Eliza covered her mouth. "She shouldn't be in there. I put her to bed."

Taking advantage of her paralyzing uncertainty, he

strode toward the barn. "That doesn't mean she stayed there."

She scanned the yard. "What if someone took her?"

He paused and looked over his shoulder. "Take care of your mom, Eliza. This isn't the night to lose the ones we love."

"Julien, wait for the fire department. You can't go in there!"

He considered a self-deprecating smile, but a lifetime of jokes and casual banter abandoned him. Choosing simplicity, he offered a tender smile to the woman he loved. "Why the hell not?"

Looking back and forth between the barn and her shaking mother, who struggled to breathe, she locked her vivid green gaze on him and nodded.

He strode toward the smoke-filled barn. Inside the structure, the hiss and crackle of the growing fire competed with the steady hum of the florist coolers. Smoke filled the workroom, drawn down by the open door. He flipped on the lights and turned toward the chicken coop. Through the haze, red heat lamps emitted a steady glow. "Skye?" He cupped his hands around his mouth. "Skye! Are you in here?"

An arc of electricity flashed high above him, and the coolers went silent. *There go the lights.* He coughed and felt his way through the eerie darkness. Hitting the far side of the barn, he coughed and turned toward the chicken coop and the old stalls. "Skye? Darlin', if you can hear me, say something." Amid the crackling emptiness, he felt his heart beat.

"I don't want Miss Guinea Heny to die!"

Her tiny wail sent hope soaring through his veins. "Darlin', nobody's dying today. Can you come to me?"

He reached out a hand. Instead of her tiny grasp, he felt the feathered warmth of a dazed chicken. Tucking the animal under his arm, he surged forward and searched for Skye in the flickering darkness. "I'll come back for the animals."

"All of them?" she asked.

He moved toward the sound of her voice. "All of them."

"Even the *nisse*?"

"The *nisse* has magic. He can fend for himself."

She crawled out of the stall and wrapped her arms around his good leg.

He dropped and scooped her against his chest. She felt as light as a feather. Stepping into the aisle, he saw her pale nightgown trailing beneath her winter coat. "Pull your nightgown over your face and tuck your head against my neck." He considered dropping the chicken but adjusted his weight. "Hold on, Skye. Your mama's waiting outside the barn."

She coughed and nodded against his neck.

Eying the blazing loft, he made his way toward the open doors. The cold snap of winter air never felt so good. Releasing the dazed bird, he drew a deep breath and relinquished Skye to her mother's arms.

Eliza inspected her daughter from head to toe. Soft murmurings escaped her lips, and she wiped away Skye's tears as fast as they could come. "Everything's okay."

"I'm sorry, Mommy." She plastered her face against Eliza's shoulder. "I was lonely."

Eliza buried her face in the girl's braids. "It's okay, Sweet Pea, The fire's not your fault."

Tearing his shirt, he grasped melted snow and held

the damp fabric over his mouth.

Eliza grabbed his arm. "Julien! Don't go back in there."

Lifting her head, Skye wailed. "He promised to save my pets."

"Julien! They're chickens," Eliza said.

"And pigs!" Skye said.

He met Eliza's gaze and winked. "I'll open the rear doors, and they'll find their way out." A gust of wind lifted sparks to the sky. They rose like a swarm of brilliant fireflies.

"What if the roof collapses?" she asked.

What if Skye's heart collapses? He faced the barn. "I have time." No longer concerned for a child, he made his way to the coop and put his weight against the exterior doors. They held firm, and burning fragments of hay drifted to the floor. *C'mon. Budge.*

The pigs squealed in their enclosure.

Sirens wailed in the distance.

He turned his body, took a deep breath, and threw his weight against the old wooden doors, praying a second chance would do the trick. They gave way, and he stumbled into the freezing air. A flush of oxygen pushed the flames toward the roof. He released the family of pigs.

The chickens flapped in the coop.

He grabbed them one by one and tossed them out of the barn. "I hope the eagle eats every one of you." Free of his obligations, he left the barn, sank to his knees, and savored the crisp air upwind of the fire.

Eliza touched his shoulder.

He looked up. "Where's your mother?"

"Catching her breath." She caressed his cheek.

"You didn't have to do that. You didn't have to save everyone."

Shaking his head, he pushed to standing and watched Skye herd the animals toward the propagation greenhouse. "If I'd left them, Skye would never have forgiven me."

Eliza rested a hand against his chest. "I'm sure she'd take you over a flock of chickens."

He covered her hand. "Well, it's nice to feel loved." His flip remark sounded empty against the crackling soundtrack of the fire.

Biting her lip, she pulled back.

Hell. He pulled her close enough to feel her chest rise and fall, tipped up her chin, and met her gaze. "I keep telling myself you don't need protection, you're more than capable of running this place, and everything's your call."

She swallowed. "But tonight?"

"I'm learning to love you, but you have to let me manage the risks of that complication. You handle everything else."

She nodded and stroked his cheek. "I'll hold you to that promise."

The barn roof collapsed, and a shower of sparks rose in the night sky.

Skye ran from the greenhouse. Stopping, she watched sparks and ashes rise from the structure fire. "The sky is full of stars."

Sirens wailed, the fire engine arrived, and Devon jumped down. He counted Eliza's family members, and relief washed over his features. He pointed to two crewmembers. "Assess Claire." Walking toward him and Eliza, he shook his head. "That barn's a loss, but we can put out the fire and do our best to salvage the contents."

Eliza scooped up her daughter. "Do what you can, but I have everything that counts."

The firefighter nodded and signaled a crewmember to run a line toward the building.

Julien walked toward where Claire sat on the ground.

Two firefighters checked her vitals and administered oxygen.

She pulled the mask from her face. "You can stay in the house."

He smiled. "You're not so bad yourself."

Chapter Nineteen

Eliza fielded questions from the emergency responders and directed the men and women toward the resources they needed. When the flames died down, the firefighters taped off the smoldering remnants of the barn and warned her about hot spots.

Claire sat on the tailgate of an ambulance.

Her heart rate refused to settle. "Will you take her to the hospital?" Eliza said.

The paramedic nodded.

She directed Julien to the guest room, bathed Skye, and tucked her daughter into bed. "Sweet Pea, you need to stay put. No more nighttime adventures."

"You weren't in your bed." Skye yawned.

"I know." She leaned down and kissed her forehead.

"Where were you?"

"Taking a chance." She would never forget the sight of Julien emerging from the smoke. Skye clung to him, and hope soared in her chest. *Who else would have done that for me?*

"Can I help you in the morning?" Skye asked.

She smiled and tucked a strand of wet hair behind her daughter's ear, vowing to braid it as tightly as Claire could. "You're my favorite helper."

"Even better than Serah and Michelle?"

"You're the best," she said.

Skye pulled her stuffed animal to her chest. "Michelle will be sad. The fire 'prolly messed up all her pretty designs."

Nodding, she tucked in the edges of the blanket. "She's very creative."

Skye closed her eyes. "Sometimes she dries extra flowers and makes pretty things to sell online. She shouldn't have stored her treasures and notebooks in the hayloft."

She stilled her hand and wondered how many other things she missed running between her obligations. "No, that wasn't a good idea."

"Goodnight, Mommy."

"Goodnight, Sweet Pea. I'll see you in the morning." Padding from the room, she found Julien standing in the hallway. "Did you hear that?" The possibilities tumbled from her mouth, but she took a deep breath. "You don't think Michelle purposefully started the fire?"

He drew her close. "Nah, she's rebellious, but she loves Skye."

She closed her eyes in relief. "I need to go into town and check on my mom."

"I'll stay here." He rubbed her back and anchored her against his chest.

She looked up. "Julien, if Michelle started that fire on purpose…"

Looking at Skye's bedroom door, he shook his head. "Fire's a destructive statement. I might pin the negative reviews on her, but your assistant's not a psychopath."

She pulled back. "I thought Warly masterminded those reviews."

He shook his head. "Keep your friends close and your enemies closer."

She laughed from his protecting arms. "What does that make me?"

"Everything." Lowering his head, he kissed her.

On a normal day, the intensity of his kiss would have chased away her fears and uncertainties. Tonight, the intensity confirmed them. *I almost lost everything.* She broke the kiss, her mind racing with possibilities and lingering threats. *Why are people so much harder to manage than plants?* "Michelle resents me."

He released her and stared at the distant mountains, silent beneath the dark sky. "Maybe so, but you have more immediate problems on your hands than an angst-ridden teenager. Morning's almost here, and I don't see how you'll provide flowers for the wedding."

She followed his gaze through the window and saw past the smoke-filled destruction of the yard. In the smoldering embers of the barn, arrangements and bouquets wilted in the coolers. Even if the flowers survived the fire, the heat damaged their shine, and the debris rendered them inaccessible. She thought about the people and resources she could marshal. "I'll find a way to make the delivery."

Following her down the staircase, he handed her the wide-brimmed hat and kissed her. "Go check on your mom. I'll stand watch."

The smell of smoke lingered in his hair. She paused, torn between two parts of her life. *I can't ask him to keep adding to his burden.*

He swatted her bottom. "Go. I have the first shift."

Driving to Mount Vernon, she tried not to remember the last time she visited the hospital. Logic said her mother would be fine, but she spent hours in a sterile room, waiting for her husband's life to end. She parked and entered the emergency room. The hygienic stillness of the halls brought chills to her skin. Standing at the nurse's station, she rubbed her arms. "My mother's name is Claire Hartley."

The nurse handed her a visitor's sticker. "Room 306."

She opened the door to the private room and pulled back the privacy curtain. Metal rings slid along the pole. Wincing, she focused on the bed. The woman lying beneath the smooth sheets resembled her mother, but beeping monitors and a neutral gown swallowed her frame. *I came so close to losing everything.*

Claire turned her head and smiled. "You didn't have to check on me."

"I worried about you." She sat on the edge of the bed and lifted Claire's hand.

Returning her squeeze, Claire smiled. "No stroke this time. Just an old woman's panic attack."

"You get as much credit for saving Skye as Julien," Eliza said.

Claire's gaze softened. "Credit doesn't matter."

She sighed and toyed with the thick cotton blanket. "I'm so scared of messing up."

Straightening, Claire cocked her head. "When I raised you, did I mess up?"

She took her mother's hand. "No, of course not!"

Claire coughed. "Sure, I did."

"But you did everything for me. Even if you made mistakes, you were always there to make them right. While I'm responsible for the farm, I don't have that freedom."

"What makes you think that way's worse?" Claire squeezed her hand. "You're her hero."

She sighed. "How can that be? She loved Erik, and these days, I barely know myself."

Claire closed her eyes and smiled. "We all loved Erik. He was a cheerful, clever man. Much more ambitious than I ever suspected"—she shrugged her good shoulder—"but he was a good man."

"Everything he did was an adventure."

"And you?" Claire asked.

"I lost my path."

The steady beep of the heart monitor filled the silence. "Seems to me, you took a beautiful detour." Opening her eyes, Claire turned her head. "Erik's gone. Your father's gone. You and I? We're still here."

She released her breath. "Without you, Skye and I wouldn't have thrived. Thank you."

"I'm not dead yet." Claire rolled her eyes.

She laughed.

"You have never been a quitter." Claire smiled. "You inherited that stubborn streak from your father."

Stubborn to the point of failure. Standing, she walked toward the dark window. Streetlights flooded the hospital parking lot. "What was it like watching your world shrink? When he started selling off land, I was too young to understand the implications. Then I was a teenager. I didn't know how to handle the issues keeping us quiet at the dinner table."

"When he sold your horse, you cried like a baby," Claire said.

She nodded and thought of the gentle mare. A box of show ribbons remained at the top of her closet. *I shouldn't have owned a horse. The money should have gone back into the farm.* "He told me I wasn't home enough to take care of Nibbles."

"You weren't. But neither of us was brave enough to confront him with the truth." She sighed. "I kept hoping he'd pull it off."

She turned, thinking of her father's bets and her mother's quiet acceptance of his loses. "A big win?"

Claire shook his head. "His dreams." She closed her eyes. "I didn't like your father's gambling, but I did my best to make his life more comfortable." She smiled. "I already claimed my dream; I had you."

Walking to the edge of the bed, she stroked the soft, aged skin of her mother's limp hand. "Thanks, Mom."

Claire raised her good arm and patted her hand. "I'll help you as long as I can, but I think you should sell the farm. Your life would be easier."

She held her breath and mentally counted to ten. "I don't think easy is the right answer."

Claire smiled. "Obviously not. You brought home a one-legged tomcat."

"Mom!"

"It's not an insult." Claire cleared her throat. "Julien's a good man, too."

"He dotes on Skye," she said.

"Skye's easy to love."

Julien's words felt too fresh to share. "He might love me, too."

"He might"—Claire raised an eyebrow—"if you let him."

She exhaled. "When he arrived, he said he wasn't looking to put down roots. Now, he plans to stay. What happens when he settles in and realizes I'm not who he expected? What if I push him away? I don't know if I can feel vulnerable all over again."

Claire stared at the ceiling. "Strength comes from the place where you least expect it." She turned her head. "Those old trees down by the river? Your grandfather sprouted the saplings and planted the trees to anchor the mud. Your dad said it was his favorite spot because it showed how long his family had been on the land. Things want to grow, Eliza. Life wants to move on."

Nodding, she braced her hands on her soot-stained jeans. "Julien wants us to expand into seed production."

"Is that why you were creeping out of the house last night?" Claire raised an eyebrow. "A business meeting?"

Heat flushed her cheeks.

"Let him love you. Do your best to love him. That's the most you can ask of each other."

She met her mother's gaze. "And if he walks away? If I push him away?"

Claire shrugged her good shoulder. "You'll still be strong."

Acknowledging the truth of her mother's statement, she let the white noise of the hospital room recall a recent dream. Julien's shaggy, black hair and tall, imposing frame stood beside her, but the anchoring weight of his presence helped her see the distant horizon. Instead of drowning in a sea of blooms, she floated, and the warm, yellow glow of highlighted possibilities she never imagined. *He could have slipped beneath the icy river waters of his pain, drowned his sorrows in vodka, or retired to the simple escape of privilege. Instead of the easy road, he weathered life's upsets, cranked his bike, and sought hope and new beginnings.* She shifted, aware of her body's reaction to the mere thought of him. *I can't deny I like the way he looks naked, but he's so much more than the sum of his parts.* Opening her eyes, she met Claire's gaze. "I love him."

Claire nodded. "Anybody can see that fact."

"Can I keep loving him?" she asked.

"You were a fierce girl, but your father's suicide struck a chord, and you came roaring back to Mount Vernon. Erik thought he could tame your wild, stubborn spirit. Julien isn't insecure about his place in the world."

"He's been through a lot." She blew her hair off her forehead. "He's not infallible."

Claire pulled the white hospital blanket higher on her chest. "None of us are."

She helped position the blanket. "You don't have to take care of us anymore, Mom. Buy a little cottage in Mount Vernon. Walk to yoga and drink hot tea with the biddies." She smiled. "Make sweet eyes at Luke."

Claire chuckled. "Luke does not make sweet eyes. He'll be more trouble than the pair of you."

She scratched her head. "Maybe you should take up charity work."

Claire met her gaze. "Ha. I'd rather die on that old farm. Maybe plant roses."

Shaking her head, she smiled. "I'm fresh out of rose hips."

"Good." Claire closed her eyes. "I'm not done yet."

She sat by her mother's bedside and thought about everything Claire experienced. When the rise and fall of her mother's chest signaled sleep, she crept from the room, spoke to the nurses, and left the hospital. *We have so much of our lives left to live.*

The sun peeked over the mountains as she turned onto the servitude and imagined acres of houses obliterating the potatoes. *Not on my watch.* Slowing on the gravel drive, she examined the remains of the barn. The walls stood, but a light breeze stirred ashes and left a haze in the air. *We'll build it again.* She found Julien sitting in the living room of the farmhouse.

He smiled, held out a hand, and pulled her down on the couch. "How's Claire?"

Scratching her scalp, she smiled. "A one-night stay for observation."

He nodded and tucked her against his side. "That's good."

She yawned. "You should get some sleep."

"I'll sleep better with you beside me." He kissed her hair.

"Skye will be up soon."

His chest rumbled with laughter. "Then stop talking. It's well past dawn."

She smiled and dropped her head. "Your shoulder's bony."

He pulled her closer. "Yeah, well, you're hard to please."

Tensing, she waited for the closeness to unravel. "Is that a problem?"

He shifted until her head rested against his chest. "Better?"

That's all life takes? Slight adjustments until two people fit together like they have years and years waiting in front of them? "Much better." She turned her head and watched him close his eyes. His chest rose and fell beneath her cheek.

He stroked her back. "Relax for a few minutes, Eliza. We'll figure out how to make things work."

Closing her eyes, she let his touch soothe her anxiety. *We're stronger when we're together.*

****

Skye slept until seven o'clock. She came downstairs, her eyes blurry, and her movements languid. "Hi, Mommy."

Eliza raised an arm to make room on the couch opposite Julien. "Hi, Sweet Pea. Do you want to cuddle?"

"Mmm-hmm." Skye nestled under her arm.

For a moment, she sat with two people she loved and absorbed the quiet sounds of the morning.

Skye looked up. "What's for breakfast?"

She smiled. "Cereal?"

"How about oatmeal with raisins?"

"Yeah, I can do that," she said.

Scrambling to her knees, Skye cocked her head. "How's Granny?"

"The doctors are monitoring her, but she'll come home tomorrow."

Nodding, Skye eyed the kitchen. "That's good. I miss her already." She looked at Julien and climbed in his lap.

Eliza tried to contain her grin. Hearing a car come down the driveway, she checked her watch and extracted herself from the warmth of the couch. "It's too early for Serah and Michelle." Opening the front door, she found Jessica standing on the doorstep holding two buckets of roses and anemones. "What are you doing here?"

Jessica breezed past her. "Word travels fast through the collective." She jerked her thumb over her shoulder. "Love what you've done with the barn."

She snorted and let the door swing closed. "Aren't you chipper?"

Putting her blooms on the kitchen table, Jessica faced Julien and Skye. "Rough night?"

Skye held a narrow length of Julien's hair in a braid.

He shrugged. "I can handle it."

Eliza smiled. *Yes, you can.*

Jessica tilted her head. "Well, I'm glad to hear it." She turned to the front door. "I have another load in my car. Be right back."

Eliza watched her leave and struggled to keep her mouth from gaping. *That's it? No editorial feedback?*

Her friend returned carrying a large box of wreath frames, heavy-duty clippers, and floral wire. She laid the items next to the blooms on the kitchen table. "Sooty chic won't fly for the wedding."

She checked the time on her phone. "I'm waiting until eight to call the bride."

"Did you salvage anything?" Jessica plucked a pink rose from the bucket.

"No, but we delivered the garlands midweek. We can pull cedar and interesting textural bits from the farm, but the greenery won't be enough for a wedding."

Jessica nodded. "My assistant scavenged the bits and pieces we have in dry storage. Lunaria, pinecones, birch, filbert catkins, ranunculus, and dusty miller. Thirty florists operate within a day's drive. Call in favors for the additional blooms."

"The bride said she wanted to use local resources."

She pressed a thumb against a rose's thorn. "I'll describe what we have and sell her on the replacements."

Jessica dropped the rose into the bucket. "She'll trust your expertise?"

Glancing at the destruction smoldering beyond her doorstep, she swallowed. "I hope so."

"What about filler?" Jessica asked. "I think we can round up wax flowers without too much trouble."

Julien left Skye on the couch and joined them. He picked up a pair of heavy-duty shears. "What's a wax flower?"

"The new Baby's Breath," Eliza said.

"Right." He raised his eyebrows and looked at the tool in his hand. "Aren't these shears overkill?"

Rolling her eyes, she claimed the tool. "Give me your opinion when you've trimmed six dozen slight, wooden stems."

Jessica laughed. "Good call."

Skye pulled the shears from her hand. "You said I could help."

Correcting Skye's grip, she pointed the sharp ends toward the floor. *She won't be this young and malleable forever.* "You can help, but let's slow down before anyone hurts themselves." Surveying her options, she calculated the time she needed to make breakfast. "Why don't you spread out the frames?"

Dropping the shears, Skye picked up the metal bases and spaced them atop the table.

Julien stared out the window. "What about the saplings?"

"The saplings?" she asked.

"The stuff in the farthest greenhouse? Can't you

string them up with lights and make the church look like a winter wonderland?"

"That's a fantastic idea." She turned to Jessica. "Do you think your assistant can roundup those super-bright LED lights? The ones on a thin silver wire?"

"Fairy lights?"

Skye squealed.

She winced. "Yeah, fairy lights."

"I might have them." Jessica pulled out her phone. "My workshop overfloweth."

"Looks like I'm on oatmeal duty." Julien walked into the kitchen and started opening cabinets. The wooden doors banged against the frames.

Following him, she wondered how a scarred man with a motorcycle could embrace the possibilities of making oatmeal. Placing a hand on his lower back, she felt his muscles shift. "I like your idea to use the saplings in the church. The lights'll make a pretty walkway, like continuing the line of Dogwood trees."

He nodded and peered into the pantry. "Use what you have."

She laid her head against his back. *I have you.*

He stilled, his arm raised to an open cabinet.

Don't I? "You're sure you want to do this?"

His breath escaped. Lowering his hand, he turned, widened his stance, and settled her between his legs. "Are we still talking about the oatmeal?"

She met his gaze and smiled. "First things first."

"Fair enough. Where the hell does Claire keep the oatmeal?"

Laughing, she reached toward an adjacent cabinet and withdrew the canister.

He took it from her and shook his head. "I'm better

389

with tools and machinery. Numbers."

"Two cups of water. One cup of oats." She pantomimed dumping the ingredients in a pot. "Turn on the heat and stir the oats so they don't stick."

He repeated the instructions.

His solemnity worried her, and she decided to take pity. "I can make the oatmeal."

Putting his hands on her hips, he pulled her close. "So can I."

She considered the dark circles beneath his eyes. "But you'd rather be outside with tools and machinery?"

"Eliza, this thing between us is fragile." He sighed. "I don't want to mess it up."

"What are you worried about?" she asked.

"Measuring up?"

She trailed her fingers down his chest. "That hasn't been an issue."

Laughing, he pulled her close. "I love your confidence in me. I'm making the world's best oatmeal, loading up the trailer with potted trees, and wrapping the branches with—"

Jessica cackled from the front room.

He winced. "Fairy lights."

"That might take you most of the day," she said. "You might need to avoid the house."

He eyed the chaos strewn over the table. "I'll stretch out my tasks."

Laughing, she pulled away. "Don't worry about the floral staff. Bang on the greenhouses or overhaul the tractors. I have plenty of resources." Smiling, she looked at the women assembled to give her a hand. "A real community is so much better than a planned one."

Chapter Twenty

Julien tasted the oatmeal, added salt, and lured Skye into the kitchen with a bag of raisins. He watched the women chatter and eat the oatmeal he made. Some type of caveman satisfaction elicited a smile, but he refused to surrender the moment to a bout of introspection. "After breakfast, let's check on the chickens and pigs. They're probably hungry, and we need to muck out the waste."

"I want to stay with my mom." Skye pouted.

He leaned back in his chair. "After we tend to the animals, I'll bring you right back. Sparkles is probably roosting on the seed trays."

Skye's widened her gaze and scrambled toward the front door.

The animals clustered on the sunny side of the greenhouse, claiming the elevated seed trays, roosting on the rafters, and eyeing their porcine subjects.

He and Skye distributed the greens, grains, and seeds he scavenged from the kitchen pantry. "I need to go to town and pick up bags of feed."

Skye held her breath and stopped petting her favorite chicken. "Will you ride your motorcycle?"

Clearing his throat, he searched for a solution. "Maybe the feed store will deliver."

She exhaled.

"I might ride the motorcycle this summer." He

added possibility to test her limits.

"You could get hurt."

Crouching, he looked her in the eye. "Skye, I promise to do everything possible to avoid getting hurt. Remember that sugar mountain?"

She kicked the dirt. "I don't want you to die."

That makes two of us. I've never had more to keep me going. He squared her shoulders. "I have lots of good reasons to live. You and your mama are special to me."

"More special than the chickens?" She met his gaze.

Laughing, he pulled her into a hug. "Definitely."

Miss Guinea Heny made a "tuck-tuck" sound, spread her wings, and landed on his shoulder.

He eyed the animal.

Skye laughed and retrieved her pet. "She likes you." Leaning against his side, she smoothed the chicken's feathers.

"She's jealous." He absorbed her weight and smiled. "She knows Foxy Soxy is my favorite." Hearing a vehicle approach, he disengaged and peered out of the greenhouse.

Serah and Michelle climbed from their dusty sedan.

Interesting. I didn't expect them both to show up.

The teenagers made a show of examining the wreckage of the barn and shaking their heads.

Eliza approached the pair.

He led Skye and her pets outside to take in the morning air. *And mind the women.* Pulling out his phone, he pressed the record button for posterity or amusement. *Hell, I'll take them both.*

The three women stood at the edge of the caution tape and looked at the remains of the barn.

Skye did her best to line up her chickens for a photo shoot.

"What a mess," Serah said.

Eliza crossed her arms and nodded. "The barn's a total loss." She glanced at Michelle. "The firefighters said it could have been arson."

She's not wasting time. He smiled until he saw Michelle mimic her boss's pose. The teenager looked like an immature version of the opinionated and competent woman Eliza worked so hard to become.

"How would they know that?" Michelle asked.

"No storms in the area. No interruption in electrical service." Eliza cocked her head. "What else could have started the fire?"

Michelle kicked the gravel. Ashes rose from the ground, and she frowned. "I'm sure your insurance will cover the damage."

Eliza shook her head. "If a policyholder intentionally creates a loss, the company won't pay out. Arson's bad for business."

"But you didn't torch your barn." Serah frowned.

Eliza kept her gaze trained on the older sister. "You're right. *I* didn't set fire to my barn. *I* didn't traumatize my mother or trap Skye in a smoke-filled building. *I* didn't put Julien's life at risk when he went inside a burning building to save a six-year-old child."

Michelle's eyed widened. "Is Skye okay? Why was she in there?"

Watching her scan the yard, he waved and jerked his thumb toward Skye.

Her shoulders relaxed, and she closed her eyes for

an instant.

That's right. The losses could have been much worse.

Eliza cleared her throat. "What were you doing up in the loft, Michelle?"

The sisters exchanged looks.

"I, uh, kept some sketches up there," Michelle said.

Serah blinked. "I thought you gave the sketches to Warly for his promotion campaign."

"Shut up, Serah. I only gave him half my designs."

Eliza shook her head. "That's not how sisters should talk to each other." She looked at Serah and raised her eyebrows. "Maybe she'll pin it on you."

Serah wiped away a tear. "I didn't burn down your barn. Nobody thinks I would do something like that, do they?"

"No, but I think your sister made a mistake." Eliza stared at the wreckage. "Who will tell me the truth about what happened?"

Michelle took a deep breath and squared her shoulders.

He nodded. *That's a girl. When your choices are admitting culpability and feigning outrage, you might as well take the high road.*

Michelle cleared her throat. "I left the barn flashlight in the hayloft."

Serah nodded.

Michelle frowned. "If you bought LED flashlights like the rest of the Western hemisphere, this accident wouldn't have happened."

"Michelle!" Serah covered her mouth.

Eliza crossed her arms. "Leaving your flashlight was a stupid mistake, but you shouldn't have been up there. You shouldn't have hidden things from me. I can rebuild the structure, but I can't rebuild my trust."

"I told you the fire was an accident." Michelle stamped a foot.

"This conversation is about more than the fire." Eliza crossed her arms. "It's about your pattern of behavior. A small army of friends will come to my aid. They know the value of hard work and community. They also know how to close ranks."

The teenager opened her mouth.

"Without my recommendation, you'll have a hard time setting up shop anywhere near Skagit County."

Eliza's crossed arms and cool determination emphasized the weight of her tenure. He knew every general in her rose-studded Farmer-Florist Collective would censure Michelle's behavior.

The teenager rolled her eyes. "I don't need your silly collective. The Preserve will revolutionize this backwoods county."

Eliza laughed. "Is that what they're calling it?"

Michelle pressed her lips into a line.

"There won't be a Preserve." Eliza rolled her shoulders. "I'll do everything I can to thwart the development. Life in Skagit County means more to me than the bottom line."

Michelle threw up her arms.

The teenager marched to the sedan, as dramatic as a slighted heron. He rubbed his lip, wondering if he should intervene. *What would I say? Listen to your boss?* Biting his lip, he suppressed a smile. *I'm in so much trouble, but damn, it's the best kind.*

"Whatever. I'm out of here!"

Left with the younger sister, Eliza braced Serah's

shoulders and spoke words he had no chance of hearing.

Grabbing his phone, Skye jabbed the screen, snapped a picture, and showed him the image.

Smiling, he took back the phone and figured the snap would make a charming screensaver. "Your mama's pretty tough."

"She looks mad. What's the Preserve? Are we making jam?" Skye asked.

How much did she hear and understand? He shook his head. "The Preserve's a funny idea that makes little sense here."

"Maybe it should go somewhere else."

"Maybe so," he said.

She frowned. "Did Michelle burn down the barn?"

So, all of it. He cleared his throat and watched Serah retreat to the sedan, exchange words with Michelle, and drive off in a hurry. "I don't know, Darlin'. It sounds like the fire was an accident."

Looking at her mother, her lip quivered. "I don't like accidents."

He rested his hand on her shoulder. "Let's go see your mama."

"Mommy!" Skye ran toward her mom and hugged her leg.

Eliza picked up her daughter and settled her on a hip.

He considered the dust lingering on the driveway and transposed the situation to Brandon's cane fields. "Michelle might sue you for wrongful termination."

She glanced at the remains of the barn and shook her head. "I never technically fired her. She made a bad decision and fled."

"You're not reporting your suspicions to the authorities?" he asked.

She shrugged. "She made a mistake. What good would it do to saddle her with an investigation?" Tweaking her daughter's nose, she smiled. "The barn's gone, and I'm ready to move on with my life."

"What about Serah?"

She transferred Skye to her hip and looked at the gravel road. "She knew her sister used inventory to create her designs. If she's more comfortable with a new job, I told her I would provide a reference, but I also told her she could come back next summer. They're like family, Julien. I can't give up on them that quickly."

No, family doesn't quit. He smiled. "Will your insurance balk?"

She brushed her bangs out of her eyes. "I made up that part."

He laughed. "It sounded good."

The eagle landed on the farmhouse roof and dangled a fat fish.

Skye's gaze widened, and she looked between him and the raptor. A slow smile brightened her face, and she laughed. "Eagles eat fish, not chickens."

He ruffled her hair and turned to the bird. "We're good."

Eliza eyed the animal. "You two are on speaking terms?"

"Animal seems a little possessive of the farm." He shrugged.

"They're migratory animals.

He raised an eyebrow. "Have you seen its talons? I'm pretty sure this bird will hang around."

Skye cocked her head and chirped at the bird of prey.

Her call would have fooled anyone at the raptor center.

The animal flexed its wings and chirped right back at the kid.

"Well, I'll be damned," he said.

Mother and daughter stared. "Don't swear."

He laughed at their mirror expressions.

Skye linked their arms. "My daddy said the *nisse* stays to help take care of the farm. He was probably the first man to live here, and he's never gone away. I bet this bird has been here a long time, too."

He frowned. *Are there three of us in this relationship?*

Eliza narrowed her gaze. "Your granddaddy loved the trees down by the river." She scanned the eagle and shrugged. "Maybe he stuck around to help us."

The golden-eyed eagle tore the head off the fish.

He smiled. *Well, that's a lot better than the alternative.*

Chapter Twenty-One

The cloudless, late afternoon sky filled the white, clapboard church with low light. Garlands of fragrant cedar gave the space a crisp, clean smell that reminded Eliza of fresh greenery and new beginnings. She watched Julien run wires to power the fairy lights while she wove pinecones and lunaria through evergreen swags. *Rustic chic would have worked, but a pulse of nature complements the new bouquets. I hope the bride loves them.*

Reverend Mark ran a hand along the tiny lights wrapping a branch. "These lights seem much safer than candles. We should incorporate them more often."

She cleared her throat. "You mean, we've already burned down one structure this week."

Putting a hand on her shoulder, he squeezed. "No one will blame you for that accident."

"Won't they? Maybe I pushed Michelle too hard. I remember how exciting independence felt. Maybe I should have tried a softer approach and listened to her ideas."

He laughed. "Remember that attitude when you're butting heads with Skye. We were stubborn teenagers, too. You'll do better the second time around."

She thought of Skye tucked away on Whidbey Island. Her daughter went through so much, but love and fairy tales reminded her to smile. Vowing to take

Skye riding in the morning, she rose and brushed off her pant legs. "I hope so."

The bride arrived wearing jeans and a buttoned cardigan. While Mark greeted her, she clasped her hands in front of her, surveyed the revised floral installation, and made polite comments. The minute he turned, her hand shot out and rubbed a garland.

Who wouldn't be nervous on their wedding day? She smiled and walked up to the bride. "When we're done, I think the church will look magical." Softening her voice, she gave the nervous bride a safe space to share her feedback. "Do you like them?"

The bride nodded, but her eyes filled with tears. "When you called about the fire, I was so worried, but I knew you could do it! I called so many of your former customers." She wiped away her tears. "But I had to see the church for myself."

She smiled. *Yep, this bride's a crier. Thank goodness she hasn't done her makeup yet. Be soft and gentle, like dusty miller.* "I appreciate your trust and confidence. Most women would have thrown a fit, but you've been very gracious."

"I thought about it, but why waste time when you can't change the outcome? What else can I do? Round up matching bouquets from a grocery store?"

She laughed and led the bride back to the wide, double doors. "Don't worry about the flowers. We have that end covered. Why don't you head back to the hotel and start getting ready?"

The bride planted her feet. "Do you think my mom can take a peek, too? She's been pacing up and down the hallways of the hotel. Her nerves are driving me crazy."

"Why don't you take pictures of the church? When you get back to the hotel, pour your mom a glass of Rosé. I'd hate for you two to miss this special time together."

Nodding, the bride again wiped away a tear. "That's a good idea. When in doubt, add more wine."

"And food," Julien said. "You should eat food."

The bride looked at him and frowned.

He shrugged. "Just sayin'. You don't want to faint on your big day."

Eliza winked. "That's good advice from a man who's never been married." Linking arms with the bride, she led her past the vestibule. "When I walked up the aisle, I couldn't stop my hands from shaking. Then I saw my family and friends gathered to support me, and I realized everything would be okay. Weddings create new families. Before the night ends, you'll hug and kiss every person you love, but Julien's right. A little food is a good idea for stamina."

The bride dabbed a tissue against her cheek. "Maybe a little protein."

"Exactly," she said. "Protein and Rosé."

"Am I forgetting anything?" The bride planted her heels. "So many things keep me up at night."

She nodded. "I know what you mean."

"You do?" the bride asked.

Ushering the woman toward the door, she smiled. "We'll move to the reception venue, install the centerpieces, and bring you the bouquets." She lowered her voice to create intimacy. "The wedding will be beautiful. You'll never forget it."

Nodding, the bride smiled. "It will be so pretty, like a sparkly, pink-rusted dream."

Julien snorted.

Looking over her shoulder, she glared at the man.

He shrugged.

She smiled and patted the bride's arm. *I assumed Skye would grow out of the sparkle stage, but maybe she won't, and that's okay.* "When we're finished setting up things, why don't I text you those pictures of the finished product? I'll send some from the reception site, too."

"Oh, could you? That would be awesome."

The big wooden door stood open to admit the breeze. She escorted the bride out of the church and waved as the woman walked down the stairs. "Not a problem. I'll see you in two hours. Go enjoy this time with your bridesmaids. Remember, your mom is looking out for you. If she panics, ask her about her wedding."

The bride waved and hurried through the dogwood trees.

Julien walked up behind her. "You're pretty good at your job."

She laughed, pushed aside her bangs, and resettled her hat in the February air. "Winter gives me time to do small weddings, but I prefer to spend my time planning the next season. Flowers rarely require this much"—she paused, searching for the right word—"coercion."

He laughed. "Oh, I don't know. I've had experience with a reluctant bloom."

Ignoring his jab, she shook her head and thought about the promise of May and June. "I love the warmth of spring and returning to the fields. The growing season is coming, Julien. I can almost feel it."

He crossed his arms and scratched the rough

stubble on his cheek. "So, you'll be pretty busy? New fields? Selling seeds?"

"You were right." She laid a hand on his arm and squeezed, grateful his support gave her the courage to expand her ambitions. "Seeds are a good idea. When I rebuild the barn, I can include space for shipping and processing."

"What's all this 'I' business? Are you cutting your partner out of the profits?"

She drew a deep breath. "I'm giving you a final chance to escape." *Even if I want you to stay so much I'm shaking in my boots.* "You don't have to be my hero."

He shook his head. "I don't want your escape clause. We'll do the research and figure out how much land we need to make a go of expanding Hartley Farms. When you exercise your options, Warly and Smith will fight you tooth and nail, but I'll be right beside you until we win."

"Good." She grinned, hearing the strength of his vow and knowing he would stand behind his promise. *He might ooze Southern charm, but his work ethic's as tight as his ass.* She felt her cheeks heat and cleared her throat. "I'm developing a taste for confrontations."

He frowned. "You'll have to start over on your children's book."

She licked her lips and thought of their night in the barn. "I backed up most of the images."

"Clever woman."

"Sometimes." She winked.

"I want you to dream big, Eliza." He shifted his weight. "I'm not Warly, but I have plenty of money."

She looked at the expensive stitching on his boots.

The day she met him in the hardware store, she noticed the quality. The tell had comforted her and spoke of his character. *Well, the boots and Luke's hardheaded insistence on pushing the two of us together.* She smiled. "My dreams don't depend on scale. They depend on beauty and the promise of new growth. Plants inspire all my projects."

"Like what?" he asked.

"Like nurturing a family and finding room for passions." She raised her eyebrows and waited for the innuendo to sink in.

The corner of his mouth quirked up, but he cleared his throat. "I'll do my best with Skye—"

The warmth of his pledge surprised her.

"—But I can't promise to keep my foot out of my mouth."

She laughed. "I don't expect you to be perfect."

"No?" He stroked her cheek. "You might be close. You have more energy than your precocious daughter, and you work from sunup to sunset, but I want you to end your day with me." He pulled her close. "I'm not getting down on one knee."

"Why not?"

Sighing, he picked her up and carried her down the church steps. "Because we're equals, Eliza. I love you, and I'll be here as long as you'll have me."

Equality sounded like the sweetest blessing she could imagine. She draped an arm over his shoulders. "Forever, Julien. I want you for the long haul. I want to share every new season and every new beginning with you."

Clearing the steps, he dropped his head and kissed her.

She arched into the warmth of his mouth. He kissed her lips with the possession and confidence she needed. His hand clutched her waist and drew her close. Bracing her hands on his shoulders, she let the tension of the prior days drive her reaction. He had stayed by her side and had been as steady as a rock. Knowing she would find pleasure in his arms, she surrendered to the desire coursing through her system. The need to find time for the two of them urged her to hike a leg around his waist or drag him down the steps, but she tore away her lips, panting and meeting his gaze. "I don't know what I was thinking." She blinked and eyed the steeple. "Julien, I just mauled you in front of a church."

Laughing, he bent and tossed her over his shoulder. "Say it, Eliza."

She scrambled to hold onto her hat. "Say what?"

The man slapped her butt and kept walking, the impacts of her fists and laughter doing little to deter his progress.

She stopped fighting and bounced along, admiring the view and recording the bright moment of happiness in her life. Tiny white dogwood buds promised the beauty of spring. Birds chirped in the air. She wondered what returning to this place year after year would feel like with him by her side.

He stopped walking. "Last chance, woman."

"Or what?" She laughed, knowing he would give her the time she needed. *But I don't need more time.*

He turned them.

She saw the ice-cold water of the reflecting pool. Clouds drifted across a mirrored image of the church. Her gaze widened. She pulled off her hat and threw it to the ground. "You wouldn't."

"Yes, ma'am, I would."

She pushed against his back and straightened.

He let her slide down his chest until their gazes met.

He gave her the most handsome smile she ever hoped to see. His loose hair and easy smile hid the strength and perseverance that could support her dreams without commandeering them. *I never knew I needed that support, but now that I have it, I never want to let it go.* "I love you, Julien Kroger."

"Good." He exhaled and tipped up her chin.

The church bells rang.

"Good? That's all you have to say?"

He pulled her close, saluted the reverend, and claimed her lips. Pulling back, he met her gaze. "I love you, too, Eliza. Never forget that fact. I'll spend the rest of my life proving how much I love you. You're not unlikeable; you're strong, and you're perfect. You do you and let me do the rest."

She nodded, hearing the love and commitment behind his words. "We have work to do."

Laughing, he shook his head and offered his arm. "Yes, ma'am."

A word about the author...

Amy Craig lives in Baton Rouge, Louisiana with her family and a small menagerie of pets. She writes women's fiction and contemporary romances with intelligent and empathetic heroines. She can't always vouch for the men. She has worked as an engineer, project manager, and incompetent waitress. In her spare time, she plays tennis and expands her husband's honey-do list.

Visit her at:

https://www.amy-craig.com
https://twitter.com/authoramycraig
https://www.facebook.com/AuthorAmyCraig
https://www.instagram.com/author_amy_craig